RIVER OF SALT

Dave Warner is an author, musician and screenwriter. His first novel, *City of Light*, won the Western Australian Premier's Book Award for Fiction. He is also the author of *Clear to the Horizon* and *Before it Breaks*, which won the Ned Kelly Award for best Australian crime fiction. Once nominated by Bob Dylan as his favourite Australian music artist, Dave Warner originally came to national prominence with his gold album *Mug's Game*. In 2017 he released his tenth album *When*. He has been named a Western Australian State Living Treasure and has been inducted into the WAMi Rock'n'Roll of Renown.

www.davewarner.com.au
@suburbanwarner

DAVE WARNER
RIVER OF SALT

FREMANTLE PRESS

For Marie, Bernadette and Nadine — my girls of '63.

Contents

1. Yuri

'It's a fucking disgrace. This country has gone down the shitter.'

Holding the offensive newspaper with his fat left hand, Little Joey backhanded it with his right, the same way he smacked around a numbers runner who hadn't made his quota. Al knew what was coming next. What had come next every morning since April, making breakfast even more stressful: Fucking Russians.

'Fuckin' Russians.'

There it was. Al nodded as if in sympathy but in truth he admired Yuri Gagarin, admired anybody who could sit in a fucking tin drum and be shot into outer space. How many Russian cosmonauts were up there just floating around? You'd never believe what the Russians told you. Could be dozens. Mind you, given the job these last few months, it might be relaxing. Every bodyguard he knew had an ulcer. So far Al seemed to have been spared but perhaps that was because he hardly felt like eating. You couldn't put two hands on a burger for fear of a bullet in the back of the head. Bodyguard used to be a good job, prestigious, but ever since Carmelo had gone on the warpath, it had turned to shit. Philly was a fucking slaughterhouse. Little Joey should have distanced himself from Carmelo but what Joey was thinking — erroneously in Al's considered opinion — was that if Carmelo won the struggle with the Don, then Carmelo would come gunning for those who had been his enemy. Joey wasn't dumb. Well, not that dumb. He knew he couldn't sit on the fence forever but he was holding out, hoping New York stepped in, said, enough is enough, you assholes can't sort out your problems, we're taking over — in which case he might be rewarded for keeping a cool head.

Al smuggled a look at the boss slurping his coffee. There was a difference between being cool and being negligent. Refusing to change your habits, that was negligent. And who were the suckers who would pay for such negligence?

Sam, sitting opposite, stopped scanning the doorway for a moment to meet his eye, thinking the same thing: We're the ones gonna take lead and all he wants to do is talk Russians.

'They got women astronauts too. Can you believe that?'

No point correcting the boss. He'd forget 'cosmonaut' by lunch. Stubborn little motherfucker. He ate breakfast here most every day. They'd made it as secure as possible: two guys at the back door, Caesar in the car out front, them in the booth so they only had to defend three sides maximum. Including staff, there were fifteen people besides them. The skinny guy at the stool in the cheap suit, some sort of insurance guy would be Al's guess, was there most days. Same for the college kid looked like Troy Donahue with the glasses. He was always reading a book or a magazine at a table by himself. Apart from them, couple of secretaries grabbing a bite to eat, a henpecked husband and his wife, the staff who were mainly Polacks. Day before yesterday had been a bit of a scare, that shiver you feel: two guys, heavy set in suits, walking in off the street. Al's hand had gone straight to his inside coat pocket. He'd felt Sam tense, the same. The guys had ordered ham and eggs and sat on the far side. In the end nothing ... but the tension, whew ...

'They'll have a woman in space before we've even got one of our guys up there.'

Joey was shaking his head. He didn't even look up at the tinkle of the front door bell but Al and Sam did. Couple of guys, looked like plumbers, no threat. Breathe out.

'You guys see Arnold Palmer on the TV?'

'No, boss.'

Al didn't own a TV. If he did, he would not be watching golf. Golf had become Little Joey's latest thing. The plumbers were getting coffee, Al watching just in case.

'The guy is amazing.'

The golf course was another place that was a pain-in-the-ass to watch over the boss. Little Joey was a terrible golfer. He swung like he was swatting flies. Al was sure his boss hated it but the New York guys had taken it up and the ripples had spread. Sam and Al spent half their time looking out for snipers and the rest of the time looking for Joey's ball.

'That's one thing the fucking Russians can't do. Play golf.'

Al's eyes followed the plumbers, backs to him now, sitting on their stools. The bell rang again. Al's eyes flicked quickly, like the tip of a whip: two guys, suits … same guys as the day before. He watched, real careful now.

'I need gloves.'

Why wouldn't he just shut up?

'Ricki says ever since he bought gloves his game has improved. I have to stop slicing. Some guys hook. I slice.'

Al sensed somebody approaching, he tensed and swung … relaxed, only Troy Dona —

If Al had had the time, he would have congratulated the kid on his demeanour, his whole technique, his patience, and of course his accuracy but he never got that far because suddenly there was an automatic in the kid's hand and Al knew he'd been bested and it was the end. He never even felt the sting of the twenty-two-calibre bullet, being already dead when the kid shot Sam through the throat. Acting on instinct, Little Joey picked up the newspaper to shield his head. The kid put two right through the photo of Yuri Gagarin — the one thing Little Joey might have approved of — into Little Joey's brain, then walked calmly towards the door.

Blake moved purposefully just like the old guy who'd once done jobs for Capone had told him.

'Never rush out. It invites the unwanted, accidents, problems. You get hit by a car, knock over a pram … people remember that. I knew a guy: he fired, turned and ran straight through a glass door. He bled out on the pavement before the guy he shot. Wear glasses. All they remember: the guy wore glasses.'

By now the door was within reach. He was aware of the sense of disbelief around him. It was too immediate for the witnesses to be afraid. They were still processing, thinking it must be some stunt, thinking, what happened just then didn't actually happen. He pulled open the door. It felt light, like a cardboard prop. The bell jangled. They should invent a bell that doesn't jangle when you're leaving, he thought absently. All his thoughts were absent or, at the most, viewed through tracing paper. It was always that way in the zone and he'd been in the zone ever since he'd first entered the diner. Only when he stepped outside did he move into technicolour. Jimmy had a gun on Little Joey's driver, who was compliant, both hands on the steering wheel. Vince was covering the street. Right that second, Blake sensed the sedan approaching. It skidded to a halt: Marcello, always on time. Vince pulled the back door open for him and jumped in the front himself. Blake slid over. Jimmy piled in quick behind him and pulled the door. Marcello gunned the engine.

Nobody spoke.

No whoops, no shouts. It was business. Jimmy clapped him on the shoulder with that big hand of his that had always been there for him, the same right hand that had knocked their booze-hound father flat on his worthless ass and scared him out of their lives when Jimmy was just seventeen. When they still had a mother. All of this passed through Blake's brain before he heard the first siren heading back from where they'd left.

Marcello finally said, 'How many, kid?'

'All of them.'

Vincent sighed. 'I liked Al. It wasn't his fault he worked for that cocksucker.'

Winter was coming. Cold air seeped in through the car body and seemed to elevate the smell of stale tobacco. Nobody had lit up a cigarette yet, even though Jimmy and Marcello were inveterate smokers. It was as if all those parts of the world not directly to do with assassination and escape had been frozen.

After twenty minutes, Marcello pulled over two blocks north of their apartment block, popped the glove compartment, pulled out a lumpy envelope and passed it across to Jimmy, who opened it and quickly skimmed the notes.

'Three hundred bucks. For a triple? What the fuck!'

'The deal was only for Joey.'

'And how else is he supposed to get to Joey?'

'No one forced him to take the job.'

'The Don can't afford another three hundred?'

'You don't know who the client is. Don't suppose nuthin'. You're on thin ice, Jimmy.'

Vincent, who was Jimmy's friend, looked deep into his eyes.

'Take the money. You guys are building a reputation as reliable. That's money in the bank.'

Blake felt his brother was about to say something. This would not be advisable.

'It's okay,' Blake said, and stepped out of the car. The weight of the automatic in his bomber jacket made it sag to the right, and for the first time since he'd used it at the restaurant, Blake thought of it as a thing and not a limb, an extension of himself. That was his secret; when he was on a job, the gun was part of him, like a little kid playing bang-bang in a back lot pointing his finger. Jimmy snatched the money and slammed the door, a futile gesture, as Marcello had boosted the car earlier. What the fuck did he care if they took to it with an axe?

The brothers stood and watched the Electra rumble away under skies grey as an elephant's belly.

'It stinks,' said Jimmy but what went unsaid was he was the one who'd made the deal. He was the one who'd quoted too cheap, forgetting the bodyguards. Blake would never hold that against him though. They started along the sidewalk. The wind probed their clothes like the fingers of a dead man. It was a mixed neighbourhood but Blake felt more at home with the Polacks and Spades than the Italians from the old neighbourhood, a lot of who were now made guys with new allegiances. This was something he had grasped a long time ago but Jimmy still didn't get it. Vincent was one of his brother's oldest pals and Vincent loved Jimmy but even to Vincent they were outsiders now. That was never going to change but his brother still thought it was like when he was the bravest, toughest kid on the block leading the Italian kids, busting heads, boosting cars. The world had grown up around Jimmy without including him.

They lived in a plain red brick block. Blake hated it. He hated the cold of Philly. He especially hated the music Jimmy and his friends listened to: crooners who sang in neckties swaying with the mike, their eyes shut. The dark vestibule smelled of some kind of oily soup and yesterday's mutton fat. Blake tried the light switch but like always, nothing happened, the globe had been dead for a month. The bonus was he didn't have to look at the peeling wallpaper that had been there since the twenties and was even more depressing than this gloom. He gripped the bannister to begin hauling himself up the four floors.

His brother spoke softly in the dark. 'I'm sorry. It's my fault. I should have asked for triple or double at least. I'll make it up to you.'

'You don't have to.'

'I will. Trust me.'

Those were two words you never wanted to hear from Jimmy.

Later they were eating steaks at the small table in their apartment. This was the extent of their celebration for now. The irony of marking his kills by eating steak was not lost on Blake — dead meat buys dead meat — but he blocked the thought so it was no more than a soft footfall at the end of a dark hallway. Some men are born to write poetry or design frocks or hit a baseball out of the park. Everybody except Blake believed he'd been born to pull a trigger. This was the fourth time in a little over twelve months he and Jimmy had sat down to eat steak after a display of his prowess, and though he did not relish his calling, he still enjoyed the steak. Life dealt you a hand, you did your best with it. Or you tossed it in.

'You okay, champ?' Jimmy's eyebrows knitted as he leaned over, concerned. 'I didn't overcook it?'

'No, you cooked it fine.'

'So, what? You want to go dancing? I could scare up Trixie, she could find that friend of hers, the blonde ...'

'Mindy.'

'Yeah.'

Blake shrugged. Dancing didn't appeal. He didn't know what he wanted to do except maybe turn on the heater but the brothers were frugal and winter was coming when you'd need every cent to pay to be warm. Unless he chased another job. But no, he'd prefer to shiver than put a bullet in somebody's brain. The cash should last them a few months at least. His mind drifted back to the car, the parting argument about the money.

'You shouldn't have said that to Marcello, about the money.'

Jimmy nodded. 'I know. But it's okay. They need us. And the Don should have fucking paid more. And I know it's my fault, I made the deal but even so ... it had to be said.'

'You think he was the client?'

Marcello had never actually revealed who the hit was for.

'Of course he was the fucking client.'

'It could have been Carmelo.'

'No. Marcello and Vincent are the Don's guys. They wouldn't have anything to do with that psycho.'

'So why wouldn't the Don go after Carmelo? Why Little Joey?'

Jimmy pushed his plate away, shook his head like his kid brother had so much to learn. 'Carmelo is expecting that. He's strong. A lot of guys like Little Joey are sitting on the fence. You try to hit Carmelo and miss ... sends a bad message, rats start to leave the ship. So, you make an example of Little Joey. "You guys think you can sit on the bench, think again." Little Joey was a warning in lights from the Don: "I got teeth too."'

Three days later Blake was walking down the hallway to their apartment, his bones brittle. He'd had to force himself to leave the local diner. It was snug in there and he liked the sound of the cash register and plates and cutlery. Outside it was grey and too cold to shoot hoops. The weather had brewed up a chill all too quick. But he'd been there close on two hours and he couldn't stay forever. Jimmy was with Vincent scoping some job, so it was just him. As he passed number seventeen, he heard music like no music he'd ever heard before. It was all twang and thumping tom-toms. The guy in eighteen was a tall, skinny white guy and Blake knew him to nod to when they passed on the stairs but that was all. There was no sign of any woman living in the apartment. For a whole minute Blake stood outside the door listening to the music. It made him tingle all over. He realised the sound must have been a record, not radio, because when it finished he could hear the click of the needle. He was going to turn away but curiosity got the better of him and he knocked. A few seconds later the door opened and the guy stood there looking like he expected a complaint, defensive but more worried than angry.

'The music ...' Blake began.

'Was it too loud? I'm sorry.'

'No, no it was ... I'm Blake.'

'Pete Lanscombe.'

They shook hands awkwardly.

'I'm in ...' Blake pointed up the hall.

'Eighteen.'

'Yeah. I've never heard anything like that. It sounded ... wild.'

Lanscombe's face lit up. 'Isn't it! I picked it up in California. I just got back. This guy was playing ... Dick Dale. It's called surf music.'

Lots of times people say, 'That changed my life.' Sometimes they mean it, like the first time they spy their husband or wife. Or when they get shot in the knee because they skimmed or didn't pay on time. Of course that changes your life: you'll walk with a permanent limp and wake in the cold, dark hours with your bones throbbing. Lots of times though it's just a filler, one of those things said for effect. That's what Blake thought anyway, but when he heard that record with the twangy guitar he felt deep down inside that it really wasn't going to change anything, even though it should have changed everything.

Sometimes you can be wrong.

ㅁㅁㅁ

'You really want to go to California and play that thing?'

'That thing' was a Fender Stratocaster and it had cost Blake all his cut of the Little Joey job, apart from what they'd put aside for rent and food. It was his pride and joy but he didn't mind Jimmy speaking about it like it was a cheap ukulele. Jimmy didn't know any better and he was trying to look interested. Blake had been practising three hours straight. He figured it must have been driving his brother nuts. His fingers were blue with cold. He looked up from the guitar.

'I know it's just a dream.'

'No, no, don't say that.' Jimmy wagged a finger in his face. 'You want to do that, we'll do that.'

'Come on, Jim, all your friends are here.'

Jimmy's head was the size of a melon that could feed an Irish family. He shook it now. 'They're not my friends. You're my friend, the only one. I don't owe them nothing.'

What had transpired to alter Jimmy's opinion from three months earlier when the iceblock that was winter hadn't yet been dropped on their doorstep, was that the Don had forbidden Jimmy's planned robbery of a large craps game run by Carmelo. It seemed Carmelo was back at the heel with all the fight gone from him and the Don preferred that to crushing him as he might have and creating yet another power vacuum. At least that's what Blake had picked up from Jimmy. Blake didn't really care about or understand the deeper machinations of that crowd.

'I'm serious.' Jimmy was hunched in his big overcoat, hands jammed into the pockets. 'I'm sick of this. Let's get the fuck out of here, go live on Redondo Beach.'

'You don't swim.'

'Yet.'

'We need a car. They say in California you have to have a car.'

'We'll get one. Play me something.'

'The only thing I can play is "Silent Night".'

The guitar was only one or two years old. Blake had spied it in a pawnbroker's window. He didn't know any musicians but he saw there were a lot of musical instruments in the shop and figured the old Jewish guy who ran it might be able to suggest somebody who could teach him from his list of musician clients.

'You don't want those guys. Nice young kid like you. They're all black, all addicts. My sister's kid has been learning guitar. I'll give you the address.'

Blake had thought the guy meant 'kid' the way everybody called him kid. It turned out though that Arnold Schleider really was a kid, thirteen years old. He charged Blake a buck for two one-hour lessons a week. They sat in Arnold's bedroom beneath a Yankees banner. Arnold's mom brought them cups of cocoa. A Mob triggerman being schooled in guitar by a thirteen-year-old Jewish kid taking cocoa breaks … the weirdness wasn't lost on Blake. Arnold wasn't exactly a prodigy, so his method was to teach Blake just how he'd been taught. That meant 'Silent Night', which was still fresh in Arnold's memory from the recent Christmas.

Blake didn't want to play it now but Jimmy was so eager, like a big puppy waiting for you to toss a ball.

Hesitatingly, he fought his way through it, only having to go back twice.

'That's great. That is really fucking good. You're a talent. You don't have to do that other shit.'

Blake thought, no, seriously, we both know I do.

Jimmy was walking around in circles now, head bowed. 'Leave it with me. This is going to happen. Trust me.'

ᗞᗞᗞ

The main thing occupying Blake's mind as he sat in the broken chair in the basement of the parking lot, the wall behind him smeared in blood, was Jimmy saying, 'Trust me.' Even if the waitress at the diner hadn't very carefully slipped him the address and whispered, 'Your brother says you'll give me five bucks for this,' those words still would have been the steaming dog turd in the dining room of his mind. He'd tried to not look hurried, finished his coffee in his own good time and pushed out into the sleet. As if he had confirmed an appointment, the Mercury slid along the snow-flecked tar and stopped in front of him. Marcello and Vincent. Marcello told him to get in.

He acted dumb. 'What's wrong? Is Jimmy okay?'

'The boss wants to see you.'

That was all Marcello had said. Vincent had said nothing, tight-lipped, strained. You didn't have to be a genius: Jimmy says 'trust me', then he doesn't come home — okay, that in itself is not unusual — but the waitress with the address written on her pad, and then the Mercury and the guys ... what the fuck had Jimmy done? The second thing occupying his mind was not the cold — that was just a harsh fucking reality, Vincent was stamping his feet and Marcello was kicking a radiator that clearly wasn't working because it was an icebox down here — the second thing he was thinking about, way back there, was that this chair once occupied a place in a fine dining room. Maybe a hotel, or a large house where dinner guests dressed in black ties and tails, and ate sliced beef off silver platters. It was now a piece of junk, creaky, sloping to the right, cut adrift from its family and left here in this freezing basement lit by a single bulb. The splatter on the wall behind suggested the last person it had supported had not left the room in the same health in which he had entered. Another chair was placed right opposite him but not matching, a bentwood, better condition. Somewhere a pipe dripped. The rumble of the freight elevator descending turned all their heads. It was one with wire mesh in front. Eventually Blake could make out the Don, Franco Repacholi, or rather his cashmere coat. His cadaverous face was in shadow. His personal fixer, 'Peste', was at his side as always. Blake remembered asking Vincent what the name meant, pest?

'The plague, silent and deadly,' Vincent replied. 'You see him outside your house, you're already dead.'

An outsider might have found it amusing, a little stagey even, but it was all too fucking real to Blake.

Trust me.

The elevator jolted to a halt. Repacholi yanked open the grille himself. Blake noticed little things like that. The Plague couldn't defend his boss if he had one hand on the grille. The Don clipped over on his leather shoes and sat on the bentwood. He wore leather gloves to match the tan coat.

'What the fuck. It's fucking freezing in here.'

It was the first time anybody had spoken since Marcello had said the same thing ten minutes earlier and just like then it made mist when Repacholi opened his mouth.

'The radiator's not working, boss.'

Marcello gave it a kick to prove the point. The Don shook his head as if to ask the Lord to give him strength. Then his eyes fixed on Blake and Blake felt his insides turn to soup.

'You're not in trouble, kid. I like you. Jesus Christ, it's cold down here. You do a good job. You keep your head down. You don't make trouble. So, I want to assure you I'm genuine. We can put this behind us, move on. Where is he?'

Repacholi pulled a cigarette case from his inner jacket pocket, flipped it open, offering one to Blake who shook his head. Blake had never smoked. People who smoked always had their hands occupied with lighters or matches or tearing cellophane and he wanted his hands to always be ready.

'Where is your brother?'

The words 'I don't know' had pushed their way to the door of the moving bus but before they could ring the bell, Repacholi pointed a bony finger at him.

'Before you tell me you don't know, which I understand, he's your brother …' Repacholi put the cigarette between his lips then produced a smooth little silver lighter and fired up, inhaling, '… I must warn you, this is a very serious situation for you.'

Somehow Blake found words. 'What do you think he did?'

'I don't *think*, I know. Same as I know you weren't involved. Eighteen top quality furs. Mink, sable …' he waved his cigarette, '… gone. I busted my balls to boost those. Flew in this shit-hot alarm guy from … where the fuck was he from?'

Even though his boss kept his gaze on Blake, the bodyguard knew he was the one being asked. 'Detroit.'

'Flew him in.' Repacholi took another drag as if the memory pained him. 'More fucking planning than D Day. And to have that taken from me, by someone in my own family, that's like … fucking Eskimo would freeze to death in here … it's like a knife going into my own nuts. That's what it's like.'

Marcello gave the radiator another kick to show he was trying something.

'Your brother knows I use the Margolis warehouse.'

'Maybe it was Margolis? Jimmy didn't come home. He probably figures you'll think it's him.'

'It is him.'

'It could be Margolis.'

Peste spoke. 'It was not Margolis.'

Blake now knew whose blood was on the wall behind him but kept swinging, his desperation palpable. 'What about the Feds? Maybe they have a wiretap. All cops are dirty. They heard about the furs …'

The boss held up his palm: desist. 'You are not guilty but because the guilty party is not here and you are family, you are responsible. However, you can discharge that responsibility. I need to know where he is. Half of those furs belong to New York. You see what I'm dealing with, son? This is an extra-jurisdictional situation. Things happen on my patch, I become responsible even though I am not guilty. There is nothing I can do for him. I won't pretend otherwise. It's too fucking cold. I can only protect you from New York if you give me your fuck-up brother. You're loyal. I like that. Don't be stupid here. We'll find him. Your brother's not that smart. But you know what, he loves you. If he were in this room right now freezing his nuts off, he would tell you, save yourself. And I promise you absolutely, this will be no impediment to you going forward. The opposite. No-one will harm you. I give you my word. Now I am going to ask you, and I want you to think very carefully before you answer. Where is Jimmy?'

Under the illumination of the headlights you could see snowflakes falling. They look like lost souls, thought Blake. He remembered a picture of a painting he had seen in a book once, scared and tortured humans falling into hell's belly. He was numb, had been on the ride over, sitting in the back alongside Vincent. Pennsport: he hadn't been in this neck of the woods for a while but it figured. Jimmy used his Irish pals for the job. They got drunk. Or their women did. Somebody blabbed. They must have been damn near caught in the act because Jimmy hadn't even made it home. He'd obviously cut out and gone to ground. And all to get him to California and a bullshit dream that was never going to happen now. It was silent in the car. They had cruised into the street, headlights off. Row houses. The address was across the way, plain brick, a jaundiced light in a second-floor apartment. Blake looked across at Vincent, stretched back, eyes closed, a revolver sitting in his shoulder holster. There for the taking. He could do it. He could ...

'Time.'

It was Marcello. He had driven. Peste was beside him, a sawed-off shotgun across his lap. Blake's heart was galloping now, his cheek cold against the passenger window, his breath misting it up.

He'll know I've betrayed him, he thought. The Don sold me some candy, a way out. I took it. Jimmy will look down from a grimy window and through the descending snow he'll see legs in dark trousers striding his way and he will know.

The click of the car doors closing, quiet as it was, made him jump. He snuck another look at Vincent, the gun still within reach. Still time. No sounds except their breathing, the others' footsteps had been snuffed already.

'You didn't do anything wrong, kid. You had no choice.' Vincent sounded resigned, like he was talking to himself. Then his voice changed a gear. 'You need to get out. I know what the Don said. I think he believes it. Now. But sooner or later he'll doubt. They always do. They should be there now. Marcello the front, Peste the back. Take my gun, hit me across the head with it and get the fuck outta here.'

Vincent's words were like a child's fist beating on the window of a car sinking in the river. They couldn't break through.

'Blake, listen to me. Jimmy is my best friend. This is the only thing I can do for him. Take the fucking gun.'

Blake snapped the pistol from the holster and backhanded Vincent across the forehead. He thought he heard the crack of bone but it was lost as he shoved open the door and jumped out, skidding on the sidewalk. For an instant he stood looking up at the window, suspended the way a tiny leaf gets snagged in a spider web. Then he started moving quickly away in a hunched run. Something made him turn and look back up. Two bright muzzle flashes lit the window. He ran.

Going back to his apartment was too dangerous. They could put a call through, send somebody. Or they might not. Who would they send? The Pest? Would the Don risk him knowing Blake was armed? But maybe there would be somebody waiting anyway. Somebody out of New York, sitting there in the dark. He couldn't risk it. But he had to. That's where the guitar was.

The cab took the last of his cash. He had it drop him a block away. He couldn't afford to think of Jimmy, not yet. He cut through a back alley. Nobody obvious at the rear of the building. The front clear too. If it was him he'd be waiting in the vestibule or the apartment, give the target two steps inside then open up. Blake could wait for some other tenant, come in with them but nobody was out. It was too cold. He pushed the door open into the gloomy vestibule tensing for shots, the pistol gripped in his right hand down by his leg. Nothing except the familiar smell of soup, and the mutter of faint television. He took the stairs carefully. The muzzle flashes snapped in his head like rim shots. Down the dark corridor now, pitch black, past Lanscombe's, with some kind of quiet jazz playing tonight. He stood outside the door to his apartment, pistol still in his right hand, key now in his left. He sniffed, inhaled. A good killer, you'd never hear a breath, waste of time trying, but tobacco, cologne … he could smell nothing. Pistol gripped and ready for action, he slid the key in the lock began to turn it. That's when he heard the door to Lanscombe's apartment open and knew he'd fucked up. He'd been bested. He was a dead man. The killer had taken out Lanscombe first. There was a gun probably with a silencer pointing at the back of his head right now. He'd betrayed Jimmy for noth—

'Hey, Blake.'

He swung around, pistol pointing, found the will to not depress the trigger. He saw Lanscombe's hands go up.

'Easy, man.'

He dropped his hand back down. The light from Lanscombe's apartment was backlighting him. He had his hand out, something in it.

'Some woman knocked on my door. Irish. She said Jimmy said to give this to you.'

It was a brown paper package, small, wrapped in string and tape. Blake took it.

'Thanks.'

Lanscombe retreated towards his flat. 'Oh, and she said Jimmy said, "Get a suntan."'

Lanscombe's door closed behind him and Blake was alone again with that odour of mutton fat. He ripped open the package. Cash, several hundred by the looks. He felt shame. He had thought his brother dumb. Jimmy had known all along how it would play out if things went awry. This cash must be some advance he'd negotiated. He knew they would grab Blake. He knew the deal they'd put to him, he knew Blake would take it and would come back for his guitar.

Trust me.

River of salt, flowing from my eyes. Blake tasted it, couldn't stop it.

2. Twang

His belly pressed flat into the board which gently rose and fell like a crumb on the chest of a snoozing giant. Blue as far as the eye could see, above, out yonder, all around. Not a day went by Blake didn't pinch himself that this was his new reality, the sun burning into his shoulders, his legs dangling in the mighty Pacific.

And all of it because of Jimmy.

He could talk to him out here where there were mostly only seagulls for company, other surfers few and far between.

'We're goin' in, Jimmy,' he would say as he felt the ocean draw in its breath. He would turn to spy a cliff of water building further out to sea. 'Come on, this is ours.' And he would smile as he imagined Jimmy pulling back, trying to get away because he always hated water and sky and open air. As he stood, he felt Jimmy with him, felt him finally giving in, standing with him, right in front, the wind ruffling his hair, a giant smile creasing his face as the power of something so much bigger than the Mob, than the whole of Philly, carried them towards the shore.

Blake had never cried since about what happened. He was too empty for that. But if he could, he still wouldn't have because he didn't want to let Jimmy down, wanted him to know he was thankful for every minute. And Jimmy was always with him, he knew that, so why cry?

As he rode to shore, he caught sight of the Surf Shack billboard and, as always, it made him swell with pride.

'We made good, Jimmy, you and me,' was his silent thought until the slope of the wave fell away and the big sign was no longer visible. He dropped down onto the plank and rode into the shallows. There were a handful of swimmers to the south. The beaches were unbelievable here, miles of them and next to nobody else. He could have chosen any of them to settle but he picked this one because it was pristine and even more deserted than most. Some kids ran by calling to their dog running behind them, a collie, they were popular here. He plucked the board from the ocean and stared east. Thousands of miles thataway was where he might have been but for fate. However, he never regretted the decision made initially with safety in mind. LA hadn't been far enough. Wise guys were always heading to California to grab some sun and bikini bait. But that had become a secondary consideration. He loved it here. It was undiscovered. He felt like a Conquistador except even better, he didn't have to learn Spanish because the locals already spoke English — well, kind of, but he liked that too, the junky way they talked.

He loved everything about Australia.

The Coral Shoals forefathers were smart. They'd not allowed anybody to build on the beach. The closest you could be was across the other side of the coast road, which was where he'd spotted the Steak Cave nearly two years ago. Later, when he knew what he wanted to do and exactly the sort of bar he wanted to own, he had remembered this location and bought the licensed restaurant.

Even though the board was a heavy fucker, he could have walked to the beach from his house, less than half a mile north, but the sand was hot under the January sun and so he had driven. He slung the board into the back of the ute. It was pretty much like a pick-up truck, useful to transport the kegs to parties around the hinterland. In the early days the hire business had been his saviour. After buying the Steak Cave, even though it was a steal, he had no cash left to do it up but Blake had spied an opportunity in hauling kegs out to private parties: weddings, engagements; twenty-firsts especially, for twenty-one was the legal drinking age and the youngsters always figured they could put away more beer than they really could. You added in the hire of glassware and coloured lights and the whole thing was lucrative enough to pay for the furnishings of the Surf Shack — which had to be exactly how Blake wanted — plus enough left over to rent a house. The best thing was, there was absolutely no competition apart from the golf club and it was harder to become a member of that than the Mob. He'd heard they balloted prospective members out with a black ball. So, unless you were over forty and well-heeled, you had to head twenty miles south before you would find another place to drink. To the north was more populated. The Ocean View Motel served dinners and had a small bar but it was a good forty-minute drive. That was the closest liquor outlet. Another forty minutes north, you hit a strip of coastal bars and pubs and then things got busier up to the sea aquarium by the Queensland border. Here at Coral Shoals, his only competition for the entertainment dollar was the drive-in, minigolf and an open-air movie theatre. The drive-in was pretty much exclusively teenagers taking the chance to grope one another away from the family house and Blake didn't serve teens anyway. There was no way he would jeopardise his licence. Sergeant Leslie Nalder had made it abundantly clear that's what would happen if Blake transgressed, even if it meant Nalder temporarily having a drop in his income. Nalder wasn't cheap, twelve pounds a week, but he was worth his weight in gold because he opposed every application by every prospective business that wished to sell liquor.

Mindful of the big surfboard propped in the back, Blake drove slowly along the coast road past the collection of strip shops that comprised the town, before turning left up Reynolds and right up Wattle. Halfway along Wattle the houses thinned, each dwelling followed by two vacant blocks. Just before Wattle dead-ended, Blake swung left up a steep gravel driveway and came to rest underneath the house he rented. The whole area was prone to huge thunderstorms and heavy flooding so most of the older houses were made of wood or fibro and built high on stilts to prevent flood damage. Up this way they called them Queenslanders. The newer brick houses with their stone feature walls, sunken lounge rooms and rolling lawns were mostly clustered a couple of miles south and west on a wide, long ridge which everybody just referred to as 'the Heights'. The golf club was located in the Heights.

Blake pulled out his board and hosed it down. Then he took the concrete interior steps from the garage up into his living area. Blake's house was unusual in that it was built like a Queenslander but made of brick, the living area sitting on top of high concrete pillars with a wide wooden deck that had once gleamed in new varnish but was now weathered. Given the house was on top of the small hill and had brick pillars for extra height, he guessed it was immune to flood damage but so far he'd not experienced that kind of disaster. It was much bigger than he needed but the houses here were bigger than anybody needed. He had two bedrooms and a big lounge room with ocean views, because across from him was a double vacant block and then sandhills and water. One of the reasons he had wanted two bedrooms was to make it feel like Jimmy was still living with him. As it turned out though, none of the houses he looked at had less than two bedrooms. This place had the view, and he could go to bed at night with his windows open and listen to the soft hiss of breaking waves. It was about as far away from Philly as he could imagine. The owner was a builder who had lived here with his family before child number three came along. He'd subsequently shifted to the Heights.

Blake stripped off and took a quick cold shower. He stood naked on his deck and dried himself. There were no neighbours close enough to worry about and traffic rarely came to the end of the cul-de-sac. Even though it was hot, there was a smell of moisture in the air that Blake had come to associate with summer in Coral Shoals. Like Florida, he guessed. It conjured images of sugar cane and lightning and tall grass growing out of irrigation ditches on the side of roads of crumbling bitumen. It might thunder later, it might not. You couldn't tell and there was no point worrying about it.

Being a Tuesday meant he was off the hook from anything major. He could while away the day practising guitar. Tuesdays, his band The Twang usually practised at the Surf Shack but the drummer, Duck, who was a plumber, had a job on in the hinterland. The Surf Shack opened Thursday to Saturday and that was enough for Blake. He wasn't complaining. It had been six long months of hard work fitting the place out so the bar had precisely the look he wanted: the booths shaped like waves, the tables surfboards cut in half — which was exactly what they were — the bar itself like it was set into a reef, and of course the giant aquarium that bisected the room and made it feel like you really might be underwater. He'd had to get a loan for all that but within a month of opening the doors it was clear he had a smash-hit on his hands. Friday and Saturday the place was jam-packed, people flocking from miles around, driving hours to check it out. Thursday was strong too.

He broke away from the deck, went back inside and dressed in jeans and a striped top. Most people said he was the spitting image of James Dean. Those that didn't said he was Troy Donahue — yes, Jimmy, ha ha. It was the quiff, that was all. He checked the time: a little after eleven. Andy, the yardy, would be at the Shack feeding the aquarium fish, cleaning the toilets; Doreen probably not. She generally liked to do all the accounts Monday and take Tuesday off.

Thank God for Doreen. And no, Jimmy, I ain't going there, she's too valuable.

While he squeezed oranges, he put a Ray Charles LP on the turntable. That guy was the man. Blake wouldn't even attempt to play that stuff, he was strictly surf twang but that didn't mean he couldn't appreciate it. He scrambled some eggs and ate barefoot on his balcony, staring out at the low sandhills in the distance and the ocean twinkling behind. Not for the first time he imagined a group of half-a-dozen men in dark suits appearing over the rise of the hills and traipsing towards him: killers who had crossed the ocean to get him. He could sit up here with a rifle and pick them off. Except he didn't have a rifle and they weren't coming. They didn't care that much about him and even if they did, they wouldn't find him.

Getting a passport had been easy. He even told his contact to find one with the first name Blake so he wouldn't have to think twice about somebody calling his name. Of course he had to give up his surname but that was no problem. That was like giving up a bad flu that had been with you forever. Blake Saunders sounded respectable. He liked being respectable. Originally he'd been thinking only of Hawaii. Shit, you were going to play surf music, you better get your ass there, right? It was in a bar in Long Beach things turned out the way they did. Blake got talking to this interesting guy who had flown in the war, survived Midway. Turned out he was flying a Catalina to Hawaii so Blake naturally asked if he could hitch a ride. The pilot, Jim — an omen, surely — was glad for the company.

'Son, you want to you can fly all the way to Australia with me.'

And that was it, like it was meant to be. No more looking over his shoulder, they would never find him in Australia. So Blake had island-hopped all the way to Brisbane, the experience of a lifetime. Jim was delivering the plane to an outfit that operated to the Great Barrier Reef. Blake could have stayed on, taken the job he was offered by Jim's contacts but he wanted to keep moving. He hitchhiked down the east coast, improved his surfing, practised guitar. Three months in he had passed through Coral Shoals and spied the Steak Cave, a restaurant that was struggling even though it was in the most glorious location. Right off he knew this was the place he could make his dreams happen. And that's how it was. The Surf Shack was making money and, more important, he was having fun doing everything he'd always wanted. Except it wasn't with Jimmy.

Blake finished his eggs and washed and dried his dishes. Doreen had told him that one of the doors in the women's toilets had a broken lock.

He'd check whether Andy had fixed it, do it himself if he needed, practise his licks later. One thing he'd retained from his previous occupation was attention to detail. The Surf Shack had to be perfect, no blemishes. People might say, one little lock, it's no big deal. But it says everything about an establishment. Besides, little things could cause big problems. He remembered the story of a triggerman in the Kansas City Mob whose chipped fingernail snagged on his suit coat pocket when he went to pull his piece. That fraction of a second was all it took. The bodyguards shot him dead. Maybe he was too slow anyway, maybe he didn't do his homework on the bodyguards but that really just proved the point. You wanted to survive in this world — no blemishes.

Andy had done a good job on the lock. Blake checked all the stall doors in the women's and men's toilets to make sure there were no other problems. More than most, Blake understood a desire for privacy. Andy was out the back now, carefully stacking crates of empties. They'd first met when Andy was helping the guys who put up the billboard. He was only twenty then, so Blake couldn't employ him during hours the place operated as a liquor outlet but he'd given him odd jobs to do during the day. Andy told Blake he had left school at fourteen and had no trade. He put his heart and soul into his job as yardman-janitor. Two months ago he had turned twenty-one and Blake had thrown a party for him in the main room. Andy's smile had lit up like neon.

'Nice job on the lock.'

Andy shrugged, bashful, like a pretty girl had complimented him on his shirt.

'It was nothing.' Then his smile faded and he stammered, 'I'm worried about Audrey.'

He was right. Something was amiss. Audrey wasn't gliding with her usual imperious style.

'You think her top fin is okay?' Blake had no qualms seeking Andy's advice. Andy spent hours studying the fish. Blake had watched him when he'd been in doing the books or rehearsing. Andy peered in at the tank, which was fifteen feet long and nearly five feet high, though only ten inches across. The main room lights were off, so the fish were particularly luminescent.

'Could be. Yeah, at the top there.'

Audrey sported magnificent black and white stripes. Doreen had named her for Audrey Hepburn. She loved Audrey Hepburn. She kept urging Blake to see *Breakfast at Tiffany's* if it ever came to Coral Shoals but that was unlikely. Films usually only made it here when they were at least five years old. Doreen had caught the film when she'd visited her sister in Sydney. Blake never wanted her to visit her sister again. If he hadn't realised before, he came to understand how much work she did. Besides, Doreen was the only one you could—

'I bet it's him.' Andy pointed angrily like a jealous lover.

'It might not be him.' Blake felt obliged to come to the defence of the Siamese fighting fish. Just because its family had a bad reputation didn't make it a villain.

'I bet it is.'

By now Blake wasn't so sure there was anything wrong with Audrey's fin. Maybe it just looked odd because she wasn't moving quite so well. Maybe she was just sick.

'I don't know there's anything wrong with her fin.'

'No. I'm pretty sure it doesn't look right. Mr Clarke called. Sorry, I meant to mention it. He wants to hire two eighteens for his son's birthday. He asked could you go see him.'

Andy sometimes forgot that he knew the locals a lot better than Blake.

'Who is Mr Clarke?'

Andy pointed vaguely to the centre of town. 'Clarke's Cars.'

There was only one car yard in Coral Shoals, a lot of acreage light on stock, as you might expect from this size town. The models reflected the inhabitants — station wagons and sedans. To his knowledge, Blake hadn't met Clarke. His own car he'd purchased at the Heads.

'Doreen been in?'

'Haven't seen her.'

'Keep your eye on Audrey for me.'

Andy had his eyeball almost to the glass. 'It's that bastard, I know it is.'

Remnants of blond hair clung around the rim of Winston Clarke's head like civilisation around an extinct volcano. At least, Blake presumed it was Clarke slapping the bonnet of an eight-cylinder Holden as he laid it on. The customer, sixty or so, was weathered and wiry-tough. A farmer, Blake reckoned. As the older man followed Clarke around the car hearing its virtues extolled, it was clear he had a permanent limp. Farm accident or Great War? His vintage, it could be either. The man Blake presumed was Clarke was somewhere in his forties. Used-car salesmen, like Jimmy's Mob connections, were always a couple of beats behind fashion, still with wide lapels and short, wide handpainted ties. Blake leaned against the counter, scoping the brick back wall of the office, the other three sides nearly all glass. Pride of place was a black and white photo of Clarke, some other guy and Bob Hope standing on a golf course, smiling at the camera.

'What have you got in mind? Something with a lotta toe. Am I right?'

The voice came from behind him and spun him around. The salesman standing in the doorway looked younger than him. His first thought was this was Clarke's son, the party-boy, but his suit was not only dated, it was cheap and it jarred that a father would throw his son a big party yet let him dress like a hick.

'Barry Leftwich.'

He threw out a skinny hand. Blake didn't extend his own.

'I'm not a customer, Barry. Here to see Mr Clarke.'

Clarke must have gazed in through the window and sensed his salesman was in trouble because he left the farmer to ogle the Holden engine and came inside.

'Gentleman says he is here to see you.' Leftwich was clearly sceptical of Blake's claim that he wasn't here to buy, like he might have been holding out for the main man who could authorise a better deal.

'Blake Saunders, Surf Shack.'

The penny dropped for Clarke. 'Oh, right.'

Leftwich was straining at the leash, throwing glances at the farmer. 'Shall I attend to the other gentleman?'

'No, Barry, you attend to the incinerator. We need to burn those boxes while the breeze is blowing from the west.'

In that heartbeat, Blake understood Leftwich, his frustration and humiliation. Clarke didn't trust him enough to close the farmer sale. Blake didn't blame him. Leftwich slunk off. Clarke was darting looks through the window, keeping a close eye on his prospective sale.

'I'm looking at two eighteens. The party is Thursday night.'

'Twenty-first? I got coloured lights, a jukebox.'

'I've got my own lights and shit. Just the grog and glassware. We're on Belvedere up past the general store, yellow wood letterbox.'

Blake pictured the area up in the hills about six miles out of town. Clarke pulled a business card from his wallet and a fountain pen from his pocket and scrawled across the back.

'My home phone number.'

'It'll cost thirty pounds including delivery and pick up.'

'That's alright. If I'm not there, my kid Tom will be. What part of the States are you from?'

It wasn't a question he got a lot.

'Pittsburgh.'

The salesman nodded. 'I lived there after the war, Los Angeles, three years. My sister married a Yank sailor she met here. He went into the movies.' His glance strayed towards the Hope photo and Blake readied for the tale but then Clarke saw the farmer looking around and finance got the better of an entertaining story. He took a step towards the door but stopped, and turned back to Blake.

'What are you driving? I got an imported Chevy Bel Air would be perfect.'

Blake nodded at his ute which was parked a way over. 'That'll do me for now.'

'Keep it in mind. You're in a business. You need to spread the right image.'

Blake was ready to suggest Clarke heed his own advice but the salesman was already outside striding back to the farmer, dangling keys for a test drive.

Blake checked his watch. Near midday, Carol should be awake.

After they came, they lay on their backs getting their breath back. It was cool in here with a sense of damp. The cottage was small, dwarfed by palms and other thick vegetation that thrived in the semi-tropical climate, so the bedroom was always in shade. Carol reached for a Rothmans King Size and lit it with a chunky nickel-plated cigarette lighter. Nothing about smoking appealed to Blake. He found himself thinking back to his former occupation, things not to do if you wanted to survive, kicked the idea to the kerb. He was glad the stream of smoke could sneak out through the louvres Carol never shut. He couldn't get over how people here never locked doors or windows. It had been like going against a law of nature but eventually he'd got into the practice of leaving open the upstairs windows of his own house. Carol was maybe twenty-four — he'd never asked — small breasts, firm, tanned. When she wasn't sleeping or tending bar at the golf club, she was sunbathing. Blake enjoyed the convenience of daytime sex. Once it was over he could leave, no strings attached. He didn't want anyone else in his house, especially not at night. He shared his bed with enough demons.

'You've got a dance competition on,' she said, flicking ash into a thin metal ashtray showing the crest of the golf club.

'Yeah. Thursday, hoping it will be busy. You?'

'Sleepy Hollow as usual.'

The golf club was a staid crowd but the tips were good. They'd met when she'd turned up at the Surf Shack looking for a job. If he hadn't wanted to have sex there and then, he might have hired her, but you didn't screw the staff, that was a line he was not going to cross. He told her to try the golf club, advised her that the tips would be far better than his place and the work easier, both of which were true. Then he took her to lunch and after, they fucked furiously on the beach. That was around six weeks ago. He saw her most days.

She sat up, as if determined to make the day begin. 'You want breakfast?'

'You mean lunch?'

Her eyes drifted to the clock, registered the hour. 'I could fix us something.'

'I'm alright.'

He was thinking he might get in another surf before rehearsal. He got up and searched for his underpants. She sucked the cigarette real long, then said, 'You want to meet up later, after work?'

'No. I'll be tired.' He sensed her disappointment, tried to soften it as he dressed. 'Tomorrow I have a rehearsal and have to get things ready for the dance comp. What about Sunday? We could take a run down the coast?' Friday she worked afternoons, Saturday was her big day at the club so he knew she'd be out of action.

'Sure.'

Like a kid who was pleased to get a Christmas gift under the tree even if it wasn't the one they really wanted. He leaned in and kissed her, tasting the smoke.

'Sunday, then.'

ㅁㅁㅁ

With The Orlons' 'Wah-Watusi' pounding out of the jukebox, Doreen demonstrated the dance to the assembled girls. Worried the whole thing might be a disaster — the dance comp was her idea — she'd spent all yesterday cruising the beach and distributing handbills promising 'fabulous prizes'. Ten had shown up for the rehearsal so as long as they all fronted tomorrow night, she'd have sufficient contestants. Some of the girls followed her moves, the others stared in amazement at her long legs. It had always seemed her destiny to have been a star netballer or a TV dancer but instead here she was, hostess and promotions manager for the Surf Shack. Unlike the frug, the watusi was simple and required no training because your feet barely moved, a total waste of the six years Doreen had spent on her toes imagining herself as a prima ballerina. When reality hit — she was too tall and not precise enough to be Dame Margot — she had shifted into chorus work but that was too much of a job so she quit. She shed no tears for her change in career path. On the contrary, it was dancing she loved, and it was more enjoyable when that wasn't your profession. The advantage of the watusi was it gave all the girls a chance whether they'd had dance lessons or not. A high ponytail and trim figure helped but all you needed was energy. The track finished. She got her breath back and turned to the expectant faces.

'You got it?'

The girls looked at one another, mumbled and nodded. Doreen guessed eight of the ten were underage but so long as none of them actually consumed alcohol, Nalder would turn a blind eye, although the little one that had modelled herself on Patty Duke could be a worry.

'Why don't you girls give it a shot?'

Three of them had come prepared and were wearing leotards, a couple in bikinis, the rest skirts. 'Everybody in swimsuits tomorrow, okay? And no alcohol. Stick to Coke, unless you're over twenty-one, which most of you aren't.' She heard herself sounding like a maiden aunt. She was twenty-five, no man, no plan. She strode to the jukebox and punched in the track, listened to the mechanical whirr give way to the click of the needle in the groove, then boom — the track exploded and the girls began to move. A blonde in a bikini was a natural, her arms pumping, her arse curved and hard as steel. The leotard girls were fair. Patty Duke was stored energy, wanting to bust out of that skirt, this club, the house in the Heights where she undoubtedly lived with her parents. Raw but with the beat of life thumping inside her ribs. Just like you were, Doreen, a decade of mistakes ago.

Most of them were going to be fine. The men would be standing on the dance floor looking up at the catwalk, checking out those bodies. Doreen didn't want her girls to suffer any kind of put-down from some wanker trying to show off to his mates, she wanted these women to walk out of here, tall, all winners. A noble sentiment but it was obvious the blonde had it in the bag. Walking along the line that they'd formed themselves into, Doreen offered encouragement, a little advice, some corrections. The song stopped.

'That's good. I'd like you all here by seven tomorrow.'

All of a sudden the girls resembled the fish in the tank behind them, bulging eyes, stunned expressions. Doreen turned to see Blake had walked onto the stage carrying his guitar. Duck the drummer and Panza the bass player followed in his wake but the girls' eyes were only on Blake. A couple whispered behind their hands to their friends. Nobody like Blake had ever lived in Coral Shoals.

'Any questions?'

Doreen gradually regathered their attention like pins spilled from a basket.

'What does the winner get?'

It was Patty Duke. She couldn't be over sixteen.

The blonde sniped, 'Won't make any difference to you, Kitty, you're only going to embarrass yourself. Why don't you go and ... sew or something?'

The other girls laughed. Kitty looked crestfallen.

Doreen said, 'The winner gets a brand new transistor radio.'

'Perfect. Todd and me can listen to it while he's sticking his tongue down my throat.'

It was the blonde with no trace of irony.

'Wish my boss looked like that,' offered a skinny girl, her eyes still locked on Blake.

Doreen said, 'A boss is a boss. Okay, ladies, be here tomorrow night at seven.'

'We're all in? Even her?' The blonde jerked her thumb at Kitty.

Doreen wasn't going to get into it with the little bitch. 'Seven, don't be late.'

The blonde sashayed out right past the stage, three of the others following. Blake was too busy with his guitar to notice but Duck beamed.

'Sayonara, ladies.'

Duck's lines always sounded like they came from a sidekick in an Elvis film. Doreen figured they probably had. Kitty was still fumbling with her things. She looked stressed. The blonde had got to her.

Doreen said, 'You sure you want to do this?'

The girl looked up at Doreen with resolve. 'Yes. I am.'

'What's his name?'

'Who?'

'The guy you're hoping to impress.'

Duck was playing drum fills now. Doreen knew she was right, knew this was all about some boy. She could imagine Kitty with a dreamy faraway look in her eyes, lying on her stomach on the carpet of her affluent parents' sunken lounge room. A romantic Rodgers and Hart song would be playing on the phonograph as Kitty slowly drew her finger around the photo of the high-school sports star in the school annual.

'Todd.' The name came out with the hesitation of a dog that knows it has done the wrong thing.

'Eva Braun's boyfriend?'

'Brenda talks through her bum. I'm not sure Todd even likes her.'

'I know something about men, and I'm guessing he probably does.'

Doreen pulled out a cigarette, leaned back and lit up. Normally she avoided smoking around Blake.

'You think I'll embarrass myself, right? Don't worry. I'm working off a low threshold here. If I fall, it won't hurt much.'

Doreen sized her up. 'Maybe we should raise that threshold.'

Kitty was breathless. 'You could help me?'

Blake had started playing. It was the new song, a sweet ballad, really different to the normal instrumental surf stuff. He began to croon:

She holds my heart in her fingertips.
Traces my soul with the sweetest lips.

'I'd love to see you wipe the floor with that bitch.'

It's bliss each we time kiss but we know.
No good can come ... of this.

'You're still at school, right?'

'Brenda's only just finished.'

She holds my soul. In those eyes divine.
Heavenly body, lips the sweetest wine
It's bliss each we time kiss but we know ...
No good can come ... of this.

Part of Doreen wanted to imagine Blake had written the song for her. The rest of her was indifferent. He was her boss, never the twain and all that.

'Alright, Kitty. You're still on holidays, right? Meet you back here at two and we'll put in a couple of hours.'

'I've done ballet.'

'I can see. The steps aren't what you have to work on.'

'What do I have to work on?'

'Sex.'

He loved this middle part, didn't know from where within him it had come. First to the F, *Though her love is a waterfall* ... then to the G and C ... *This man's heart is but sand* ... He wondered what Doreen was talking about with the girl. Maybe explaining she was too young for the competition ... And here it was, the part that really kicked, where it goes to the E minor ... *She still thinks she can have it all* and right on up to the D ... *But she'll rue the day* ...and back to G ... *Love came to stay* ...

His focus drifted back out. The side door had opened and a shaft of light speared in ahead of two men in wide trousers and sports jackets that had seen better days, not cops ... more like the types Jimmy hung out with, low-lifes that would sell their sisters for a packet of smokes. They draped themselves on the bar stools. After Doreen had farewelled the girls she approached them, must have asked what they wanted. Then she turned and pointed at him. Their eyes followed her ass as she exited in that stylish way of hers, like a graceful cat. Blake kept the interlopers waiting, finished the song, then ran through the surf numbers that would back the watusi dancers. Duck sped up on the toms, slowed down on the snare. His eyes were redder than a Santa suit.

'You've been smoking that funny stuff again.' Rehearsal was done. Blake carefully laid his guitar in its case.

'It relaxes me.' Duck was short, and his grin always reminded Blake of those mechanical toy monkeys that banged cymbals.

'Relaxes you too much, man, you were behind the beat.' Panza was the opposite of the drummer, over six foot, skinny. Blake had found him in a trad-jazz band up the coast playing double bass.

'No man, you were ahead of the beat. It's the German in you, you got that blitzkrieg thing going on.'

Panza's great-grandfather had been German — Dieterling — and Duck gave him hell about it. Around here, rhythm sections were scarcer than hen's teeth and Blake smelled potential for disharmony. He stepped in.

'Lay off that stuff before the show, Duck. And no peddling it to the chicks. Nalder doesn't like that shit.'

Only then did he climb down off stage to see what the two guys wanted.

'How may I help you gentlemen?' Now that he was close, he saw his initial suspicion was on the money. Grubby trousers, sweated-up shirts. They exuded ex-con.

'Actually mate, we were thinking we could help you.'

If one could be described as the better looking or more civilised, it was this one. He was six foot, around there. The other was shorter than Blake with a five o'clock shadow, low forehead and broad shoulders. Blake snuck a look at his fists, like sledgehammers. The spokesman gestured Blake should join them at one of his own tables. He thought about remaining standing but decided he would play it cool. The last thing he wanted was trouble.

He said, 'I'm very happy with my current suppliers.'

His mind was moving fast. He expected they were going to offer him cheap — obviously stolen — cigarettes. He'd probably take some to get rid of them.

The apish one said, 'We're more in the insurance game.'

Most Australian accents sounded the same to Blake. Not this guy. He was coarse as a bum's blanket. So, this was a good old-fashioned shakedown.

'I have insurance.'

'Harry and Steve.' The taller one with a crooked smile introducing himself first.

'Blake Saunders.'

Harry didn't offer surnames. He said, 'Blake, there's insurance and then there's … insurance.'

'Protection against accidents that could see your staff, or even you yourself, meet with a nasty accident.' Steve gave the pitch he'd clearly learned by rote.

Blake was pretty sure he wasn't their first customer. He leaned back in his chair. 'I'm not accident-prone.'

Harry pointed a nicotine-stained finger at him. 'See, that's the thing about accidents. You can't tell when they're going to happen. That's why they are called accidents.'

Blake was considering how to play this, trying to suss them out at the same time. They'd been doing this for a little while. Maybe they couldn't cut it in the city and had been forced out to find clients. Or maybe there was some other organisation behind them, something like the Mob.

'I'm not interested. But I thank you, gentlemen, for your time.'

. The squat Steve lunged at him like an attack dog. 'Listen, wanker ...'

Harry placed a restraining hand on him. 'That's okay, Steve. Let the bloke be.' Again he offered that crooked smile and nice as pie said, 'Fifty quid per month, that's all. It's really a drop in the ocean. Think it over.'

Steve leaned in. Blake could smell his bad breath. 'Yeah, have a good, hard, think.'

They stood. Harry said, 'I'm sure Mr Saunders is going to. Everybody's luck runs out sooner or later. Right, Blake?' He stared right into Blake's eyes and Blake felt that old familiar chill he'd first experienced hanging with Jimmy in low-grade bars where guys could break your jaw for glancing the wrong way. But he'd been around tougher guys than these bozos. He said nothing and watched them head out.

Doreen must have returned and been watching from the shadows. 'What was that about?'

'Insurance.'

She looked at him like that didn't fit. He changed the subject.

'The dance comp is looking okay?'

'We'll be fine. There are some good movers.'

'I wanted to try the new song.'

She scooped up her clipboard. 'Well, I'll leave you to it.'

He let her get halfway towards the door before calling after her. 'What did you think of it, the song?'

It was like she was running it again in her head. 'I liked it.'

The ocean was an inkblot. The sun had fallen like a body sliding down a wall after a hit, life ebbing, darkness in the wings. Sometimes he thought of what had happened to Jimmy after they'd shot him. His soul, not his body. Even if there was a heaven, odds on he and Jimmy wouldn't be heading there. He imagined the worst things: Jimmy adrift out there in a black, cold sea, forever, calling for help, calling his name. Blake pulled back from the open door, the sea breeze following him into the lounge room. He walked to the stereogram, picked up an LP, Dakota Staton, weighed it on his fingertips, extracted the platter and placed it on the spindle, clicked the switch and let the mechanism do its thing. Slow bass like a heartbeat, a piano that trilled and then her voice dragged him back to clubs with small round tables and cold streets outside. He could almost smell the cigar smoke and whisky under his nose. It was those guys, the shakedown mutts, that was what was bugging him, bringing back this space in his head. Everything was going so good. But them turning up, it was like you had bought a brand new car and walked out to find it had been sideswiped. The image of the car led him to the farmer in the car lot earlier. If life was a wick, his must be burned down a long way but the guy figured he had enough of a future to buy a new car. Maybe that's what came of a life of dirt and hard work. A farmer's life was honest. Not like his. He had taken the easy option: pulling a trigger a lot easier than working a machine ten hours a day. Bottom line, he didn't deserve this ... the Surf Shack, Doreen ... paradise.

He shoved aside the niggle for now. He would grill up some lamb chops. He could even drive out to the golf club, pick up Carol after work. Wednesday was a slow night, that's why he never even bothered to open the Shack.

Dakota could sure sell a song.

She was worried he'd identify her car engine if she drove to the end of the street so instead she parked on the ocean road and cut through vacant blocks of scrubby sand on foot until she was on the sand dune closest to his house. It was dark, the moon was thin and there was no way he'd spy her. Doreen didn't know why she put herself through this, didn't know what she wanted, what she didn't want, only that she felt this need to be here. Sometimes she sensed it in him, the same yearning to connect. But how could they? Why ruin what worked. He had his women. Like the one at the golf club with the sloppy nail polish. Doreen had her own admirers. Every night at the Shack at least half-a-dozen men asked her out. Occasionally she accepted and, sometimes, even enjoyed herself. Yet never so much as here, sand over her feet, the cold breeze across her face, a heart quietly beating in darkness, the hush of the ocean in her ear. In a way she was alone but not alone. She felt connected, like some long strand of cotton ran all the way from his lounge room to here and she could feel the vibrations from whatever song he was playing. She sensed in Blake the same depth as the ocean at her back, a cold darkness deep down. But when you jumped into the sea you felt exhilarated, you weren't worried that on the ocean floor some weird fish with eyes on stalks was patrolling a marine graveyard. She'd been engaged once, but not with a ring or anything, the kind of fake engagement where a boyfriend says 'when we get married ...' and you play along. You believed for a little while, in romance, knights in shining armour, happy endings. But it always turned out the same. Her lovers were still at heart schoolboys looking for a mum to make their lunch, or worse, wankers always wondering if the blind auction bid they'd put in was too high, if there was somebody better for them than you. And when you caught them out, they promised to change but never did. Blake was neither of these. He was his own man, unique. Women wanted to change men, mould them. She didn't want to do that. She wanted to stay like this always, her feet in the sand, the ocean breeze kissing her back, and him over yonder, a mystery, playing music she couldn't hear but didn't need to, with nothing between them but space, both part of the same pulse of sweet night.

3. Watusi Stomp

It was a big house built facing east on a large property, high up on the escarpment, further north and deeper inland than the Heights. You drove up a long dirt driveway from the west, arriving at the rear of the house. Orange and lemon trees, untended, formed a natural border to the north before giving on to a bushland of tall gums. On the house's south flank was a disused tennis court. Its surrounding fence was still up and, though the grass court was overgrown with weeds, the net poles, while rusted, looked intact. The wide back lawn also needed a trim but compared to the rest of the property seemed manicured. Blake had slept well. In the end he'd not gone out to the golf club. He had no plans to end things with Carol but one day that would happen — maybe her choice, maybe his — and it was always easier to cut a line than a net. He pulled his ute up on stubbly lawn occupied only by an old wooden clothesline and an aqua EK Holden. He guessed it was Thomas Clarke's. Winston Clarke had said his son would be there. Blake climbed out and enjoyed the isolated mechanical sound of his car door closing in what was otherwise a noise-scape of pure bush — unseen birds, a slight rustle of dried, brown gum leaves. He stood, hands in his jean pockets, taking in the rear of the house. Unlike the Queenslanders in town, its stone foundations sat directly on the ground. Cement steps led to a high but small back porch. About ten years old, estimated Blake. He tackled the steps, waited at the back flywire door and called out, 'Hello? Anybody here?'

No radio to suggest a teenager in occupation. Maybe he'd got lucky and Thomas Clarke was out with a friend. He stepped onto the linoleum floor of a large kitchen. The smell of toast still clung faintly to the room. He walked through and into a short corridor and called out again.

No answer.

He turned right and came to a large sliding door that gave onto the lounge room. He stepped inside and found himself looking out over rolling bushland through concertina doors. They were still closed and the room was hot from the late-morning sun. He saw they opened onto a low concrete porch that sat on level ground, not a deck. He realised then that the house had been built on the top of the hill, probably into the back of the cliff with the rear built up to reach this level, hence the concrete steps. The lounge room itself displayed all the untidiness of bachelor living: newspapers and *Man* magazines strewn about, a couple of cushions on the floor, a sofa that had been expensive once upon a time but was now worn. Father and son living. In one corner was a bar, Blake caught sight of himself in its mirror. There was a Pye TV in the opposite corner and a large radiogram with LPs scattered on top; Sinatra, Ray Conniff, Julie London; Winston's taste not the kid's.

'Who are you?'

He'd not heard a sound. In his old game, he'd be deader than manners. He turned. Thomas Clarke had an ugly block head, small rosebud ears, small eyes, and was wearing shorts and singlet. He was also holding a cricket bat ready to swing.

'Blake Saunders. I'm supplying the booze for your party. I called out.'

Clarke lowered the bat. 'Sorry. Dad didn't say.'

'Nice place.'

'I'm only here for the holidays.'

No way was this kid twenty-one.

'You finish high school?'

'Last year.'

So this was for the kid's eighteenth, not strictly legal but on a private property, supervised by the old man. Nalder wasn't going to fuss.

'Any idea what you're going to do?'

'Not really.'

Blake knew that feeling, wished he could go back, make a different choice than the one he made when he was eighteen. But maybe you can't. Maybe it's all written in stone where the gods hang out.

'Well, Thomas, I have two kegs to set up. I'm thinking on the back lawn there would be the best spot. I don't reckon it's going to rain anytime soon. It might help if you had a table or something?'

'There's a trestle table and chairs in the shed.'

'I didn't see a shed.'

'It's around the side of the house.'

'Good, we're in business.'

He was just finishing the set-up when a pink-and-white Chevy Bel Air rolled up the driveway. Left-hand drive, he noticed, as it pulled up on the grass beside him. It was gleaming, not like the ones he remembered. Winston Clarke climbed out. His shirt was crisp white, his tie broad royal blue, handpainted showing a scene from some bay in LA or Mexico, cacti in the foreground looking down over yachts.

'No problems finding the place?'

'No. I figure it's not going to rain.'

Clarke ran his eye over the set-up, nodded approval. 'This is a good spot for it.'

'How many you got coming?'

'About thirty I think. He lives up at Clough with his mother. Quite a few are coming from there. They can park all over the lawn.'

'If the kids aren't twenty-one, you know that's not legal.'

'Come on, I'll be here.'

'What you're telling me is that this alcohol is for you and your friends and those above legal drinking-age only.'

Clarke got the drift, his eyes twinkled.

'Of course. I've got soft drink for the others.'

If one of the kids did something stupid and wound up in hospital, at least Blake could assure Nalder that he'd checked.

'I was just about to do a test pour on this one. You be alright with the other?'

Clarke chuckled. 'Oh yeah, I've tapped a few kegs in my time. Why don't we wet the baby's head?'

Blake obliged. He pulled two glasses out of the box and poured them each a beer. The flow was nice and even. Clarke raised his glass.

'Here's to the good old US of A.' They both drank. 'You're about the first Yank I can think of around here. There're a few older guys up at the Heads, came for the war and stayed.'

Blake shrugged. 'Australia's a long way away.'

'I might have told you. My sister married a Yank, moved to California. I went over and worked there a few years. Paul's in the movie business, started as a refrigeration mechanic, wound up making movies. Land of opportunity.'

'Plenty of opportunity here.'

'Tell that to my son. Where is he? On his bed reading a comic, I'll bet.'
Clarke took a deep gulp, finished the glass right off. 'No, it's too damn
dead here. I was your age, I'd be in the States, but then again, I hear that
bar of yours is doing good business.'

'I can't complain.'

'What brought you out here?'

'A girl.' It was the easiest lie.

Clarke shook his head sympathetically. 'Yeah, they can fuck everything
up. Still with her?'

'It didn't work out.'

'Best thing for you. You got the bar, no ties.'

'I best be heading back.'

'Of course.'

'I can leave everything an extra day if you like. Just give me a call.'
Clarke caught him admiring the Chevy.

'Could be yours, I'll do you a good deal. Like I said, you want to
project the right image.'

'It's probably a little more than I can afford.'

'You ever want to talk terms, I'm sure we can look at some arrangement.'
Blake offered a noncommittal smile.

Clarke called after him, 'You play golf?'

'No.'

'Well, no matter, I'll drop in to your bar sometime. Come into the
yard tomorrow morning, I'll fix you up then with cash, if that's okay.'

After setting up Clarke's, he'd gone to the Surf Shack and with help from
Duck and Andy prepared the stage and the go-go platforms for the
evening competition. It was only a Thursday night but the vibe around
town was building strongly and he was expecting a big crowd.

'Audrey seems to be doing better.' Andy was pointing her out. Blake
reckoned he was right, the glitch in her swimming had gone.

'Fingers crossed, Andy.'

Duck joined them. 'I've got a job in the Heights, better be going.'

Blake dug two pound notes out of his pocket for him and thanked
him.

Duck said, 'What time tonight? I'm judging the contest.'

'You?'

'I come cheap.'

'Be here by seven.'

'Is The Beachcomber on tonight?'

'If I can find him.'

Blake left Andy to clean up, got into his ute and headed north seven or eight minutes before swinging off the road onto a beach-side track among thick trees, maybe blackbutt, he wasn't sure. About a hundred yards in, he stopped and turned off the engine and climbed out. Built in the grove was a small shack constructed of tin, hessian bags and a few bricks. A couple of sheets of rusting corrugated iron propped between branches and some wooden uprights did for a roof. He pushed away the two hessian bags tacked to a horizontal piece of ply and peered in. A bamboo mat lay on the flattened earth beside a small kerosene stove and lamp. Three empty wine bottles stood neatly beside a cardboard box of books and a suitcase, which he knew contained men's clothes. A pyramid of shells of all shapes and sizes provided decoration. There was no sign of the shack's inhabitant. Blake backed out and walked through spiny grass to the beach. It was narrower here and a little rocky so the tourists rarely came, preferring the broader, cleaner sand to the south.

The surf was even as a metronome but the tide was out. He should have realised Crane would be out scavenging from the detritus of a world he had rejected. Blake started off north but abandoned that pursuit after about ten minutes when he'd made it around the little rocky point and still could see nobody on the long beach ahead. After backtracking to his original position and walking five minutes or so south, he saw a figure stooping in the shallows, pants legs rolled up to the thigh. He called out and the figure became erect, waved and started wading in. Crane was aptly named, around six foot, thin as a rail. He had his left arm through something doughnut-shaped, carrying it like that because he had his hands full, almost certainly with shells. A shirt knotted by its sleeves was around his throat, the rest of it covering his back. His chest was bare except for a clump of white hair. Locally he was known as the Beach Bum, but he'd taken pseudonyms 'The Beachcomber' and 'Robert T. Menzies' for his weekly Surf Shack performances. He beamed at his visitor.

'Ah, the footnote Hemingway declined to write.'

Because of his penchant for complicated words and flowery expression, most people assumed Crane had been a lawyer or teacher but he'd told Blake he'd been a pastry chef before signing on to the navy in the war. The only thing Blake knew for sure about Crane was that in the dark hours he was a slave to alcohol. Now Crane was closer, Blake could see that the doughnut hanging from his arm was a toilet seat. Crane displayed it with the pride a conqueror might have brandished the severed head of an adversary.

'The treasures the sea yields up are wondrous indeed.'

Blake realised he must have pulled a face, for Crane chided, 'Oh come on. You Americans ... Neptune himself could have sat his arse on this throne.'

Crane walked on to his shack, dumped the shells and let the seat slide off his arm into the sand. 'Probably a damn sight cleaner than the ones in the public lav I'm normally subjected to. I tell you, friend: Shelley, Wordsworth, Tennyson et al. are valueless unless one can sit down and have a decent shit while reading them. You literally — like the literary play on words? — you literally may as well wipe your arse with them. Sherry?'

'No thanks.'

'Of course you won't. Don't mind me though.' Crane ferreted through his part-empty bottles until he found the one he was looking for. Blake thought he better get in quick, before the night's path was set.

'You feel like doing a spot tonight?'

Crane had popped the cork on the sherry bottle already. The aroma was calling him, his focus was loosening. Blake drove on.

'You'll be able to buy two full bottles of that tomorrow.'

That brought Crane back. 'Deferred gratification?'

'I guess so.'

'You know how to torture a man.'

'Two bottles. I'll throw in breakfast.'

'How fucking ingenuous. You know I don't eat breakfast till lunch.' It was the usual banter between them and normally the highlight of Blake's day. 'For a man named after the most wonderful poet of them all, you are more than a disappointment.'

'I wasn't named after the poet. I told you.'

'But why should I believe anything you tell me?'

Blake pulled out two one-pound notes. Crane smiled.

'Ah, that's why! The currency of currency. Perhaps you could pay me upfront?'

'I think not. Well?'

Crane pushed out a bottom lip and reluctantly recorked the sherry. 'I'll give you ten minutes but I want to be on no later than eight-thirty. I will have drinking to catch up on.'

Ten minutes of Crane's weird-shit poetry was about all his audience would take. Blake hadn't been game to put him on a weekend but it worked great on the Thursday, and even if the kids hated it — plenty did — Blake dug it. What was the point of owning your own bar if you couldn't run with what you liked yourself? And the counterbalance of the spoken word with his own twangy guitar just somehow worked.

'Done. See you at eight.'

'Two bottles of your best plonk and a kiss from the delightful Doreen.'

'In your dreams.'

'That's a place you would not want to visit, believe me.'

Blake did believe him. Sometimes, after a bad binge, Crane looked like a painting on the wall of a haunted house.

'You want me to get the guys to pick you up?'

'I shall make my own way.'

'Eight. Don't be late. We have a dance competition too. You might enjoy that.'

Crane curled a lip. 'Dance is for those who can't talk. That ...' he pointed at the toilet seat, '... is far more edifying.'

ㅁㅁㅁ

Kitty had barely slept. Last night she'd spent over an hour in the bathroom practising in front of the mirror all the things Doreen had shown her in the afternoon. In the evening, the bathroom was the only safe haven in the house. She could lock the door, pretend she had period pain and was taking a bath. Days were usually easier, especially today because it was her mum's tennis day. The trouble was she was tired now from no sleep but when she tried to shut her eyes, she was still buzzing. Todd Henley was going to be there for sure, checking out Brenda. And that meant Todd would also be checking out her. At school he'd never noticed her, not once. Of course she was two years below him, so why would he? Brenda was that irritating one year older than her, and the sub-leaving and leaving years went to the same dances and social functions, which gave Brenda so much more opportunity to toss her stupid straight hair in his face and push her tits up with her elbows. Brenda was actually small-breasted, especially compared to her, and that was one thing boys noticed ... or two things as the joke went — boobs. Todd had just done his first year of engineering at university. Maths was one of Kitty's best subjects, she could talk to him on his level ... though of course he would know so much more about life now having lived in the uni college in Brisbane. All the same, what she had lacked up until now was opportunity, but that would all change tonight and Brenda with her skinny legs and cute little bum was in for the fight of her life.

Kitty swung up and sat on the pink bedspread that had covered her body for so many nights as she'd slowly transformed from a little girl to a young woman. The shelves her dad had built for her sported Barbies whose accessories were all still neatly packed at the ready in a little wooden treasure chest. Her hockey stick rested against the wall where she had practised her arabesque and her wardrobe door bore the pencil marks made by her dad recording her annual height, a practice which regrettably had been abandoned two years ago when her body had refused to move past its peak of five foot three. Nothing in her external world had changed all that much but inside everything was suddenly incontrovertibly altered and all she could think of was Todd's amazing, glorious lips… and him kissing her as he held her in his arms. As for what happened after that, well, Kitty really wasn't too sure. Naturally she knew the basics of sex: the penis, the vagina, sperm, egg. She also knew she wouldn't be having intercourse before she was married. Poor Ginny Herrison had made that mistake and been forced to drop out of school and start wearing smocks. She'd disappeared for a month or two then come back and now worked in the bakery. The baby had been adopted — or so Mary Cunningham said and Mary knew most everything, like what college at university Todd was boarding in. So no, Kitty wouldn't be going 'all the way' with Todd but she was sure she could keep him happy if she could get a hint or two about what to do after the kiss. Perhaps Doreen could help? When Kitty was thirteen, while the parents were drinking beers on the back patio, Brian, her kind-of-cousin had put his hand on her breast, but she was wearing a jumper and bra and all she felt was a bit of pressure on it, as if she'd dropped to the floor during PT push-ups.

She mustn't get ahead of herself though. First things first. Make it through tonight's heat at least: three were going through, seven would miss out. Brenda was a certainty, much as Kitty hated to admit it. That left two spots out of nine. The tricky thing was how she was going to get to the Surf Shack. In the end she decided to do what she had for the practice: ride her bike. It was mostly downhill from here so she wouldn't sweat up too badly. She'd told her parents that she was going to a beach barbecue with some of the kids from school and that she expected to be home by eight but not to worry if she was late because they might all go over to Geraldine Wilson's. The advantage of Geraldine was that she did not have a phone and Kitty's parents and their crowd had nothing to do with the Wilsons, who were poor but not wild criminals-in-waiting like, say, the O'Haras or Moores. That would have brought a straight-up ban from her father. With nothing better to do she went into the lounge room, neat as a pin as usual from her mum's vacuuming efforts, and put the soundtrack of *South Pacific* on the stereo. Her mum loved the record and played it all the time, which was naturally annoying because there was no space for her to squeeze in her own Paul Anka 45s, but how could you not want to sing along with 'I'm In Love with a Wonderful Guy'? And so she played it now and danced right around the lounge room imaging that she was in a faraway place with nobody around but Todd.

For a Thursday, the place was packed. Doreen was being run off her feet. Thank God when Blake had arrived and seen the line of kids queued up before the doors had even opened, he had told her to serve no alcohol in the main room until the contest was over. It would have been chaos. Any adults who wanted a drink, she'd invited to dine in the Conga Drum, the small restaurant serviced by the back bar. She had taken it upon herself to offer each diner a complimentary drink and Blake had better not complain or she would drop one of these crates of Cokes right on his head. She was ferrying the soft drinks through the crowd — no mean feat in stilettos — to the fridges in the back bar because the stock of cool ones in the front bar would soon be exhausted. Blake's first set was coming to a close. The dance floor was a heaving wave of young bodies. She'd hired a photographer who was busy snapping left, right and centre. She wished she could have taken it in. Blake was playing better than he'd ever done. She handed over the Cokes to Jeff in the back bar and turned back, almost colliding with Kitty.

'I'm so scared, Doreen.'

'You're going to be fine.' Kitty was wearing a kind of car coat. Her hands were trembling. 'You got your bikinis on under that?'

Kitty nodded, spat out words. 'He's here. Todd's here.'

'That's what you wanted, right?'

Doreen had no time to linger, she had to push back into the main room. Kitty was a limpet.

'But what if I'm hopeless? Then he'll never be interested in me, ever.'

Doreen said, 'Kitty, sooner or later you have to take that risk.' The guitar and drums were building to a crescendo. 'You need to get backstage, now. You're on in ten.'

Kitty managed to nod unconvincingly. She turned to start back. Doreen grabbed her hand. 'And you're not going to be hopeless. You're going to cook, right?'

This time Kitty managed a thin smile before moving off. She was quickly swallowed by the crowd which erupted as Duck crashed a final cymbal. The screams and applause gradually settled. The three musicians took a bow. Duck, who fancied himself as the Shack MC, grabbed the microphone.

'Not long now before the watusi comp, but in the meantime hot-dogs and kitty-kats, the one, the only ... Beat-comber.'

Wearing what had once been white tennis pants and shirt, and topped by a panama, Crane shuffled on halfway through a deep drag on his cigarette. There was a smattering of applause. At first Doreen had hated Crane's abstract poetry but he'd grown on her. He could be hit-and-miss but there was something about his couldn't-give-a-fuck-attitude she admired, like he'd been in a deeper hell than anybody in his audience could imagine so he didn't need your kind words or admiration, like he knew how to separate artifice from truth in himself and offered only the latter.

On stage Crane regarded the microphone like it was an alien space-ship. He started in sudden and sharp like a knife thrust:

> Please, pretty please, give me these, to be the bees' knees
> I need things, rings, not words or ideas,
> Even a bum can have those, but clothes
> Give me those, not a rose, not a plant, not a moon ...
> Anyone can have a moon over their head, or a star, but a car!
> Shows who I are what I've got, what you're not,
> So please, gimme, gimme, gimme, gimme these ...

Doreen felt a sharp pinch on her arse. She turned to find a group of young guys smiling up at her. The offender, a clean-cut kid from the Heights, probably just finished high school, licked his lips and said, 'Choice,' with a shit-eating grin. Doreen took the Bic biro from where it always sat work nights, behind her ear, and jammed the point into the kid's thigh. He yelped.

'Just remember, handsome. The pen is mightier than the sword.'

His friends hooted in delight.

Blake was back of the stage, carefully wiping down his guitar. He'd given over the dressing-room to the dance hopefuls but he didn't mind. He would have come out anyway to hear Crane who was rolling through his verse even though the dance floor was long empty. Doreen loomed out of swamp smoke. In those heels she was like a skyline.

'You good to go in five?'

'Panza and me are cool. Duck's somewhere out the back.'

Almost certainly smoking the funny stuff. He'd been good tonight, right on the beat.

'He's supposed to be our MC.'

'He'll be cool.' Blake put more certainty into that than he felt.

'You know the format?'

Of course he knew the format. She'd drilled it into him for what seemed like an hour straight.

'Duck introduces the contestants. Five-minute song while they dance. The judges eliminate four girls. We go again. Three more girls eliminated. Ten-minute break, then back for the finale. And here he is.'

Duck was coming in from the back door. Blake smelt the acrid, sweet smoke follow him in.

'How many we got in the Conga Drum?'

'About a dozen, and birthday party of six.'

'How are they handling it?'

'Fine. I offered them all a complimentary drink.'

'Good thinking.' She'd looked prepared for a different reaction.

'I better get back there. Make sure he knows what he's doing.'

Blake watched Doreen head back out to sea. He turned to his drummer.

'You know what you're doing?'

'Shit yeah.'

For just a shard of a second, Blake thought of Jimmy. Trust me.

The stage seemed a long way up anyway but the platforms that rose either side were scary. Doreen had run them through it one more time just before they got called out. They were to line up across the stage in order of their numbers from one through ten. Kitty was number eight, Brenda number seven, which meant they were side-by-side. Doreen was going to stand side of stage and indicate when they were to move to the platforms.

They would do that in pairs, one girl each side on the platform, the other eight keeping their position on the main stage. That meant she'd be up against Brenda on the platform as well. Each girl got one turn on each of the platforms so everybody could see them no matter what side of the room they were. The trip from the dressing-room up onto the stage had been like walking on a thick mattress, like Kitty wasn't connected to anything solid and could have just blown away with a gust of wind. Her stomach was twitching too but all of these feelings were distant, baffled as if they belonged to somebody else imitating her. She tried to look for Todd in the crowd but with the lights in her eyes it wasn't possible to make out anybody. And then everything just completely stopped except her pounding heart and, *boom*, she felt, rather than heard the drums and bass and the stage was vibrating and everybody around her was moving including herself. The routine she'd practised over and over again was somehow still there but so was the disconnect, the feeling she was a mere shadow. Then Doreen was gesturing it was her turn and she felt Brenda peel to the left and she went to the right and scaled the ladder and stepped onto the tiny platform so high that had she been wearing a high pony like Brenda she would have been worried about it hitting the ceiling.

But suddenly up there it all went clear in her head again. The music was in her bones, fizzing her blood and she was filled with an urge to paint the whole room with what she knew: her limited, precious, prescribed, boring life of pogo sticks, and pretty pink frocks, dolly tea parties, of spread woollen picnic rugs and flies that had to be shooed, and a Goofy ball that rolled lopsided on a buffalo grass lawn that would always bring her out in red itchy blotches on summer nights when mosquito slaps sounded from distant corners of an ill-lit back-lawn barbecue, of shared bunks in a Christian camp where with an illicit pocketknife the girls cut initials into criss-cross beams that spoke of loves long forgotten or stillborn, of cold homemade swimming pools, and woollen pyjamas staving off the cold of cracker nights while a Guy Fawkes of some father's socks burned with the slow progress of a piano lesson. This was the rhythm of her life, such as it had been so far, and her shoulders and thighs and arms beat it out like a confession. And it no longer mattered who was watching, or who knew because she was beating on life's door and yelling, 'Open up, open up!'

It was like that great feeling you have walking across a frozen lake, everything white, snowy, and you're feeling so good, and then right in front of you, you come across a pile of dogshit. Not that this had happened to Blake before, but that's what he imagined it would be like. He was on a high. The dance comp was killing it, the band was smoking, everybody was having fun. And then he looks up, and there they are coming through the door, the would-be extortionists. Deep down he'd known they'd be back. He forced his way through the crowd, found them at the back of the main bar.

Harry scanned, pushed out his bottom lip and said as if with real appreciation, 'Well, this is really cooking, Blake.'

'Thank you. I'm sorry but I thought I made it clear, I didn't need insurance.'

'Actually mate,' Harry gestured at the crowd, 'I reckon with all these kids here you need it more than ever.'

'Yeah. Imagine if a fire broke out or something?' Steve shook his head as if already choking up at the tragic consequences.

Blake could see Duck mounting the stage, getting back behind the kit, ready for the last set. He told himself to stay cool.

'Gentlemen, I am sure there are other businesses that would really appreciate your services but as I said before, I'm good in that area.'

'You're making a big mistake, Blake. I feel trouble is just around the corner for you.'

Blake said, 'I have to go to work. Why don't you enjoy a drink on the house?' He caught Ken's eye, ushered them towards the Conga Drum. 'Ken will look after you.'

Harry said softly, 'You're gonna be sorry.'

Blake started back to the stage. If only Jimmy had been here.

He found Doreen down by the dressing-room, hustling the three finalists out. He pulled her aside.

'Something I want you to do for me. Those guys who turned up the other day trying to sell insurance, they're in the Conga Drum. When they leave I want you to follow them, find out where they're staying.'

'What am I? Sam Spade now?'

He ignored that. 'And be careful. If they stop somewhere, drive on by.'

'What's going on?'

'Please.'

Why couldn't she refuse him when he looked at her like that?

'You owe me.'

He squeezed her arm tenderly. 'I know.'

She found a position halfway up the room where she could watch the stage and keep an eye on the bar at the same time. One look told you those blokes didn't fit. She wondered what their game was. They were sitting on bar stools mumbling a few words to each other, ogling the waitresses. Then the band started and she swung back to the stage. Kitty, Brenda and one of the leotard girls, Vanessa, had made it to the final. Kitty was more confident each time, and in the previous heat Doreen had noticed her playing up to the audience, shaking her backside at a young man, the same young man Brenda had been pawing earlier. Odds on, this was Todd. He was good-looking and knew it. Doreen sighed. Kitty was a toddler playing with matches. Doreen shot a look at the Conga Drum. The blokes hadn't moved.

They were still there when the song was over and Duck finished conferring with his fellow judges: a couple of surfer regulars. The expectation in the room had been wound high, everybody had stopped what they were doing. Duck came to the mike.

'Firstly we would like to say all the girls were amazing and our finalists were incredible. Vanessa, Brenda, Kitty you were all brilliant but there has to be a winner. And that winner is … Kitty!'

Doreen's gaze fell not on Kitty but Brenda, who, after an instant of blinking disbelief, knitted her brow in a good old-fashioned scowl. While the other runner-up, Vanessa, politely applauded, Brenda's hands knotted into fists.

'Thank you, thank you, thank you.'

Kitty bearhugged her. Out the corner of her eye Doreen caught Brenda gesticulating at Todd and storming off.

'Don't thank me. You earned that.'

Doreen noticed the two blokes she was supposed to tail were climbing off their stools. Kitty was pouring excitement.

'It's unbelievable. The best thing … Todd asked for my number.'

'Are you sure that's such a good thing?' The men were halfway to the door.

Kitty was confused. 'Of course. He's a dream.'

'But he's asking for your number when he's here with his girlfriend?'

'He probably got sick of her. Who wouldn't?'

Doreen started moving. The men were at the door now.

'I gotta go. Well done, Kitty. Keep dancing.'

Doreen pushed out the back door. Crane was sitting on a low brick fence by the area where they stacked the empties, smoking. Her Falcon was parked there.

'Don't know what your poems are about, Crane, but I liked them.'

'May the stars always shine upon your crown, Doreen.'

Doreen opened her car door. It was dark out here but the Surf Shack sign threw enough light to catch the unmistakable shape of the two men heading for an FJ Holden. Doreen fired up, no choke needed on a night like this, almost balmy. She heard the car doors close, there was a beat then the headlights ignited. The car swung left in an arc. She waited a few seconds then dropped the car into first and followed, catching sight of the vehicle at the exit. It turned left, heading north up the coast road. She slid after it.

ooo

'They started north up the coast. They stopped at Greycliff and went into the Toreador.' Doreen sipped her gin and tonic, the room lit only by the fish tank and bar signage, bare like a carcass stripped by ants. It was after one now. Blake had finished the tidying up in here nearly an hour earlier. He'd even done the carpark, including a used condom. More than once while waiting for her, he'd cursed himself for allowing her to do something so dangerous. The sight of her headlights swinging into the carpark flooded him with relief.

'How long did they stay at the Toreador?' Blake had eaten there, a small steak restaurant with a decent bar.

'Ten minutes.'

Not long enough for a pitch to a new customer, sounded more like an existing client.

Doreen continued, checking a small notebook. 'They then drove straight to the Heads and called in at Chez Fifi and the Sandcastle. They ate a complimentary dinner at the Sandcastle ...'

'How do you know that?'

'They were inside twenty minutes. I went in and had a look.'

He flashed, 'I told you just to tail them.'

'I needed to wee and my legs were cramped, okay?'

'How do you know it was complimentary?'

'Put it this way, they didn't offer to pay.'

'After that?'

'They turned around and drove back south, through here and then took the turn to Barraclough.' Barraclough was a small logging town with not much more than a general store. 'Eventually they turned off on Cockatoo Ridge Road. You know it?'

'Winding climb, lot of trees?'

'That's the one. There's a few old places up that way the workers used to live when the sawmill was bigger. The rest is farms. They took the third driveway on the right. I kept going in case they were watching me.'

'Good.'

'Then I parked and hiked up through the bush.'

'What?'

Jesus what had he been thinking asking her to do this?

'You owe me a pair of fishnets.' She pointed to where hers were torn.

'That could have been dangerous.'

'It was. I nearly got wee'd on by the short one. I was in the bushes. The place is surrounded by them. He came down the back steps, wooden, rickety things. I thought, oh hell he's spotted me. To be honest, it was a good thing I'd gone to the ladies back at the Sandcastle. I didn't know whether to run or stay. I was frozen. He came right to where I was hiding behind this tea tree but he was obviously drunk, weaving. And then, well, he pulled it out and started spraying. Then he stumbled back up the stairs and I got out of there.'

'Was there anybody else there beside those two?'

'Just them from what I saw, and only their FJ at the house. The back of the place has a window you can look right in.'

He should have skipped his last set, done it himself. He told her he was sorry.

'No need. I actually had fun.' She finished her G&T.

'The dance comp was great. That was a really good idea.'

She made a dismissive sound. 'Maybe.'

'Was there a problem?'

'Kitty, the young girl.' She looked at him like she was going to explain and then just shook her head. 'Don't worry. It's just a girl thing.'

'Perhaps you shouldn't have rigged her to win.'

'Huh?'

He liked it when she acted dumb. He said, 'She was very good. But you had three male judges. And the other one was blonde. How much did it cost you?'

There was no point her lying. Duck would give it away soon enough. You could never get anything past Blake. She wondered what his background had been that he knew people so well. All he'd told her was that he'd worked in a factory where his brother was the foreman but his brother had died in a work accident and Blake needed to get out, find something new.

'Less than six pounds all up.' Six pounds she couldn't really afford if she was going to buy herself a television set. But then again, it was worth it for the look on Brenda's face. Blake reached into his pockets and pulled out ten pounds.

'Petrol and hosiery,' he said with that wicked smile of his.

The transistor radio sat on her bedhead directly behind her. It was Japanese and had a little aerial you could pull out, and you needed it here because the signal was weak. Kitty levered herself up with her elbows to take one last look at it before dropping back down and trying to sleep. She didn't dare turn it on because then her mum would want to know where it came from. What she would do was, she would hide it. Meanwhile she would start saying how she was going to save up to buy one from her pocket and babysitting money. It was the happiest night of Kitty's life. Winning the competition and shoving it right up the nose of that bitch, Brenda, that was one thing, but then to have Todd actually ask for her phone number ...

She let out a little squeal and her legs kicked furiously under the sheets. Why would he want her number unless he was planning to ask her out? There was no way now she could sleep, she'd be lying awake the whole night because perhaps tomorrow, the phone would ring.

4. Membership

Blake drove south towards the meeting place, a picnic area five miles out of town. Sensibly, Nalder did not like anything open to public scrutiny and the picnic spot had always been deserted on their previous meets, which were traditionally set for around ten a.m. It was a fine clear day, the humidity not yet roused as Blake turned off the coast road and headed inland along a gravel road that ran to the river. He was surprised to see Nalder's car pulled over to the side, well short of the picnic area. Through his windscreen he could make out Nalder about a hundred yards ahead in his sergeant's uniform standing in calf-high grass looking down at something. Blake parked behind Nalder, got out of his car and advanced. Halfway there he saw Nalder was holding something flat against his leg ... a tyre iron. Nalder looked back at him, waiting till he was almost level.

'Dumb bastard.'

Now Blake saw that lying in the grass was an injured kangaroo.

'Ran out in front of me. Lucky it didn't break my headlight. Can't leave it like that, though.'

A large man with a sizeable beer gut, Nalder was sneaking out of his forties, having disguised himself for many a year as early-fifties. He raised the iron and struck down hard: one, two, three times on the head of the roo. He got his breath back, seemed to realise he had nothing to wipe the tyre iron clean.

'Bloody things are everywhere this summer.' His eyes met Blake's. 'You said it was urgent.'

The sudden violence had shaken Blake. He thought the animal had quivered after the first blow and had been forced to pull his gaze away.

'Two guys turned up trying to shake me down. I think they're running the racket up the coast to the Heads at least.'

'And you tell me this because?'

'Because I pay you twelve pounds a week. And you're a cop.'

Nalder still looked at a loss with what to do with the bloody tyre iron. For an instant Blake thought he might use it on him.

'Your twelve pounds a week is, I think I've made clear, insurance that you will get no competition in the liquor business. Anybody applies for a licence, I object. Makes my life simpler, yours too. Now, I am prepared to turn a blind eye to the occasional underage drinker or public urinator emanating from your establishment — call it goodwill — but as you know, I will not tolerate drugs or depraved acts. Nor does your twelve pounds entitle you to have me act as your private security.'

'I'm not the one breaking the law.'

'I only have your word for it. The parties involved will deny it.'

'I'm not the only place they're pulling it.'

'You're the only one who has come forward and complained. And the Heads is out of my jurisdiction. Look, what do you see before you: a policeman in a suit, a detective?'

'No.'

'No, you see an ageing sergeant in his uniform. That's the way I like it, the way we both should like it. You start reporting anything above a little larceny or common assault, our crime statistics rise. Some wanker in an office somewhere decides they need a CIB division in Coral Shoals. You don't want that. Neither do I.'

Blake told himself to take this very slow and calm, like the Massimo Benetti job when he found himself on the creaky landing and had to slip off his shoes. Benetti was in the lavatory. Even now he could transport himself back in time and hear a radio from somewhere else in the building. It was playing old music, Glenn Miller. He'd waited in the shadows. When the toilet flushed, he'd slipped his shoes back on for the exit. The door opened on Benetti standing there in his singlet. A look passed between the men that said everything about their respective roles: You are going to kill me. Yes.

Blake shot him twice in the chest. He never knew what Benetti had done wrong.

He had to be just as calm now. Getting hot under the collar never helped anybody. He needed Nalder. He put himself in the cop's shoes, caught a whiff of Nalder's logic.

'So what am I supposed to do?'

'Take care of it. Make your choice: pay up or find another solution.' Nalder's eyes bored into Blake's. 'Sure, you look like butter wouldn't melt in your mouth, but I know you, Saunders. I've seen a thousand Blake Saunders since I started this job. Well, maybe not ones as smart as you. You're a businessman. Thankfully I am but a humble policeman. You will have to make a business decision.' The matter as such was clearly at an end so far as the cop was concerned. 'I believe you had a large crowd of youngsters there last night?'

'Yes. Of course no alcohol was served except in the restaurant.'

Nalder lay his heavy mitt on Blake's shoulders. 'See, that's what I mean, a businessman. Now, regrettably I have to return to the station to protect the good citizens of this principality but perhaps you will save me the trouble of a return trip?'

Blake had come prepared. He handed across the envelope containing the twelve pounds.

Nalder smiled. 'Watch out for the roos.'

On his return, Nalder deliberately diverted past the golf club. The fortunate were out in their short-sleeve Gloweaves, nothing more on their minds than a pesky insect as they were lining up to putt to the background click of reticulation. Tonight would determine whether he could join their number. His application for membership would be considered … again. With Rob Parker nominating him this time, he felt sure he had a strong chance. As a solicitor, Parker carried weight. More clout than Jack Hitchcock who had been his champion last year. Jack was a nice enough fellow and well respected by the RSL blokes, but he didn't mix with the young professionals who really controlled things at the golf club. It pissed Nalder off that he had been rejected last year — you had to wait twelve months before you could reapply — but, on the other hand, what made the golf club so desirable was that it didn't just let in anybody. Once you were in, you were 'in'. He had always had a strong desire to belong to a group: a clan.

As a younger man, Nalder had flirted with the idea of joining the Masons. The police force had two strong groups, Catholics and Masons, and he was no Mick. That Freemasons had arcane rituals appealed greatly to him but then he met Edith and soon enough they were married and had the two boys and then war had broken out. Nalder had joined the navy and spent three years on a minesweeper that had never seen action. There was much about the comradeship of the navy he had enjoyed but as a club it offered no entrée to higher status. For that you needed to be an officer. He left the same rank as he went in and returned to policing. When the Coral Shoals job came up, he was the only one to put up his hand. The others had seen a tiny station, no chance for advancement, a frontier world. He, on the other hand, had smelled potential. Going on for ten years now, his word had been law here. There were only six of them at the station and he was the most senior. He was more or less the sheriff of this strip of coast and the adjacent hinterland. On the few occasions when a more serious crime had been committed, the regional detectives came down from the Heads and attended but they knew their place. You wanted to build flats or shops in Coral Shoals, you wanted to operate a liquor licence or drive a taxi, you wanted to so much as fart in Coral Shoals, you needed Nalder's approval. Oh sure, it might seem like it was the mayor, Tom Street, or the town planner, John Duggan, who was calling the shots but it was him.

Street had been his servant ever since he'd found his son drunk as a skunk having just crashed into Harrison's furniture store. Nalder had been able to keep the kid's name out of it and make Harrison happy by goosing the insurance. Duggan had smacked up a prostitute after the Heads' race-day carnival two years ago. Nalder had called in a favour from his colleagues to the north and everybody had walked away happy. Well, perhaps that wasn't strictly true. Duggan wasn't happy once it was his turn to repay the largesse displayed by his local policeman. However, the constant threat that his wife could be made aware of his deeds had made him compliant. At first he'd not wanted to approve the George Street shops on what had been set aside as a public carpark for beach patrons, running a whole lot of claptrap about aesthetics. Nalder had been forced to remind him about the aesthetics of fucking around on one's wife with a prostitute. Tony Puglise the developer was grateful of course and saw to it that one of the shops, the hair salon, was titled in Edith's name. The rent wasn't going to make them millionaires but every penny helped; the shop, the tithes from the Yank and a couple of other businesses, various one-off contributions from ratepayers looking for council approval on this or that, all swelled the coffers. Originally he'd thought he'd be using the money for Brian and Andrew to go to a private school up in Brisbane but neither showed any academic aptitude. It would be throwing good money after bad. Instead he'd bought a caravan park down the coast and that was ticking along nicely, the proceeds enabling him to buy three vacant blocks within a couple of hundred yards of the beach. Nobody else here seemed to appreciate the value of land so close to the water with a booming population. Well, it might take twenty years but there would come a time when he hung up his boots for good and when that land would enable him to live like a king.

He was galled by the knowledge that he was worth as much or more than many of those members of the golf club who thus far had rejected him. Regrettably, it was not possible to know who had voted against him. Each member who attended the nomination meeting had a black and a white ball, black for 'no', obviously, white for 'yes'. They dropped them in a ballot box and then these were tipped out into a tray. One black ball was enough to nix you. Though members weren't supposed to reveal details, he had been told that four black balls had been issued against him. Had Duggan been there, he would have been an obvious suspect, however, Nalder had been secretly watching from the carpark and had noted Duggan was not present. So he had at least four other enemies. It could be anybody. As a policeman you were bound to have run-ins with people, although his gut told him it was probably just some bloody snobs who thought a policeman wasn't up to their level. That's where Parker should help.

He cruised down the tapeworm road that took him back to the heart of town, and for the first time actually considered what the Yank had said about the extortion racket. It wasn't good but his hands were largely tied. If he did anything official, there would have to be a report. Powers-that-be would read it. One of them might even realise that Coral Shoals existed. If any policeman more senior than him got posted here, bang went the gravy train. On the other hand, tangling with crooks direct was not a course of action compatible with where he saw his life heading. In fact it was the direct opposite of what he should be doing, enjoying a top-shelf whisky in the dead of winter before a blazing fire, cosy in a lamb's wool pullover in the company of the good men of Coral Shoals, talking real-estate deals, and looking at the tight arse of the waitress to the hiss of a soda siphon. Or enjoying a cold beer on the terrace on a summer night, like tonight, smoke from his cigar drifting among fluttering moths, a yellow moon trying to catch their men-only jokes. There was, too, a certain attraction in the accoutrements of the game itself: the little wooden tees that you could push into the spongy earth, the gleaming steel shafts of the clubs, the gloves, soft leather that matched perfectly the style and swirl of brandy in a balloon glass. All of these made the experience more than a mere game. They formed a language that bonded the chosen, the powerful men of the community, and that set them apart and made them brothers. Once he was in the club, Nalder would no longer just be the local cop. He would be Leslie, 'Les', their valued equal.

In one way it didn't surprise Blake that Nalder had stiffed him regarding the shakedown guys. Life was like that. It was never as easy as you wanted. There was always shit to clean up. One look at Leftwich made him think the salesman would agree wholeheartedly. Jacket off, Leftwich was vigorously polishing the duco of a Holden with a chamois in the prescribed circular motion. It looked like he'd already done a whole row of the vehicular bargains available on the lot of Clarke's Cars. Blake saw a smear of ash over the last two cars in the row and thought he'd figured out why this was occupying the salesman's morning. Leftwich had clearly lit the incinerator at the wrong time, forgetting about the prevailing wind. Blake was almost at the door of the office when Leftwich called out.

'He's not in.'

Blake angled his body at him.

Leftwich said, 'I think it was a big night last night at the party. He called at nine to say he wasn't coming in.'

'I was supposed to get paid.'

'Sorry, you'll have to speak to Mr Clarke about that.'

Blake didn't think he looked sorry at all.

Blake went back to his car and drove to the beach. There were only two other boardriders out there. Even from the shore he could recognise Pete and Dave. They all got on fine but today he didn't feel like talking to anyone. He might understand Nalder, was not surprised by his attitude but all the same, he didn't like it. If he'd have had Jimmy with him, those bozos would have taken one look and cleared out, but they looked at him and they saw 'easy target'.

He climbed back in his car and drove fifteen minutes south. The break wasn't as good here but at least he would be alone. As usual when things niggled at him, the water changed everything. This is life, infinity, God, he thought as he let the power of the ocean lift him up and propel him. He felt good again, cleansed by the river of salt.

Just under an hour later he was in Carol's cool room, the smell of her hair mingling with the fragrance of a warming day outside as it squeezed through the shutters. They fucked like beggars fighting over a scrap, neither giving an inch, both knowing whatever morsel they got would be never enough to not have to go through the same ritual again. What had led her here to this point, what failures or half-won dreams, he never inquired. He really did not care, did not want to jeopardise the sanctuary that he found when inside her. All he knew was that for a short time the throb was morphined out; the snow of Philly, the bare room with their chipped plates, the apartment building's dark vestibule smelling of stew, the weight of the revolver in his hand, the mist of his breath in the back of the car outside the flat where Jimmy was holed up, the flash of the gun, all that was blotted and there was only skin and heartbeat and the relinquishing of control ... and for the flimsiest time, peace.

They sat at her formica table — here they called it laminex — sipping instant coffee. She wore a singlet and panties. Because his swimmers were still wet he was naked.

She said, 'I didn't expect you this morning.'

'That bother you?'

She looked at him across the top of her black brew. She was still wearing last night's make-up. 'No.' She cast about for cigarettes, seemed to decide against it. 'I might have had company though.'

This was true. He should have considered that.

'I apologise.'

'You wouldn't have been jealous?'

He toyed with his cup. 'No.'

She sat back. 'No, I don't believe you would have been. Must be good to be that ... free.'

'You don't get jealous.' It was a statement. She'd never seemed possessive.

'I don't show it.'

This genuinely surprised him. He wondered if this was the beginning of the 'girlfriend' talk. He'd experienced a few of those in his time, didn't like them at all. But she didn't pursue the subject.

'How was your night last night?' she asked instead.

'Good crowd, all young. You?'

'Could have fired a cannon. You know *The Honeymooners*, that TV show?'

'Jackie Gleason, sure.'

'Is it really like that? People live in those tiny apartments and other people drop in?'

'The big cities in the east.'

'Why do they live like that?'

'They don't have a choice.'

ㅁㅁㅁ

Edith had cooked sausages for dinner, with mashed potato and peas. No fish on Friday here, this was no Mick house. Normally Nalder loved his Friday dinner. He would drain a chocolate soldier, then he and Edith would sit out on the back porch, sometimes turn the radio up so you could hear it through the window. Tonight though, he'd had to pretend how much he enjoyed the meal. For the umpteenth time he checked his watch: 7.16. They would be just filing into the room at the golf club now, free jugs of beer on the table no doubt, ham and mustard sandwiches, probably. He had not told Edith about his renewed application. He'd made that mistake last year, expecting naturally enough he'd be accepted. When he had failed, she'd made all the right noises about them being snobs, and who would want to play that silly game anyhow et cetera? She just didn't get it. Quite frankly she was probably pleased. Edith wouldn't be comfortable in those dresses they wore to their balls and dinners but, dammit, she deserved it. And he definitely deserved it. He'd served this community ... another quick check of the watch ... 7.18. His doorbell rang. Could they have decided already? Had somebody declared there was no way they were voting for him and so that was it? Game over? He rose quickly from the old cane chair and walked through into the dining room. Edith, who had been engrossed in a *Pix*, made to get up but he stayed her.

'I've got it.'

'It's probably Phil wanting our mower tomorrow. Tell him to buy his bloody own.'

The house reflected none of Nalder's steadily growing assets. He'd been sorely tempted to buy a Rover but had thought better of it. When ordinary policemen started to spend up, they stopped being ordinary. He yanked open the door, determined to confront his fear as soon as possible.

He was taken aback to find two men in suits and hats who just had to be ...

'Sergeant Nalder?'

Shit. Had they come to arrest him?

'Yes?'

'We would have called but nobody had your bloody number and there's no answer at the station. Detective Inspector Ian Vernon,' the spokesman tapped his chest. 'Detective Sergeant Tony Apollonia. Homicide.'

The ballad had gone down well, couples on the floor taking the opportunity to dance close after the more frenetic surf rumble. The room was almost as full as the previous night but with an older crowd of liquor drinkers, profits would be higher. Blake couldn't enjoy it though. He was still on alert, scanning the crowd to see if Harry and Steve had turned up. Maybe they would leave him squirming a little longer?

He stiffened. He'd caught a glimpse, suits moving through the crowd heading his way. Then he saw they were wearing hats, realised Nalder was with them, in uniform. Cops. The crowd was doing the Red Sea. Doreen loomed to intercept but Nalder waved her away and took the lead, reaching Blake first.

'Mr Saunders. These are detectives Vernon and Apollonia from Sydney. Can we speak privately in your office.'

The office was small. A desk and a couple of chairs with a lot of crap jammed on the perimeter. Nalder looked over to the fairer of the detectives — Vernon, Blake was guessing. Vernon put his hand out and the other detective slipped a large manila envelope in it. Vernon opened it over the desk. Glossy eight by ten black-and-whites spilled out. Blake caught images shutter speed: a motel room, blood on the walls, the bed, the floor, a naked body, a young woman's face close-up.

'You know the Ocean View Motel?'

'Sure.'

He was getting some kind of an idea now why they were here. The Ocean View was the closest of the few motels between the Shoals and the Heads. Vernon's finger stabbed the close-up and manoeuvred it to the top of the pile.

'Sometime last night or early this morning in room ten of the Ocean View, this young woman was murdered.'

'Stabbed at least twenty times.' Apollonia speaking for the first time.

Blake's focus eased in and out. The ferocity of the attack obvious. The cops not sparing the dead girl's modesty, splayed, naked.

'Who is she?'

Vernon took the lead again. 'We were hoping you might tell us. She checked in using the name Susan Smith but there's no sign of any ID. Queensland plates on her car, we're looking into that.'

'Why would I ...?'

Apollonia tapped a close-up shot of the night table: a matchbook, Surf Shack. Blake's head was still ringing.

'We had thousands of those printed. She could have been in sometime or got it from anybody.'

'You don't recognise her?' Nalder offering something other than beery breath.

'No. My manager Doreen knows faces. She's your best shot.'

Vernon said, 'There was also this,' pointing at a roach in an ashtray. 'I'm sure you're familiar with marihuana.'

Blake didn't like where this might be heading. 'What do you mean by that?'

'You're American. You run a bar. You are some kind of musician from what I hear. You telling me you don't know this "grass"?'

'I'm telling you I don't tolerate narcotics of any sort in my establishment.'

Apollonia moved in closer. 'That's funny because we've been up and down the coast the last few hours and people have said they've heard about weed being used here.'

'People make up stuff. Sergeant Nalder will tell you, we run a clean place.'

Vernon was not to be snowed. 'You're saying to the best of your knowledge, nobody in this place smokes the stuff?'

'That's what I'm saying.'

He was going to kill Duck.

'And if we shook down everybody here, nobody would be holding grass?'

Blake conjured a room with a radiator that didn't work and blood on the walls. He'd been in worse places. 'That's right.'

Vernon regarded him from top to bottom, looking for something wrong about him. 'Where were you last night after your bar closed?'

'He was with me.'

Doreen was standing there. The men noticeably straightened.

'This is my bar manager, Doreen Norris.'

'How do you do, Miss Norris?' Vernon scooped up the photos with practised ease. 'You were with Mr Saunders last night?'

'That's correct.'

'How long, may I ask?'

'All night. Till the early hours. That's not against the law yet, is it?'

Vernon appraised her with a smile on his lips. 'Certainly not.'

Apollonia and Nalder smirked at the joke. Vernon carefully peeled off the photo showing the victim's face in close-up.

'You recognise this girl?'

Doreen studied the photo carefully. 'No.'

'She wasn't in here last night?'

'Not while I was here. I went out for an hour or two.'

'May I ask why?'

Vernon was no fool. Blake could almost hear gears whirring.

'I was checking on the competition up the coast, see how they were doing.' She rattled off the places she'd been.

'So it's possible, this woman came here in the time you were absent?'

'Yes, it's possible.'

The detectives swapped looks: more work.

Vernon turned back to Blake. 'We'll have to interview your patrons.'

'Of course.'

'Thanks for your time Mr Saunders, Miss Norris.'

'Anything we can do.'

Doreen said, 'If you have a spare of that photo I could put it up in the club by the entrance?'

'That would be of great assistance.'

'You don't recognise the girl?'

'What? No!'

He had Duck up against the wall behind the old outdoor toilet, shoving the photo under his nose.

'Last night, you were out here, smoking that shit in the break.'

'I might have been.' Duck was squirming.

'Did you meet this girl and give her a joint?'

'Did I …? No, no, I told you … I don't recognise her.'

Blake tried to control himself, eased back. 'Would you?'

Duck was less confident. 'Probably.' He realised his error and scrambled to cover. 'I mean shit, it's dark, there's girls … sometimes I … but not last night.'

'Anybody else? Did you give that stuff to anybody else?'

'Last night?'

'Yes, last night. Or any night.'

'Not last night.' He flinched at Blake's gaze. 'Look, sometimes, a guy or a girl, I might let them have a puff.'

'Did you sell any to anybody?'

'No. Man, come on, you're grilling me like a fucking cop. Next thing you'll bring out the phone book.'

'The girl was murdered. Like something out of *Psycho*.'

'Yeah well, there was a matchbook there too, that mean you did it?'

'They could close us down. You get that?' He tapped Duck's head. 'I don't want you ever, ever bringing that stuff in here again.'

'Okay, I swear. Scout's honour. Listen, it's not like I'm the only person in the state who smokes weed. There's loads of it. You know that.'

'And you never saw the dead girl here last night? Or a car with Queensland plates?'

'No. I was judging the contest. I came out in our break for a quick puff. I spoke to a young guy, I didn't offer him anything … that's it.'

Blake stepped back, Duck pulled out a cigarette.

'I love you, man. I wouldn't put you in the shit. And I swear, no weed near here ever again.'

'What did Duck say?'

They were in his office, Doreen handing him calico bags of the night's takings. There was just the two of them. He could hear Andy cleaning and straightening the main room but it was past two and the bar long closed.

'Said he didn't recognise her. Admitted he was smoking weed last night but never gave any to anybody else. You didn't have to do that, you know … cover for me.'

'You saying you had somebody else could alibi you?'

Sometimes when she looked through those long eyelashes he thought his heart might thaw out from where it had been frozen so long.

'No. But I didn't do it, so …'

'So you were clear?' She invested it with disbelief. 'I missed the intro but it seemed like Vernon was interested in you. I thought it best to be on the safe side.'

'Thank you, anyway, called for or not,' he said. 'You're right. I don't need some cop giving me grief. Nobody recognised her?'

'None of the staff. I don't know about anybody else. There weren't many from last night in tonight.'

That was true. The dance comp had brought in underagers.

He said, 'Nalder told me they would likely be back tomorrow asking around town.'

'She could have got the matchbook from anywhere.'

He liked Doreen trying to reassure him.

'Yeah.' But what he didn't say aloud was what he reckoned she was thinking too: the girl may not have been a customer here, but maybe her killer had. 'I can follow you home?'

Doreen brushed that off. 'I'm alright. Once they identify her, they'll find it's her husband or boyfriend. Queensland number plates on her car. She was probably heading south, picked up the matches in the Heads. I left a bunch up there last week.'

She swayed out of the office, pulled the door to. Though he had a safe in here, he decided he would take the money home with him. He hadn't forgotten Harry and Steve. More vermin threatening his paradise. And now Nalder would be even less likely to change his mind and intervene.

Doreen wasn't being quite as noble as he thought. She had been on the verge of telling him that she knew he was alone because she'd sat across the way and watched him like she did regularly. Thought maybe she could confess it in one shocking rock-through-a-window moment. But didn't. What was he going to think — she was some desperate woman stalking him? The Surf Shack matchbook didn't mean anything, really. They'd had hundreds printed and dropped here and there up the coast. It could have even been left by some previous guest. These motels were cleaned about the same level as a bus. She'd often found somebody's shampoo in a bathroom cabinet or a magazine under a couch. Still, even though she was sure the murderer would prove to be some man who knew the woman, she did cast around the carpark when she reached her car. That wasn't something she did normally, too busy thinking about staff and shifts and next week's advertising. She climbed into the car. She was looking forward to getting back in her little place, kicking off her shoes. Lately she'd been thinking she had to have that television. Maybe with a TV she wouldn't feel the need to go sit outside Blake's? She already had money saved and they had some smaller models she could buy. No way was she doing hire-purchase. As she pulled out of the carpark, she was contemplating whether the young woman who had been killed up there in the Ocean View had left hire-purchase agreements. She guessed she probably had.

By the time the detectives left Nalder, it was a little after one-thirty in the morning. He'd played the assiduous local cop kissing their arse, how he'd have loved to have been a detective but wasn't smart enough, blah, blah. They lapped it up. He'd driven them around town and shown them the likely places where they might get a witness who recognised the dead girl, if she had indeed passed through.

He also gave them the run-down on a half-dozen locals with some kind of form for violence and sex crimes.

'What about Norman Bates?' The Italian cop had asked.

'Who? I don't think he's on our files.'

The two of them had started laughing then. At him.

Trying to quit the hysterics, Apollonia had said, 'You know from *Psycho*, the motel guy in the movie. Janet Leigh gets stabbed to death in the shower.'

Nalder had never heard of the movie. He and Edith almost never went to the movies. Earlier this year they'd gone up to the Heads to *The Music Man*. If they did go to a movie, it wouldn't be one about a woman getting hacked to death. He felt small, a country bumpkin. They were thorough. They went to the station and made notes and skimmed files. They were staying in Opal, halfway between the Heads and the Ocean View Motel, and said they would canvass that area first. The only thing pointing them here had been that damn matchbook. And the narcotic. It made him look bad, people saying you saw that stuff at the Surf Shack. Saunders would need a very serious talking-to. In private, the cops had admitted that they'd heard the same about other places up near the Heads, and in the river towns inland, so it wasn't actually a black mark against him per se, but when you put it with the matches it didn't look good.

The house was cool when he entered. Edith always left the windows open even though he'd told her not to when he wasn't around. All night he'd been busting to ring Rob Parker and see if he had news for his nomination. It was too late now. But maybe he had called here? He clicked on the kitchen light, saw the dark blur of a moving cockroach making for a corner. His feet hurt. He walked lightly on the lino so as not to wake Edith. There on the little pad beside the phone under the Goodbye Cruel World cartoon of the bloke about to flush himself down the dunny was a message written in biro. He needed his glasses to read it properly.

'Rob Parker called. Sorry, no. Call him tomorrow.'

In that instant he felt insubstantial, made of straw or less, chaff, like he could dissipate in the night air, like there was no centre of him anymore, like Leslie Nalder had ceased to exist, may never have existed, was just a volume of space that had split asunder without leaving a mark of his existence on the world.

He felt ashamed.

Quietly he opened the fridge and took out the half-consumed bottle of beer. Not flat yet. He carefully removed one of the beer glasses with the frosting around the outside and sat down at the kitchen table, poured a beer and raised it to his lips. He endured the bitter liquid rolling over his tongue, swallowed it. His old man had worked for the railways. Tough as nails. Nalder sensed his judgement: 'That'll teach you for trying to muscle into the dress circle. They've wiped you away like a stain.'

He saw the scene as a camera would: kitchen chair pulled at a laminex table, a half-full glass of beer, and above, looking down over the tableau, an ironic poster of a man about to flush himself down the toilet ... but no human presence, no subject, so that it seems a work of still life, unless peering very, very closely you detect ... There! A variation in the light as if something otherwise invisible, some pulse, some near undetectable half-life, might actually exist.

Here's to you, Les.

5. Cockeyed Optimist

The last thirty-six hours had been a roller-coaster, like the big one she and Dad had gone on when she was thirteen — didn't that seem ancient history — up the coast. Same holiday they went to the marine-life place and she got picked out of the crowd to feed the seal. She was wearing a polka dot dress and thought she was the ant's pants but now she cringed at the memory. Braces too. God, polka dots and braces. Yesterday, Friday, had been an absolute misery. The phone had not rung despite her willing it. She had closed her eyes and asked God to help with this one.
The phone had not rung.

She picked it up and listened to confirm the dial tone was there. It was. It was after ten-thirty in the morning before it jangled. She'd rushed to the phone, breathless, but it was only Jean Rossiter after her mum's recipe for tuna mornay. She'd battled on through the morning listening to the radio but by lunchtime she was down the well. She couldn't eat, even having had no breakfast, her appetite just wasn't there. Bumps, the family's white Persian cat, seemed to scold her for being so stupid. Kitty could almost hear her voice: 'As if Todd Henley is going to dump Brenda for you.' She rode her bike around the streets and dropped in on her friend Jenny who was experimenting with a facial mud pack. Complete disaster. She couldn't laugh. The night was a funeral procession. Then, this morning, she didn't even run for the phone, resigned. Her mum answered and put on the voice she did when people she didn't know very well called: like an ABC announcer.

'It's Todd Henley for you.'

Her mum couldn't hide her own excitement. It wasn't like Kitty hadn't had dates — she'd been out to the movies a few times with a couple of boys her own age but this was different. Todd Henley went to university. His father was some businessman involved in chemicals for farming or something.

Kitty'd tried to sound relaxed but her voice was all constricted and high when she greeted him.

And then right in, no messing around, he said, 'I was wondering if you would be available tonight to go to the drive-in?'

They were his exact words. 'Available', like she might already be taken.

'I would love that, Todd.'

Her mother was hovering. They talked only for a short time. Todd said he was helping out at his dad's work for the holidays. Saying she would be ready at a quarter to seven as requested and after explaining where she lived, she finally relinquished the phone. Todd had his own car. She had never, ever been out with a boy who owned his own car. She was ready to hitch a ride on cloud nine but first there was her mum to deal with on cloud one.

'The drive-in?'

In her mum's brain, the drive-in equated to a Roman orgy. Under normal circumstances it would have been a complete no-no. She'd already been told many times no drive-in until she was seventeen. But these were not normal circumstances. She had pleaded: Todd goes to university. You know the family. Todd's father is successful. Her mother said she would talk to her father.

That meant the deal was sealed. Her dad would do whatever her mum wanted him to do. Cloud nine was here.

She had a bath, shaved her legs singing 'A Cockeyed Optimist' and 'Some Enchanted Evening' at the top of her voice. Her dad's so-called safety razor was lethal. One small nick, that was all. Underarm was hazardous but she got through it. She'd narrowed her outfit choice to five possibles. She brushed her teeth twice while she debated what to wear. No way would she eat before the date. Make-up was going to be an entirely different challenge. On stage the other night, Doreen had helped her with some proper stage make-up that made her eyes huge so the crowd could read her expressions. But this was going to be too close and … intimate for that.

And that's how it was heading as late as three o'clock, everything on track, a few slight concerns over mascara. Then her mum came back from shopping in town and went to the phone and rang every acquaintance she knew as she told with ghastly pleasure of her encounter with *real* police detectives who were asking everybody if they recognised a young woman who had been stabbed to death in the Ocean View Motel.

That's when the penny dropped. This was going to be a problem. And it was.

Her mum guessed what was on her mind as she saw her daughter approaching. She rang off from Mary Stevens and said, 'Darling, you know this changes everything.'

She protested. No, no, no. You can't do this. Her mother pointed out that a girl had been stabbed to death.

'The Ocean View Motel is like … Queensland. It's fifty miles from here.' An exaggeration of course but Kitty felt she needed to throw everything she had at this.

'There's some madman running around.'

'I've got Todd to protect me.'

'Todd's not your father.'

This was the most superfluous statement her mother had ever made. Even she seemed to realise that. She guillotined all discussion.

'Not while there's a murderer out there.'

And so Kitty had plunged off the cloud without a parachute, down through cold, chill air. All because some girl she'd never known, never met, got herself stabbed to death. It would almost certainly turn out the girl was a prostitute or something. She'd probably been entertaining men in her motel room. Now because of this stupid woman …

She pulled herself up. Deep breaths. Maybe it was a madman, maybe the girl was minding her own business but she clearly didn't have a guy like Todd to protect her. And that's when, right at the nadir of the plunge, she came up with a new strategy.

'It's incredibly offensive to the Henleys.'

'What is?'

'Virtually accusing their son of being a killer.'

'That's rubbish. It's nothing of the sort.'

'Okay, so … you're saying he's not a killer but if the hypothetical situation arose where this killer of some woman we don't know, fifty miles away … if that madman decided out of all the cars at the drive-in to target Todd's, that Todd wouldn't be able to defend me. That he'd what … run away and save his own skin?'

'I'm not saying that.'

'That's how it's going to sound. That Todd would be so scared he wouldn't even be able to lock the doors. He wouldn't think of driving off, he'd just sit there and let us both get stabbed to death.'

The longer the ensuing silence went, the more optimistic Kitty had got. Then, capitulation.

'Fine. You may go with Todd, straight there and straight back, no stopping off for malts at the milkbar, no getting out of the car for the snack bar.'

And that's when she felt that gravitational rip in her stomach as she started climbing again for the stratosphere. Five forty: time to paint nails.

◻◻◻

Nothing was going to stop Blake's ritual. Despite everything, he was up at seven and out for a surf. He was still touched by Doreen's loyalty. She was the best. If only she didn't work with him. She was beautiful, sexy, but he never ever thought of her naked, having sex with him. In fact, he never really thought of any women like that, not like some guys did, Jimmy for example. Sure, once he'd actually had sex with a woman, it was different. Then he only had to smell their perfume, or catch sight of their thigh when they crossed their legs and he'd be feeling the need in his loins. But until then it was their mystery that drew him in. They were so different to him, to men. They might barely move an eye and that could tell you more than sitting for a thousand hours in a bar with some guy. The trouble with Doreen was that if they got close he might want to share, to tell her about who he had been. That would be disastrous because she could never love him then. Never trust him. How could you trust a man who had let his own brother perish? He could lie but that was cheating, just as wrong as if he was sleeping around. Now, it was okay to lie if you had to, to save your skin, or in a business situation. But if you fell for some girl, or she fell for you, then lying was weak, the coward's way.

He would not bother to visit Carol today. She started her shift at eleven-thirty and besides, it would set a bad precedent. Tomorrow they would drive up the coast. He only barely considered that was near where the girl was murdered. Before he'd dropped off to sleep he'd already decided that Doreen was right. The girl was from Queensland passing through and had just picked up the matchbook at the Heads. That still left Nalder to deal with. In that regard he would let sleeping dogs lie.

And there was still Harry and Steve.

Meantime, he wanted to try Crane on a spot tonight. He'd changed his mind about him being too weird, got to thinking Saturday could be a good night for Crane. Arty types from the hinterland north and south made their way to the Shack. It wasn't a lot of people, maybe only twenty all up, but put Crane with them and it would give the Shack the flavour he wanted. He couldn't describe that flavour exactly but he knew what he didn't want — those nightclubs with the silver shimmery curtains and some Californian Poppy dude crooning about the moon. Crane was as far away from that as you could possibly get. As he towelled off, Blake sensed a change in the air, moisture, a build-up. It might take a few days but somewhere along the line, it was going to dump.

Crane was lying on his back on a thin mat on the floor of his shack. He did not look good. There were some cuts around his face and on his arms.

'What happened to you?'

'The vagaries of life.' He didn't try to sit up.

'What specific vagaries?' After a while you got to learn this was the best way to speak to Crane.

'After the last gig and the excellent plonk you bequeathed me I became inspired to stretch my legs, walk up that old logging road off Salisbury Drive. There's a little hut up there the loggers once used. Regrettably I lost my sense of direction and fell right off the ridge, through a thankfully thick bit of foliage that cushioned the worst, no broken bones. I landed like a cat, literally, you know they can fall out of a window and land fine?'

'So you're not up for tonight? I'm thinking Saturday could work well.'

Crane registered the offer and visibly brightened.

'Au contraire, Monsieur Americano, I'll be there with bells on. My weekend rate —'

'An extra bottle.' Crane's smile was as good as a handshake. 'You hear about the dead girl?'

He had not. He hadn't been out of his place since he hobbled back. A truck driver had given him a lift for all but the last mile or so. Blake told him what he knew.

'"Life stains the white radiance of Eternity till Death tramples it to fragments." Shelley.'

'Meaning?'

'Whoever she is, she is in a far better place. Then again Shelley was more pissed than me most of the time, so who's to say? It will give me something to work on for tonight.'

'You need anything?'

'Aspirin. I have toilet paper, water and books, the essentials.'

Blake went back home and spent an hour practising the guitar. Playing guitar and sex were the only times he felt immune from his past, innocent, like when he was a kid and Tommy Ioppolo let him hold his pigeon. He could still remember the pumping heart, the soft feel of feathers, life. Then images he didn't want crashed in: *smash, bam*. A newspaper, Yuri Gagarin. A hole appearing right in the middle. Blood. His phone rang. It was Winston Clarke.

'Sorry about yesterday. It was a big night Thursday, and we just kind of kept at it yesterday.'

'No trouble.'

'The kegs are ready for pick up when it suits you. And I have your money here right now.'

'I'll come on over.'

Though it was a Saturday morning, there were only a couple of guys kicking tyres on the lot when Blake arrived and parked by the office next to Clarke's Bel Air. In the distance he caught sight of Leftwich, nodding his head in a phony way to a prospective customer. Clarke must have been waiting. He bustled out brandishing an envelope.

'Thanks, mate, I'll use you again.'

'You know where to find me. Everything went well?'

Blake leaned back on the Chevy to check the cash in the envelope. Long ago he learned to take nothing for granted. As he glanced down, he saw the Chevy's fender was dented.

'Too well.' Clarke pointed at the fender. 'One of Tom's idiot mates. But what are you going to do? You're too young for kids, right? Don't worry, one day.'

The money was all there.

'You need a receipt?'

Clarke waved that away. 'Cash is cash. We should get together some time. Talk about the States.'

A chance for Clarke to try and sell him a car. He went perfunctory. 'Sure.'

'Speaking of the States. What about Jackie Kennedy? Is she something or what? How could you concentrate on running the country with that waiting at home?' One of the tyre-kickers was heading over. 'I gotta go. Everything's ready for you at the house. They broke a few glasses.'

'That's covered.'

'Thought so.'

Clarke strode quickly to the stranger, hand extended automatically, gold watch gleaming. Different world.

There was an old FJ and a Zephyr slumbering on the lawn. Up here you could see the purple of the clouds more. Maybe it wouldn't thunder today, but soon. Clarke had disconnected the kegs and packed up the glasses. They'd done well, got through about one and a half of the kegs. Blake loaded up the ute. Thomas Clarke appeared at the top of the back steps shading his eyes. He wore footy shorts and nothing else. Even from this distance Blake could feel the weight of the kid's hangover.

Clarke managed to slur, 'Oh, you. Just checking.'

Like the kid could have done anything if it wasn't.

Blake said, 'You enjoy your birthday?'

The kid looked like he was going to be sick. 'See you.'

He retreated into the house. Blake thought he heard retching. Well, he sold them the beer but didn't put a gun to their head to drink it. Only as he was driving away did he realise the irony of that sentiment. He tried to recall his own eighteenth birthday, got an image of Jimmy, Vinnie and him catching a train to Penn station. They had wound up in Little Italy where they drank some really rank, strong stuff, grappa or something like it, who the fuck knew? Vaguely he remembered some craps game. Yeah, that's right, it was coming back, though it might have been his nineteenth birthday. He won, rolled seven three times in a row. Made his point, the ten. They kept calling him birthday boy. Vinnie and Jimmy went off with some hookers and he had to wait by stinky trash cans in an alley. But it was his nineteenth, he was certain of it, for his eighteenth he now remembered he'd spent at Tommy Hanlon's apartment watching the Giants playing the Phillies. He was certain because the next year the Giants headed west, which was a pity. He liked the Giants more than his home team who were crap. Jimmy was supposed to be getting there but never showed up and Blake had to walk back home by himself. It turned out Jimmy and Vinnie were boosting some truckload of liquor for the Mob. Their payout was a box of booze. That's probably why they'd tried to make it up to him the next year with the New York trip. He wished he could go back, spend a night sitting on crates in a New York back alley twiddling his thumbs, or watching a snowy TV screen seeing the crap Phillies get beat up again, knowing it didn't matter how shitty the night was, because sooner or later Jimmy would be there.

Miss you, brother.

ooo

Eventually Kitty had decided on a lovely white summer frock with little cherries and matching red shoes. She was watching through the curtains of her bedroom for the telltale headlights in the driveway. 6.44, right on time, twin headlight beams speared at her, and she had to pull back in case her face was snared. She heard the engine switch off and the door close, made herself remember to breathe. The plan was her mum would greet Todd and say 'I'll let Kitty know you're here.' Her father would do the man-to-man thing, shake Todd's hand, ask him to be particularly careful with a potential maniac on the loose.

Her mother appeared in the doorway, didn't need to say anything, just raised her eyebrows.

'How do I look?'

'Beautiful.'

Her mum stepped back and allowed her to make an entrance into the lounge room. Todd swung back from where he was standing with her dad and smiled as she mustered her best 'hi'.

They stood there awkwardly for a moment.

Her mum said, 'Well, you don't want to miss the start.'

Her feet got the cue and started moving.

'We'll wait up for you. Please don't be late, Todd, not with ... you know.'

'Don't worry, Mrs Ferguson. I will take good care of Kitty.'

'Give my regards to your father.'

'I will, Mr Ferguson.'

The only one in the house not gushing was Bumps. She had a scowl on her face.

The door closed and they were suddenly outside in the perfumed, humid night. Todd's car sat in the driveway. Kitty didn't know anything about cars, what model was what or anything, but it looked reasonably new. She waited at the passenger door and was electrified by Todd's fingers as they rested gently on her lower back. He looked into her eyes.

'You look terrific.'

She melted. He opened the door for her and she slid in, the way she and her friends had practised when they were pretending a couple of years back. But this was really happening. Kitty guessed her mother would be sneaking a peak through the drapes and would be impressed that Todd had opened the door for her 'like a gentleman'.

They reversed out. So far she had hardly spoken to him but she knew that you were supposed to ask boys — men, she corrected herself — all about them.

'So you were working with your dad today?'

'Yeah, he has a factory warehouse. It's all fertilisers and stuff, pretty boring.'

'University must be interesting.'

'We do a lot of drinking, that's interesting. The rest of the time it's a bit like school except no uniform and it's harder.'

'It can't be as boring as here.'

'I don't know, you don't have some girl stabbed to death there. How was that, eh? Like twenty times or something.'

Kitty hadn't heard that detail and asked how he knew. 'Someone said. I only found out when I got home from work. I bet she's a prostitute.'

'You think so?'

'Otherwise what was she doing in a motel by herself?'

'I heard she was quite pretty. The police showed my mum a photo. You see one?'

'No, I got home, had a bath and got ready.'

That's something she would have liked to witness. She steered the conversation away from dead girls. This was her first date with Todd, she didn't want it ruined by morbid talk.

'You know anything about the movie?'

She'd looked it up. *The Man Who Shot Liberty Valence* was playing. She'd heard the song on the radio but it wasn't her kind of thing.

'It's a western.'

'Oh.' Her heart sank. Even a spy film had a little romance. Horses and guns was such a boy thing. Todd looked over and grinned.

'Don't worry. We might be too busy to care what the movie is about.'

She felt herself blush. There was something she had to know though before any kind of ... activity ... was going to occur.

'Do you mind if I ask you something?'

'That depends. If you want to know if I have been thinking about you all day, the answer is a definite yes.'

Here goes. 'What's the situation with you and Brenda? Are you like, going steady?'

'With Brenda Holsch? Is that what people think?'

'It's what Brenda likes people to think.'

He was shaking his head vigorously. 'We went out a few times, that's all. She got really clingy, like we were engaged or something. She asked me to come, check her out on Thursday, which I was happy to do. She's a good mover. She was real pissed off when I said you deserved to win.'

It was better than Kitty could possibly have hoped for. To prove her fairness she offered, 'She's attractive.'

'Oh yeah, she's that alright. But you know, I'm not ready for an engagement yet.'

'Of course not.' Darn.

By the time they joined the queue of cars they knew a little bit more about each other. Todd liked sailing and still kept a VJ at his parents' house. She'd confessed that if she could have a wish to be anything, she'd be an actress, but for now she was thinking of working in a bank: secure job, reasonable pay. Todd parked in his 'favourite place' over on the left-hand side by the trees.

'Nobody can see us here,' he said with a smile. It took a bit of time for him to position the car just right on the hump. Then he got out and organised the speakers. The drive-in was about half full but not many people were getting out for the store. Kitty guessed most of them were a bit spooked too. She was glad she wasn't working in the store. Todd reached down and slid the seat back. The ads were playing and the lights were on half.

On screen, an attractive woman was spraying her perfect beehive with Gossamer. For a fraction of a second Kitty imagined the woman at the motel doing that, waiting for her lover, ignorant of the truth that in a few minutes some maniac would be plunging a knife into her.

'What are you doing way over there? I'll need a loud hailer.'

Todd lifted his arm off the back of the seat by way of invitation and she snuggled over. He put his arm around her. Everything was perfect. Then the lights went way down and the titles started rolling.

Todd said, 'Darn, I think I've got something in my eye.'

She turned away from the screen to look at him. His eyes were staring right into hers. Before she knew what was happening he had lunged at her and his mouth was fastening onto hers. This was not like any other kiss she'd ever experienced. For a start, she couldn't keep her lips closed. The pressure of his mouth, his tongue ... Oh my God, they were French kissing!

And wow, it felt good.

She had barely time to breathe when he was back at it again. She had not planned any French kissing on this date. Not that she'd ever done any before except practising with her friends. Her heart was pounding and things were happening all through her body, weird sensations, all of them good. Eventually Todd broke it off. She was half-relieved and half-disappointed.

'You're a fast worker,' he said and smiled.

'Me?'

It was funny. Todd was amazing. Handsome and funny. They watched the movie for a while but her mind wasn't on it at all. Then Todd swung to her again and she put her arms around him and pulled him into the kiss. After that, the script got thrown away. At some point Todd started nibbling her ear, nuzzling her neck. Her body felt like a volcano, the car a steamy jungle. And then his hand was on her breast. No, no, no! She tried to pull away but the way he was kissing her made that almost impossible. Desire was bullying reason. With a determined effort she managed to break off.

One day, out at the clothesline beneath Jenny's mother's and father's damp underwear, Jenny's older sister Leonie had prepped them for this situation.

'If you're with a boy and he starts groping your tits, you grab his hand and firmly push it away and say "I'm not ready for that yet." The "yet" is important if you like him because you're not saying "never", you're establishing a few rules.'

Tossing her hair around to show she was now back in control of emotions that may have temporarily gone AWOL, Kitty delivered her line just the way she been told: with a certain haughtiness.

'I'm not ready for that yet.'

Todd said with determination, 'But I am.'

Oh shoot, shoot, shoot! That wasn't supposed to happen, he was supposed to ...

He was grabbing her again now, kissing her aggressively, his fingers of one hand fiddling with the zip at the back of her dress, while the other had started probing her thighs.

This time she pulled away and actually slid back a fraction to her side.

'Todd, please. I don't want to.'

'Why not? I thought we were having fun.'

'I was but ... but I don't want to do those things ... yet.'

She still had enough control to remember to emphasise the 'yet'.

'Life is moving fast, Kitty. Soon we'll be old.'

'Todd, I'm a virgin.'

She hadn't expected to have to own up to this. Not so soon anyway.

'I can help you with that.' He nodded solemnly. 'No one needs to know, believe me. I will never tell.'

She was speechless. Her alarm grew when he pulled something out of his pocket.

'And don't worry about getting pregnant. I have these condoms: the best.'

'We're not doing that.'

She tried sliding back to the passenger door but he had her tight and she was going nowhere.

'Kitty, I've bought the tickets. I've dumped Brenda. You kissed me, we've gone halfway. We are going to do it.'

In his eyes was a crazed determination that drilled into Kitty's bones. This was real. She couldn't reach for the door, her wrists were totally in his control.

'Come on, I'll be gentle. You know you want it.'

Bang.

Something slammed into the window, a crazed face, distorted: Brenda. She was battering something into the glass ... her shoe, screaming.

'Shit.' Todd flew out of the driver side. 'Leave the car alone, you crazy bitch.'

Kitty didn't think about it. She opened the passenger door, it swung back in — the speaker cord pulling it, she shoved again, heard the loudspeaker thump into the window beneath Brenda's angry wail, jumped out and ran and didn't look back.

ᗡᗡᗡ

Crane stood in front of the mike, boogie-woogied his shoulders. Panza and Duck were chewing through some avant-garde jazz stuff Doreen didn't get at all, the brushes slapping the snare and cymbals with no rhythm, the bass like a drunk falling. The crowd was off tonight by about a quarter. Having the two detectives moving among the audience wouldn't help bury the fear. Blake was shadowing them, keeping a wary eye from a distance. Most of those here were busy smoking, talking, tracking the cops with their eyes but some had seen Crane before and were waiting for what crazy shit he'd deal tonight. He did an Elvis hip-swivel, pretty damn well actually, pointed to nowhere.

> *Hey man, welcome to Never Never Land. Dig it.*
> *Hubcaps spin, and the grins of cool cats form*
> *One long piano all the way to Melbourne.*

A few claps and a couple of whoops from the aficionados. A rat-tat-tat snare from Duck.

> *Steel and rubber, gasoline screams,*
> *The blood of dinosaurs, mainlined courtesy JP Getty. Dig it.*
> *Young souls juiced on Walt Malt, Disney jism, here in Fantasyland,*
> *Sliced and diced and laid upon the altar of cheap motel floors. Dig it.*

Doreen watched the cop, Vernon, straighten, turn around and face the stage, noticing Crane properly for the first time. Which was what Crane was probably after. Jesus, what did Crane think he was doing? She'd heard women gossiping in the ladies, as much scared as excited now by the murder, the reality sinking in. She felt the same thing herself, arriving for work tonight: some maniac was roaming around out there having stabbed a woman to death. He might have been in this very room. Might be here now. This shit from Crane was going to sabotage business. Blake was going to have to rein him in.

'Psst.'

Doreen looked to the back door, Andy was motioning her. She walked over.

'Got someone who needs you.'

'I couldn't think of where else to go.' Kitty was dabbing uselessly at her tears with the man's hanky Doreen always kept in her glovebox. Her own dainty one and Doreen's were already sodden. They were in Doreen's car. She didn't dare take Kitty into the club with cops around. Kitty had already gushed everything out, the words garbled like debris swept up in a flood, but Doreen had got the sense of it all. It was an old story and one Doreen and every woman she knew was too familiar with: Prince Charming turns out to be an ogre. The only twist was the evil witch as surprise saviour.

'You ran all the way here?' It was a good three miles.

Kitty managed to nod. Her mascara had run. She looked like an urchin from *Oliver!*. Kitty tempered her breathing, was able to half-gasp, 'About halfway I remembered about the dead girl. A car slowed for me but when I heard a man's voice asking if I was okay, I just kept running. What am I going to do?'

'Don't worry. It's going to be alright. When you settle down, I can drive you home.'

'Really? Oh, thank you, sooooo much. I feel so stupid.'

'You're not stupid.'

'You warned me.'

Doreen wasn't taking credit for being jaded and cynical. There were good men out there. Just not the ones she'd picked. Kitty took a deep breath and blew her nose.

'You going to tell your parents?'

Kitty let out a long deflating groan. 'They mustn't know.'

This is how our secrets start, thought Doreen. She wasn't going to bully the kid, hell, she'd do the same ... *had* done the same.

'Mum will be looking out for a car. Only, it's still too early.'

They calculated what time the drive-ins finished, a while yet.

'I should be going back inside.'

'Please don't leave me.'

'I can lock the car.'

Kitty nodded, grateful. A yellow wedge cut into the night at the back door of the Surf Shack. Crane shuffled out and lit up a roll-your-own. He was sucking deep on it when she saw Vernon and Apollonia emerge and start questioning him.

'I'll come back and check on you. You get scared, honk the horn. I'll tell Andy our yardman.'

'Thanks for everything.'

The poor kid looked pale. Doreen climbed out of the car and watched Kitty lock the door behind her.

She passed close enough to the cops to hear them with Crane.

'Currently unemployed. Except for my occasional gig here.'

'Were you here Thursday?' It was Apollonia.

Crane saw Doreen approaching. 'Remind me, Doreen, was I here Thursday?'

'Yes.'

Vernon tipped his hat and smiled flirtatiously. 'Evening, Miss Norris.'

'Evening, detectives.'

'Did you see this girl?' Apollonia shoved the photo at Crane.

Doreen slid inside. Blake was on stage firing his guitar. The dance floor was pretty full but at the bar women were sticking close to their men. Thursday night everything had been fun, the dance comp raging, Kitty full of dreams about her and that shit, Todd. Forty-eight hours on, that had all gone. You can only keep the wolf away for so long, thought Doreen. You can play piano, sing, be merry but sooner than you think the lights will be extinguished, the guests gone, the party as cold as lamb in the fridge. Then you'll be curled up in bed, face near the wall, listening to the howl just the other side of your window.

ㅁㅁㅁ

Just as she had done Thursday night, Kitty lay in bed unable to sleep. Only everything was different now. Despite the stickiness of the night she had pulled her sheet up to her chin. She thought she had carried it off okay. Her mum and dad had both been in the lounge room, waiting for news of the big date, although her dad had nodded off in the armchair. Scratches the Pekingese who had been banished to the back porch earlier because he stank, had wormed his way back in and was lying on the newspaper her father had dropped on the floor. Kitty smelled fresh baking, knew her mother had a sponge ready in case Todd had come in. Hoping to pump him, no doubt. Kitty had thwarted that, got Doreen to drop her at the end of the driveway. If her mother was watching she wouldn't be able to see if Todd had climbed out of the car to open the door for Kitty. She had asked though.

'Did he open the door for you at the end of the date?'

'Of course.'

'That's what I said: a gentleman.'

Her father had roused himself. Her mum had not let him put on his slippers.

'How was the film?' She could tell he was uncomfortable about asking anything intimate.

'You would have liked it, a western.'

'She wasn't worried about the film.' Her mum smirked. 'You want some sponge?'

'No. It's been a big day. I think I'll go to bed.'

'Did you make plans with Todd for another occasion?'

Yes, a nutcracker applied where it hurt.

'No, Mum. I'm not sure we're all that suited, you know?'

She sensed the disappointment in her mum. It quickly turned to puzzlement tinged with annoyance.

'He's good-looking, good family, smart: plenty of girls would be suited to that.'

She was not going to engage. 'Good night.'

God, how stupid she had been. As if play-acting dates with her equally ignorant girlfriends had given her grounding and experience. She had been way out of her depth. 'Boys only want one thing': you heard it all the time and dismissed it — maybe they only want one thing from you because you are dumb and boring — that's what she'd thought in her arrogance. Doreen had told her not to think all men were the same but advised her to be careful and go easy on the dating front till she was a little more experienced. Well, there wouldn't be any of that. She would likely now die a shrivelled old maid. Her eyes played across the room: the hockey stick against the wall, the stuffed Goofy, the Barbies-in-waiting. Suddenly she longed for the security of what they had brought her and wished they could spark in her the same excitement they once had. They were impotent but she wouldn't throw them away, she wouldn't cut that line, not now. Life was scary out there and it dealt out a certain justice that your parents' house kept you from. Out there, nobody thought you precious: you transgressed, you were punished. She'd been only too happy to try and lure Todd from Brenda. Maybe Brenda didn't deserve sympathy but perhaps she did deserve Todd. Kitty had meddled with a certain natural order and it had reared up and bitten her. She wondered about the dead girl in the motel. Had she also transgressed?

She realised she was trembling under the sheet. She fought it, finding words in her head:

When the skies are bright canary yellow,
I forget every cloud I've ever seen,
So they call me a cockeyed optimist,
Immature and incurably green ...

6. Aquarium

Carol's car was gone. Blake had not expected her to be out so early on a Sunday because Saturdays she was on her legs all day. It was near eleven a.m. He'd fallen asleep on the couch about two a.m., listening to Charles Mingus. Thunder had woken him around an hour later, the long-threatened storm finally arriving. Some of the fat leaves of Carol's front garden were still beaded with rain but the sun was already on low bake and the air was steamy. Perhaps she'd gone to the shop to pick up a few picnic supplies. Blake got out of the car and sauntered over to the little house. Down the street somewhere a kid was hitting a tennis ball against a wall. On his way over he had passed station wagons of families coming back from church. The heathens were easy to spot, polishing their cars on front lawns. He thought he might make himself an instant coffee, tried the front door just in case. It was locked. Sensible with all that was going on. He wondered though if she had been as careful with the back door. He walked up the side of the little weatherboard, feeling good with life. A macadamia tree hid a fair part of the wall. Through a lopsided wooden gate he entered the dense back garden and followed a narrow path to the back door. He tried the loose brass knob on the door with its blistered paint but like the front door it was locked. Unusually, the louvre windows were closed. Maybe the murder had got through to Carol. He walked back to the car and waited half an hour. When she didn't turn up, he decided to cruise town but even though the Sunday streets were pretty deserted he could not see her VW Beetle anywhere. One last time he drove back to the house but the car was still not there. Only then did it occur to him that she may be working. The Sunday shift paid more but the longer-serving workers made sure they had that nailed down. Every now and again, however, somebody was off sick or had a wedding or christening to go to, and Carol got a call up. She probably didn't phone him, knowing he'd had a long night. Or she had phoned when he was out surfing. He decided he would go to the Surf Shack and help Andy tidy up. There was always something to do.

Andy's bike was propped against the back door as usual. Blake parked and climbed out. There was no sign of Andy in the yard.

'Andy!' he called out as he swung into the Surf Shack via the unlocked back door. He was half expecting the noise of the vacuum cleaner — that was what Andy usually started with. A strong smell assailed him. Pond water. Until then he hadn't realised the aquarium was no longer there. Now he saw the steel stand, a frame without a window, glass littering the carpet like snow, the bodies of tiny fish. He ran towards the dark centre of the room, was about to call out again, caught sight of something white near the gents — Andy's sandshoes. Blake's eyes focused. Andy crumpled into a ball, a crimson halo, head caved. His fingers drove through blood. He checked Andy's neck: a pulse. First thought, call an ambulance. Second, it would be too slow. A trolley stacked with Cokes waited at the bar, probably Andy restocking. He pushed the trolley up, dumping the crates, more shattered glass. He jammed a foot against the back of the now free trolley, rolled Andy onto it. The kid weighed no more than his clothes. Blake ran back the way he came, through the rear door, up a short ramp, yanked open the passenger door of his ute, poured Andy into the seat. Now he was covered in blood himself. He jumped in, fired up the engine, stamped on the pedal. The closest hospital was thirty miles south and inland.

Don't die on me, Andy.

ㅁㅁㅁ

When Doreen came through the ward door, it was like somebody had stuffed all his organs back inside and he was half real again.

'How is he?' She was carrying a shopping bag, breathless.

'They're still not telling me anything more: broken ribs, probably a broken arm, bruising on his legs. The main worry is his head. He hasn't regained consciousness yet. He'd lost a fair bit of blood.'

She bit her lower lip, trying to stay strong. 'I called Nalder at home after I locked up and cleaned up the fish tank. I couldn't see anything stolen.'

Blake hadn't expected there to be.

'Who would do this?'

Blake looked straight at her. She read his eyes. 'Those guys you had me follow?'

'That'd be my guess. I've seen injuries like this from a baseball bat.'

'Those bastards. Andy wouldn't hurt a fly.' She handed him the bag. 'I stopped off at your place. After I saw the blood, I thought you might need a shirt.'

'How'd you get in?'

'You don't lock the downstairs door in your garage.'

She knew things about him even he didn't know.

By the time he'd changed into the clean polo shirt she'd brought, Nalder had arrived. He was in civvies. Blake asked Doreen to wait while he and Nalder went outside. They found a quiet position screened by a hedge.

Nalder said, 'He see who did it?'

'He wasn't conscious when I found him.'

'Doreen says nothing seems to have been taken.'

'They smashed the fish tank, beat up on Andy. I don't think robbery was a motive, though I won't be surprised if there's a bottle of scotch or two missing.'

Nalder rubbed his chin, thinking. 'Those protection low-lifes sending a message?'

'That's what I'm thinking.'

Nalder scratched the dirt with the toe of his shoe. 'Officially there is not much I can do unless Andy can identify them or some other witness comes forward.'

'I think they'll have made sure there were no witnesses around.'

Nalder nodded. 'Also, I don't need to tell you it's not a good time ... with the homicide and all.'

'I'll handle it.'

Nalder studied him. 'You think you've got the juice for that?'

'I'm not worried about them.'

Nalder clapped him on the shoulder. 'Good. For now let me write it up as a break and enter: Andy surprised them, they beat the shit out of him. If he doesn't pull through ...'

'He's going to pull through.'

'I know … but if he doesn't, then it's a different game, you understand?'

'Yeah.'

Nalder turned to go, paused. 'You don't think these two …?'

'The Ocean View Motel? They know what time she died?'

'Close to midnight, no later.'

'Then it's not them. I had eyes on them. Your cop friends any closer?'

Nalder sighed, pained. 'They have a couple of sightings of the car Monday at Greycliff and Toorolong.' Both towns within thirty miles to the north. If true, it meant the victim had travelled further south than the Ocean View. 'The servo bloke at Greycliff is sure it's the car he filled up, woman on her own driving. We've also got a girl on her bike who reckons she saw the car Thursday evening just a few blocks from your place but she is less credible.'

None of this was good.

Nalder continued, 'On the other hand, they've interviewed a stack of people and nobody says they saw her at the Shack.'

That was something. 'Sounds like she's been in the area a while.'

'Yeah. Somebody knows a shit lot more than they are saying but so far there's no ID on her.'

Nalder said he had to go but asked to be kept informed.

'You told his parents?'

'I don't even know his last name.'

'You're kidding me.'

'I gave him a job. I pay him cash. He's just Andy. Doreen probably knows.'

'Leave it with me. I've seen him talking to the Greeks in the fish and chip shop. They'll be open for lunch.'

Doreen did know Andy's last name. Of course she did, she knew everything.

'Wellard.'

'You know where he lives?' Even when he'd thrown the party for Andy, the only guests had been the other staff and the band.

'He talked about the Baxter shops being his local.'

There was a public phone box out front of the hospital. Blake walked out and waited patiently while a middle-aged woman made three calls. She had been crying so Blake didn't hassle her. Perhaps her husband or mother was really ill, or had died. Hospitals were all about loss. Except for maybe the maternity ward and he'd never been in one and never expected to be. He took the phone book and scanned for Wellard. Only one Wellard was in the book. All he could think of was exacting retribution on those two who had done this. Andy had counted on him to protect him, and he had failed. Just like he had failed Jimmy. But exacting justice, that was something Blake could do. He called the number for Wellard but the phone rang out. He got his coin back and dialled Nalder's home number. His wife answered. Nalder wasn't back yet. Blake passed on his information and returned to the hospital and Doreen.

It was another hour before the surgeon found them. He was clinical: brain damage was the main concern. The skull had been fractured but Andy was not in obvious imminent danger, although the unexpected could occur with these sort of injuries. They'd reduced swelling of the brain and were taking precautions to prevent a blood clot, so far so good. They were debating whether he might actually need structural support for the skull but for now it was wait and see. They were keeping him sedated, allowing the body time to heal.

'Is it true you stuck him on a drinks trolley?'

Blake admitted it was.

'Lucky you didn't kill him. As it is you've probably given him a good chance to maintain all his functions.'

Doreen asked how long before Andy was likely to regain consciousness.

'We don't know. Some people never do but like I say, we got to him early, the skull is cracked but intact. He might be conscious and able to interact in a couple of days, couple of weeks … months.'

'Can we see him? Sit with him?'

The surgeon considered Blake's request, assented.

The sight of Andy lying there unconscious swathed in bandages made Doreen cry. Blake felt doubly useless. He squeezed her hand and the tears slowed. They sat side-by-side for a long time. It was the first time he had held her hand.

'Have you done much of this?' she asked. Her voice was unusually dry, like a brown leaf off a gum tree, crumbly and scratchy. 'Waiting by a hospital bed?' she added, in case he hadn't understood.

Yes. He'd done more of this than he would have liked. He was fourteen when his mother caught pneumonia and died. He and Jimmy sat like this for two straight days. At the end of it they were orphans. Science could put a man into space but it couldn't save a forty-three year old woman from a chest infection.

'Not so much,' he said. 'You?'

'I've been lucky. My grandmother was sick but I was really little and we didn't stay long. Your brother died, right?'

'Yeah but it was quick. Hit by a truck.'

'You have other family? Your mum, brothers and sisters?'

'Dad ran out on us when we were little kids,' Blake said. 'We didn't know that then. It was still wartime. Mum said he'd gone to fight in the Pacific. More likely he'd gone to fight at the Tiki Bar with other drunks.' That was all the truth.

'Your mum is still alive?'

'Lives in Pittsburgh with her mum, my grandmother.'

'No other brothers or sisters?'

'No there was just Jimmy.' That was all he'd ever needed.

'I've got a younger sister and an older brother.'

'They say the middle child is always difficult.' He liked that she smiled at him when he said it.

'I think Andy has a brother. In the army.'

'Two,' he enlightened her. At least he remembered some things. 'Both older. The other one is a builder or something. We talk, Andy and me.'

'About what?'

'Mainly about the fish. I just didn't know his surname.' It still worried him that she might have thought he didn't care about Andy as a person.

'You talk about the fish in the tank?'

She had this kind of cute smile on her face.

'Audrey is his favourite. He's going to be heartbroken.'

'We'll have to get some more.'

He liked that she included herself in that. Yes, she was right. They would get some more fish. He was going to take care of everything.

He found an envelope under his windscreen in the hospital carpark. They must have known he would come here sooner or later. Inside was a badly printed note on a page torn from a school exercise book. It said he should drive to the point near the toilet block at the beach at four o'clock. DO NOT SPEAK WITH COPS was written large. It was five to four already. Doreen had stayed with Andy's parents who had turned up a little after two o'clock when they'd finally been contacted. The parents looked like poor Okies. Blake had already told Doreen to open a savings account in Andy's name. He would pay Andy's wages into that till he could come back to work. He didn't tell the parents though. The lessons he'd learned about human nature and money suggested that people could always find a reason why somebody else's money should be theirs. He crumpled the note in his fist: case in point.

The wind was blowing in strong off the ocean and the skies had clouded over again. There weren't many people left but a few families were still goofing about in the water and on the sand. The car was easy to spot, a light blue FJ. He pulled in beside its driver side. Harry was working his mouth with a toothpick. From the passenger seat, Steve looked over with lizard eyes. Blake wound down his passenger window.

Harry said, 'Hear your bar had one of those unfortunate accidents we were discussing the other day.'

Easy, Blake told himself. He was ready to explode, but years of dealing with wise guys tempered his behaviour.

'What do you want?'

'What we've always wanted, to offer our services.'

Steve piped up across the way. 'But it'll cost you more now. You should have taken the deal.'

Harry said, 'He's right. Our costs have increased because it looks like your business really is in need of some serious protection.'

'How much are we talking?'

Harry looked over at Steve and they grinned at one another: got the sucker.

'Thirty pounds deposit, payable immediately. After that it's only ten bob a day. Bargain.'

Three and a half pounds per week. Fourteen pounds per month. That was about half Doreen's wage.

'I don't have thirty pounds lying around. Tomorrow midday is the earliest.'

'Don't be late. See you at your bar tomorrow midday. On the dot.'

Harry started up his car and reversed. Blake watched them in his rear vision mirror as they faded up the coast.

Just because you think you are the only shark in the aquarium doesn't make it so.

He knew what he was going to do, had known since that first moment he clapped eyes on poor Andy. Once before he had walked away, taken the easy option. Not that this was easy. He had thought he'd travelled far enough away, thought he'd left his old self behind along with everything else that was corrupt and wrong, thought he had found paradise. Well, no, he had found paradise. He looked out now at the ocean in the last throes of the day.

'I wanted you to see this, Jimmy. To be part of it, to be proud of me.'

He might have said the words or just thought it. What did it matter? The truth was he had not discarded that part of himself of which he was ashamed, and he was even more ashamed right now because he was glad it was part of him. He needed the him that had waited calmly outside Benetti's apartment block looking for any telltale sign that he might be expected, that word might have got out, that he might have walked into that building and had his guts blown out with a pump-action. He needed the quiet resolve that had allowed him to sit at the table in the restaurant for a week, letting Little Joey's boys come to see him as no more than an empty chair. He needed the him that understood one failed day at the office meant he was maggot food, the him that had been hidden away like a baseball mitt in an old cellar, waiting for winter to pass, but when you brought it out and slipped it on, nothing had changed, the magic was still there; it was your glove and nobody else's, shaped by a thousand hours together.

The stepladder was folded flush against the wall of the broom cupboard. He brought it out, carried it into the bedroom, stood before the wardrobe, travelling back in time to the mouldy, scratched door of the wardrobe in his room in Philly. Now he opened the ladder and climbed it. He pulled down the suitcase that he'd stored on the top shelf at the back, noted it was a little mouldy and the lock clasps were rusty. They were slack and did not readily spring open when he slid his thumbs in and squeezed, so he had to really force it. When the suitcase opened he placed it on the floor. On top was a bunch of old clothes. He dug through them and hefted out the tin, which was far too heavy for the fading biscuits depicted on the lid. It had to be prised off with effort, more corrosion. Inside were two items, soft cloths wrapped around something deceptively heavy. He lifted the cloths off: the Beretta .22 or the Browning? Both looked good as new. He checked them out quickly, likely one of them was never coming back. He decided on the Browning.

Doreen's directions were spot on. He had parked on the lower arm of Barraclough road and hiked three miles uphill across an adjacent property to wind up exactly where he wanted, in the bush out the back of the target house Doreen had described. The houses on the ridge were farmhouses now, spaced acres apart and on a Sunday night there was no traffic about at all. This wasn't like a hit in a Philly restaurant where you needed to worry about identification and exit routes. It was a clear sky, the thunderclouds having rolled on, the moon a low-watt pearl globe, Blake just another rat in the basement. Earlier he had stripped the pistol, finding it clean as a whistle. He still had a couple of boxes of cartridges, which he retrieved from his garage. He had driven south to deserted bush. There he had raised the weapon and pointed it at a tree trunk twenty feet away. Surely now he would feel something? He didn't know what exactly he thought this would be: excitement, shame, fear? But there was an absence of any emotion. He felt nothing except the familiar weight of the gun, natural as it had always been, like it was his own palm grown suddenly heavier. In a way it disappointed him, mocked his concept of himself as a musician, a businessman, a surfer. Put a gun in his hand and he had not changed at all. In a practical sense that was a positive but all it said about him was that he was incapable of anything more than the primal. He was no better than Harry or Steve when it came down to it. There is a world that exists outside of me, he thought, a world he could not step into, as if some giant soap bubble was always between himself and it. Doreen was in that bubble. And Andy and Carol, and even Crane the bum, but he was trapped outside of it.

He raised the gun and fired a spread of shots. Even under a half-moon he did not miss.

So here he was now, squatting at the back of the bungalow with prickles up his ass. Just as Doreen had described, a wooden staircase ran to the back door. In Queenslander style, the wooden house was built on stumps high enough for the car to be parked under the house in an open garage. Blake couldn't imagine there was a flooding problem this high up but he supposed it helped cool the house on hot days. It was past eleven-thirty, and he had expected Harry and Steve might have been asleep but he heard them clinking beer bottles and calling out to one another, with a boisterousness that suggested a skinful of grog. Though he would not have hesitated to wake them from their sleep before shooting them, he preferred it this way. He waited nearly an hour. A bare-chested Harry came to what must have been the kitchen window at the back. Looking straight out into the night he poured himself a glass of beer. Then he turned back inside. It was time.

Blake left cover and moved quietly as cancer up the rear steps, waiting on the landing, pistol ready at his leg. Through the flywire door he could see parts of the kitchen, an old meat safe, a rough wooden table. The smell of cooked chops lingered. Conversation ebbed and flowed. He guessed they were in some kind of lounge room in the centre of the house but every now and again they were coming back towards the kitchen.

'... I said fuck that. Remember that?' Harry.

Followed by a mumbled response and a loud burp. The voice came closer. Blake caught a glimpse of shorts.

'That wharfie prick. Took care of that bastard.' Topping his beer. Then, '... need a piss.'

Outside on the small landing, Blake tensed, remembering Doreen's story, expecting Harry to head towards him through the kitchen to piss outside. He raised the Browning ready, but instead of heading through the kitchen, Harry walked down the hallway past the open kitchen door, staring at his feet. A door banged. Make that the dunny, as they called it here. So there was an indoor toilet after all. Blake quietly pulled open the flimsy back door with its window of flywire and slipped into the kitchen. The floor was warped, the lino cheap and chipped. Leaning against the wall was a cricket bat, edge stained with blood. Dead ahead, the doorway led to the narrow hall which ran left and right, dunny to the left, lounge room to the right. He heard the clink of a glass from that direction, turned out of the kitchen and started walking down the hall, turned into the first room on the left: low light from a standard lamp, sofa with its springs out, Steve sitting back, singlet and trousers, glass of beer in his hand, sawed-off shotgun resting on the arm of the sofa. Blake could have shot the dumb shit right off when Steve looked at him with the confused expression on his ugly mug but he waited for the reptilian brain to warm.

'What the fuck ...?'

He brought up the Browning, aimed. Steve reached for the shotty. Blake pulled the trigger, put a bullet through the thug's forehead. He walked to the shotgun, checked it was loaded, swivelled at the sound of rushing feet. Harry stopped dumb, the shotgun facing his bare chest.

'Hang on. We can sort something out.'

'You crossed a line.'

'We work for people. They're gonna ...'

Blake had not worked with a shotgun before but at this range he could not miss. Both barrels. Harry's chest spread open, the force knocked him back. He lay on his back gasping for air, his lungs shredded.

Just like Audrey, thought Blake. The sucking sound continued in the background while he picked up his spent .22 cartridge. Most times he never got the opportunity to tidy up but this was important. He looked for more shotgun cartridges and eventually found them in a kitchen drawer. He reloaded the shotty. By the time he walked back in the lounge room the sucking had stopped. He stepped over Harry's body and advanced to Steve. Blake pulled a stick of kid's plasticine from his pocket. He broke off two pieces and shoved them in his ears. He stuck the barrel of the shotgun right over the bullet hole the Browning had made, picked up Steve's limp hand and manipulated it onto the trigger. Then he squeezed.

ㅁㅁㅁ

Sometimes you hear people saying so and so looked peaceful when they were dead. Blake had seen more than his fair share of dead people and none of them looked peaceful. They looked caught out, like they were passengers in a bus and a driver had slammed on brakes and they'd been thrown this way and that and then just frozen haphazardly. But Andy looked peaceful. Maybe because he wasn't dead. He had tubes rigged up, he was bandaged but his head was on the pillow and he could just have been in a deep sleep. Blake had come straight to the hospital. It was three fifteen in the morning and there was nobody around, nobody to stop him from dumping the flowers from the glass vase in reception and then using the vase to scoop a goldfish from the ornamental pond right outside the front door, nobody to see him walk up the hallway to the ward. The only sign of human habitation had been the hollow echo of a door closing somewhere and the squeak of a wheelchair or trolley. No sister or nurse was at the ward desk, so he'd invited himself in. Any family had long since taken off. Blake cast his mind back earlier. Just him and Doreen here, and he'd reached out and squeezed her hand and that small gesture made him feel so good and so human. Of course it couldn't last. He had no idea if Doreen would approve or not of his actions. It didn't matter either way. You simply could not live your life based on what you thought other people wanted, no, you had to set your own rules. In his case, those rules had been set in that car with Vincent with his breath steaming up the window. What he had done, or not done then, was going to define the rest of his life. Maybe, even if Harry and Steve had not beaten up Andy, he would have arrived at the same course of action. It was moot. They had made their choices.

They had to live — and die — with them. He placed the vase on the little bedside table so that if Andy woke, the first thing he would see would be the goldfish. Blake felt sorry for that fish all by itself but the sacrifice was necessary to make somebody else's world better. That was the thing with aquarium life. You all had to find your own space, deal with what the world threw at you. There was a food chain and you never, ever knew where you resided in it. That was just life.

Blake relaxed, sat back in the chair and listened to Andy's ragged breathing. Only then did he remember Carol. Monday was her day off. He'd go and see her first thing. He closed his eyes. Sleep was welcome.

7. Paradise Lost

Both Carol's front and back doors were still locked. A worm of concern was eating into him. There was no evidence Carol had been home since his last visit. He had no idea who she rented from so he decided to check the most obvious places a key might have been left — under the mat or in the meter box. Bingo: the front door key was in the box. He opened the door, caught that slightly stale smell of a house closed a short time.

'Carol?'

He had not expected an answer but called anyway. The lounge room revealed a rumpled sofa, a newspaper carelessly open. He checked it, Friday's. He retraced his steps to the hall and advanced to the kitchen at the rear of the house: dishes had been washed and left to dry in a rack but it was perfunctory; the Trix not put away under the sink, the cutlery drawer not shut tight. It suggested haste but there was no sign of breakfasting today. Carol's bedroom was the one at the back adjoining the kitchen, she always liked having that mess of plants and trees outside her window. He clicked on the light. The bed was stripped, the bedclothes on the floor in a heap. The old-fashioned wardrobe was open. The locusts had been through, coat hangers and nothing else. The bathroom was a similar story, a near-empty Pears shampoo in the bin, the cabinet cleaned out. The spare bedroom was, as always, untouched. He felt relief. No bloodied corpse, which, he could admit to himself now, had been his gravest fear. It looked like Carol had got up and left in a hurry. Not so extreme she had left dirty dishes around but she hadn't tidied the lounge or cleaned the bathroom properly. Carol wasn't what you'd call houseproud but she was neat and he would have figured considerate enough to leave the house spic and span if she decided to move on. He did a quick search but found nothing at all to suggest a forwarding address. She had never maintained a phone so he couldn't call the golf club from here to see if somebody there knew anything. He locked the house back up and checked the trash can: old eggshells and vegetables but not paperwork.

'If you see her, tell her not to bother turning up again because she has no job.'

Blake knew Ray, the golf club bar manager, reasonably well. They weren't really competitors. Each helped the other out if they were short of stock. Ray was stacking crates out the back of the building. 'Never turned up Saturday, our busiest day, never called, nothing.'

Blake helped him with a couple of crates, dug for more info.

'She never showed Saturday?'

'Nope.'

'But she was fine Friday?'

'Good as gold.' Ray took a break from his labours and studied him. 'Rooting her were you?'

'We were acquainted.'

Ray gave a knowing chuckle. 'You might want to get your dick checked. You weren't the only one.'

Blake didn't care, didn't want to own anybody. He'd liked Carol, he got her, she got him.

Ray embellished. 'Couple of the members, older blokes.'

It quickly ran through Blake's head that perhaps there had been a problem in this regard: a wife finds out about her husband in a small place like this ...

'Do you know who she rented off?'

Ray did not.

'If you really need to find out why she split, try Gloria. She works at Gannons during the day and does the night shift here. She and Carol are thick.'

Gloria was diminutive with a small unremarkable face, a clearing beneath thick, curly brown hair. Blake put her age at late thirties.

'You're the Yank she's always going on about.'

'I guess so.'

They were at the back of Gannons, which purveyed everything from groceries to fishing gear. Gloria sucked on the very last of her cigarette, dropped it, ground it out, looked back up into Blake's eyes searching for some indication of deception.

Finally she said, 'She didn't tell me anything. She never told you she was heading off?'

Blake told her no, she had not.

'You didn't do the dirty on her?'

Blake decided to answer obliquely. 'Everything was good. We were supposed to be going for a drive Sunday.'

Gloria shrugged. 'I dunno. I expected her Saturday. When she never showed, I thought she must be sick and too crook to call in. Then I thought we'd hear something yesterday. She's not the kind of girl puts down roots, know what I mean, but I really thought she'd hang around. For you. She liked you. A lot.'

'You know who she rented off?'

'Try Gardiners.'

Gardiners was the bigger of the two real estate agents in Coral Shoals and was only a block from Gannons. He thanked her.

'You ever get shorthanded at your bar, you know where to find me. And if you hear from her, tell her to drop me a line.'

'I will.'

'You heard any more about the woman was killed?'

Blake said he hadn't. He felt obliged to add, 'I was worried ... about Carol, you know? But all her things were gone. I don't think anything bad happened.'

Gloria gave a half-grunt. 'Girls like Carol, something bad always happens.'

George Gardiner wore a crisp white shirt, gold cufflinks and watch, striped tie. He had indeed rented the house on behalf of a client but had no idea the house had been vacated.

'She'd paid to the end of the month, ten-pound bond. She'll forfeit that.'

'Did she leave a forwarding address?'

Gardiner went to a filing cabinet and looked through, pulled out a form, scanned.

'Post-office box in Toowoomba, Queensland. You want it?'

Blake couldn't see himself writing to her, he'd never written a letter in his life. He declined Gardiner's offer and took his leave. That was it, a dead end. For some reason Carol had up and left. Maybe he was the cause, but then why agree to see him Sunday? If one of her family had fallen ill suddenly, wouldn't she at least leave a message? Gloria was right. A girl like Carol always had some kind of trouble stalking her. He was kind of zoned out standing on the footpath — as they called it here — the air getting steamy again, when a shadow skidded through his vision like a dolphin through a wave and stopped in front of him. It was Nalder in his police van. The passenger window was half-down. He leaned over.

'Come here.' Nalder indicated something secretive. For the first time since last night, Blake thought about the bodies up there in the hinterland. They must have been found already. He lowered his head to the window. Nalder darted looks around, making sure he was secure.

'Vernon and Apollonia just arrested the Beach Bum for the girl's murder.'

ᗢᗢᗢ

'You have to admit he is weird.'

Doreen was squeezing oranges for a fresh juice. A Blake she had never had an inkling of had turned up at her place. Not the ice-cool, soft-spoken, logical Blake.

'They've arrested Crane,' he'd said, then run his mouth nonstop on how dumb and ignorant the police were. Five minutes on he continued to pace around the kitchen, still saying the same words. 'Crane didn't kill that girl.'

She thought twice about saying anything but did anyway. 'You sure about that?'

'Yes.'

'Just because he's a friend ...'

'Forget that. How did he even get there?'

She poured him a glass of juice and handed it to him, tried to be neutral. In honesty she could never say she liked Crane. He was smart, sure, he used words like a rich woman used her purse, as if knowing the contents would never run out. But he was a beach bum for a reason: he didn't want to fit in with society.

'What do the police say?'

'According to Nalder, they say he was with the girl in her car. She gave him a lift to the motel. He killed her and walked back. It's bullshit. He had scratches because he fell down Cockatoo Ridge. That's what he told me and I believe him. They say it was her clawing at him.' He looked at the juice, finally drank some.

'They have any evidence: fingerprints at the motel, something like that?'

'Nalder told me on the quiet that Crane's fingerprints were on the outside of the car. So what? It was parked out the back of the Surf Shack. Some witness says they saw him talking to the dead girl.'

'What witness?'

'They wouldn't reveal that to Nalder. It's a fit up. They want to clear the case so they go for the easy target, Crane. I spoke to a solicitor in Sydney, David Harvey.'

Alarm bells were ringing for Doreen. The business was doing well but Blake wasn't shy to spend. Sydney solicitors didn't come cheap. Blake was already into his story, how he had visited the local solicitor, Collopy, first.

'The guy flapped about like a wounded seagull, saying the case was way out of his league. "If they've taken him to Sydney you need somebody there. At this stage you don't need to engage a barrister." At least Collopy explained the difference between the hot-shot who went to court in the wig and the guy who did the legwork. For now we need legwork.'

'What did Harvey say?'

'He was honest. He said if the cops had arrested and charged Crane, they wouldn't be bothering about doing any other investigation, they would try and make everything point at Crane. He told me most Australian juries convict because they believe what the cops tell them. But for now, what he could do was visit Crane and tell him to clam up, say nothing.'

That didn't sound promising. She said as much.

'It's not. Harvey told me Crane's best chance of getting off is if it's some psycho who kills again. Great, huh?'

She didn't look him in the eye, just stirred the juice slow. 'You can afford Harvey?'

'Not for more than a couple of weeks. He advised me the most important thing was to get Crane good counsel now, in the early days, stop him from digging himself in a hole. But I have a plan.'

She was worried he was going to go into debt over Crane. 'You're not going to get a second mortgage or anything?'

'Money is not going to save Crane. I'm going to find out who did it.'

It made sense to Blake that if anybody could figure out the killer, it would be him. After all, the one thing he knew a lot about was killing people. He wasn't proud of this but it was a fact that very few killers had his degree of professionalism: they got sloppy, they made mistakes. For a start, many knew the person they killed. They were married to them or related to them. They left a trail. It was of utmost importance therefore that he knew the identity of the young woman who had been murdered.

'Valerie Stokes, twenty-four, convicted of prostitution three years ago in Kings Cross.'

Nalder had agreed to meet him at Crane's beach shack. The cops had been through it, trashed it. All that was left were books, tossed and left in the sand and scrub like scattered bones. The revelation about Valerie Stokes charged Blake.

'It's obvious. She met a john at the motel and he killed her.'

'I don't disagree but Vernon and Apollonia like the Beach Bum. He's got no alibi, he was messed up, his fingerprint is on the car.'

'In it or on it?'

'I'm not sure. I heard on the outside, but they might have found something on the inside too. Why are you wasting your time with this no-hoper?'

'I like him. He didn't kill her. The real killer is wandering around free as a bird.'

'According to Vernon, Stokes hasn't been in the game for at least two years. She's been working in a bar in Brisbane.'

'Boyfriend, husband?'

'Sort of boyfriend. He has an ironclad alibi. Says Valerie told him she was visiting a sister down this way. No sign of any relatives north of Sydney. She left Brisbane on the Sunday, the thirteenth. That night she stayed alone at the Heads in a motel. Left early next morning, also alone.'

Monday the fourteenth, there had been sightings at Greycliff and Toorolong. Then on the Thursday her car had been out the back of the Surf Shack.

'So where has she been in the meantime, Monday night through to Thursday?'

'So far they haven't been able to find out. That's your mate's best chance. Maybe she was turning tricks at motels.'

'Or shacked up with whoever killed her.'

Nalder conceded that would explain why the police could find no sign of her.

'On the coast, she would have been seen but up in that hinterland ... farms, shacks, no neighbours for miles...' Nalder's gesture intimated she might as well have been on the moon.

'It's not likely she just headed south on spec. She knew somebody. Does she actually have a sister?'

'In Newcastle. That's where she was from originally. The family haven't heard from her in years. One day she piked school and never came home. They thought she was dead till a few years ago when a family friend said they'd seen her in Sydney. But she never got back to them. Wild girl, from what they said.'

But if she had been heading back to Newcastle she would have kept driving south, not turned back up north to Brisbane via the Ocean View.

'How much money did she have on her when she was found?'

'Congratulations. I missed the part where you joined the police force and made detective.'

'Somebody has to find the truth.'

'If I were you I'd be concerning myself with those strongarm pricks that beat up your yardy.'

Blake ignored him, old news. 'How much money was she carrying?'

'Just under thirty-five pounds.'

A lot for a barmaid to have. She had to have been back on the game. Already his brain was working on it: somebody who knew her from before when she was a hooker, who lived within about fifty miles. Maybe they weren't the killer, maybe she'd left them, was heading back, decided to pick up a little more cash, picked the wrong john. He saw a weakness in the case against Crane.

'If it was Crane, why do they figure he left so much money? He's a bum. He'd take every cent he could get his hands on.'

'They'll say he's a bloke who doesn't care about money. Or he panicked.'

In other words, they would say whatever fitted their theory. He'd wasted enough time.

'Will you keep me posted?'

Nalder sighed. 'I feel bad about your yardy but it's still not my job ... but yeah, I'll let you know what I know.'

Though Blake had never stayed at the Ocean View Motel, he had driven by it a few times. If you were on the inland road that ran from out the back of Cockatoo Ridge, you took the turn-off to Billings on the coast. As he was already on the coast he just followed the road up to

Billings and then took Banksia Drive, which ran about halfway up the low cliff that overlooked the small town. Banskia Drive was narrow and winding, with a half-dozen properties perched on the top level of the cliff accessed by driveways. He got caught behind the garbage truck and had to wait while they emptied the trash. It would have been a bitch hauling trash cans all the way down from the houses but the views more than compensated. One white-haired resident was waiting to collect his emptied trash can. It was banged up. He must have thought Blake a sympathetic soul. He started talking to him through his open window.

'Buggers get a skinful and then overshoot the corner. They mangled my bin.'

Blake wondered if he would ever get old and rich enough that his biggest concern was a dented trash can. He hoped so. A vision of Doreen came to him at her kitchen table, handing him the orange juice. If only it were possible …

The rubbish truck jolted forward, the driver managing to get far enough to the edge of the cliff that Blake could squeeze past. He carried on about three hundred yards to the crest of the road where a tall sign 'Motel' ushered in the passing traveller. He turned into the short driveway past an entrance of stone and greenery. Reception was dead ahead but he kept going down the drive. The motel was single level and L-shaped but unlike most motels, which were bare, this one had planter boxes filled with lush plants either side of each room door. These offered screening and privacy from each neighbour. You might see what car turned and parked in front of a unit but you wouldn't see who got out. There was only one vehicle in front of any of the units, number two. It was hardly surprising, business was unlikely to be thriving given the circumstances. Number ten was the very last one on the short arm of the L, the furthest from reception, closest to the road. Blake made a three-point turn at the end of the strip and headed back to reception, parking in an empty bay beside an older model Holden. When he got out, he could see the ocean through a gap between the reception building and the accommodation area. Obviously the units offered views over the Pacific, as promised. He walked up a short, lopsided path. Birds were trilling, the humidity intensifying. Jasmine or some other sweet scent hung like incense. He entered the deserted reception area and saw, beyond the high desk, a small dining room and bar. He was about to hit the bell when a door at the back of reception opened and a gaunt man, straggly hair, wearing slacks and a sweater stepped through.

'Hello. Looking for a room?' The man's voice was flat and high at the same time. Blake put him in his late thirties.

'Not exactly.'

The man waited for more.

Blake said, 'I want to take a look at room ten.'

'You from a paper?'

'Yeah. The police finished with it?'

'As of yesterday. It hasn't been cleaned yet.'

'Good.'

'Ten quid.'

'Five.'

'Okay. But no pictures. I got to rent that room sometime, you know what I mean?'

'Deal.' Blake pulled out five pounds, asked if he owned the place.

'My in-laws.' He had picked up keys and was heading towards the door. Blake followed in behind him.

'Did you meet the girl?'

'I checked her in. She gave a false name. A lot of them do.'

They were back outside now, walking diagonally towards the unit.

'She was alone?'

'She checked in alone. I never saw the car.'

'What time?'

'Ten-thirty or thereabouts.'

Blake said he guessed the police gave him a going over.

'Oh yeah. I was lucky my wife and mother-in-law were with me.'

'You never heard anything?'

'Like screams or something? No.'

They had paused at the door. The motel guy pointed around the step.

'There was spew all over here. I had to hose it down.'

This was something Blake had not heard before. 'The cops think it was the killer?'

'That's what I heard them say. They were whispering but I've got good hearing.'

So whoever did it couldn't handle his own handiwork. Or maybe there had been more than one person here?

'Were you busy that night? Many rooms taken?'

'Four, counting her. We had a travelling salesman and two couples. The police got all their details.'

'What rooms were they in?'

'The couples were in one and three, the salesman in six.'

'Did she ask for the furthest room?'

'Yes. She said she wanted the far room, that's number ten.'

'She make any impression on you?'

'She seemed … I don't want to speak ill of the dead … but like, not the kind of girl you want to marry but you'd love to take her to the drives.' He opened the door, and said he wasn't coming in. 'Once was enough. Don't take anything.'

Blake gave him a scout's sign. Doreen had taught him that. He stepped inside the room.

With the curtains closed, it was black as the inside of a stove. He clicked on the central light. Like a giant's ulcer had burst: blood trails, rusted, crusting. It was a good thing the body had been found early. In this humidity the stench would never have cleared. Even with the front window left open, a sickening odour lingered. Immediately to his right was a narrow door smeared with blood, the knob still dusty with print powder. He was guessing bathroom. With a handkerchief, he pushed open the door. Small bathroom as expected: sink, open glass shelves above it, a toilet and a shower stall. Whatever belongings had been left here had presumably been taken by the police. The floor was of small hexagonal tiles, the walls plaster. It was clear of blood, at least anything obvious. Blake pulled the bathroom door to and settled his stomach for the hard part. It was a slaughterhouse. The gold-brown nylon carpet was disfigured by what resembled a large burn mark not three feet from the door: caked blood. Good luck cleaning that off. There was a small writing desk to his left, two cane chairs with curved arms on the left-hand side of the room. The material back and cushions on one were clear but on the other were streaked with dark brown, more blood. The double bed occupied most of the room, its bedhead resting against the right-hand side wall, closest to the road. Directly in front of him, at right angles to the bed, a window looked out over the ocean but there were only glimpses. A lot of vegetation was growing out there. The sheets had been stripped but the bare mattress was splotched dark brown. Streaks of blood were all over the wall to the bed side of the room and there were more patches on the carpet. Blake imagined it going down. The photos showed Stokes naked. If she answers the door like that, she's expecting someone. But then again it could have happened later. The killer was with her. Perhaps they had sex. She got up to go to the bathroom or grab a drink. Or they argued, she got up angry and the killer nailed her. From the photos he couldn't say whether she'd been stabbed from in front or behind. And where had the knife come from? Had the killer brought it with him? Was it hers? What Blake did know was that this was done in an angry frenzy. He remembered what it looked like when Tino Sanchez stabbed Charlie Regan at the Miracle Pool Hall. It was a thin blood trail, width of a wasp, that was all, because Tino was a master knifeman and didn't even get blood on himself. Whoever did this must have been covered in blood.

Blake opened the bathroom door again and checked inside, this time as close as he could around the drain and near the hot and cold faucets. He still couldn't see any blood but the cops had special instruments that could pick up what you don't see with the naked eye, microscopes and things like that. So, according to them, Crane either showered, then got back into his old clothes with no blood traces or what, discarded his clothes? How did he get back to his shack? Had anybody found the clothes he'd supposedly got rid of?

Blake had seen all he needed. He had to find where Stokes had been Monday night to Thursday evening. Solve that, there was a good chance he'd be able to find the killer.

There was one more thing he needed to do.

After thanking the motel guy and taking his phone number, Blake climbed back into his car and took the inland route south on Dayman Road. About eight miles before Coral Shoals, the road split. You could take Belvedere, which took you through the hinterland past farms, eventually to the Heights, or you could continue on Dayman. About two miles on from the Belvedere turnoff was the turnoff to Salisbury Road. It ran back down Coral Shoals joining the coast road about a mile south of his house. Crane had mentioned a logging track and Blake thought he knew the one, just a mile or so on from the Dayman turnoff. He found the track leading off into thick bush, parked and climbed out. It was damn hot now and the air smelt of future rain. The track curled along the ridge line in a semicircle. A lot of timber had been stripped from here to build sailing ships, or so he had been told. Many of the tall trees had gone but there was an abundance of ferns and bracken. About twenty minutes into his walk, he found a cabin. He was pretty sure this was the one Crane had talked about. It was made of rough wood, probably seventy or eighty years old but still provided shelter. Compared to Crane's beach abode, it was a palace. Just like Crane had said, on its south side, the level ground on which the cabin had been built fell sharply away but you couldn't see the drop unless you pushed aside the topmost ferns of the dense regrowth. When he did this, he could clearly see a drop of around twelve feet to the next plateau preceded by a trail of small broken branches and flattened fronds, just as if somebody had fallen. Of course it could have happened some other time. Crane could have made up this elaborate lie.

Blake did not believe so.

□□□

Just because Crane was weird didn't mean Doreen thought he could be responsible but she didn't want Blake getting involved. Yes it was selfish but she had found a tiny corner of paradise here, and now everybody wanted to tear it down. Those men who had beaten up Andy, what was going to happen to them? Were they going to come back and beat her up next? Or Blake? She had enjoyed their time this morning, Blake in her kitchen drinking a juice she'd just made. What if it really could be like that between them? He hadn't gone to anybody else, not that little number from the golf club. Her phone rang. She answered it quickly, expecting Blake with news.

'Doreen? It's me, Kitty. Can I see you?'

They met at the Heights tennis club. Kitty had ridden her bicycle and was wearing tennis whites.

'Mum's at home and this is good cover,' she explained as they took a seat on the quiet side of the terrace, the gentle rhythm of an unseen game somehow comforting like an aunt's lullaby.

'I just needed to see somebody.' This was not the bubbly, confident Kitty of a week ago. Doreen tried to angle her body to offer intimacy but was hampered by the furniture. The tables and chairs were of heavy iron frames and legs, the tops and seats made of wood slats painted different prime colours. It made her think of those iron flamingos in her uncle's garden, of family friends who had returned from the war and spent weekends with bags of concrete, wheelbarrows and welding torches. She would practise her steps and dream of being a ballerina while the men churned cement with thick shovels.

'It's horrible what happened but you're going to be fine.'

'I feel so stupid.'

'Innocent is not stupid.'

Kitty picked at her dress. 'Even if a boy asked me out … I don't know …' she fought tears.

Doreen reached over and took her hand. 'What I like about you, you're a really gutsy kid. This is not going to stop you. That creep is not going to fuck up your life. I won't let him, and neither will you, right?'

The tears squeezed out but there was a smile too. Kitty managed to nod. Doreen found a handkerchief and passed it across. Kitty blew her nose, composed herself.

'Did anything like that ever happen to you?'

'Maybe not that bad. But one boy, my brother's friend, he asked if he could feel my bosoms. This was up in our back shed. I was about thirteen, I really didn't have any bust anyway so I was almost flattered but it was wrong, so I said no. He grinned and tried again. I grabbed Dad's hammer off the bench and slammed it down on his other hand.'

Kitty was laughing. 'He stopped?'

'He started crying. I felt a bit bad actually. For years he avoided me but we ended up kind of friends. I mean it's not the same at all …'

'No, thanks.'

Somewhere glassware rattled, a rally ended. Doreen was filled with a sense of inadequacy: she'd be a terrible mother. She tried, 'Not all boys are like Todd.'

Kitty deadpanned. 'Not all boys are like Blake.'

At least Kitty's humour hadn't been extinguished.

'No, they certainly are not.'

Kitty seemed to have climbed out of the depths. 'You like him, don't you?'

'Yes, I do. But I work for him.'

'So?'

'It messes it all up.'

'Does he like you?'

A question she asked herself regularly.

'He likes me but I don't know if it's romantic.'

Kitty dwelt on that, said, 'Perhaps you don't want it all tarnished, like me with Todd.'

Maybe Kitty was more perceptive than Doreen was. There was a part of Blake like the other side of the moon. He wasn't evasive exactly about his background but Doreen could read people. There were things Blake didn't reveal, not even to her. Kitty jumped across to another line though.

'I hear they arrested the Beach Bum for killing that girl.'

'Apparently. That doesn't mean he did it.'

'They must have some evidence though.'

'Or maybe it's just because he doesn't fit.' Doreen was aware she was turning one-eighty degrees.

Kitty sighed, squinted up at the sun. 'Well, anyway. I hope it's him. Otherwise the killer is still out there.'

8. A Trip South

The solicitor, Harvey, finally rang him at home. It was late in the afternoon, the sea breeze waving a steamy towel over Coral Shoals, the excited squeals of young children on a day at the beach giving way to stifled yawns and the dull throb of departing vehicles.

'Is there any chance I can see him?' Blake had been noodling on his guitar the last two hours, waiting for this.

'No chance. I'm the only one the police will let within a bull's roar and believe me, they wish they could keep me away too. He's been charged with wilful murder. Tomorrow they are going to move him out of remand.'

'What's he say about talking to Stokes?'

Now that Crane had seen a photo of her, he was able to vaguely recall chatting to a young woman who may have been her, out the back of the club after his set. She seemed to be looking for somebody. He asked if he could help and she looked horrified. Crane couldn't give an exact time but thought it might have been after one of the dance heats. He seemed to think there were people coming and going. One of these, Harvey believed, must be the witness. Crane confirmed too that at any time on his way to or from his gig he might have put his hand on any number of the cars in the carpark. When Harvey had shown him the vehicle Stokes had been driving, he took a long time thinking about it. Eventually he had said he was pretty sure intercourse had been taking place in the car.

'He saw shapes in a car like that and then a French letter tossed from the window.'

That rang a bell, cleaning up the next day.

'You asked him if he recognised anybody?'

'Of course. All he saw were outlines. But it's good. He swears there is no way his prints can be inside the car. We can establish that even if his fingerprint is on the outside of the car, there are other, I assume, unidentified prints inside the car. I asked him if there was anybody else around at this time. He couldn't recall but he did say your yardman was going to and fro at various times of the night. Can we speak to him?'

Blake explained the situation.

'That's too bad. Obviously, if he regains consciousness ...'

Blake assured Harvey he would be right onto it. He ran through what he'd found out.

'You're good at this, Saunders. Did you get pictures of the hut and the bush?'

Not that good. He admitted he had not.

'Probably doesn't matter. They'll just say it happened some other time.'

Harvey was able to clarify a few other things. The police had found traces of blood, the type matching Stokes', in the shower fittings and drain and a towel. This led them to believe the killer had showered after the murder. They had also found a knife at the scene but, he was guessing, no fingerprints.

'If they had prints they'd be laughing at me. You ever known Crane to carry a knife?'

Reluctantly he had to say yes.

'Couple of months ago some hoons were giving him a hard time. He was looking out for himself.'

'Crane told me about that. Unfortunately he waved the knife at the little wankers and when they found out he'd been arrested, they contacted the cops.'

'Doesn't mean it's the same knife.'

'Of course not, but by the time the cops finish with them, the kids will have remembered it as being just like the one that killed Stokes.'

It was as if a concrete block had been dropped from a great height onto what had been a little bud of hope, squashing it flat. Blake scraped together what he could, tried to shape something from what he'd heard and seen. After all, he had more experience of violent death than likely anybody involved in the case, the cops included.

He said, 'You know there was vomit out front?'

Harvey was aware of this but hadn't seen any significance.

'I guess they killed in a frenzy, saw what they'd done.'

Blake explained what jarred. 'Well, the killer slashes her, showers and redresses, then goes outside and vomits? That doesn't sound like the right order. Or why not vomit in the bathroom? Maybe there was somebody else there.'

'And they were the one who vomited?' Harvey conceded it made sense but wasn't sure how that advanced them. 'What we need is an alibi for Crane or somebody else in the frame. Crane doesn't recall seeing anybody or anybody seeing him after he left the Surf Shack and headed inland, so that's not a lot of help.'

'What about the truck driver he says gave him a lift?'

'Even if we find him — and that's a big if — it's too late in the timeline to help. Although, if we could establish that Crane was wearing the same clothes with no blood on them, that might assist us. On the other hand, after his tumble, if he was bleeding a little, the Crown will make a couple of spots of blood sound like a giant pool. It could backfire. We have to tread carefully. If the police found fingerprints in that car other than those of Stokes or her boyfriend, that's a positive.'

Blake said, 'I aim to find out where Stokes was from Monday evening till Thursday.'

Harvey agreed that would be extremely helpful. Blake ran his theory about some former client of Stokes paying her to spend some time with him.

Harvey was sceptical. 'It's a long shot but you never know. You'd have to go to Sydney, try and find somebody who knew her back then.'

As if he hadn't already figured that.

Harvey wished him luck, asked to be kept informed.

'So what are his chances you think?'

'Better than they were. Just because he was talking to the girl means nothing. Especially if his prints aren't inside the car and others are. But don't get your hopes up. A case like this, the public wants to believe the killer has been caught and the police want to believe it too. Vernon is no dummy, he'll be looking into Crane's background. Any little slip-up, like the knife, will be magnified. I'll send you a copy of my file with the police reports and photos. You never know, something might click.'

He wasn't long off the phone to Harvey when it rang again. It was Doreen and she was excited.

'Andy's conscious.'

By the time he got to the hospital, Andy had drifted off to sleep again but he wasn't covered in tubes or anything except a bandage around his head. He looked like normal Andy, sleeping. Doreen was lit up like the big Christmas tree in New York he and Jimmy had once seen. She was truly beautiful. He wished he could have taken her on his arm for a stroll down South Street. Jimmy would have been impressed.

'He smiled at me, squeezed my hand, managed to say my name, but he was a bit out to it. The doctor said that's the drugs.'

'Andy say anything else?'

'One other thing: Audrey.'

Shit. That was something he would have to take care of. Only then he noticed his vase had been replaced by a proper goldfish bowl, the fish still swimming.

'Where did the bowl come from?'

'I worked an arrangement with an orderly. I'm guessing that the vase was you.' She had a smile on her lips. He owned up.

'The other night. So he's going to be alright?'

'They say he's not going to need a plate or anything else. Once they reduce the drugs in his system, he'll able to hold a proper conversation but he shouldn't work for a few weeks.'

'Of course not.'

What he wanted to do was seize her and kiss her, not like with a girlfriend — although maybe there was a bit of that too — but because it just seemed right. He did nothing at all. All of a sudden it felt awkward.

'What about the family?'

'I left a message with a neighbour.'

'I'm driving to Sydney,' he said.

'When?'

'Now.'

'That's a bad road at night.'

'I'll take it easy. There's things I have to check out.' He told her about his conversation with Harvey. He nodded at Andy. 'He might have seen something. Everybody forgot about Andy but he was there all the time.'

'The doctor said he might not remember anything about the attack or even days before.'

'I know. But he might.'

After the hospital, he had one more visit to make. Nalder had been eating steak. He had a napkin stained with worcester sauce tucked into his shirt. He wasn't happy to have Blake knocking on his door.

'You shouldn't come here.'

'It would be weird if I didn't.' He told him about Andy.

'Well if he can identify the men who beat him up, I promise I'll do something.'

'That's not why I'm here. I'm going to Sydney.'

'To help Crane? You've got rocks in your head.'

'Stokes worked as a hooker. I think maybe she had some special customer, could be our guy, or at least could help if she spent time with him.'

'What do you want from me? And make it quick, my mashed potato is getting cold.'

'I need somebody who can tell me where she worked, who her friends were.'

Nalder picked steak from a tooth. 'There's a Vice cop I know down there, might not be averse to earning an extra quid or two.'

□□□

Detective Sergeant Ray Shearer had shoulders like axe handles, heavy hands. One look told Blake he was vastly more dangerous than the weak punks who'd beat up Andy. Blake had already folded seven pounds into a wad in his palm and when they shook hands Shearer transferred these to his own with practised ease.

They were in a small dining room adjoining a cramped bar somewhere in the Cross. After driving for around five hours, Blake had reached Newcastle near midnight. There he slept on the beach like he had when he'd first arrived in the country. He'd cruised to Sydney, called into the Kings Cross police station and met Shearer, who had suggested a lunch meet at the pub.

'What's a septic tank doing up in Boomer's patch?' Shearer didn't bother to check the notes he slipped into his jacket.

'Surfing, running a bar.'

'Half your luck. How is the bastard?'

Their earlier meeting that day had been succinct. Blake had established that Nalder had been known as Boomer in his younger days, that he had played rugby with Shearer, and that for seven pounds Shearer would find out what he could about Valerie Stokes, her criminal record and associates.

'He's like the sheriff up there.'

Shearer chuckled. The waitress arrived with their food. Shearer winked at her, began sawing meat.

'This bird, Val Stokes, got done in.'

It was a statement. Blake hadn't told him that.

'That's right.'

'And you want this information why?'

If he told the truth, Shearer might shut up shop. But what choice did he have?

'They've arrested a guy I know. I think he's innocent.'

'The drifter?'

'He's not really a drifter.'

Shearer added copious salt and waved his hand. 'I don't give a stuff. Vernon and Apollonia have tags on themselves. Always strutting around, "We're big Homicide D's".' He reached into his jacket and pulled out a sheet of paper. 'Valerie Stokes' charge sheet. I'll be honest, I didn't remember her, don't think she was in the game long. Worked at one of George Shaloub's brothels.'

Blake scanned the sheet. There was a perfunctory arrest report. Not much to go on.

'How do I get to Shaloub?'

'You don't.' As if he knew Blake was going to argue, he held up a warning palm. 'Please, trust me on this.'

Blake understood: Shaloub was some kind of Aussie mob boss.

'So what do I do?'

Shearer ate some more, chewed thoroughly. There was a neatness and efficiency about him.

'I've made some enquiries on your behalf. Shaloub's bodyguard is a giant, name of Granite. Granite's no professor but he remembers absolutely every piece of tail ever set foot in the Cross. He remembers Stokes. He says you should speak to a girl called Jill. She's still on the game but she and Val Stokes used to room together. I've written the address on the back. She doesn't start work till two.'

Blake said he didn't want to seem rude but he wouldn't stay, he wanted to get onto it straight away. Shearer told him no offence was taken.

'Tell Boomer I might pay him a visit one day. Thanks for lunch.'

Perhaps this was a mistake, a waste of time and effort. Perhaps he should have let it go, left it to Harvey to get it right. But he couldn't, just the same as he couldn't turn the other cheek when those bozos smashed up Andy. Crane was his responsibility, that's the way he figured it, same as Jimmy had been, and he'd let him down, right, Jimmy? He did not deserve any of this: playing his guitar in his own bar with a beautiful woman like Doreen working alongside him, surfing in the crystal ocean, watching the sun rise like a gold coin over a sheet of pure silver. He'd suspected all along it hadn't just been gifted to him, that there must be more to it, some fine print like on a winning lottery ticket. This was the fine print. You have to help those who cannot help themselves, you have to protect and serve those who serve you. Maybe it wouldn't stop with Crane, maybe there would be another hurdle he had to clear.

The address Shearer gave him was half-a-dozen blocks away, downhill in a cramped quarter of apartments and old triple-storey terraces where damp washing was strung on lines and the road suffered from acne. After following directions from a woman with a scarf knotted over her head, he found himself in a minute kitchen at a tiny table beside a caged mechanical canary. Jill wrangled a kettle on a gas cooker, Viscount between her lips, a housecoat with Chinese blossoms. Her brown hair ran wild like the bracken around the back of Carol's house. He put her age at thirty, give or take.

'Can't believe it.' She poured hot water into an aluminium teapot, closed it up, shook it around. 'Stabbed?'

'Brutally. Sorry.'

She sighed, continue to motion the pot.

'Can you think of anybody who might have hated her ...?'

She looked up sharply. 'You said the cops had a bloke.'

'I don't think he did it.'

She considered him long and hard. 'Why are you here?'

'I want to find out who did kill Valerie. Otherwise I think whoever murdered her is walking around laughing.'

She was thinking about that, he could see it.

'Hey if I'm wrong, you've done good by her anyway. Did the police speak to you?' She shook her head, began to pour tea into two odd cups. He decided his best shot was to keep talking.

'She left Brisbane on Sunday, stayed at the Heads Sunday night then, voom, disappears from Monday afternoon until Thursday evening. I think she must have stayed with somebody, maybe a former client. Maybe they killed her, or would know who did.'

Jill brought the cups and saucers over and sat on the other chair.

'Stokesy was a good kid. She was a bit lost, needed to work a few things out. I think she knew this wasn't the life for her. What's she been doing?'

'Barmaid in Brisbane.'

Jill nodded like that made sense.

'Can you think of anybody she had a special connection with?'

Jill added three spoons of sugar, stirred slowly. 'Sorry. She had a couple of regulars but ...'

'What is it? Somebody come to mind?'

'Not exactly somebody. She came back one day grinning like the cat that swallowed the canary.' Jill realised what she said, nodded at the cage with a smile. 'Not that one. I did have a real canary once but it got out.' Blake waited patiently. 'She came back from wherever she'd been, happy as Larry with twenty quid or so. That's a big haul. She'd spent a few bob already too. She was very mysterious about where it come from but I knew she couldn't hold out. Later she tells me, she met a couple of fellas on the street. They look her up and down, ask if she wants to be in a film. You can guess what kind of film.'

'Was it the one time only?'

'One other time, a month or so later, she said they'd contacted her and she'd done another.'

'She give any names?'

Jill sucked the last of the fag and stubbed it out. The lipstick on the butt reminded him of the bloody smears in room ten.

'Tell the truth, I wasn't sure if I believed her. I never heard of anybody recognising her in any movie.'

'You think she made it all up?'

'Not all of it. I remember she had cash, more than normal, but the girls always want to talk it up a bit, you know? Especially with film stars. So and so screwed David Niven or sucked off Tony Curtis. My arse. And the prime minister or premier, of course ... mind you, those ones could be telling the truth.'

He couldn't see a phone in the flat.

'How would they have contacted her? You have a phone back then?'

'No. They would have just driven around till they spotted her. Usually she was working Darlo on the other side of William. She was new, so she didn't get prime territory.'

Dead end. He tried another line. 'She say anything at all about this movie? Who else was in it?'

'Said it was suck and fuck in front of a proper big movie camera. The bloke in it with her was one of the ones who fronted her, about forty she said.'

'She say where they filmed it?'

'I think she mentioned around Alexandria or Zetland. Some warehouse with a bed and mattress set up. They told her this could be the start of a big career.' Jill gave a derisive snort.

'You think she made all this up?'

'I think she exaggerated. Maybe it was a film but a private one for these jokers to get off on. The so-called second time, she wouldn't talk much about because I think she knew I didn't believe her. I think she just made up that to save face.'

But if there was a second time, Blake was thinking, maybe the guy gave her his number or some way to stay in touch. But how could he have contacted her? She would have to have contacted him at some point. Brisbane would have to be his next stop. Her words broke into his contemplation.

'You look like that movie guy: Troy Donahue.'

'Thank you.'

'You want a freebie? Little memory of the Cross?'

The answer was no, he did not. But if he said that, he risked offending somebody whose help he may need again. A thought dashed across his brain that he could pay her for her time without the sex but he dismissed that as insulting.

'Sure,' he said. 'Why not?'

Mile after mile of bush. Gum trees standing straight and silent along the side of the road like ghosts sitting in judgement on the living: on him. It was amazing you could drive so far and see so few people. With each passing minute, the sun slunk lower, as if embarrassed by the outcome of the day. Light that had been pale, almost white when he set out, turned the colour of urine. My life is like this, Blake thought. I keep driving on in my car, removed. I don't get out and touch what's around me. Little by little, things get darker and you don't really know where you are any more, you just follow white posts and try not to crash.

Sometimes you fuck up, though. He caught jagged memories of the house on Cockatoo Ridge: muzzle flash, blood, gaping bone.

Darkness was always coming for you.

He saw a brick apartment block, his breath on a misted window. You tried to stop it, to head west, to outrun night, to put distance between your actions and your future, but it was as relentless as age.

9. Edward

South of Taree with his tank on empty, the hour hand almost at the point where gas stations shut up shop, he saw a Neptune sign and pulled over. The attendant was a young raw-boned guy in overalls. Blake heard himself talking and joking with the guy about the drive ahead, around four hours to go still, but it could have been somebody else, a puppet, doing his part. It was still hot and the smell of the gum trees was as overpowering as Jimmy's Californian Poppy used to be when he had a date. Jimmy. What the heck would Jimmy have made of this country where you could drive a full tank and pass a handful of cars? The idea of them camping out on some picnic rug, ants biting Jimmy's ass, brought a smile to his lips.

He'd left Sydney at three in the afternoon, little wiser than when he had arrived. He had tried to find Detective Shearer again to ask about a potential blue film starring Valerie Stokes but was told by the station cops Shearer was out. The way they said it warned against him asking again. His theory that some former client might have hired her had no support, so the movie line was all he had and that was as thin as the paper on a roll-your-own. The attendant gave him his change, wished him well and went back to finish up in the garage. A car hummed by. He felt like a fly trapped in one of those displays in that big New York museum he'd visited as a kid; a rare outing with his mum and aunt who lived somewhere near Cleveland. Like the whole world could be painted and put inside a cube, and it was beautiful but the only thing that was actually real was that dirty little fly. He remembered a card from his aunt and uncle after his mum died, Jimmy ripping it up, chucking it in the bin. He wondered now if they had offered to look after him or something. Jimmy had dismissed the card as crap.

'Where were they when she needed some help? I'm looking after you, nobody else. We stick together.'

But his aunt, Jane was her name, she had been nice that one time in New York. They had stopped at a café and Aunt Jane had bought pie for him and his mum. Jimmy wasn't there of course. He was already in too much trouble. Maybe he was in juvie at that time? Too late now. He could not remember the taste of the pie, nothing like that, not even if it was apple or something else but he remembered he liked it, almost as much as those glass cubes with the world inside them.

As he was about to climb back into the ute he saw a shape coming towards him from the south along the side of the road, moving in uneven jerks. He thought for a moment it may have been a roo but as it drew closer realised it was a man walking with an uneven gait on account of the big swag he was carrying across his back. As the man reached the station area, Blake saw he wore tattered clothes and shoes with no socks, and then last of all that he was Aboriginal, and only Blake's age. Blake had had nothing to do with Aborigines. It wasn't like back home where there were actual laws in some places keeping black and white from mingling, but all the same there was a real demarcation and the 'Abos', as everybody called them, seemed to have the thin end of the stick. On his travels he'd caught glimpses of black people living down by riverbeds or in parks. He'd been drinking in pubs where they'd been shooed out even though they weren't noisy or drunk. He had never seen an Aboriginal person in Coral Shoals. This guy looked like he'd been walking for a long time.

'Where you heading, man?' he asked when the guy was nearly level. The guy stopped, looked nervous.

'I'm just passing through. I'm not stopping.'

He said it like if he stopped it was going to offend Blake.

'But where are you heading?'

The young guy looked away, didn't meet his eyes, said, 'North.'

'Me too. You want a lift?'

The guy blinked. 'In your car?'

'Yeah.' Blake slapped the roof. He wondered if maybe the guy was a bit simple. 'I'm heading to Coral Shoals. I'm Blake.'

He stuck out his hand. The guy hesitated then took it.

'I'm Edward.'

'So Edward, you want to take a load off? I could do with the company.'

Edward smiled for the first time. It was like a full moon coming out from behind clouds.

'Me too, Blake.'

They'd been chatting easily all the way to the outskirts of Coral Shoals. The moon had been hung out like a lantern, birds had faded from silhouettes to invisible. Edward told Blake this was only the third time he'd ridden in a car and the first time ever in the front seat. Apart from that it was the bus or the back of the police wagon. He said he was originally from Wagga Wagga but he'd left when he was sixteen. He wasn't exactly sure where America was but he knew about Mickey Mouse and Coca Cola. He slapped his knee at Blake's accent.

'That's funny.' He amused himself trying to sound like Blake.

'What are your plans from here?' Blake asked. They had just passed a sign that said five miles to Coral Shoals.

'Plans?'

'Yeah. You got a job lined up?'

The idea of a job seemed foreign to Edward. He explained after leaving Wagga Wagga he'd gone fruit-picking but eventually he had to move on and since then he hadn't worked much at all.

'It's not I don't want a job. People don't hire us.'

'My yardman is in hospital. I need somebody. You want the job?'

Edward looked anxious. 'You run a pub. I'm not good with the grog. It messes me up.'

'Well, stay off the grog.' Blake told him the sorts of things Andy did for his wage. 'I'll pay you exactly the same as I pay him. Okay? Deal?'

Edward found enough confidence to nod.

'You can start tomorrow. We need to find you a place to sleep.'

Edward said he was fine sleeping under the stars and tapped his swag. 'Got everything I need right here.'

Blake was thinking that would be fine for a night or two. After that Edward could hire a caravan at the caravan park. He pointed out the Surf Shack sign, not illuminated because it was closed. Edward was impressed.

'I never worked in a place like that before.'

Blake felt bad dropping Edward at the river near where he and Nalder met but Edward was delighted.

'I'll pick you up at nine-thirty tomorrow, get you some clothes, show you the ropes. Okay?'

Once again Edward seemed worried. Blake asked what was up.

'How am I going to know when it's nine-thirty?'

Blake took the watch off his wrist and gave it to him. Edward's jaw nearly hit the floor.

'I won't steal it, mate, I promise.'

Blake told him he knew that. Edward was still thanking him as he drove away. In truth he wasn't sure Edward would be there; he knew well enough that despite our intentions to change, sometimes we couldn't, sometimes we are gripped in a current that takes us where it will. But he also knew that every man needed somebody who believed in him. Jimmy had believed in him and he had ultimately failed his brother. He would try and not let that ever happen again.

□□□

'A fish tank? Where has he gone to get that?'

Nalder had never been Doreen's favourite person. Not just because he was a cop who strutted around like he owned the town, though that didn't help. It was that he always turned up when she was busy and made a nuisance of himself. Here she was trying to get the bar and tables ready and Nalder was just hanging around at her elbow asking dumb questions. Still, she had to answer. She knew Blake must be paying him off, just not how much or what it covered.

'There's a guy in Greycliff. He made the last one.'

'Those blokes never showed up again?'

'No.'

She was thinking it had been three weeks now since everything went pear-shaped: Andy getting bashed, that girl murdered, Crane arrested. She wrangled a table into position. Nalder didn't offer to help, just used the toothpick he had taken from the little shot glass she had just set out, to work his mouth.

'How's business going?'

'Last week was pretty much back to where we were before.'

'People have short memories. Speaking of which, has Andy been able to remember anything? If he confirms those guys attacked him, I can do something official.'

'His memory is coming back in dribs and drabs but hardly anything about that day.'

'How much longer are they keeping him in?'

Nalder was following her now as she went around to the back bar to make sure there were replacement bottles if any of the spirits were low.

'He'll be out any day.'

Nalder speculated that the men who had attacked him had probably realised they'd overstepped the mark and done a runner. She stood on a milk crate and checked all the spirits, said she hoped so. In the mirror she saw Nalder sneaking a look at her legs but then quickly looked away as if that was out of bounds. His one redeeming feature was that he actually seemed to love his wife. She stepped down, the squeak of a trolley made them both turn. Edward had brought in two crates of small Cokes.

'Where you want these, Miss?'

'Just in the fridge there, Edward, thank you.'

Nalder eyed Edward suspiciously. Edward averted his eyes from the cop, finished his job and got quickly out of there. In the meantime she'd been able to wipe down the jukebox.

'What's he thinking, employing an Abo?' Nalder went to the fridge and helped himself to a Coke.

'Edward is a good kid, hard worker.' She started cracking coins from their cardboard cylinders, imagined with pleasure that the counter was Nalder's scone.

'People around here don't like it.'

'Blake doesn't pay much attention to what people like or don't like.'

'So I've noticed but he doesn't want to get people offside. Gannons employed that Abo and look what happened.'

What happened was some arsehole hoon had been sitting on his car bonnet talking shit about Aborigines and flicked his butt right near the Aboriginal man's feet. The man told the hoon to watch it. The hoon had asked if he was going to make him and, with a couple of lightning fists, the man had. He'd lost his job and wound up in jail.

'Edward wouldn't harm a fly.'

'They're different with drink in them.'

'You know what's funny? So are most men.'

Nalder didn't like her cheek, she could see him bristle. He took his time to finish his Coke.

'I'm only looking out for him. Tell him to drop in when he's back.'

It was her turn to ask a question. 'What's happened to Crane?'

'He's still in remand. They won't bail him. Your boss isn't still thinking of heading up to Brisbane, is he?'

'Thinking about it.'

'Talk him out of it. He's already wasting good money.'

She'd said something similar but wouldn't give Nalder the satisfaction of revealing that.

'And I wouldn't leave cash lying around.' Nalder inclined his head to the door, intimating he was referring to Edward. She felt guilty that when Edward had started there she had raised the same concern to Blake, who had shrugged and said, 'You don't show a man trust, he will steal from you.'

He said it in a way that told her he had come to this opinion from some personal experience. She would have liked to have the courage to ask about it but she didn't. So many things I lack the courage for, she told herself. It was just too hard to risk losing the little joys you have for riches you might never get.

Blake rang about an hour later to say he was going to spend the night in Greycliff.

'The tank won't be ready till tomorrow morning. I may as well spend the night here.'

'Where are you staying?'

'The fella has a sofa in his shed. Or there's the car.'

'I'm going to see Andy later.'

'Give him my best.'

That wasn't why she was mentioning it.

'Every time I go out there he says he wants to come back to work. He can't wait. What are you going to do? About ...'

She looked around, no sign of Edward, but she whispered anyway, '... Edward.'

'I was thinking that I could pay both of them for a little while. I don't want Andy trying to do too much. After that, maybe Eddy could work in the kitchen washing dishes and stuff.'

She told him what Nalder had said about people not liking him being there and added, 'I've heard people say a few things too.' She had kept this from Nalder.

'What kind of things?'

'You know: "I don't want to drink in an Abo bar", shit like that.'

'I thought I got away from those crazies and crackers. Why can't a man ever just be treated as a man?'

'You sound like that Negro preacher, King? And his civil-rights stuff.'

'I don't know him but if that's what he says, I'm on his side. Edward has never done me wrong. I like him the same as Andy. Nalder and everybody else can get screwed.'

There was nobody like Blake Saunders, or at least nobody she had ever met. The man made up his mind. He acted. He did. Others talked but never did a darn thing. She parked the Beetle in the hospital carpark, felt a pang that he was up there in Greycliff alone in some shed. It was a lovely day, the sun spread like butter with just the right amount of thickness. She smelled cigarette smoke, looked over and saw Peg, one of the nurses she'd come to know from her visits, leaning back against an old Holden, smoking. Peg was probably mid-thirties, piano legs, Scottish skin, always joking. She was in the late stages of pregnancy.

'Beautiful day,' Doreen offered.

'I'm enjoying it while I can.' Peg indicated her stomach.

'It'll be a joy.' It was just one of those things you say.

'You got kids?'

She shouldn't have felt embarrassed when someone asked but she always did. Before she could answer, Peg said, 'No of course you haven't. Not with a body like that.' She didn't say it in a nasty way, more like she admired Doreen. 'I've got three. Believe me, I would have kept it that way but I was too late.'

It was the first time Doreen had seen Peg anything but cheerful and it threw her. Peg flipped up her Rothmans for another cigarette but the pack was empty. She crumpled it and tossed it.

'Have mine.' Doreen opened her handbag and handed over a packet of Viscount.

'I'll just take a couple ...'

Doreen waved that off. 'Please. You've been so good to Andy.'

'He's a nice kid.' Peg pulled out a cigarette, offered Doreen one from what had been her packet but when Doreen shook her head, slipped the packet in her pocket. She lit up again, drew in deep. 'Been a rough day today. Lost one of my favourite patients, Lilly. She was eighty-one, a trick.'

And once again Doreen felt that her own life was slight, shallow. Even though her words sounded trite, she spoke them with genuine belief. 'It's important, what you do. What I do ... show people to a dinner table, organise a dance contest …' she sighed, not bothering to waste words on a pointless mission.

'We should swap some day,' smiled Peg.

'We should.'

'He's in the garden in his favourite place.'

'Thanks.'

'Thanks for the cigs.'

As Peg had indicated, Andy was sitting in a wicker chair in the sun in the little back garden of the hospital. Lately it had become his favourite place. This was the first time though he was out of his dressing gown and in real clothes. The bandage had gone from his head. He told Doreen as he ate the lamington she'd brought for him, that he just needed to build a bit more strength.

'I can only walk for a little way and I have to sit down.'

She reminded him he'd been nearly a month off his feet. She asked him about the day he had been attacked.

'Nalder called into the Surf Shack and asked if you remember anything yet.'

He pulled the cake away from his mouth and looked sad. She was sorry now she had troubled him with it.

'No. Nothing, but I did remember something from that night Blake kept asking about.'

'The night the girl was killed?' She was on high alert. Andy had been the one important witness the police had never interviewed.

'Yes. I was out the back just washing glasses and stuff. I saw Crane talk to her — the girl whose photo Blake showed me.'

'You did?'

'Yeah. Maybe she asked him for a light or something. I'm just starting to remember things in like, little flashes.'

'How long did she talk to him?'

'I don't know. I just remember I saw the girl and Crane, and I think he gave her a light or she gave him one.'

She asked if there was anybody else around at the time but he could not remember.

'Will I still have my job when I get out of here?'

'Of course.'

Andy began fiddling with his hands, agitated. 'I heard the boss has hired some Abo.' Andy was looking at the ground where ants were crawling from a small pyramid of dirt. Word might ride a donkey not a freight train in Coral Shoals but it still travelled.

'Blake promised you. You'll get your job back.'

She did not want to be the one to tell Edward he would have to go. Blake could do that himself.

ㅁㅁㅁ

It was afternoon by the time he got back from Greycliff and installed the new tank. The clouds were low, purple and full of rain. The air pressed in on his chest. He was dead-ended on the Crane thing. The case file had arrived from Harvey and he flipped through it but didn't find anything that stuck out. Crane was still in remand and Harvey said there was nothing more he could do for now. His only move from here would be to travel to Brisbane and make enquiries there but the boyfriend of Valerie Stokes had an alibi, and when Blake had telephoned him he had said he did not want to talk to him — the police had the killer and that was that. If that wasn't bad enough, there was this shit about Edward. Coral Shoals might be beautiful on the outside but it seemed it wasn't a million miles from Klan territory when you stirred the pond. Apart from the Mob guys hating President Kennedy, Blake knew shit-all about politics but he thought he'd be safe from it here.

The sight of the ocean opened a valve, let off steam. He pulled in to his favourite spot, took a deep breath. No matter how bad things were going, no matter what you did wrong in your dumb life, the water and the salt healed it. Holding his board, he waded into the sea, let it melt him, make it one with itself. He surfed for just under an hour, would have kept going but the bar was open tonight. He was putting the board in the back of the ute when the unmistakable hue of Duck's van materialised. Duck pulled in fast beside him.

'You better get into town. Your black mate's pissed and going to get himself arrested. I just saw him wobbling across the street shaking his fist at passing cars.'

It didn't take Blake long to find Edward. He was sitting in the sandpit of the kids playground on Archer Street sucking on a bottle of sherry. It was devoid of children or parents. Blake was hoping Edward hadn't scared them off.

'What's going on, Edward?'

Edward glared at him like he was going to throw the bottle at him. Then his face crumpled and he started crying.

'I'm sorry, boss. I'm sorry.'

Blake helped him up, dropped the bottle in the bin and eased him into the car. They drove to the caravan park in silence. There Blake put him to bed.

'I'll see you tomorrow, Edward,' he said and pulled the door shut.

It was just Doreen and him now. It had been a good night, good turnover, though people were still talking about the crazy psycho-killer who used to do poetry there. Despite everything, or maybe because of everything, the band had played well tonight. Like when he held a weapon, the guitar was an extension of his arm. Energy flowed through it into the world. Unlike with a gun, when he'd finished, nobody was lying dead.

'You going to sack him?'

'I don't know.'

'You know why he ...?'

'He's an alcoholic. They don't need a reason, just a bottle.' He asked her how Andy was doing.

'Still worried about his job, asking about the fish.'

Blake hadn't been out there nearly enough. He would go tomorrow, buy him a few comics.

'And something else. He's remembering things.'

'That's good.'

'Maybe not for everybody.' She told him about Crane and Val Stokes.

'You going to tell Nalder?' she asked.

He told her it was probably better they said nothing to anybody about it.

Next morning when he arrived at the Surf Shack after a surf and breakfast, Edward was hosing and sweeping. He couldn't look Blake in the eye.

'I'm sorry. The drink gets to me.'

'Did anything happen? Anybody pick on you? What started it?'

Edward shook his head, still looking at the ground. Finally he looked back up, right into Blake's eyes.

'Nobody to blame but me. I was laying on my bunk and I just started thinking about a drink. Like the devil put it in my brain. "It's alright, Eddy, it's alright to think about it." That's what I tell myself, "It's only thinking." But I keep thinking. And then I start walking ... And then I see a bottle all shiny and perfect and I think, "How can that little bottle be bad?", like Eve and the apple, you know? And then I start drinking …'

Blake said, 'I'm not paying you for last night, seeing as you missed. You do it again, I won't have a choice, I'll fire you.'

Edward nodded. 'It won't happen again.'

ㅁㅁㅁ

Nalder looked up from the form guide; it was the races tomorrow and he liked to get in early. Constable Patrick Denham stood waiting, fists clenched, nervous. Nalder had been assiduous in making his juniors aware of his ill temper at being disturbed during lunch.

'Yes, Constable.'

'Sorry, Sergeant, but we have another one. Mr Bentley, he wants to speak with you.'

Nalder made a show of slowly folding his newspaper before walking out to the front desk. Tim Bentley was the fourth resident of the Heights who had stood there this week looking exactly the same: annoyed, powerless.

'What did they take?'

'I've made a list. A radio, a lot of records …'

Nalder took the list off him. He was pleased. Even though it was handwritten and he would have to type it, it would make the report easier. 'Your golf clubs?'

'Spaldings.'

'Bastards.' Nalder made a show of sitting down by the typewriter. 'What's your address again?'

Bentley gave it and Nalder typed two-fingered.

'How many others have been burgled? I know Tom Leonard got broken into.'

'Took his TV. I think you're the fourth. Were the doors and windows locked?'

Bentley shuffled. 'Women. Margaret went out to have her hair done, left the laundry door unlocked.'

Nalder tut-tutted. Bentley threw his hands around.

'She should have but … what's the world coming to? Having to lock your door?'

'I know, different times now.' He methodically copied the list.

'Can I go?'

'You got to sign it, sorry.' The Bentleys had been in the area forever.

Tim's father had run a bicycle shop, his mum had been the town florist. Tim Bentley had bought a hardware shop down in Sutton. Nalder was pretty sure Bentley had voted against him at the golf club, at least the first time. Bentley hopped about, checking his watch.

'I can drive up later, fingerprint the place but there was nothing at the others. You insured?'

'Yes.'

'They may not pay out if the door was unlocked.' Nalder yanked the paper out. 'Sign here.'

Bentley did as he was told.

'We'll keep our eyes out but they are pros by the looks of it. Don't leave us much to go on.'

When Bentley had gone, Nalder thought to himself, there will be more, definitely more. He tried to return to the form guide but his enthusiasm had waned. Saturday was the day he should be out there on the golf greens putting, not sitting hunched at his kitchen table listening to the ponies. You tried to make something of your life, somebody was always there to block it. He called out to Denham, told him to mind the fort, he was heading out. He strolled down from the station into town and entered the Victoria Tearooms where he ordered a pot of tea and a vanilla slice. It was quiet in here. The only other customers, a woman and a girl, he assumed her daughter, stared out the window without making conversation. Genteel, that's what it was here. There was almost nothing in the world that a strong pot of tea and a vanilla slice couldn't put right, even the slight that those who sought his help when the world turned against him did not want him in their club. Rather than sink his spirits, this anomaly buoyed him. When the enemy is at your door, hypocrites, you come running to mine and ask me to defend you. And so he sipped, mildly content.

The ceiling fans in the Victoria were the best in town but even they were struggling with the build-up today. It was going to rain, that was for sure.

You didn't imagine policemen having tea and cake, thought Kitty, looking at the big sergeant at the other table. Ministers or priests, yes, you imagined them having tea and cake but not say, standing in a pub drinking. She wondered what kind of things the policeman would be thinking about. What he wouldn't be thinking about was that he had to sit here having tea with his mum because that was the only place he could go now. Yesterday she was at the Olympia malt-bar with Jenny and Leonie having a milkshake when that bitch Brenda had walked in with

Todd and she just had to get out of there, like, that minute, or she was going to faint. It was like hot pins and needles through her whole body. Brenda the cat that swallowed the cream, Todd putting on that nice act of his — she knew now that's all it was, an act. Jenny and Leonie thought it was just because the date hadn't worked out, that was the lie she had told them, because the funny thing with girls her age was no matter how much they said they loved you and they were your best friend, sometimes if they had some juicy information they just couldn't keep it to themselves. Kitty knew Jenny too well. She would have been on the phone to everybody: 'Guess what ...' The only person she trusted was Doreen. So she'd had to get out of there as quick as she could while maintaining a little dignity. She knew what the others were thinking: poor Kitty, she was so over the moon for Todd but he was never going to ditch Brenda. Part of her wanted to correct them but she'd been smart enough to resist and play along, accept their sympathy. Her mother had been talking about something but she had not been listening.

'What?'

'The Bentleys were robbed. You think you-know-who would be out looking for the culprits.'

Her mother slid her eyes towards the policeman.

'The Bentleys have everything that opens and shuts, they deserve to be robbed.'

'They are very nice people. That's ridiculous, you are talking like a Communist.'

'At least they're fair.'

'Stealing from everybody who works and giving it to layabouts who wouldn't work in an iron lung. You think that's fair?'

It was stupid, juvenile, the whole thing, her mum trying to talk politics and, yes, what she was saying herself. She really didn't give a rat's about who had money and who didn't. She hated politics. She liked JFK, he was good-looking and vibrant and Jackie was glamorous, kind of like Doreen only richer, but Menzies was an old man in a suit who looked like he'd stepped out of a painting where the men had fob watches and the women parasols. The Labor man, she couldn't remember his name, he was like one of those old blokes you see staggering home from a pub after closing. She hated politics, she hated this town, she hated who she was and where she was, she hated Brenda and she hated Todd but most of all she hated herself.

The thunder started about eleven that night. Lightning flashes began half an hour later as the core of the storm came closer. Kitty slipped out of her bed and changed from her shortie pyjamas into shorts and a top. The ignominy of being found in those pyjamas was too much to contemplate. It was easy to get from her room out the back door and to her bike resting against the back verandah pole. She wheeled her bicycle as quietly as she could along the side-path past her parents' bedroom. Once out on the street she pedalled steadily towards the golf club. Everybody always said that golfers got hit by lightning because they were in the open space on high ground. There was not a car on the street and the boom of thunder was terrifying. The lightning by now was coming in jagged bolts, making the sky look like a dinner plate cracked down the middle. She reached the back of the golf course, dropped her bike and ran up the incline. Rain had begun falling in big droplets, you could hear it on the piles of fallen gum leaves she passed. She emerged onto the green and walked to its centre where she stood, arms out like a scarecrow. A clap of thunder sounded directly overhead and the whole area was lit ethereal white.

'Come on, take me,' she urged the elements and closed her eyes. Take me, take me, take this stupid idiot.

But the next boom was nowhere near as loud as its predecessor and though the crack of lightning was powerful, the area lit was close to a half-mile south. In a whoosh the rain descended and she found herself in wet darkness.

That's your answer, she thought. The gods don't deem you worthy. Her tears poured down her cheeks but she couldn't taste them because of the torrent pounding her.

ㅁㅁㅁ

'So, you're all ready?'

Blake had brought the ute to the front of the hospital. Andy was standing dressed carrying a Gladstone bag that contained his possessions.

'This is it.'

Blake had promised to drive him home. Andy climbed in and sat the bag on his lap. Blake rolled away from the hospital. It had been just over five weeks since he'd been admitted.

'When can I come back to work?'

'Don't rush. How about next week? Give yourself time to get your strength back.'

'I'm strong now.'

'Well, I feel responsible. I don't want anything bad to happen, and I'm paying you.'

It was a pleasant day. The run of storms had finally cleared.

'Doreen is going to call in on you once you're settled.'

Andy smiled. Then a shadow crossed his face. 'How's Audrey doing?'

'She's fine. I've been looking out for her.' The truth was he'd only got the replacement the day before yesterday. He still wasn't sure the ruse would hold up once Andy was back at work.

'Doreen said it was a couple of blokes but I don't remember.'

Blake assured him that was not a problem. The men were most likely miles away by now. 'They're not coming back.'

'They do, they'll be sorry.' Andy punched a fist into his palm. 'I've been remembering stuff, you know. Just bits and pieces.'

'I know. That's good. The doctor said you'll probably remember almost everything eventually.'

'One thing I remembered just this morning as I was about to leave, because there was a man there with a shirt … and it reminded me.'

'Of what?'

'That girl that was killed. I saw her with Crane.'

'Yes, I know.'

'But I saw her with someone else too, some other bloke.'

Now Blake was totally focused. 'Who?'

'I didn't see his face. They were over near a car and I saw his shirt from the back. It was short-sleeved and had big crabs and crayfish over it.'

Crayfish was what they called lobsters here. He was thinking he had seen that shirt somewhere. At the club maybe?

'Have you seen that shirt before do you think?'

Andy scrunched up his face, bit his lip. 'I don't think so.'

'Do you think you might have seen the guy's face and just can't remember?'

'Maybe but I doubt it. It was the girl I was looking at, you know?'

Valerie Stokes was the kind of woman a young guy like Andy would notice.

Blake wanted to make sure he had this right. He was too excited to think clearly, so he had to repeat everything, straighten it out in his head first. 'Crabs and crayfish?' Doreen had come in to do the accounts and found him as he was feeding the fish, just like he'd promised Andy he would.

'So Andy said. He didn't see the man's face but he was certain he was talking to her by the car. You've never seen that shirt?'

'No. But I was busy chasing those wankers that night.'

Doreen had an amazing memory. If somebody had worn the shirt in here when she was present she would have remembered. Perhaps Duck or Panza would recall it, or Crane himself might have got a look at the guy. He'd ring Harvey first thing, let him know. This had to be good for Crane, a witness saying she was talking to some other guy.

'The problem,' Harvey said in that measured way of his, 'is that from what you say, this witness has effectively had brain damage. He can't recall everything, only bits and pieces. The Crown will play on that. Do you know if it was before or after he saw Crane with the girl that he saw the man in the shirt?'

Blake explained he hadn't thought to ask that. It was possible Andy wouldn't know for sure.

'It's very important. If she was with the man after talking with Crane, it is much better for us.'

The way Harvey said it, was like he was hinting that *should* be what Andy remembered. Much as Blake liked Crane though, he didn't want to put that pressure on Andy. He told Harvey he would check tomorrow and hung up deflated. He would try Duck and Panza, see if they had seen the guy in the shirt. Duck was always sneaking out for a cigarette so there had to be a good chance. They were rehearsing tonight, so he could ask them then.

'You know I don't pay much attention to shirts … blouses that's another matter.' Duck was fiddling around the jukebox with a new 45 he wanted Blake to hear. 'And I didn't see the girl.'

Panza did not recall seeing a shirt like that. Blake couldn't shake the idea that he had seen one like that somewhere.

'Maybe back in America,' said Duck. 'It's not like it would be the only one ever.'

Blake was already giving in to that idea. 'Anyway, are you sure that Beach Bum didn't do it?'

Sometimes he could imagine putting a neat hole in Duck's forehead. He shook off that idea because it took him back to the house on Cockatoo Ridge and a world he thought he had escaped.

'What is this record?' He asked as much to distract himself as out of curiosity.

'Last year I was in Sydney and I saw this group on *New Faces*. They're instrumental, like us.'

'Who are they?' asked Panza.

'Called The Atlantics. The single is "Moon Man".'

Blake listened with interest. An Australian group writing and recording their own material was almost unheard of. The track wasn't special but there was something in the sound, the guitars. He liked it, not enough to cover but it got him thinking, maybe he could actually record those couple of tunes of his.

It was a good rehearsal, nothing but music in his head for an hour or two. It was easy to forget how good it could be here.

ᴏᴏᴏ

It had been a while since she had watched him from her perch on the sand dune. Last week it had been too wet and wild. She asked herself if there was something weird about this. Well it was obviously weird, but was it some psychological condition? It slipped into her mind that sometime in the future there might be a house right here on this block. It would be a shame, her old sand dune no longer there. Maybe this would be a kitchen, kids smeared in Vegemite. Or a bedroom, a couple making love, and perhaps somehow, her spirit from this moment would still be haunting the space, coating it in ... what? Longing? Would he still be there opposite, older in slippers, his hair thinner, alone?

She got up and dusted herself off. She did not feel like going home yet. There was nothing there for her except a kettle and a bed. She had girlfriends but they were trending younger as one by one the older ones got engaged or moved. It scared her: that is you in three years. She was making progress saving for a television. That might make things less lonely at home. The golf club would be open. You had to be a member to play but the public could drink there and a pianist plied his trade Wednesdays. It would mean wearing a dress though and that would mean going home to change but at least it was on the way.

There were about a dozen drinkers in the golf club — only one other woman, who was with a man likely her husband because they barely said a word to each other as they sipped gin and tonics and listened to the pianist play 'Moon River'. She felt the eyes of all the men on her, noted a perceptible but short halt in their murmured conversations about golf or business as she took her stool at the bar. The barmaid she knew as a woman who worked in Gannons. She ordered a brandy and dry. The pianist switched to 'I'm in the Mood for Love'. She was halfway through her drink when the first man took his chance. He was wearing a suit that looked like it had spent a substantial time in a car. She guessed he worked up near the Heads. Wedding ring said he was married but then the men here all were. He introduced himself as Gary, said he was an accountant, made small talk. Did she live here? Where did she work? She answered politely. He asked if she would like a drink. She was only halfway through the brandy and declined.

'We should go for a drive,' he suggested hopefully.

'*You* should go for a drive ...' she corrected him, '... home.'

He took it well. A man used to plenty of rejection. He placed his empty glass on the counter.

'Nice meeting you, Doreen.'

The man in the dark suit on her left, whom she had barely noticed because he'd been so quiet, spoke with a mellow voice.

'Doreen meaning "gift". From the Greek.'

She felt obliged to say she had never heard that before and asked if he was Greek. He did not look Greek but he must have been fifteen to twenty years older than her and had grey at the temples, which for some reason she associated with European men.

'No, I'm not Greek,' he laughed and she enjoyed his smile. 'Adrian.'

He offered his hand and they shook. 'My name is from Latin, Adrianus. You know the English Pope was an Adrian?'

'I didn't know that.'

'When I was a young man,' he said, 'I worked at a magazine for a time. One of the things I had to do was a column on names. I've never forgotten.' He ordered himself another whisky and politely gestured whether she wanted another drink. What the heck. She finished her brandy and thanked him. 'It's remarkable how something trivial you do in your teens or twenties is marked indelibly on you for the rest of your days. I bet there is something you remember?'

'My father loves the Melbourne Cup. He used to run off all the names of the winners. I learned from him. Only from nineteen-thirty, mind you, Phar Lap.' Their drinks arrived.

'Go on then,' he urged. She felt foolish but at the same time it was fun to remember being a child.

'I'll give it a shot.' She rattled them off and was going like a storm until 1951 when she hit a blank. At the last second, the name jumped out at her: 'Delta!' From there it was easy an easy run home.

'I backed the winner of the Melbourne Cup last year,' Adrian said. 'It was a complete fluke. When I was at school we had a tyrannical headmaster, Mr Stephens, who was proud of the fact he could deliver the cane with either hand with equal proficiency. We nicknamed him Even Stephens.'

She toasted him and for the first time their eyes met in that other way that men and women seem to register instinctively.

'Fate,' he said, 'is a strange beast.'

The bar was closing. Everybody else except the staff had gone. She wasn't sure when the piano had stopped. Doreen still didn't want to face her house alone. She shouldn't have said it.

'I've got a bottle of Starwine at my place.'

She saw him running through the same scenario in his own mind. He had a wife, almost certainly a family to go home to. His hesitation was like a nick received in battle, it stung but was not fatal; she would recover.

'I'll follow you,' he said.

It did not occur to her until they were actually inside her house — she was far too worried about whether it was too untidy to entertain — that as far as she knew Valerie Stokes' murderer was still out there, that this 'Adrian' could be him. The thought was no sooner through her brain than she felt his hand rest on hers beside the glasses of wine she had just poured. Her heart nearly burst into her mouth and she turned and opened it ready to scream when he gently kissed her on the lips. Crazily, she responded; the brandy and the night and a lone pianist had conspired to bring her to this point and she wanted and needed this moment because this was her house in the here and now, her body, her blood, she was not just some phantom spirit who had once sat on a dune where the house now stood, longing for connection.

□□□

Blake was at the back of the bar washing his ute, Edward doing a good job with the chamois, when Nalder drove in. Blake had not told Nalder yet about the man in the shirt. He was thinking that could backfire. Until he could identify the man, all the police would do was what Harvey had said — concentrate on Crane being with the girl, saying Andy's memory was messed up. So what was Nalder up to? He looked serious as he got out, put on his hat and walked over carrying something in a bag.

'Morning, Sergeant.' He kept it formal between them in public. Edward was scooting around the back of the car, trying to dematerialise. 'How can I help?'

'Actually, Mr Saunders, it's your friend I need to speak to.'

Blake wondered where this was going.

'Turn off the hose, Edward,' he said.

Edward did as he was told. Not surprisingly he was nervous.

'You reside in a caravan, lot five in the caravan park, do you not?'

Edward looked to Blake for reassurance. Blake nodded go ahead.

'Yes, sir. I mean I don't know the lot number.'

'The caretaker says it's yours. Do you recognise this?' Nalder reached into the bag and pulled out a large National transistor radio. Blake noted the look of panic on Edward's face.

'I found it,' he blurted.

'Where's this going?' Blake felt he had to try and intervene.

Nalder shot a scorching look at Edward. 'The last few weeks, ever since around the time he came to town, we've had property and valuables being stolen from houses. Mainly up near the Heights.'

'I didn't steal that. Honest to God, I found it. Honest, boss.' His eyes pleaded for Blake to believe him. Blake tried to remain calm. Nalder was worse if you got him offside, but maybe he could reason with him.

'I don't understand. Why did you check his caravan anyway?'

'The caretaker heard music. He was aware of the robberies. He took a look.'

'He can't do that!'

'It's his property and if he believes it is being used for illegal purposes he has every right. This radio is from one of the houses.'

Edward was scared stiff. 'I found it, day before yesterday.'

'Where?'

It was Blake who asked the question, not Nalder.

'Down where you dropped me that first time, near the river. I went down for a swim and it was just lying there.'

Blake asked if there was anything else he found.

'No, just that, lying on the ground like somebody dropped it. And I tried it and it worked.'

'You should have handed it in, boy.' Nalder could be a stern prick. For the first time Edward looked a bit guilty.

'I thought someone had thrown it away.'

Blake cut in and asked if anything else had been found in the caravan. Nalder confirmed nothing had been. Blake asked what other things had been stolen and Nalder ran off a list.

'So where is the iron and the television and the watches and cufflinks and all the other loot? Up his ass?'

Nalder's reptilian look told him he had gone too far. 'Maybe he hocked them.'

'Maybe he's telling the truth.'

Nalder retorted, 'Maybe he is but that doesn't help any of us. Fact is, he is in possession of stolen property. I could lock him up for that alone.'

'Or you could believe him.'

'I don't do anything, you know what happens? Some bugger decides to take the law into their own hands. It's not safe for him here.'

'What are you saying?'

Nalder sighed. 'Best all round if he clears out. I won't charge him, his record's clean. If he stays there will be trouble.'

'He didn't steal anything. He's not going.'

Edward said in a clear voice, 'No. He's right. It's the best thing. You got your boy coming back anyway, you don't need me.'

'You could work in the kitchen.'

'That's not me, boss. I don't like living in a caravan and washing dishes. This is better.'

'Too right it is. I've got his swag in the van. We're settled?'

Nalder scanned both of them but fixed on Blake. Blake looked back at Edward who gave a nod.

Blake said, 'Yeah, we're settled.'

Nalder turned on his heel, went to his van, brought out the swag, walked back and handed it to Edward. Without a word he then trudged back to the van, climbed in and drove off. Just like a sheriff in the Wild West.

After they had settled up, they stood in the shadow of the Surf Shack sign.

'Tell Doreen goodbye from me.'

'Yes, Edward, I will. She'll miss you.'

'It's for the best. Time I moved on but.'

Another few seconds passed. Edward put out his hand and they shook.

'It's not fair,' said Blake.

Edward shrugged as if to say 'it is what it is'. He went to move off.

'Wait.'

Blake slipped his watch off his wrist and put it on Edward's.

'I can't take this.'

'It's mine to give. I want you to have it.'

'No. I mean I can't take it. I'll get arrested for stealing it.'

Blake was about to bite when he saw the smile breaking over Edward's face. This time they clasped one another tight.

'Thank you,' Edward whispered and put the watch on his wrist.

'Stay off the grog.'

'I'll try, boss.'

Finally they separated. Edward started walking. Blake watched him all the way out of the carpark and down to the coast road and along, with that slight limp, leaving his life just the way he had entered it.

Nalder turned off the road and drove down the track towards the river. He reckoned the radio must have fallen out when he'd got out to take a piss. Well, this would be the last trip. It had worked out well, the blackfella going. Sooner or later there would have been a problem with him and he didn't want to lock up the poor bugger for something he knew he hadn't done. He pulled into a quiet bend and reversed the van. This was where the river was deepest. Sooner or later some kid diving down would find it but it wouldn't matter. The important thing was that they had suffered. Six of those bastards who'd voted against him either this time or the last. He opened up the back doors of the van, hauled out two kids bikes and tossed them in. Next a record player and a bunch of LPs. He was tempted to keep Andy Stewart but knew there could be no trace of anything stolen in his possession. In a town this small, coincidence was bound to happen and someone would find it one day during a barbecue or a church fete. An oil painting from that poser Lamont's wall — looked like shit a kindy kid could have drawn — was next to go in the drink, followed by some tools out of Bentley's shed and, last but not least, the Morgans' vacuum cleaner. He watched it all sink, shut up the van, climbed into the driver seat and started up. Revenge was a dish best served cold; speaking of which, Edith had promised cold lamb for dinner. With a lager to wash it down, that would be just perfect.

10. Death and Resurrection

A sense of injustice regarding Edward's treatment had been clawing at Blake but it fell away like cut fern when he saw Andy rush to the aquarium and begin pointing out the fish he thought he recognised. Unsurprisingly, he picked up on a couple of little missing zebra fish and a black molly which he had called Chubby after Chubby Checker, the only Negro other than heavyweight boxers that most Australians had heard of. Doreen had played along, explaining those fish had died of natural causes. It was the Friday after Edward had gone, four days earlier for Andy to be back than Blake had intended originally. So long as he kept an eye on Andy, he figured it wouldn't do any harm. Also, if he was honest with himself, it meant he could continue to pump Andy about the night Valerie Stokes had been murdered. Perhaps by being back in the venue, his memory might be triggered quicker. For his part, Blake was still convinced that somewhere or other he had seen that shirt described by Andy but neither Duck, Panza nor any of the other staff recalled it, and definitely not Doreen, who had been acting a little off-key herself the last couple of days. According to Harvey, whom he'd spoken to the previous evening while making himself hamburgers, Crane had no memory of any guy in that shirt. The upshot of all this was that he couldn't go to Nalder or anybody else and start throwing out theories about who really killed Valerie Stokes.

'You know that man you mentioned in the shirt?' he asked Andy as they were fixing the leg of a table that had gone slightly wobbly.

'Yes, the crab shirt.'

'That's the one. Do you remember if you saw him before or after you saw Crane talking to her?'

Andy hemmed and hawed but he just couldn't remember.

'That's okay. Don't worry about it.'

Around two, they were both feeling hungry so he volunteered to get pies while Andy stayed and sorted the empties from last night. He thought he would buy Andy a pastry matchstick, which was the kid's favourite. He joined the light traffic that was typical of the town, humming the beginnings of a new tune. It was as he passed Clarke's Cars that he was zapped by the thunderbolt that made him almost run up the back of the slow-moving truck in front.

He knew exactly where he had seen that shirt ... hanging on the wall in the car yard's little office building in a photo of Bob Hope, and the wearer: Winston Clarke.

He U-turned and drove up into the lot, parking by the office. He had to satisfy himself there was no mistake, that it wasn't some flight of fancy.

The photo had not been shifted. The shirt was plain for all to see, crabs and lobsters, the kind of Hawaiian shirt you weren't going to find a double of this side of the Pacific.

'Hello, Blake.' Clarke emerged through a door in the little office behind the reception desk, followed Blake's eye-line. 'Yep, that's right, me and Bob Hope. I never sold him a car, unfortunately, but I did play a round of golf. You thinking of trading in that ute of yours?'

Clarke dabbed his mouth with a handkerchief. Blake realised it must have been a one-way mirror set in the wall so Clarke could eat lunch without missing a customer.

'Actually I have. Or not so much trading-in, I still need the ute, but I thought I'd just test the water on something else.'

'Women don't like utes, right?' He winked knowingly. 'So what are you looking at? New? Second-hand?'

'I think it would have to be second-hand.'

'Got a terrific FB that has only got two thousand six hundred on the clock. Fellow had a heart attack, wife won't let him drive.'

Blake said he'd take a look. Clarke led him out to the lot.

Blake said casually, 'I think I saw you at my bar the other week. Didn't get a chance to buy you a drink.'

Clarke frowned. 'Haven't made it to your bar yet. Should have, but Friday I'm normally at the golf club, and the weekend with my boy here, we've been doing dad-and-son shit — out in the bush, up to the Heads last weekend.'

They stopped at a two-tone FB Holden sedan.

Blake cooed appreciatively, then said, 'I'm sure it was you. It was the Thursday of your kid's party. I thought you must have got the hell out of there.'

'And leave that lot? No, must have been someone else. I will drop in though, promise. We could have a celebratory drink when you buy this baby.'

He let Clarke take him on the tour, rubbed his chin and shook his head at the price. Clarke knocked off the obligatory ten percent.

'I'd love to but ... it's out of my range.'

'I've got some others. Nice little Zephyr.'

Blake begged off, said he had to see a friend in hospital but he was glad he'd put out the feelers. Clarke said he was more than happy to let him test-drive any of his cars any time.

Leftwich passed them with a spring in his step, and a couple trailing behind.

'Showing them the FB,' he grinned.

'It won't last,' Clarke said knowingly to Blake. They walked back to the office.

'Your boy is still here?'

'Got him till the end of the month. And if his mates wreck my car again, it's coming out of his pocket money. Look at that.' It was only then that Blake realised he'd parked next to the Bel Air. 'Good as new.' Clarke ran his fingers across the gleaming chrome bumper. 'You ever need some body work done, give me a hoy.'

Blake drove without thinking, found himself down at the point where Crane's little hut had stood. It seemed a century ago. The white gums were like bones poking from a graveyard towards a grey heaven. He'd walked beneath a thousand of these skies in Philly but there you'd be wearing coats and gloves. Nothing matched here. You had a grey sky overhead but the air was as humid as a subway car in summer. He wanted to think it all through, see if he could piece how Clarke did it. The *why* he might never figure out. Trawl back: it's the night of the kid's birthday. Clarke has paid for the grog. Maybe he gets sick of the youngsters, thinks he'll head out, trawl town for a woman. Perhaps he heads to the Surf Shack because that's on his mind, he knows it's open and has never been there. In the car lot he meets Val Stokes and puts a proposition to her. Or he already knows her from her hooker days. Maybe the whole time from Sunday to

Thursday she was at Clarke's house, got out because the kid was coming home? Either way, Clarke drives to the Ocean View Motel and it all goes screwy and he butchers her. Whoever did it had to be covered in blood. If he was naked he could have showered after, then puts his clothes back on, driven home like nothing had happened. The kids would be drunk as skunks, they likely wouldn't even notice he'd gone.

There was no time to waste. Blake was playing tonight but Clarke had said that every Friday he went to the golf club. The boy, Thomas, was still staying at the house but if he was anything like every other teenager he knew, there was a big chance he would be out with his pals, surfing or drinking on the sly. The house would likely not be locked. He could poke around.

Blake took the road that ran directly through the hinterland onto Belvedere. His brain was assembling the pieces with the methodical manner in which his hands assembled a gun: Valerie Stokes had been staying somewhere in the region, why not Clarke's? It made sense she would have left before the party. Clarke arranges to meet up with her at the Ocean View. Snap. He leaves the party. Something bad goes down at the motel. Snap. Clarke kills her, gets the hell out of there but in his haste clips the trash can. Snap. He would have been covered in blood, he would have to get rid of his clothes, shoes. He gets back home, acts as if nothing happened. If the kid knew about Stokes being there, he tells him to say nothing but probably the kid never even met Stokes.

It took Blake forty minutes to reach the Clarke driveway. He parked off Belvedere on a track in thick scrub and scuttled through bush parallel to the driveway until he reached the back of the house. The sun was drifting lower, the air sticky as blood.

Damn. The kid's car was parked on the back lawn. He thought about turning back but only for an instant. He broke cover and moved swiftly across the lawn, and up the stairs to the back door. It was open, just the flywire between the landing and the interior. He strained his ears for a sound. If Tom Clarke came his way now he could still run but once inside there was no way to explain his presence. He waited for close on three minutes. Counting time in his head was just one skill he'd developed in his days as an assassin. Moving silently was another. He opened the door and slid inside the dark kitchen where he had been the day he brought over the kegs. On the table was an empty beer bottle. He moved to the door that led into a passageway, longer to his left than right. Dead ahead was the lounge room. He edged forward, saw Thomas Clarke's feet poking over the end of the sofa. He was fast asleep, a comic across his chest, an empty beer glass on the floor. Blake edged to the right, came to a laundry on the left. Opposite was a bare brick room, concrete floor, offering the hot-water system with wood cut and stacked at the ready. A golf bag leant against some meccano-like steel shelving where a couple of cricket bats and a set of stumps had been placed flat. The hallway dead-ended in a toilet. Blake turned back down the hallway and snuck back past the lounge room. Beyond it, on the same side, was a bedroom, or at least he imagined that's what was there under the sheets and dumped clothes and shoes. Odds-on it was the kid's. The room next to it was clearly Clarke's bedroom, large with windows looking out over rolling hills. One wall was built-in wardrobes and cupboards. Noiselessly he pulled open the wardrobe doors, saw an array of shirts both business and recreational, jackets, slacks, all very neat and ordered.

But no Hawaiian shirt with lobsters and crabs.

He searched again to be sure. It wasn't there. He rifled drawers in the wardrobe and bedside table looking for anything of interest, found an electric razor, pens, rubber bands, coins, nothing else of import. Opposite Clarke's bedroom on the other side of the hallway was the bathroom, recently used, the showerhead, green with mould, offering a slow drip. He checked the shelves for any sign of female occupation but there was none. Turning out of the bathroom, he looked left down the shadowy hallway which dead-ended. He was about to turn back when he saw something on the floor, some vague shape. Moving closer, he saw it was a small padlock attached to a recessed handle. He cursed himself for coming so ill-prepared. He could pick this lock with a paperclip. An idea came to him. He eased back up the hallway. The kid was still asleep in the lounge room. Blake moved into the room with the boiler and scanned the shelves of tools, found what he was after: fuse wire.

It took him about three minutes to pick the simple little lock. The trapdoor creaked when it lifted on hinges and revealed an internal staircase heading to some kind of basement. A string hung off to the right to activate a light. He waited for any sound to indicate the kid had stirred. Satisfied the kid hadn't moved, he pulled the string. A low-watt globe lit up. He started down the narrow concrete steps, pulling the trapdoor after him. Now he was enveloped by cool and the smell of rock, understandable since the wall to his right was the original rock wall of the hill, smoothed in patches by concrete. The dull bulb had illuminated a basement, at least twelve feet high, concrete floor. The other three walls were brick. Apart from some vents in the rear wall, the room was airless and musty. This looked like another storage room. Blake made out the tennis nets bundled in a corner, old tins of paint, a lawnmower; but there was a small sofa in the forties chintz style and stacked beside it 78 records. On a paint-stained table facing the sofa was an old gramophone and then … up against the wall — what was that? It looked like …

Blake headed over, his heart beating more fiercely by the second, galloping as he saw his suspicion confirmed: it was a portable movie screen. His conversation with Stokes' roommate Jill flooded back — Stokes claimed she'd shot a blue movie. Blake made his way around a heavy punching bag bolted to the ceiling. He was looking for a projector, film cans. No luck. Propped against something was a phalanx of large framed oil paintings, rural scenes. He pulled them back to see what they were leaning against — a large old trunk secured by another small padlock. He wasn't going to stop now. He picked that too. How long would the kid sleep? He pulled back the lid of the trunk. Shoeboxes of various photos, old negatives. He flipped quickly through a bunch: Clarke as a younger man in a double-breasted suit, a wedding. His? Maybe not. The bride bore a family resemblance. More photos showed the bride cheek-to-cheek with another man, dark-haired. The same man, now with Clarke, posing in a convertible auto beneath high palm trees. Blake had seen those palms, Los Angeles. More shots, a house, likely LA, the dark-haired guy in overalls smiling in a workshop as he tinkered on machinery, a background sign. The brother-in-law maybe. Fragments of a conversation coming back about his brother-in-law in the movie business. Blake put down that box, turned his attention to another one that had been slipped into a brown paper bag, slid it out.

Nudes.

Young women, mainly topless, a few full-frontal, posing like for a magazine spread. Something amateur about them, the women, not the photography, that was professional enough. Some looked recent, taken in the bush or maybe down here where a bed had been set up, the old iron-frame type. One photo made him stop cold: Carol, topless, lying back in the bush, smiling.

Queasiness, anger, terror, flushed through him all at once like the debris at the bottom of a creek bed churned by a flash flood. Possibilities shot out at him: her leaving was staged, she was dead, Clarke had killed her too. He folded the Carol photo and shoved it down his shirt, closed the trunk harder than he meant and winced as it thumped. He held his breath … no response yet. Quietly as he could, he replaced the paintings. Time to get out. He needed to think. He was about to start up the stairs when he saw, half-obscured behind a collapsed camp stretcher, an old hatbox. He shoved the bed aside, unclipped the box. Jackpot: a silver movie can. He grabbed the movie can, replaced the lid of the hatbox, froze. From above had come the solid tread of feet. He moved as quickly as he could to the stairs, seized the dangling string, pulled down, plunged the room into ink. He had already memorised the room, knew there was a clear narrow channel to behind the sofa but it took him further away from the room's only exit so he remained exactly where he was on the stairs, his left foot one step above his right. He followed the steps as they approached the trapdoor. He tensed. If the kid — he guessed it was him — reached for the light-switch cord he could grab him, pull him down …

The steps turned and moved away down the other end of the house. Maybe he was going for a weapon? No time to hesitate, Blake was still holding the film can. He pushed up and out of the trapdoor, caught the sound of a toilet seat being flipped up. He snapped the lock shut, and was about to hit the exit when the toilet flushed. He stepped back as far as he could into the shadows at the north end of the hallway. There was enough light to show up Thomas Clarke as he left the toilet and went to the kitchen. Maybe he was going out? But instead of the flywire door banging, what he heard was the fridge opening and closing. More beer? There was a long pause, then more noise and Thomas Clarke was back in the hallway. He peered down right at Blake but Blake never moved a muscle. He knew that from that distance it was just shadow. Thomas Clarke crossed the hallway into his room. Blake slid along the far wall straight past the kid's room back into the kitchen, out the flywire door.

He made his way back to the car, pulled up the lid of the film can: coiled film, negative. A quick look, naked flesh, faces too hard to make out. Not smart to hang around, he fired up the ute and headed back to town. It was only when he was on the outskirts that he realised poor Andy was still waiting for his pie, so he stopped at the fish and chip shop. All he could think about now was Carol. She had known Winston Clarke and most probably that had cost her her life. But should he go to Nalder? He needed to think it through.

'I was worried you had an accident.' Andy devoured the fish and chips in a frenzy. Blake apologised, said something had come up and he couldn't get back but all the time his mind was working on what he needed to do next. He'd never encountered this problem where you actually needed to keep somebody like Clarke alive. You just ended it all with a shot to the head or heart or both. But that wouldn't save Crane nor reveal if Carol was dead. The only person he trusted was Doreen but when she turned up, he resisted spilling any of it. Friday was a big night. He would tell her after.

ᗡᗡᗡ

The last few days since that night at the golf club had been weird. She didn't know why she had done what she had, slept with a complete stranger. Up until then when she had slept with men there had always been some kind of relationship: dates, a few dinners or shared outings that grew into something — never satisfactory. The last boyfriend had been six months ago, Michael. Three months of weekends watching him fix cars and play rugby had been enough. She didn't know what she wanted to do but definitely not that, and not dancing in nightclubs anymore, cramped dressing-rooms, the smell of hairspray that hung like chemical warfare. When Blake told her he had something to talk with her about after they finished tonight, her first thought was that he'd found out. Probably the barmaid at the golf club or one of the other men who had been there. She had not been prepared for what he was telling her now under the green glow of the fish tank.

'Winston Clarke? The car man?'

He ran through it all. The photo of the shirt, the film can he'd taken.

'Jill, the girl Valerie Stokes worked with in Sydney, told me she boasted of doing a stag film. I think it was with Clarke. They renewed their acquaintance and made another.'

'Why kill her?'

'I don't know. Maybe he's a psycho. There's another girl, Carol, from the golf club.'

She knew all about Carol. He laid out his suspicions, that Clarke had killed her too.

'If he's really killed two women, you don't have a choice, you have to go to the police. But are you sure that's Valerie Stokes on the film?'

'I can't tell. I'll have to get it printed.' He considered. 'You're right. If that's not her, I've got nothing.'

'Even if it is her, he might have an alibi for when she was killed. He could have been back at his kid's party.' She was getting the hang of this now, working the logic. She might have acted impulsively the other night but here she could be measured, pragmatic. 'First, you need to prove he knew Valerie Stokes. Then that he hasn't got an alibi for when she was killed or Carol went missing. Are you sure about Carol?'

Men could be dumb, maybe even Blake. Just because no woman had dumped him before didn't mean it wasn't going to happen ever. She was thinking Carol could have got into debt, or felt her past creeping up on her. There were a dozen reasons she might have bailed. But Blake just shook his head.

'She would have told me. I think something bad has happened.'

If it had, then it worried her: first Andy, now this girl who was intimate with Blake. She could see herself right slap bang in the middle of things.

'You want me to run you home?'

Of course she did. She had read the copy of the police report Harvey had sent down and it gave her shivers. But what happened if she said yes? Would he need to offer to escort her home every night for her not to feel slighted? She didn't want that strain. She'd take the wheel spanner from the boot, carry it with her.

Long after Doreen had declined his offer for an escort home, Blake continued to sit in his office thinking. He would have to get the film printed as soon as possible. If, as he suspected, Valerie Stokes featured, it was a step in the right direction but it wasn't proof that Clarke was her killer and he knew enough about cops to know they were very fucking reluctant to change their opinion. What he needed was something hard and irrefutable. Something like Clarke's blood-soaked Hawaiian shirt. It had to have been blood-soaked because it was no longer in Clarke's wardrobe. He'd buried it or burned it. Pity. Blake could see it all unfolding now in his head: the meeting, the murder, Clarke's desperation to get away.

But was it enough? His eyes ached, his brain was numb. He switched off the lights and locked up. It was somewhere near three thirty when he made it to his own bed, fell onto it fully clothed.

Blake woke fifty minutes later. A dream, fresh as bread from the oven, came back to him. He was in the bush and he had a pistol in his hand like he was readying for a hit but he couldn't remember who it was he was supposed to kill. He knew time was running out and it had to be done but who was the target? Next thing he remembered looking up behind him and there were Harry and Steve grinning as Harry dropped a match in a pile of dry gum leaves. He tried to shoot him but the gun wouldn't fire and the flames were advancing fast. He turned to run back the other way and there was Winston Clarke in that damn shirt. Winston did exactly the same as Harry. He torched the bush and then it was all closing in on Blake, the circle of bush around him that was not aflame dwindling by the second. The smoke was rearing at him like a cougar. He couldn't breathe.

That's when he woke up.

The smoke seemed to still linger in his nostrils. Was the house on fire? He jumped up and quickly checked but there was nothing burning. For an instant he thought it might have been a bushfire somewhere that he'd smelled but by the time he'd completed the thought the smell was already gone. But there was … something. His brain had relaxed with sleep and had yielded up some deep secret. What? Smoke, flame, death … the shirt. Why did he keep fixating on that shirt? Clarke had burned it, yes, that made sense. But not in the bush. The last thing you needed was to start a fucking bushfire.

So you burned it in an incinerator.

An image jumped at Blake: Clarke's salesman Leftwich grumbling because he had to clean windscreens … again. What day had that been? He couldn't remember but what if it was the morning after Stokes' murder? Hadn't he dropped in to say they could keep the keg if they needed? Regardless, if I'm Clarke, my clothes soaked in blood, what do I do? I go to my car yard and burn the evidence. Blake raided his kitchen cupboards for a brush and pan, grabbed a couple of calico moneybags from his table, then his keys and lit out.

Ten minutes later he was outside the car yard. He'd not passed one vehicle. The cars on display, presumably disabled, were locked in behind a wire fence at the front and sides. At the back of the car lot, behind the office was a high paling fence. A lane gave access to it. He took a left down the side street then another left and cruised down the lane. Fuck it. He stopped the car, jumped out, pulling with him the brush, pan and bags. He lobbed the pan and brush over the fence. Then he scaled the fence, just like old times when Jimmy would lead a raid on the Emeralds. The incinerator, a big cast-iron thing, was right there at the side of the office. Who knew if anything was still there, but you had to try, right? He threw open the grate. It was wide enough to take the pan. He shovelled out ash into the calico bags, hoping to see fabric of some kind. Sometimes that stuff didn't burn. There might have been fabric there but it was still dark and he'd need to wait till he got home. Something clanged on the pan, some piece of metal. With a torch he could have seen better but it was too dim to discern exactly what it was. It looked small, about the size of a fingernail. He threw it in the bag and kept shovelling, found a little bit more metal, which he suspected was a blackened paperclip. Not wanting to linger, he knotted the bags and tossed them over the fence, dropped the pan and brush in the nearby trash can and re-scaled the fence.

Rather than drive back to his house, he drove to the Surf Shack. It seemed only an instant since he'd been in here. He grabbed a couple of trays from the bar and tipped the contents of the bags into them. He had no way of knowing whether the incinerator had been cleaned out since. Mostly it was just paper ash. Some wedges of cardboard at the extremity of the incinerator hadn't quite burned and there was something that looked like a strip of material about three inches long by half-an-inch, scorched but not totally incinerated. He wanted to think it could be the shirt but in truth it was impossible to tell. He retrieved the paperclip and a few staples and pins he'd missed. The small metal object he could now discern was some kind of small badge like men wear in a buttonhole, Rotary or one of those clubs, but it was impossible to say for sure because fire had blackened it. All that was left was a diamond shape. He dropped it into an empty tin he kept for paperclips. Automatically his focus returned to the material. It could be part of a shirt, for sure.

ㅁㅁㅁ

Before leaving for the Heads he had gone home, caught three hours sleep and made himself a quick breakfast. No chance for a surf, and he missed that keenly. The Yellow Pages had given the address for a film lab and after two and a half hours of straight driving he had located it relatively easily. From here though, things might prove delicate. It was, after all, a stag film. The lab was obviously just a backroom processing place, a basic brick building with minimal bevelled glass windows up high, no retail signage. It was in a street of similar buildings. He could hear the clang of hammers from a body repair shop a few doors away. It was near eleven a.m. and he guessed whatever staff were there would be getting ready for weekend fun. He stepped into a room with a lino floor and a long, low deserted bench at the front. A curtain hived off this modest reception from what he guessed was the processing area. There was a bell which, when he hit it, gave off a dull tink. A young guy with Tony Curtis hair, wearing a lab coat, appeared.

'You process sixteen-mil movies here?'

'Yes, sir. Normally we can do a reel in a day but not over the weekend.'

'Who does the processing, your boss?'

'Yes. Mr Hampson or John.'

'Are either of them in?'

He disappeared out the back. A moment later a tall guy with a side part appeared. Early-thirties or late-twenties, face slightly pitted. Blake was guessing John. John asked how he could help.

'I have a film I need processing as soon as possible.' He held up the can.

'We could do it by end of business Monday.'

Blake leaned in close and spoke in a whisper. 'Thing is, it is … risqué, I think is the word.'

John looked around to see if the teen was listening. 'If you mean …'

'Yes. I do. So I'm guessing I might have to pay extra. And as I would be paying extra anyway, perhaps it could be done … sooner. Tonight?'

John shook his head. 'Tonight is not possible.'

Blake found that encouraging, not an outright no.

John said, 'This time tomorrow, that's the earliest I could do it.'

'How much?'

'Twenty, cash in advance.'

Blake had no leverage to bargain and John knew it. Though he had braced for thirty, he'd been hoping closer to ten. He handed the film across, pulled out his wallet and found the money.

'I'll be here at eleven tomorrow.'

'There's a bell in the wall.'

It was early enough that he could drive back, do his gig tonight and then return tomorrow. On the other hand he could sleep in the car or by the beach. Saturday night was solid whether the band played or not. He was still tossing up what to do as he tootled slowly down the beachfront where Neptune's World, the marine park, was located. Being a Saturday, it was frantic. Even though school had been back a couple of weeks the guesthouses were still full. He found a place to park and started walking towards the concrete pool and viewing area that comprised Neptune's World. On the beach there must have been five hundred teenagers doing a hokey-pokey competition. He'd seen the porpoise show on that very first trip after getting in from the States. In truth it was a little underwhelming, a group of porpoises flipping a beach ball around in a concrete pool. It was fun for the kids though, especially if they got to feed them. He felt a sudden desire to bring Doreen up here one day, maybe Andy too. Andy would love it, he was just a big kid. By now Blake was out front of Neptune's World. Maybe he would go in after all.

'Oh God. I don't believe it! Blake.'

The voice was American and female. He swung around and saw a woman about his age he vaguely recognised. She wore a big sun hat and a summer dress with a plunging back, high-heels and a lot of lipstick.

'You remember me? Mindy, Trixie's friend.'

He did now. She was gushing like a fire hydrant somebody had cranked open on a sweltering July day.

'I can't believe it. I thought you'd be in Florida.'

He was lost. 'Florida?'

'With Jimmy. Vin said Jimmy had gone to Florida. Oh gee, it must be years. What are you doing here?'

He grabbed the first idea that popped its head up. 'Vacation. What about you?'

'I'm dating a really nice guy, Mike. He was a marine in the war stationed up in Brisbane. He kept talking on and on about this Great Barrier Reef, said it was the Grand Canyon of the south and I had to see it with him. And it is, it's amazing except I got real seasick on the boat because you go out to it on a boat. Have you seen it?'

'Not yet.'

'This is so crazy.' Her fingers fluttered, in what he guessed was an imitation of particles of craziness.

He said, 'You still see Vinnie and the gang?'

'Oh yeah, all the time. Well, not quite so much. Mike's from Pittsburgh. You'll have to meet him, he's a nice guy, though you know, he might be jealous because I told him I was sweet on this guy, Blake.' She cosied up to him when she said that.

'So where is Mike?'

'Fishing with some other guys. I said I ain't going out there on account of I get sick as a dog. I said I'll go see the dolphin show. He's gone for the night but he'll be back tomorrow. You still single?'

'Yes, still a bachelor.'

'So you're at a loose end tonight too?'

There was no escaping the implication. 'I'm supposed to be heading off. You're on your own?'

'Yes. I'm staying at the Bella Vista guesthouse up the road there. Room eight. I'd love to hear about Jimmy and everything.'

His assassin's brain had run well ahead like a scout noting possible enemy ambush zones. It told him: don't be seen with her, when she is found dead they'll be looking for anybody who might have been with her. It told him: you have everything you need to know, get out of here. Now!

'I don't think it's going to be possible, Mindy. I've got a friend I have to meet. I'm real sorry. I would love to have caught up.'

'Oh, me too. I've always had a thing for you, you know that.'

Again she angled her body at him. It was a fine body.

'I'll see what I can do but, you know ... room eight, Bella Vista. No promises.'

He held her and kissed her on the cheek. She was wearing a lot of perfume. It was a long time since he smelled this kind of girl. She reminded him of snare drums, wise guys at small tables, cigars.

'If you don't make it, give Jimmy my regards.'

He promised he would and started off in the opposite direction to his car, turned and waved. He would kill her tonight. He would have to.

For a time he wandered aimlessly to the south away from the crowds. Before he had felt hungry but not now, now there was nothing of him that was human, no hunger, nor thirst, no thumping head or aching leg, no repetitious tune he'd heard from a transistor dangling off the nut of a beach umbrella, no satisfaction that would come from patting a dog, no fear of God; no urge to look his best, to comb his hair, apply cologne; no desire to hear the lilt of a loved one's voice; no relief to take a load off and put up his feet and chuckle at a dumb cartoon. This was him as he had been before, in those days when he sat day after day in a diner becoming invisible so his target, a Mob captain, would think of him as part of the furniture. This was him as he had been to so many people, a wisp of wind, an insubstantial thing, a curse, death. Here, all his considerations were technical. He had brought no gun with him and a knife was too messy. He had no clothes to change into, nowhere to dispose of those soaked in his victim's blood. Garotte or strangulation it would have to be. He would arrive latish, say after nine, so the likelihood of bumping into neighbours was diminished. He would knock quietly. She would answer the door and let him in. If there was anybody else present he would have to postpone the event but he doubted there would be anybody else. He could not linger, just establish who she may have talked to about him since their earlier meet, what that person might know. Then he would have to kill her. He would leave the body and get out of there, maybe leave a window open, take some money to make it look like a robbery gone wrong. He would drive down the coast and wait, pick up the film tomorrow and return.

It was only much later, a good two hours on, as the sun was off the stove and cooling, that he found a way through the robot's metal carapace and into the wiring where he could cause a spark, ignite his humanity for a second and ask the most obvious question: did he really need to do this? Would she tell Vinnie and the others she had met him in Australia? Would they bother about him? Did anybody still care? In answer to the first, she had said she was spending more time in Pittsburgh but she also was clearly still in contact with Vinnie, Marcello or whoever. If she saw them, she would mention it. And then all of this, all of his carefully won freedoms, his anonymity, would be gone. Would they actually bother to try and track him down? Australia was a long way, but then it wasn't so far Mindy hadn't made it here. Blake made himself think like them.

Vincent might keep it to himself if he was alone when she told him. But if she told him and there were witnesses, he'd have no choice. Somebody would tell Repacholi. Would he despatch Peste all the way here just to have him rubbed out, save a bit of face — nobody walks away, all that bullshit? He might. And he might also think, what angle has the kid found over there? Is there a market he should be looking at? Then he would send Peste or somebody like him and they would look for him and eventually, as they always did, they would find him, and they would say, 'We like what you've done here, we want a piece of your bar because you owe us.' One night they would kill him or force him out or demand he go back to his former profession.

'You're too good to waste playing a fucking guitar. We need guys like you.'

He could hear it already. But now that his blood was warm and circulating and he was no longer aluminium and tin, he was forced to consider a whole truckload of uncomfortable questions. Like, how would what they were asking him be any different to what he was going to do tonight? If he had to kill an innocent woman, to stop him having to kill other people, innocent or not, what was the gain? How was that different, and maybe wasn't it worse, even?

And he had to say, yes, of course it was as bad or worse. He'd never killed a woman before. Mindy had never done anything bad to him. She had a life ahead of her, kids, a good husband. Was he prepared to take that from her to protect his life here? A life, where, let's face it, he'd already lapsed once, no matter how justified that had been. But if he let her be, took the risk hoping nothing would happen but was wrong, and the Mob did come for him, then what happened to Jimmy was for nothing. Everything was for nothing. There could be no going into the ocean to be reborn. Dreams of coming up here with Andy and Doreen, forget it. He'd have to get rid of Doreen, not kill her, no, fire her, find some excuse. He couldn't expose her to that, couldn't let her see who he had been ... who he still was.

Shit. He was fucked a thousand ways sideways. If he killed Mindy tonight, could he live with that? Yes, he could. The world, fate, dealt you a hand and you had to play it as best you could, for your own sake. Not to kill her was simply too risky because everything he loved about the world would be blacked out if they came here.

He didn't want to do it. He wasn't angry with Mindy. It was just an equation of the shit stuff you had to do if you wanted to have life's good stuff. At the end of the day Mindy was nobody to him. A girl he once knew in a city far away. She wasn't even that sweet or pure really. He was sure she had been coming onto him so it wasn't like she held any moral high ground. But, and he made himself face this question, how would he be any different to Winston Clarke? Clarke brutally murdered women for his own gratification, and sure, there was nothing like that in what he would have to do if he killed Mindy, no sex or anything, but what it boiled down to was, he would be killing her for his own sake, just like Winston Clarke.

What do you say, Jimmy?

He literally walked in circles trying to solve this conundrum. Time spun out like candy floss. The sun was down now. He hadn't yet warned Doreen he wouldn't be back tonight. He retrieved the car and drove the back blocks till he found a public phone. Like every other public phone box, it smelled of piss and damp. He pumped a heap of coins into the slot. Long distance cost an arm and a leg. He punched in the Surf Shack number, heard it ringing the other end. Doreen would be flat out, the early drinkers and diners already there. Somebody picked up, the coins fell with a clunk.

'Surf Shack, Doreen.'

'It's me.'

'Where are you?'

'Out and about getting that movie developed. I'm not going to make it back tonight. Tell Duck and Panza. They can do some of their jazz stuff if they want. Is everything okay?'

'Yeah, fine. You'll be pleased to know Carol's not dead.'

The words cuffed him about the ear like an angry teacher. 'What?'

'She called a couple of hours ago. When I said you weren't here she said to let you know she was fine, she was sorry she left without contacting you.'

'She say where she is? What she's doing?'

'She's working at the Heads. I think she's flipping burgers because I heard somebody in the background calling out orders.'

'Did she …'

But that was as far as he got before the call timed out and the line went dead. He checked his pocket for more coins but had nowhere near enough for another call. He stood in the phone box, its fug clawing at him like a beggar. He was impervious, his head spinning … Carol was alive. Clarke hadn't killed her. Nobody had killed her. He had been unable to accept the simplest truth in front of his face: she'd lit out of town because that's what girls like Carol did, not because she was cold in the ground at the hand of Winston Clarke.

It took him only about half an hour to find her. It was the third café he'd tried, a couple of blocks off the main drag. It was at the tail end of the family-dinner trade, hungry kids like crocodiles watching dads fork cash out of their pockets for the pile of wrapped burgers on the counter. She saw him pretty much as soon as he entered and seemed surprised as hell. She didn't look much different. Her hair was a bit messy like it often was and she'd been grabbing a bit of sun, more tanned than before. All of a sudden he was hungry. He scanned the blackboard menu and ordered a steak burger with the lot from the other girl working there in the same kind of mauve pinafore as Carol. While he was waiting she slid past him and said, 'Fifteen minutes, I'll take a break. Head down the lane on the left.

It runs all the way to the beach. There's a seat facing the ocean.'

He did as he was told, cradling the burger, warm through the grease-proof wrapping, like some cheap god holding his tiny world. It was a good spot, solitary. There was no humidity here, the ocean breeze sweeping it away. He slowly chewed his burger: steak, egg, lettuce, onion, beetroot and cheese. It was so calm out there, so beautiful, but dark, and you couldn't see but could hear the waves tumbling, catch a little moon glow off the ocean here and there, salt in the nostrils, a hint of pine. He heard the scuff of a rubber thong on the sandy path, felt her in the vibration of the air and then she was beside him.

'How was the burger?'

He smiled inwardly. That droll sense of humour hadn't changed.

'It was very good.'

'You were smart to get it from Mary. She's more generous with the onion.'

Only then did he turn to her. It was about a half-moon tonight and her face was in shadow.

'You've been sunbaking,' he said.

'Not much else to do here.' He heard rather than saw her pull out a cigarette. 'How did you get here so quick?' She struck the match.

'Coincidence. I was here already.'

She sucked on her cigarette. He could imagine her nodding to herself. 'So you didn't come for me?'

'I had some other business. I've been worried about you. That girl ...'

'I'm sorry. I didn't want to see you in case I changed my mind.' She took another drag. 'That Saturday morning I was going to head off for my shift at the golf club. I stopped to get a few things. The detectives were there outside Gannons asking if anybody knew this dead girl. They showed her photo. It could have been me, same age, same ... look. I got back in my car and all I could think of was, what am I doing here? — working at a golf club for randy older guys, screwing you but only when you felt like it. Emptiness, that's what I saw. People say, how did that girl end up there being stabbed to death? It's easy, so easy to end up there. How the fuck *don't* you wind up there? That's the question I asked. Well, you get out. I packed my things soon as I got home. To be honest, I didn't think you'd give it a second thought. I'm flattered you were worried. But that surprised me. After a time I thought about it, decided it was wrong to just walk out on somebody who hasn't done you any harm. So I called. I really didn't think you would be worried but it was bad manners to do what I did.'

He let her words soak him. The ocean waves continued to roll as they had for all time. How should he approach the subject of Clarke?

In the end he said bluntly, 'I think Winston Clarke murdered that girl, Valerie Stokes, that's her name. You know him, right?'

'He didn't kill that girl.'

He had figured it could have gone either way with her. Thought she might have been scared of Clarke but no, she wanted to defend him.

'He was seen earlier in my carpark, talking to her. I think she'd been staying at his place, maybe making a stag film.' He looked her right in the eye, her mouth was making a small *o*. She flicked her lit cigarette in the sand. She said, 'Winston Clarke called me about six o'clock at the club that evening. I was doing my Thursday shift. He was pretty drunk. He's a member. I knew him from there. I'd been out to his place before ...'

'You mean ...'

'I fucked him. Yes. I would have preferred it was you but you had limited availability. You think you know what it's like to be lonely and you probably do. But being a woman of a certain age and lonely, that's a whole other world. One minute you're young and beautiful and you think every man is on his knees wanting to propose and you have endless choice. You want to have fun. You don't want to be some Bex-and-lie-down wife at thirty-three with three screaming kids, chopping kindling for a boiler. You think you can cheat, you can have your cake and not gain an ounce. Then you wake up one day and the scenery has changed and there is no choice. No good one. And you meet somebody, some man who is different to the others, darker but deeper too and you can feel something ... some pull like in a deep current. And you just wish you were the one for him. But you're not. All of a sudden three screaming kids and a boring husband who buys you a vacuum for Christmas doesn't look so bad. But you're stuck, you can't quite get there now, so it's night after night alone or a little company.'

Blake felt her pain, he did. He just didn't know how to alleviate it. 'He called you that evening?'

'Yes. Said he had this party on for his kid and he felt like company, did I want to come over when my shift finished. I said I'd see how I felt. I wasn't going to go. I actually drove back to my place but then ... I felt lonely. You weren't an option. I cruised over to his place, must have been around eleven-thirty by then. The party had broken up. I walked up to the house. The door was open. There was a kid flaked out on the lounge. Clarke was in his bedroom snoring his head off. He couldn't have killed that girl.'

He heard her words clearly enough but wanted to gather them up and hurl them far out to sea. No. No. No. His theory was right, dammit.

'How long were you there?'

'I made myself a coffee. Fifteen minutes later he was still asleep, so I left. Maybe he went out earlier, met the girl in the carpark like you say, but if she died between ten-thirty and twelve-thirty, he didn't kill her.'

The Bella Vista was a big old wooden rooming house of three floors, six rooms to a floor. Room eight was on the second floor up a short flight of stairs from the entrance hall and along a narrow hallway, two doors down on the right. Blake let the shadows drape over him like a hood. It reminded him of Philly, of standing in dark hallways and the kind of smells — cabbage and grease — the low churn of TV talk and radios behind closed doors, a kid being spanked, tears following. It reminded him of men with singlets with holes in them, chest hair poking through, of large trousers with cuffs and braces. He remembered Trixie and Mindy now, some kind of fair they'd all gone to. Jimmy wanting him to show off by shooting ducks and winning the girls prizes but he resisted that and shot hoops instead, didn't win anything. Jimmy told him he was a dumb mutt, he should have taken out the ducks, but later Mindy still wanted her to kiss him, and he did, in a hallway just like this. Felt her up, his fingers probing up her thigh, inside her panties. They were satin and so soft against his fingertips that were used to metal. She moaned, wanted him to do it there, up against the wall but he couldn't. He really didn't even know why he was doing what he was, other than he could and maybe everyone including himself expected it. He'd kissed her and told her he had to go and that's where they had left it. He'd seen her once again, maybe twice, but in a group and nothing had happened but she was keen. She made eyes and whispered they could go out to the alley. It was just before he had a job, which one he didn't want to remember, didn't want anything interfering, didn't want to feel a girl's hot breath in his ear, her body on his fingers, to know life, to cherish anything in the world, wanted it to stay bleak and cold and metallic because how else could he do his job? And that was how it was again now, in this hallway. He was the tin man.

Except he wasn't any more. He had friends like Andy, Edward, Doreen; people who when they smiled touched something deep in him, made him want more. And Carol who was all human, not a skerrick of hard metal. He had been wrong about Clarke killing her. It didn't seem possible that he could have been, but clearly he was. Clarke couldn't be in two places at once. And if he was wrong about Clarke when he had been so sure, how could he be certain he wasn't wrong about Vince and Repacholi too? Maybe they'd laugh, say screw it, leave him be.

Just the width of a cheap door separated Mindy and him. His heart was beating fast but he stilled it. His knuckle rose to meet the wood, stopped. If he ever found a way to tell Doreen about who he was, what he was, had been … she might find a way to understand. Even Harry and Steve. But not this, this would be something she could not forgive because he could not forgive it. His hand returned to his pocket. He spun on his feet and walked silently back down the stairs and out to the warm moon.

11. Forest For Trees

Giselle, the stonemason's daughter, was neither pretty nor wise, and though she was honest enough to concede the former, she was foolish enough to disbelieve the latter. All the girls in the village dreamed that one day handsome Prince Tyrol would ask them to be his bride and Giselle was no exception. Though Tyrol could choose whomever he wished, she reasoned that her plainness need be no impediment. After all, the richest man in the town was certainly not the most learned. Her chance, she believed, would come at the town festival where the single women all danced in the Prince's honour, for one thing Giselle could do was dance. Her greatest rival was clearly going to be the beautiful Hilda. Hilda paraded around town wearing a golden pin in her bonnet which she said the Prince had given her. Giselle believed that Hilda was in fact a witch, her beauty but an apparition. The pin, which indeed looked like those worn by the Prince, may have been his after all but Giselle believed that it resided with Hilda through sorcery not merit.

The day of the festival arrived and so too did Prince Tyrol. The girls of the village swooned and the dancing was called upon to begin. One by one the young women performed, one by one they were eliminated, until only Giselle and Hilda remained. Hilda did everything in her power to sway Tyrol but Giselle's belief was stronger than any witch's spell. Much to Hilda's anger, the Prince chose Giselle as the winner. That night he invited her for a ride on his wonderful carriage.

Giselle's parents were beside themselves. This was the greatest honour anybody could imagine. Giselle's heart beat in rapture as he drove her deep into the wood, his strong arms and wrists raising and then slowing the tempo of the horses until he hushed them to a halt beside a silver stream.

'How fortunate I am,' she thought. But no sooner had the thought crossed her mind than Tyrol had begun forcing himself upon her, ripping at her pretty dress, intent on taking her virtue. Gone was the handsome prince: Tyrol was revealed as a vile monster. She realised then that everything she thought she knew was false but it was too late now. Hilda flew at her, dragging her from the carriage and stabbing her again and again with Tyrol's pin. Terrified and shamed, Giselle ran for her life but she had no idea where she was heading. The forest was dark and seemed to close in around her with every step.

Doreen finished reading and handed the paper back to Kitty.

'You see the mark I got? C! "Child-like" is what the teacher called it. I would have got C minus except for my good spelling and punctuation! You know, animals can smell evil but we have no idea. We can't see what's in front of our face.' Kitty folded her arms angrily. Doreen had been worried how Kitty was going to cope going back to school. A month into the school year, it didn't seem good. This was the second time this week Kitty had called and asked to meet.

'What about your friends? Have you told them?'

'As if. I eat lunch with Jenny and Amanda. Jenny said she saw the witch strutting around town like she owned it. She's got some job in the chemist.'

Doreen watched Kitty rip the cardboard coaster into confetti. It wasn't the same girl she'd met back in mid-January. She wished she'd never had the stupid watusi contest, felt obliged to offer something.

'The only advice I can give you is work hard and get good marks.'

'And be what, a primary-school teacher?'

'That's a great job. Kitty, the worst thing about school is that you can't go back.'

Kitty exhaled as if exhausted. 'Sorry, it's not your problem.'

Nalder entered, looked over and nodded at Doreen.

Kitty said, 'He'll order a pot of tea, he always does.'

'What about your parents?'

'Mum was so disappointed it didn't work out with Todd, Dad too probably. Mum thinks the best thing in the world is to have babies to a rich man. I mean, that's her goal in life. For me.'

Doreen said, 'I'd settle for it.'

Kitty scrunched up her face. 'You're kidding?'

Was she? She wasn't so sure any more. She loved her job at the Surf Shack but would she still want to be doing that in three years? Five? Sometimes a life devoted to cooking and gardening had a lot of appeal.

'We're not men, Kitty. We can bellyache all we like about it but that's a fact.'

'Why should it be that way? Why shouldn't you run an insurance company or … be a mechanic?'

'I'm not saying it's the way it should be, just that it is. Maybe you can change it. It needs somebody smarter and stronger than me. Although to be honest, I have no desire to be a mechanic.'

Kitty gathered her things. 'The Russians are talking about putting a woman in space.'

'Guess they realised they needed somebody to clean the lavatory.'

Kitty smirked. Doreen always got a kick when they shared an in-joke. She stood, said, 'I have to get back.'

Kitty hefted her bag, indicated Nalder, who was pouring tea. 'Told you.'

Nalder was enjoying his habitual pot of tea in the Victoria. Saunders' girl had passed pleasantries with him briefly before she had gone, leaving the whole room to him. His solitude was short-lived. Denham's face peered in at the window, searching for his boss, tagged him. He entered, eager as a puppy that had discovered a squeaky toy.

'Sorry, Sarge, I know this is your break.'

'What is it, Constable?'

'Just got a call from Pasquale Tonorelli out th'ere on Cockatoo Ridge. His mower had broken down so he went next door to see if he could borrow one.'

That would be the old Carmody place, if Nalder had it correct.

'No one answered but there was a car there, so he went in. There's two bodies.'

The last sentence came out like air when a tyre has been slashed — which was something Nalder had been considering doing to the cars of those at the golf club who would reject him. Nalder picked up his hat and stood up from the chair, leaving the exact amount for the tea plus a threepenny tip.

'We better go and take a look.'

Long before he reached the back door, Nalder caught the stink of bacteria that confirmed death and delayed discovery. It was still hot and humid, even at night. There would be truckloads of maggots. He'd called Doc Sorrow — his real name was Suwarrow but everybody shortened it — and asked him to get up there as soon as he could. The Doc passed for the official police doctor in Coral Shoals and surrounds.

'Stay here,' Nalder told Denham. He didn't need him losing his lunch all over the steps. That's what had happened to Nalder when as a rookie he attended his first murder-suicide. Not that he was pre-judging what he was going to find but when you got two bodies in a farmhouse, that was always the outcome. He knew of a couple near Armidale who had died because of some problem with a heater that had asphyxiated them but the three times prior to this when he had attended a scene with multiple bodies it had been a farmer taking out himself and his wife. Tonorelli was waiting by his old truck upwind of the smell. He was one of those wiry Itie types, probably in his sixties but strong as a bull.

'You know anything about them?' Nalder fiddled with his top pocket and notebook out of habit.

'No. I seen a couple of blokes in the car a month or so ago.'

This was news to Nalder. 'It's two men?'

Tonorelli shrugged. 'I think so. This heat, the flies ... one was in men's shoes, the other bare foot.'

Nalder understood: bloated, maggot-ridden, the features of the corpses would be indecipherable. He looked over at the car, a light blue FJ. Something sounded in his brain. Got it. The standover guys who Saunders said beat up his yardman. He could check the rego with what Doreen Norris had supplied. He left Tonorelli, crossed to the house and started up the steps. He'd never smelled anything this bad. He pulled out a handkerchief, held his nose and entered the kitchen. Empty beer bottles tried to stand straight on sloping lino, baked bean tins in the bin.

The carnage had taken place in the lounge room. Two lumps of goo remained, one on the lounge suite and one on the floor. The size of the feet told him it was two men. The drone of the flies reminded him of the model aeroplane club he used to take the boys to. At the feet of the body on the couch was a sawn-off shotgun. The head had been pretty much obliterated. Goo — blood, brain and whatever the flies had done to it — was spattered on the faded curtains behind. He edged over toward the other body. Head more or less intact. Unless fingerprints told a different tale, he ran it this way: the one on the lounge shoots the other one and turns the gun on himself, murder-suicide, thank you very much. The sash-window at the front was halfway open, easy access for the creepy crawlies but it had helped a little with the smell. He shoved it all the way up, stuck his head outside for a deep lungful of warm air. He carefully retraced his steps looking for anything like bloody footprints but, as he expected, saw none. He moved down the hallway, located a dunny. The hallway bent at right angles, a room each side. He turned into the one on the right, very basic. A camp stretcher bed, a pine dresser. On top of the dresser was a wallet and a few coins. No identification inside but there was a receipt on top of the dresser. In scrawled writing he made out 'rent' with a Toorolong address stamped on it. Above the drone of the flies he heard a car arriving. Doc Sorrow, thank God. They could get on with removing those things out in the lounge room. He didn't envy whoever had the job of trying to get rid of the smell.

Since his trip to the Heads, Blake had been rudderless. Before, he had felt some kind of purpose: freeing Crane, bringing Clarke to justice, restoring his Garden of Eden. What had happened there had been like some horrible myth where the hunter snuck up on the cave of the evil monster, only to be confronted by the spitting image of himself. Carol had not been killed and disposed of by Clarke after all. She'd simply realised that when she tapped Blake Saunders, he was a hollow log. She ran, just as he had run from Philly, that simple. But he had been prepared to murder an innocent woman to maintain his illusion of freedom, of control. The worst thing was, part of him still regretted the decision to let Mindy be. There was that song, 'Cast Your Fate to the Wind'. Well, that was what he had done, abandoned control of his own life.

All week he'd been drifting, the can with the printed film unopened in his garage. True to his word the film guy, John, had the developed print ready for him for pick-up by eleven a.m. the previous Sunday. All the way back to Coral Shoals he had driven, the canister at his feet, the phrase 'Clarke didn't kill Carol' repeating over and over in his head. Harvey must have called again by now. He didn't know for sure because he hadn't answered his phone. He didn't want to face Harvey, admit his failure.

By Wednesday, even though he had no interest in viewing a porn movie featuring the now deceased Val Stokes, he had scraped enough resolve to do so. A new idea had sprung up like a shoot in the desert. Perhaps her co-star or stars might not be Clarke himself. If that were the case then there could be more viable suspects. Duck had said that he could lay his hands on a sixteen-mil projector from the local scouts — he used to be one apparently. It transpired, however, that the projector had been loaned out to a group from Greycliff and not yet returned. Blake's enthusiasm died like a fire built only of kindling. He told Duck to let him know when it was back and played a perfunctory set at the Surf Shack. Carol's alibi of Clarke he confided to Doreen. She worked hard to show she too was disappointed that his theory hadn't worked out but he was certain that already she was measuring Crane for a prison cell. Not even Dakota Staton was helping his mood as he mooched around the house. The phone rang, Nalder.

'Meet me at the usual. I've got news.'

Frogs croaked, the smell of river water overtook that of gasoline around Nalder's van, a leak somewhere, Blake thought absently. It was too dark to see each other's faces clearly.

'Harry Wakelin and Stephen Schneider.' Nalder leaned back against the bonnet of his van, pleased with himself.

'They never gave me their last names, just Harry and Steve.'

'That's them, sure and certain. Looks like one shot the other and then blew his own brains out. They had no ID but I tracked them through a receipt from the people who rented them the property. There were lots of empty beer bottles. Probably got pissed, argued. They both had records, Queenslanders. They'd only been out of jail a couple of months.'

Nothing in that surprised Blake. 'So it looks like it turned out okay.'

'Yes it does. I get the feeling you're that kind of bloke, Saunders.'

'What kind of bloke?'

'The kind that things always turn out okay for.'

Blake wasn't sure if there was an edge there, a hint. 'Not always,' he said. 'I thought I had something that would clear Crane. It hasn't panned out.'

'Perhaps that's because he did it.'

'You really think he somehow cadged a lift with Stokes, brutally stabbed her without his clothes being soaked in blood, then found his way home without somebody noticing?'

'It doesn't matter what I think. It's what twelve strong men and true think.' Nalder opened his car door. 'At least you can tell your yardy that he can sleep easy.'

Blake watched Nalder drive away. He'd shot two men dead and, whether they deserved it or not, nothing was going to happen to him for that. Crane on the other hand was looking at life behind bars. So much for justice. The unicorn was more real.

He went home and got drunk. A rare occasion for him. Music eased the melancholy. Maybe he was already dead? Maybe this was hell? He could make a case for it. Suppose back there in Philly at Repacholi's garage he had ratted on Jimmy and they had shot him. Next thing he's in the car being forced to see the result of his cowardice. Then he thinks he gets away but he doesn't of course, because this is hell. The devil gives him a glimpse of what he might have got, had he deserved it: his own bar in a paradise, good people. But, little by little, that world is dismantled, like stage props being taken away, until all that is left is him: rotten, stinking, worthless.

He fell asleep in his lounge chair, woke sometime and dragged himself to bed. He got up at seven feeling like the way the Phillies played, forced himself into a listless session with the waves, skulked back to his house. He was putting his car in the garage when the garbage truck rumbled by. The guys in their footy shorts ran to different sides of the street. One stocky guy hauled his trash can up and ran back to the tipper with a cheery 'g'day', dumped his trash in then ran it back. It should have been one of those trivial moments that make up your day that you don't even register. So why was it that he felt it was important? A memory there. He dredged. Something was glinting in the mud, pulling him towards it, closer, closer ...

'Did I see his car? Who, Clarke's?' Carol sounded annoyed. Perhaps she'd thought he called her for something more personal. He'd been going crazy killing time, waiting till she came in for work. The guy who answered the phone at the café said she wouldn't be in till just before midday. At three past, Blake had called. He tried to encourage her.

'Yes, when you drove in that night to his house. Was his car there?'

'As if I would remem—' Her denial was cut short as she recalibrated. 'Wait, no. No, I didn't see his car because my first thought was he couldn't be bothered waiting for me and had gone out. But there were a couple of cars there. I guessed he might have driven a different one from the yard. But he was there asleep, I told you. I didn't imagine it.'

This was critical now. 'You said there was a kid asleep on the sofa. Was it his son?'

'I guess. I never met his kid.'

'You didn't see Clarke at his place anytime between the previous Sunday and that Thursday when Valerie Stokes was killed?'

'It wasn't like a regular thing with us. He might have come to the golf club. His son was coming to stay with him. But you know that, right? Because he booked you to provide the keg.'

It only occurred to him now that she had been the one who had pushed Clarke in that direction.

'That was you, sent him to me?'

'I reckoned you could use the business. Listen, I have to start my shift.'

'Do you know what day Thomas Clarke arrived?'

'Sorry.'

'The kid you saw on the couch, do you remember ...' He searched desperately for ideas. '... what colour the kid's hair was? How big he was?'

'I don't remember his hair. He wasn't so big he couldn't fit on the lounge.'

Blake had once seen Tom Clarke asleep on the sofa. 'You said the kid fit. Were the kid's feet way over the edge?'

'I don't know. How am I going to remember that?'

Well, *he*'d remembered. She sounded stressed. 'I have to go.'

The clunk of the receiver cut out any chance of another question. Tom Clarke was big. Maybe it had been one of Tom Clarke's friends she'd seen asleep on the sofa? Maybe Tom Clarke was out of there.

Something else clicked into place. He grabbed his car keys.

'Let me see.' Harold Travers stood on his porch, which looked high over the Pacific and, down to the left, the Ocean View Motel. Travers was a man about sixty-five who wore a cardigan even in summer. 'It had to be a Thursday night because I put the bin out for the rubbish men and it was dented when I went out there on the Friday.'

'Seven weeks ago? The seventeenth?'

'That's when your car was hit too?'

This was the tale Blake had spun after he'd walked up the long driveway and knocked on the door.

'Yes, late on the seventeenth. I was parked down the road there. I remember because it was the night that girl was killed down there at the motel.'

'Of course,' said Travers with a shiver. 'Ghastly thing. Some vagrant, I believe.'

'Apparently.' Clearly Travers had never understood the significance of his dented bin.

'They come around that curve going downhill and get in too close to the kerb. Good luck catching him, though. He could be anywhere.'

'I suppose I just have to look for a scraped fender.'

They both chuckled like it was the veritable needle in a haystack. But Blake had already pricked his finger. He knew which haystack and exactly where to look.

ㅁㅁㅁ

Kitty had been lunching with Jenny and a couple of other girls but it was just going through the motions. Their excited chatter about what boys they liked and which ones had looked their way made her feel resentful, angry. Today she couldn't face it any more so she headed to the library where nobody would disturb her. To make it look like she was there for legitimate purposes, she peeled a book off the shelf, opened it at random and began reading, an activity never high on her list. It wasn't that she disliked reading, more that she didn't want to waste time she could spend on her true loves of dance and drama. She'd always wanted to be a ballerina, but if that didn't work out, an actress would do. At first the words were just inscriptions on paper. She was reading but nothing was soaking in, her brain stuck on a loop of a drive-in screen and that maniac attacking the car. And then, without any preamble, the words in front of her coalesced and inveigled her to forget everything else. She read without realising it and was still reading when the bell went. It was a book by a woman, Edith Wharton, and though it was written many years earlier, it spoke to her no less clearly than Laurey Williams in *Oklahoma!*, as if some all-seeing person had been able to distil her life — Kitty Ferguson's — and record it in this book before she had been conceived.

That night when her head touched the pillow and she closed her eyes, for the first time in weeks she was not assailed by Gene Pitney's haunting 'Liberty Valance', or visions of a banshee swinging a shoe, or the sense of helplessness against the iron hands of Todd, but of brownstones and bonnets and the slow tick-tock of grandfather clocks. She gave into it completely, let it take her where it would. As if her history had been written on a seawall, then wiped smooth by an eternity of tides, she released everything she had been, offered herself free and clear to be whatever nature's forces decided she could. For the first time in what seemed forever, she looked forward to tomorrow.

12. A Shirt Returns

White light on a screen that could be pulled from the ceiling, the clatter of projector gears in the cool emptiness of a wooden hall, mislaid scout hats, cub caps, a sweater and a lunchbox abandoned on dusty seats. Blake and nobody else unless you counted the deceased Val Stokes on screen. When he'd picked up the projector, Duck's pal, Manto, had shown him how to thread the film and now he stood watching. Black and white, one fixed camera, no Cecil B. deMille. Almost certainly it had been filmed in the underground 'cellar' at Clarke's, converted for the movie into a studio boudoir. Stokes appears in front of the camera wearing a bikini. Ham acting: it's hot, oh so hot. She takes off her top, fans her bosoms but clearly it's still too hot for her. Her eyes focus on a Kelvinator fridge, unusual for it to be in a bedroom but not to Stokes, who doesn't bat an eye. She opens the door, removes a tray of ice cubes, pops one and traces it over her breasts. That's better. She's giving her nipples a work-out and now there's an actual zoom in, so somebody is working the camera. Nipples erect she throws herself on the bed and starts to play with herself but her bikini bottoms are still on. After a few moments they're gone too. Plenty of close-ups now, then back to a single focus as she's writhing in ecstasy. Somebody walks toward her from camera, a man in a suit, Clarke, he can tell, even though his back is to camera at first. This next part is going to be edited out no doubt. Clarke adjusts her in front of the lens at the angle he wants, nods for her 'action'. More ham acting: she cowers. He slaps her hard. With trembling fingers she unzips his fly. He points threateningly. She pulls out his penis, transfixed like it's the first time she's seen such a thing. He meets her gaze and nods with authority. She sucks ... amazingly she is converted instantly, going at it like it's her favourite ice cream. Her desires seem to increase rapidly from here, sucking replaced by Kama Sutra stuff that goes on until Clarke's eventual climax. The acting over, Stokes relaxes. You can almost read her lips: 'How was that?' For his part Clarke seems pleased enough. He walks to the camera and the screen goes black as he switches off.

Blake stood there under the tin roof thinking on his next move. He was confident his theory was correct but alone could do little. He needed help.

Nalder was starting to wonder whether Saunders was worth the trouble but on the phone he'd been insistent he meet him at the scout hall. Nalder parked a distance away, walked there in his civvies. It was still light but wouldn't be for much longer. He remembered bringing the boys here all those years ago, marvelled how time had wriggled out of his grasp like a greased piglet. He walked up the three short steps and tried to open the door. Locked. Whatever it was, Saunders didn't want unannounced guests. He knocked.

'It's me.'

February was already gone, the humidity leached out of the air, but experience told Nalder there would be one more rousing charge by the rain god. The door opened, Saunders welcomed him with a single word greeting and locked the door again with a long key. It was little more than a rectangular hut, although at one end was a four-foot high stage that Nalder remembered building with a few other dads while Edith played tennis with the other wives in the courts at the back screened by tall gums. An era of homemade lemonade, Lew Hoad on the radio.

'So what is so important?'

Saunders said, 'I know who killed Val Stokes.'

He saw that rocked the policeman, at least temporarily. But Nalder wasn't going to make a fool of himself by any clamour.

'Who?'

'Got something you need to look at.'

He pulled the chair across and gestured Nalder sit. When the cop did, he played the movie. Nalder didn't say a word during the film.

When it finished Blake said, 'That's why nobody has found Stokes during those critical few days from Sunday to Thursday. She was at Clarke's shooting this. I don't think it was the first time they'd worked together.' He told Nalder about what he'd learned in Kings Cross. 'Clarke told me he was in the movie business in LA with his brother-in-law. I'm guessing these were the kind of movies. I wouldn't be surprised they film here and distribute in the US.'

The cop considered it. 'They look pretty chummy at the end. You think it soured and he killed her?'

'Andy saw a man in an Hawaiian-style shirt with crabs and lobsters on it, out the back of the Surf Shack talking to Stokes on the night she was killed. There's a photo of Clarke in that exact same shirt hanging on the wall of his office.'

'Doesn't mean he killed her.'

'I don't think he did kill her. I think his son did.'

Nalder, still seated, squared around. 'Young Tom? You got to be joking.'

'I've got a witness called around to Clarke's house about eleven p.m. Clarke was snoring his head off in his bedroom but his car wasn't there. There was a kid asleep on the couch but I don't think it was Tom.'

'Did your witness check every inch of the house?'

'Come on, who else is going to have the old man's car? Next morning it was back with a scraped fender. Clarke told me one of Tom's friends had backed into the car. I think that's what Tom told him. Around midnight, some car knocked over a trash can a couple of hundred yards from the Ocean View Motel. I had to pay but I've got it. I took a trip over to the smash repair place Clarke used. They still had the old bumper. They did a simple replacement on his car. I'm just an ordinary Joe but the dents look like they match to me.'

Now Nalder was listening, calculating what was in his best interest. This was the critical point. 'Why are you talking to me? Why not Vernon?'

'They might bury it. I want to clear Crane. I want a confession.'

Nalder stood. 'That's not my domain. You need to speak to Vernon, or Crane's lawyer.'

Blake pressed. 'I think when Tom Clarke arrived to stay with his father, Stokes must have still been there. She was probably planning to head back home, nicely cashed-up. I don't know if Tom Clarke knew about the film but he's eighteen and she's a sexy broad. It was his birthday. He wanted to give himself the best gift an eighteen-year-old boy could get. I think he set something up, took Dad's car, met Stokes out the back of the Surf Shack, wearing his dad's shirt. Kid wanted to make an impression.' He could still remember borrowing Jimmy's shirt and jacket for a date so he looked older, worldly.

'It's thin.'

He could tell though that Nalder was considering it now.

'There's no sign of the shirt in Clarke's wardrobe. I think it was soaked in blood and Tom had to get rid of it.'

'How do you know about the wardrobe?'

Blake watched Nalder solve that question for himself.

'Jesus. You broke and entered.'

'Door was open.'

'That where you got the film?' Nalder spread the sarcasm thick. 'The film was just lying around? If that film's stolen, we probably can't use it.'

'We say it was stolen but not by me. There's been a spate of house thefts, right? Like Edward and that radio he was found with. We say we found it tossed on the side of the road. You tell them you took a look at it, realised the significance. Only that same day the yardman at the Surf Shack had told you about the shirt he'd seen. A shirt you recognised. Hell, Vernon and Apollonia hadn't questioned him. You were just connecting dots. I can put you in touch with the witness who noticed the Chevy missing. She gave you her story, it got you thinking. Maybe the shirt was there at the Surf Shack carpark that night but not Winston Clarke. You thought you'd just have a word to the boy ...'

'Alright, I get it: this whole thing just unravelled before I could call in the Homicide boys.'

'Exactly.'

The big cop rolled the idea like a lozenge, sucking on the implications. 'If Clarke knew his kid had met Stokes, he must have told him to shut up about it.'

'If he did.' Blake hit the 'if'. He wasn't sure Clarke knew. He informed Nalder how the car man seemed unguarded about the Chevy when he was talking to Blake. 'If he'd known he was covering something, he probably would have acted differently.'

'So Winston Clarke may or may not know.' Nalder paced, stopped, probed another crevice. 'Who's the witness?'

'Name of Carol, barmaid from the golf club. The whole thing freaked her out and she's up the coast now.'

'Clarke was banging her?'

'Yeah.'

'And you know this because ...?'

Blake could see him connecting the dots again.

'You were going there as well?'

Blake said, 'Does it matter?'

'Everything fucking matters when you ask me to hang my dick out and piss on Vernon and Apollonia. How do I know you didn't put her up to this?'

'If I wanted to do that, why not just get her to say Clarke wasn't there when she called around?'

Nalder appeared to give him that, muttered to himself. Then he came to a decision. 'It's not enough. Not yet.'

'Come on, we've got the trash can, the car missing, the kid absent ...'

'I want it airtight. I don't want to piss off HQ. You get me more, I'll run with it, take the bin, make up some story, see if they can get some match on it with the bumper.'

This must be how you feel when a steamroller flattens you, Blake thought, as he cruised aimlessly around town. Every so often the anger spouted out of him and he cursed the fat, dumb cop and slapped the top of his steering wheel. Near the minigolf place he spied Duck's van. Duck was probably trying to canoodle with one of the young women from the bank or hairdresser, showing them how to putt, his arms around them. Normally he would crack a smile but tonight Blake couldn't manage that. He drove back towards his place, slowed and threw a U-turn.

Bossa nova music played in the lounge room. Doreen had been mending a stocking. She didn't seem like that kind of girl, too glamorous and nightclub for a needle and thread, but then that's what set her aside from Carol, say. There was a homeliness about Doreen even though she was sexy. Actually it made her more sexy. He thought of the women he'd always dated, like Mindy. They could be fun but there was something so brittle about them, as if just sending a deep thought their way would break them like one of those little glass straws they sucked their martinis with. Doreen was stronger, mysterious, durable. If she was a country, she could be Russia.

'What's up?' she asked, showing him in, and then before he could reply adding, 'You've been in another world since you went to the Heads. You want a tea? Brandy?'

He told her he'd have what she was having. Doreen grabbed a couple of tumblers from the cupboard above and poured two brandies. She was wearing shortie pyjamas and it excited him when she stood on tiptoes to get the glassware. There was something beautiful about a long-limbed woman on bare tiptoes. It reminded him of the lamp old Repacholi had in one of his studies: French apparently, a silver nude, stretching holding the world above her head. From the fridge Doreen brought out a large bottle of ginger ale and added it.

He had to this point told her nothing about the film other than he had acquired it but not looked at it. She'd asked him 'Why?' and he'd fobbed her off with the fact he didn't have a projector.

'I ran the film tonight.' He told her about it: a stag film featuring Winston Clarke and Val Stokes in lead roles. He told her his theory, told her about Nalder. Confession done, he swallowed the brandy.

'You can get all this to Harvey.'

'My worry is Nalder. If I can't get him involved, I won't get Vernon. That leaves it up to the jury.'

As she often did when she was thinking, she closed her eyes, stretched her neck, delicate and lean. It belonged in that church in the Vatican with the painted ceiling. Her eyes opened again. In this light they were jade.

'There might be a way to swing Nalder.'

He swigged eagerly. 'How?'

'He's desperate for membership to the golf club, applied twice, knocked back twice. You convince him that solving this will get him in, then he might be prepared to stick out his neck.'

It was a different part of his anatomy Nalder feared losing, but it showed she was thinking like the cop did.

She said, 'Tell me again what Carol said.'

He ran through what Carol had told him, added uselessly, 'It can't have been Clarke senior.'

'What about the kid? The other one.'

It was self-evident, yet he'd completely missed it, Nalder too.

'The kid on the lounge?'

'You get to him. He might be able to confirm that his mate Thomas wasn't around.'

'Carol didn't recognise him.'

'But she got a look at him?'

'Not really. She didn't remember his hair, said he was small enough to fit on the sofa. Which is why I don't think it's Tom Clarke.'

To her, the next step seemed obvious. 'If we find somebody who knows Thomas Clarke they might be able to say who this kid is.'

'How are we going to do that?'

'I don't know him or his friends that well but I saw them down the beach a few times.'

Doreen had thought it was better to intercept Kitty on her way to school rather than meet up at the Victoria Tearooms where Nalder could be ensconced. Blake injected himself into the conversation.

'This guy is probably not that tall. We're guessing he might be average to slim build.'

Kitty pursed her lips. 'Not much to go on, Sherlock, though you might get lucky: most of Clarke's mates are big guys like him, rugby and all that. You could try Paul Sommerville and Doug McGee. I haven't seen McGee since school went back. I think he might be at uni. Paul Sommerville delivers telegrams.'

Doreen thanked her, promised they would soon catch up.

'I have to get the Shack ready for tonight,' she explained. Kitty was eager for gossip.

'So what did he do, Sommerville?'

'We just need to talk to him about something.'

Kitty smirked. 'You lie like my parents,' she said, and swung off towards the school.

It had been something of a revelation that her parents lied. Not about the Easter Bunny and Tooth Fairy but about loads of things: they lied to her, to themselves and most surprising, to each other. None of this she would have realised if she hadn't made that fateful trip to the library and found Edith Wharton. It was like the English in the war cracking the German code. All of a sudden, the mystery fell away. Instead of gawking at amazing sets, you could see how the pulleys and winches worked, how the flats were painted. After that first time at the library, she had gone home still thinking about the book, its world, its people.

Next day she had waded patiently through morning classes and when lunchtime came, had avoided Jenny and hurried to the library where she retrieved the book and started to read it from the beginning. She had finished it by Friday. There was only one other Wharton book there so she took it home and read it over the weekend. After that she would graze, read a few pages of something and if it took hold, keep reading. This way she found Somerset Maugham, John O'Hara, Henry James; whispering in her ear, showing her how to study, pick up clues about those around you. She returned to lunch occasionally with her friends, listening more keenly than she had ever listened, noticing nuances she'd previously missed, omissions, prevarications, things that told her just how vulnerable they all were. This new skill she found she possessed, fed upon itself, increasing progressively by the day. What shocked her most was that she was suddenly more aware of her parents' relationship, tensions, the occasional unspoken condemnation on both their parts. Her mum's obsession with tennis, canasta, bridge, musicals, even the artistic use of driftwood could be understood now as an attempt to fill in space and time. Stripped of these, her life was a void filled only by her daughter. Her dad's complimenting his wife's cooking — Kitty had always thought that sweet — she understood now was simply a password to camp after a long day on the battlefield with other men. His thoughts were on the next day and the day after that, where to move the artillery, when to retreat, who to form an alliance with, who to declare war against. She realised now that his returns late from work often included stopovers at watering holes. Her mother was thirty-six, her father three years older. Their adult lives had been spent together. When she fell pregnant, her mum was only two years older than Kitty was now. Their lives had been mapped out for them, a recent past of war instilling a desire for stability. Their habits had given their lives a structure that was clearly more acceptable than Japanese invasion but the external threat had diminished and fear was no longer calling the shots over reason. Kitty was grateful to be free of all these past horrors, had no craving for security, or peace, but for new experiences. She saw her generation as having more in common with the bohemian crowd of the nineteen twenties and thirties.

Horrible as her encounter with Todd had turned out, it had led to her changing, to understanding the world around her so much faster. She would not squander it. These were her last months of school. After she aced her exams she planned to literally get out of town. She reached into her school bag and switched on her transistor, walked with a swing of her hips. They were calling for auditions for the school play: this year *South Pacific*. Perfect.

ㅁㅁㅁ

Blake walked to the back of the red-brick post office and waited. Doreen had offered to do this, and while he was sure the kid would be putty in her hands, he already had an angle that he thought was likely to win cooperation. It was about fifteen minutes before the kid he figured was

Sommerville freewheeled down the path to the rear door. This was better than if he had been going out. He got off his bike, threw a curious glance Blake's way and was about to enter through the back door when Blake said, 'We need to talk, Paul.'

Sommerville looked both wary and curious but more the former. He edged over. Blake gave him no time to stabilise.

'You were at Tom Clarke's eighteenth,' he stated.

Sommerville swallowed, guilty. Almost certainly he'd been underage drinking there.

'What of it? Who are you?' He grouped the sentences together like that would give him more protection.

'You could be in deep shit, kid, so a few manners wouldn't go astray.'

Sommerville was nervous now. Blake remembered when he was this kid's age. He remembered which guys scared the crap out of you and which guys didn't. Well, it was pretty easy. Any of Repacholi's guys scared the crap out of you and they just told you, do this, do that, knowing you dare not refuse because the last thing you wanted was to be on the wrong side of those men. Blake had the kid where he wanted.

'The night of the party, around eleven at night, there was an accident. Property was damaged by a speeding car.'

Sommerville was eager to distance himself. 'I don't know anything about that. I crashed at Tom's at about nine-thirty.'

'You were pissed?'

A sulky look. The back door of the post office banged and a man with scaly, Celtic skin and wispy hair came out wearing a PMG sweater. He threw a look at them and then started walking off: morning tea-break most likely.

Blake continued, 'I have a witness says the car was a Chevy Bel Air. I don't need to tell you old man Clarke drives one of those. But he wasn't driving that night. Another witness puts you and Tom in town around nine.'

'I wasn't there, that's a lie. I was pissed. I stayed at the house.'

'Tom was wearing a shirt with crayfish and crabs on it, right? What did he do, wait till his dad fell asleep then nick the car?'

'Listen, I don't know anything about an accident. That's the truth. Tom wanted to head into town. He was trying to impress some girl.'

'Which girl?'

'I don't know. Some older bird, a prossie.'

'A prostitute?'

Sommerville gave it up quickly. 'Tom borrowed money off me, three pounds. That's why I had to sleep there anyway. I didn't have enough to get home. I wasn't the only one he hit up.'

'He was getting money to pay the woman?'

'Yeah. But he said it all fell through and next day he gave me my money back. He never said anything about any accident.'

'He wore his father's shirt?'

'I think so, yeah. Look, I haven't done anything wrong.'

Blake laid it out in his head: Tom Clarke had worn his father's shirt, he'd borrowed his father's car, met with Val Stokes out the back of the Surf Shack where they'd had sex before he'd followed her to the Ocean View. He had left in haste and collided with a trash can a hundred yards from the murder scene. Tom Clarke had viciously killed Val Stokes and now he was going to pay.

ooo

The Sommerville kid was the clincher. Blake Saunders had been thorough and lined up all the ducks for him. If he was ever going to write his name in the town's history, this was it. He put on his sergeant's cap, walked to the post office and called the kid out of the delivery-men pool. Outside he swore him to secrecy, gave him a tip: tell anybody at work who is nosy, that we're speaking because you were witness to a traffic accident. After Sommerville's official statement was taken, confirming what Saunders had said, there was nothing for it but to go after Thomas Clarke. It could backfire of course. Anything could backfire. If life had taught him one thing, it was you can't count your chickens. However, life had also taught him you had to seize the day. What were those pumped-up pricks at the golf club going to say when he, Leslie Nalder, the local plod, delivered the killer that the Homicide boys had missed?

What they were going to say was: please do us the honour of joining our club, sharing in our nineteenth hole conversations, eat our salami and sweet gherkin savouries and rest your expended toothpick with ours.

Edith would be proud. That would, in turn, make him happy. For years they had been looked down upon: the local cop and his missus, not clever enough or smart enough to be asked into the inner sanctum. That would change. According to the Sommerville kid, Thomas Clarke was going to be staying at his dad's place for the weekend, arriving Saturday morning.

At ten thirty a.m. Saturday, he picked up Saunders. They cruised past the car yard. Winston Clarke was attending to customers under little triangular red, blue and white flags that fluttered in a light breeze. That was good. It would be much better to have the kid alone. They rolled out of town and up Belvedere Road.

Nalder didn't look at Saunders when he said, 'You're here as a favour. Don't get out of the car.' He'd already made the ground rules clear but it didn't hurt to reiterate.

'How did you go with the bin and the fender?'

'Bumper bar, mate, we're not in Texas. Sent if off yesterday. Couldn't make it look like I had too much advance knowledge or they'd say I should have alerted them earlier. We'll check out the house first, see if he's there yet.'

They drove in silence, and turned up the long driveway. They were in luck. A Holden was pulled up near the back steps. He cruised in behind it.

'You wait here.'

He climbed out of the car and put on his police cap. He stretched, savoured the morning air. Though summer's sharpest point was blunted, it was still hot and the eucalypts were bone dry. Thunderstorms had been absent for a few weeks now.

He slowly ascended the steps and knocked on the screen door. He could smell toast. A shape emerged from the gloom of the kitchen: Thomas Clarke mid-bite, peanut butter from the looks.

'Dad's not here. He's at work.'

'This isn't about your dad, Tom. May I come in?'

The kid looked worried now, the toast drooped. He opened the door.

I'm gonna scare the shit out of you, son, he thought as he squeezed in. He pulled out his notepad, slowly, watched the kid track it. Tom Clarke was a big lump of a kid, broad across the shoulders, slightly pudgy.

'What's the problem?' he asked. He must have noticed that the toast was shaking so he put it down.

'Your birthday party ...'

'Dad was here the whole time. It was just a private party.'

The kid still hoping it was about underage drinking.

'I have a report that you were driving your father's car.'

'What? No.'

The kid was a bad actor.

'Son, best you tell the truth here. It was involved in a minor accident and we know it wasn't your father driving, but you.'

He sensed the kid's relief. 'There were no other cars involved. I hit the kerb, that's all. Knocked a bin over.'

'Almost directly outside the Ocean View Motel.'

He wasn't prepared for it. The kid was quicker than he looked, lunging straight past him and ripping open the back door. By the time he moved to follow, the kid had vaulted from the back steps and was running through fruit trees towards the bush.

Blake was sitting there drumming his fingers when he saw Thomas Clarke burst out the back door, jump from the stairs, land on his feet and dash into the bush. Without thinking, he threw open the car door and went after him. The kid might have looked big and unfit but sometimes body shapes lie. He was fast, probably a school athlete who had softened up during the long break but could still power. He didn't bother about paths but just went crashing off into the dense bush that sprawled over uneven terrain. Blake followed. Spiky vegetation ripped at the back of his neck, the pockmarked ground pitched him like a rolling deck. He couldn't see Clarke ahead but the sound of him was Blake's compass. Then he heard a startled deep oath and a thump of body hitting dirt. He broke through a curtain of brown foliage in time to see Clarke getting back to his feet and trying to continue but he'd done something — twisted an ankle, bruised a knee, whatever — and couldn't accelerate in time. Blake threw himself at him, smacked into his back and pulled them both to ground. Clarke tried to break free but Blake had him. Somewhere in the background, Nalder was calling out for them.

Blake's chin ground into the back of Clarke's shoulder. He snarled into the kid's ear, 'You killed her, you son-of-a-bitch. You chopped her up and let another guy take the fall.'

Clarke managed to roll over, his eyes were wide with fear and he had ceased to struggle.

'No, no. I didn't kill her. When I got there, it was horrible, like an abattoir. She was already dead.'

The drycleaner was a thin man. Too thin. Blake figured him for an alcoholic or a cancer sufferer. He looked suspiciously at Blake like he just knew he wasn't the same guy who had left the article of clothing there. But Blake had the ticket.

'I'll just go and check,' the drycleaner said before slipping out the back through a dusty salmon-pink curtain. The story the Clarke kid had given them was plausible. Plausible in exactly the same way that a killer who'd had nearly two months to prepare his story would make it. The kid had admitted in front of both Blake and Nalder as they stood over him in the bush, that he had indeed spied Val Stokes leaving his father's house as he had arrived. He'd caught her as she was about to jump into her car, assumed she was a pro servicing his old man and asked how much for sex. She'd looked him up and down and told him twelve pounds. He'd hastily arranged to meet her in the Surf Shack carpark around nine thirty that night. Because he didn't have twelve pounds on him he'd been forced to borrow from his mates.

The drycleaner emerged. In his right hand was a coathanger. On the coathanger was a shirt featuring crabs and lobsters. So much for the incinerator theory.

Now the shirt hung in a room in the police station. Blake assumed the sparsely furnished room was Nalder's office. He'd never been in here before. They'd entered via the back door, a back lane direct into a rear carpark. The two constables were out. Down the hall in a bare brick cell was Thomas Clarke.

Blake said, 'Do you believe him?'

Nalder snorted. 'That he didn't butcher her? Of course he's going to say that.'

'He says he threw up after he saw her. That would account for the vomit out the front of the motel unit.'

'He might have done that after he slaughtered her.'

'True. But the shirt would have been soaked in blood, right? I mean, his story that he took the shirt to the drycleaner because it got some puke on it, makes sense. He wanted to hand a clean shirt back to his old man when he noticed it missing.'

'He might have taken the shirt off, fucked her, killed her, put the shirt back on, puked when he went outside.'

That was a possibility Blake could concede. But would Val Stokes have had sex with the kid unless he'd paid? And he'd given the money back. Mind you, he could have got that in the meantime.

'Your trouble is, you don't want anybody to be guilty,' Nalder said. 'This is sure as shit going to get Crane off unless you kybosh it. You start saying the kid didn't do it, Vernon is going to go straight back to theory number one. Your beach bum mate got a lift with Stokes and killed her. The kid turned up and found her.'

All that was true.

'Listen,' the big cop leaned in, elbows on his desk, knuckles like boulders rolling against their brothers. 'His old man will pay a shitload for a lawyer. You don't think he's not going to go through all this too?'

It was true. Blake didn't figure it was his job to get everybody off.

Nalder picked up his telephone receiver. 'I'm going to call Vernon. Tell them they might have the wrong bloke. You want to stop me?'

As Nalder's fat finger turned the rotary dial, Blake got up and slipped back out the way he had come, walking through the open rear area of the building.

'Hey, Yank.'

Blake looked around and saw pale skin behind a small barred window, high up. It was Thomas Clarke. Blake just wanted to get out of there but he relented, and walked over.

'The shirt checked out, right? I told you I didn't burn it. She was fucking dead.'

'Save it for the cops.'

Blake turned and started walking.

'I didn't kill her. I didn't.'

The words bounced off Blake. It wasn't the first time he'd walked away from a desperate man. It got easier. Thomas Clarke continued to scream his innocence but all Blake heard in his brain was the rush of the past.

13. Glow

My worst fears have nothing to keep them at bay but the limp pages of an out-of-date *Post*. That's what Doreen thought as she turned the pages while sitting on a chrome kitchen chair. Surgeries were all the same. Surely no-one read these things, they were just something to do with your hands. She soaked a minute or two with the spot-the-difference sketches but some selfish prior patient had circled most of them in biro. Anyway, once you'd tried a few you knew where to look: the fingers on one hand, whether one shoe was further forward than the other, if somebody was wearing glasses. The other woman in the room sat perfectly still, her gloved hands resting on her matching handbag. From the region of the doctor's rooms came an annoying and persistent cough. It was autumn now, Anzac Day only a week away but the sun was still strong. You think things are going well and then you get punished for relaxing. You wind up here on a chrome kitchen chair with an out-of-date magazine in your hands. Her mind drifted back over the last six weeks: the sense of shock when they arrested Thomas Clarke. Nalder had taken to strutting around town. Even places where he'd never been spotted before got paid a visit so townspeople could pay homage. There was never any mention of Blake but she knew that's what he wanted. He'd gone back to surfing in the morning, rehearsing with the band and mooching around his house at night. It was colder now on the sandhill but not so chilly she'd broken the habit. Kitty had finally found her feet. She was enjoying school, short-listed for the lead role in the school play, loving life.

I can take a little credit for that, Doreen thought.

It made her feel better about herself. Right now she needed that. The nights could be so lonely. The television helped. She'd had it for nearly a month. The picture still seemed odd, egg-shaped, but what did it matter? For too long she had driven past silent houses, the blue-grey glow of the screen sneaking out of the curtains, beckoning. The salesman had suggested Pye. Maybe he was on a commission but she didn't mind. Everybody does what they have to. It had been so much more fun than she had imagined. There were a lot of westerns but surprisingly she enjoyed them. *Maverick* was her favourite and yes, that's because James Garner reminds you of Blake, she told herself. Paladin on the other hand wasn't a thousand miles from Nalder. Miss Kitty in *Gunsmoke* was of course, herself, and Andy was kind of like Chester but she couldn't see Blake in James Arness.

The door from the inner surgery opened and both she and the older woman with the straight back looked up expectantly. Doreen had arrived first but she'd been early and you just never knew about appointment times. The nurse-cum-receptionist exited with the cough culprit, a middle-aged woman in a dowdy cardigan. That's how we treat each other, Doreen was aware of thinking, like other people are just some impediment, the sooner they are out of the way the better. The cough woman shuffled off.

The nurse announced, 'Mrs Waters?'

The other woman got up and followed her in. The door closed. Doreen was back alone. She drummed up enough empathy to consider this must have been how Crane had felt, alone in a cell. Now Thomas Clarke would be experiencing the same fear: a life that was essentially over. In his case, he deserved it. Poor Valerie Stokes, knife blows raining down on her, thump, thump, thump. Doreen shuddered. A life was supposed to be sacred but Valerie Stokes had found fame as a subject of lurid gossip. Some ghastly people, as many women as men, had decided she'd got what was coming to her — and so far the information about her starring in a blue movie had not come out. No doubt that would emerge in the trial that hadn't yet started. Nalder had revealed Clarke was pleading not guilty. She'd expected Crane to return on his release but when he didn't, she'd asked herself, why would you? With the exception of Blake, everybody here, including her, had judged him guilty on the flimsiest of evidence. Guilt. A distorted, friendless word. It implied sin, crimes committed. In truth, guilt was only experienced by somebody who cared about the lives of others. Her mind drifted: her primary-school playground, the war still fresh, boys arms extended for Spitfire wings, girls clustered under the big gum playing doctors and nurses, pushers and prams everywhere when the handbell was rung and mums came for their brood. Baby boom. Her own class of 1939 births swamped by little 'uns conceived in the frenzy of peace. Finding yourself a minority before you knew it. Rural families. Kids who walked home and fed chooks and horses, bathed brothers and sisters, helped get tea on, chopped wood. All the older girls like her doting on the grade ones. Most of her classmates would be mothers now. Hell, half of them were married before she'd finished school. She on the other hand had loaded up with jet fuel, torched everything on the way out of her past.

The door opened and Mrs Waters strode out briskly, either because she had nothing to fear or the opposite. Nobody else had arrived so the nurse looked at her and smiled through her carefully shaded not-too-red lipstick.

'Miss Norris.'

ㅁㅁㅁ

The reaction had been as good as he might have hoped for in his wildest dreams. People in the street who normally averted their eyes when he passed stopped to say 'well done'. Rob Parker had had a quiet word to him to assure him he was a 'lock' for membership of the club. Of course it hadn't just happened by itself, all this recognition. He'd been forced to spread the word that he was the one who had acted swiftly upon certain 'discrepancies' and loose ends such as a car running into a rubbish bin near the murder scene that otherwise might have gone unnoticed. The local paper lapped it up: uniform cop with breakthrough. They couldn't say too much because the case was yet to come to trial. Vernon and Apollonia were not impressed. Fuck them, their boss was. He'd personally called to congratulate him on some 'sharp' police work. And because Crane hadn't yet come to trial and the matter could be easily dropped, Vernon and Apollonia didn't have as much egg on their face as they might have, so while they clearly resented him inserting himself into the case, in the long run they still got to mark a kill on their job sheets. The Clarke kid was, as expected, pleading not guilty. Winston Clarke was playing it cagey. By now he would have realised that the film can was missing but he'd not reported it stolen. He was probably hoping like hell it was in another country but he must have harboured some suspicions about its disappearance.

Nalder walked up the steps and into the station, hitching his pants at the back where they tended to slip. His gut had been expanding with the free pies the bakery was throwing his way. A bald man in a dark suit was sitting on the wooden bench with a briefcase at his feet. As Nalder entered, Denham signalled him from behind the counter for a word. When Nalder leaned in, he whispered, 'Man named Oberon. Says he wants information on the two dead guys up at Cockatoo Ridge.'

Now Nalder looked over at Oberon. He never liked men in suits with briefcases.

Oberon got to his feet, put out a hand. 'Timothy Oberon. I'm representing the estate of Harold Wakelin.'

There you go, a lawyer. As usual his gut instinct had proven correct. He pointed at his office. 'Like to come through.'

Oberon followed. They entered the office and Nalder took his chair behind his desk. Padded green leather for his arse with studs around the perimeter but it didn't swing. Oberon helped himself to the wooden dining room chair that waited off to the side for just such interviews.

'Where are you from, Mr Oberon?'

'Mathews, Snell—'

'No, not what firm, I mean what town?'

The solicitor pulled up. 'Brisbane. Mr Wakelin was Brisbane-based for most of his life.'

'In Boggo Road, from what I recall.' Nalder made sure the solicitor enjoyed his smirk.

'He made some mistakes.'

'Being friendly with Schneider his biggest.'

'Did you ever hear of any motivation for the killing?'

'Crooks don't need motivation. They fall out, they tend to harm or kill one another.'

'So you never made any enquiry?'

'Open and shut case, Mr Oberon. My door was open to you but it will be shut soon. Is there a point?'

'Sorry, Sergeant, it's just legal rigmarole. Wakelin had a life-insurance policy and for his estate to collect we need to make sure there was no suggestion he killed himself.'

Nalder could smell bullshit. But he smiled all the same. 'The blast came from where Schneider was found sitting. Then Schneider blew his brains out.'

'That usual for it to happen like that? The killer not even moving after he's fired?'

'Nothing's usual. Maybe they were pooftas. That happens a lot in prison, bum-buddies. They get out, one of them wants to carry on like before but the other one wasn't really queer, just needed to get his end away. Schneider's heart is broken so he kills Wakelin, turns the gun on himself. Or, they got pissed and they started to argue about who had gone to the fridge the last time to get the beer. That's all you need. Now if there's nothing else?'

Oberon stood and extended his hand. 'No, thank you very much for your time, Sergeant.'

There was as much chance of Wakelin having a life-insurance policy as Nalder singing soprano. He pulled the heavy phone towards him and dialled Brisbane. An old navy mate of his, Bull Thompson, worked up there in juvenile delinquency.

Bull himself answered.

'How you doing, you old bastard?' Bull asked. They swapped stories for a minute. Despite his new-found popularity, Nalder didn't want to rack up interstate phone call costs.

'Listen, you heard of a solicitor named Oberon.'

Bull went quiet. 'Tim Oberon. I sure have. He's Charlie Hennessy's fixer.'

The Yank, of course, had never heard of Charlie Hennessy. They were meeting at the old spot near the river. Nalder was pleased to see parrots out and about. The farmers couldn't stand them, would take pot shots with their .22s but they always cheered him up, reminded him of when he was a kid and kept a little exercise book with the names of every bird he'd seen.

'Charlie Hennessy is the biggest bookie in Brissy and from all reports a deadset cunt. He's got a monopoly of extortion in the Valley up there and my mate tells me he's also set up shop on the Gold Coast, a bit of prostitution but mostly strongarm stuff. I suppose he has those blokes on call to collect from late payers anyway, so he figures he might as well make use of them.'

The Yank didn't seem to react but Nalder knew he was thinking under that pretty face. He spelled it out.

'You got lucky with those two taking care of one another. They'll send somebody else.'

'You're not going to do anything about it?'

Truth was, he found himself on what they called the horns of a dilemma. He fucking would not countenance Queenslanders meddling here but he did not want to draw any attention to his neck of the woods. He tried to make Saunders understand.

'Obviously these wankers worked for Hennessy who wants to push into northern New South Wales. That visit was all about finding out if there was competition, see if they'd been offed by some other crew from say, Sydney.'

'What would have happened then if they had?'

'I don't fucking know, and I didn't want to find out. But here's the problem. If I tell Hennessy to fuck off without alerting the department, he will at best, offer me money. If I take the money, I am vulnerable. I lose control. On the other hand, if I tell the department about Hennessy, some crooked cop with a link to Sydney's equivalent of Hennessy will spill the beans, and they'll decide to take over from Hennessy.'

'You're saying one way or the other, I'm going to get fucked over.'

'It's possible some pressure might make Hennessy bypass Coral Shoals. I can make it unpleasant for his people: traffic fines, other infractions. He might decide it's cheaper than paying me off or risking me going to his competition if he tries to heavy me. But only a real prosecution will get him out of here and that would take somebody — a pub or restaurant owner for example — to testify. You feel like doing that?'

As he expected, the Yank said nothing.

'I didn't think so. I thought you should know.'

He could see the Yank was thinking things through. In the end he'd probably pay up. That's what he'd do if he was in his position. Saunders parked whatever he was thinking.

'What's the latest on the Thomas Clarke trial?'

'It's probably still a month away. He's pleading not guilty, no surprise. He now claims that just as he'd been about to turn into the Ocean View Hotel, a van was turning out.'

'He's going to say somebody else must have done it.'

'Exactly. Something else I learned from my new mate the Assistant Commissioner. The forensic people found three fingerprints from a hand on the inside roof of the car.'

He demonstrated the position of the hand: fingers pointing back like you would carrying a tray.

'Clarke's?'

'No. That's the pity. They're not Clarke's, or his old man's, and not Crane's. They're not in the system. How do you think they got there?'

He saw Saunders had already thought that through.

'I'd say somebody was sitting on the seat, likely while Stokes was straddling him. He put his hand up.'

'You should be a cop. That's what I reckon too. Of course they could be months old but Clarke's people are bound to bring that up, say they're the killer's. They'll raise your mate the beach bum as a suspect again.'

'Did they find those same prints at the crime scene?'

'No they didn't. Nor Clarke's, not at the scene or on the murder weapon, which was wiped down with a pillowslip. There are other unidentified prints around the room but who knows who was in there the last few months. We'll say he wiped his prints to support his story, he'll say the opposite. The jury will decide who to believe.'

After what Nalder told him, Blake was brushed with a sense of unease, like when you're in the ghost train at the fair and somebody tickles you with a feather in the dark. Everything had been starting to go well again. The Surf Shack was getting stronger each week. The band was playing a whole lot better. Panza knew about some recording studio in Sydney. Blake had been thinking they could actually cut a record. What a hoot that would be. But from what Nalder said, it could all be turning to shit again. This bookie from up north would send his guys. Blake couldn't complain, couldn't take it to court. Questions would be asked about where he was born. How he got here. He couldn't risk that.

And the Ocean View thing still didn't sit well with him. The kid probably did it. But what if he hadn't? What if he was just like Crane, in the wrong place at the wrong time? Crane saw somebody in the car fucking Val Stokes but if the fingerprints were from that occasion then it wasn't Thomas Clarke. Whoever it had been could be the killer.

He had the board in the back so he drove to the beach and paddled out. The swell was up, the waves had bite. He wondered about Mindy and Mike, where they were now, if Mindy had gone home to her mom in Camden or somewhere to tell her about her vacation. Imagined them drinking root beer and then Mindy deciding to show Mike the town, bumping into Trixie. 'Hey, you remember Jimmy's kid brother I was sweet on? I found him in Australia.'

He felt the power of the sea behind him, timed his paddle, jumped on the board, stood. You might as well try and surf against the muscle of the ocean as try and control your fate in this world. It was impossible, no matter how much you told yourself it wasn't. The only thing that you had going for you, the only thing, was those people who loved you or tried to protect you. He'd given Jimmy up because he told himself he had no choice but maybe you couldn't alter the course of fate anyway, you were doomed to just repeat your mistakes again and again.

Doreen's car was not in her driveway. He'd really wanted to see her, to feel real. She'd been asking him to come around and watch television but television wasn't his thing. The bad guys were never like the guys he knew back in Philly, who weren't plain bad but either fuck-ups who did bad things or businessmen who punished you for your mistakes just as they rewarded you for victories. Okay, maybe Peste was the exception. He was just evil. TV cops were always squeaky clean, which was bullshit. He was guessing, even though he hadn't fought in the war, that it was a similar thing with the Germans: they weren't any worse than us. He bet they were just like the Jersey Mob trying to grab some of your territory. Sure there was stuff with the Jews but he doubted that was your average German soldier. That was Hitler. People always thought they wouldn't make the same mistake, they would be more pure, they would be all moral and say 'I refuse to do it'. But he'd seen firsthand what happened when you thought you could say that to somebody more powerful. That guy 'Snake-Eyes', for instance. They called him that on account of he always bet against the shooter in any craps game. He was a standover guy for Repacholi. Repacholi was trying to bully some longshoremen into working for less money which, as a boss, was naturally his job. But an Irish fellow named Brennan welded them all together. Brennan wouldn't take a bribe for himself so Snake-Eyes was told to teach him a lesson but Snake-Eyes' old man and uncles had been longshoremen and he said, 'Not this guy. He's just trying to put food on the table. Sorry, boss, no.'

Blake heard about this from Jimmy and Vincent who were there at the time. How Repacholi looked at Peste. He seized Snake-Eyes and right then and there he chopped off the three middle fingers of each hand. That was the boss's idea of wit: the two fingers corresponded to snake eyes on the dice. They made sure Blake understood, so that when Repacholi called him over to his parking-garage basement and told him to clip Brennan, he did not even think of refusing. His tool of trade was a gun and Peste, who always carried, was standing right behind him. Blake did not want to do it. He wanted to say 'I refuse'. But the wave had already decided for him, was lifting him up, forcing him in the direction it wanted. The job itself might have presented no problems if Blake had been prepared to shoot Brennan in front of his kids. It could have been literally a walk in the park, but this was something Blake would not countenance, and so he'd been forced to wait. He finally shot Brennan during the seventh innings stretch of a Phillies v Cubs game when Brennan was coming back to his seat with a hot-dog. Used the smallest pistol he could find, a little two-shot, walked right up behind Brennan, kept walking when everybody else thought the guy with the hot-dog had stumbled or maybe had a heart attack. So, getting back to the German soldiers, he understood why they might have done what they did. All the same, he was disappointed to miss Doreen. It was one of those days when he could have done with her just being there.

□□□

It was definitely her. Even though it was a couple of months since she'd seen her, she recognised the awkward gait, the fair complexion that suggested milky cups of tea and shortbread somewhere back in the family line. She was attempting to arbitrate over some dispute between siblings in a poorly appointed playground: one rusting slide and two swings that had seen better days. The ward sister at the hospital had said everything had gone well with the birth. The pram wherein the new arrival must be was in arm's length of Peg. The sister had given Doreen the address, a street of weatherboards in a low section of town where the water stayed in deep pools after downpours. Doreen had walked through abandoned tricycles and upturned toys to the front door but before she knocked the neighbour, who was watering her roses, had told her to try the park. So here she was. There were a couple of pods of mothers and children but nobody in the immediate vicinity. This is the other side of the shopping aisle, she thought with a pang, the one where mothers buy White Wings mix and family size Weeties. The terrain here was miniature sandwiches with the corners cut off, coloured pencils, Disney comics, vaccinations, burping, bunny-rugs. She got out of the car and started over, was almost there when Peg turned and spied her.

'Hello,' Peg said, surprised, seemingly pleased. Doreen handed over the little fluffy toy chicken she'd bought at the florist.

'For you.'

Peg was flabbergasted but accepted it like she had the cigarette packet that time.

'Is this her? Or him?' Doreen was already on her way to peer into the pram.

'Her. Yvonne.'

Visible, just a head with a halo of thick black hair. She looked perfect.

'She's beautiful.'

'And then they grow up.' Peg indicated the other two, a boy and girl probably around five and three, they were yelling at each other because each wanted the same swing.

'James, let your sister go first.'

'She went first last time.'

'Do what you're told or I'll let your father know.'

That did the trick. Doreen said, 'I'm hoping you can help me. I'm pregnant.'

As she tidied up, out of the corner of her eye she watched the test pattern on the TV. She imagined what it would be like: tidying up ceaselessly, putting away toys strewn around the house. Then she put on the kettle and sat in her favourite armchair and watched the kids shows — *Superman*, *Crusader Rabbit*, *The Mickey Mouse Club*. She longed for those days when you felt you could be whatever you wanted: a princess, a cowgirl. Night dropped like a careless word in a tense conversation. You wanted to push it back into your mouth but you couldn't, time had moved on. Unlike the last few weeks when her appetite had run rampant, tonight it couldn't be hauled out of bed. She forced herself to heat a tin of spaghetti and ate it with toast. The news came on. She did her dishes, pulled out the ironing board and set to work on her small pile of clothes. She ironed dresses she'd bought in the city, imagined they were party frocks. There was no *Maverick* tonight but *Perry Mason* was on. Perry was smart and invariably left the prosecution guy with egg on his face. She felt sorry for that guy: always outsmarted. The advertisements were split in two for men and women. For women, soaps you should buy for the family, soap powder you should buy to wash the family clothes, washing-up liquid to clean the family dishes and what cleaning spray you should use for your bench. The mothers all had bobs and pleasant faces. The cigarette and car ads showed men in suits being admired by women who looked nothing like the women obsessed with cleaning but who, given enough time, soon would.

Life, for women, was all about erasing stains.

She watched her little egg-shaped screen until it went back to the test pattern. She imagined others driving by outside and seeing the little blue-grey glow from beneath her curtain. She would miss that.

14. The Trouble with Secrets

He'd decided to head further south because it was throwing a nice right-hander. About a half-hour into his surf he saw a figure on the beach in white. He knew the shape and took the next wave in.

'You're back.' Self-evident as that was, he couldn't help but yell it as he ran out of the surf, the plank under his arm.

'You seem surprised.'

Crane looked different, better, not so much younger as less resigned to defeat.

'I am.'

'Prison gives you time to think. Actually, not so much prison as no alcohol. I have a daughter and son. I felt the need to visit.'

It was cool on Blake's back but the wind was slowly drying him.

'How did that go?'

'One forgives me, one doesn't. You must think I'm an ungrateful bastard.'

Blake cast quickly through his brain, couldn't remember ever expecting anything from Crane. He just said, 'It was wrong. They wanted a patsy. If you weren't there, it could as easily have been me.'

'Well, thank you, anyway. I'll never be able to pay you back.'

'I don't need the money. You can do a month of free shows if you feel like it.'

'My inspiration has dried since I've been abstemious.'

'You're on the wagon?'

'I don't want to talk about it because the disappointment will only be greater when I lapse.'

'You might not.'

'Our sins define us, Horatio, not our good qualities. But I think you already know that.'

That was the thing with Crane, putting it out there, one sinner to another.

He said, 'Word is that Sergeant Les Nalder is my saviour but I don't believe that for a minute.'

'Andy is your saviour. He saw Stokes with the kid in the Hawaiian shirt, which I recognised as his old man's. That set the ball rolling.'

They were ambling back towards where Crane's shelter had stood before. What the hell, he may as well try. He asked Crane, 'You didn't see whoever it was in the car with Stokes?'

'No.'

'The Clarke kid denies it was him. Says he went off to scrounge together money to pay Stokes. And they found some prints in the car that don't belong to him or Stokes.'

They had reached the place where the shelter had been. Nothing was built but Crane had made a start, collecting forty-four gallon drums and some sheets of tin.

'You're welcome to stay at the Surf Shack.'

'Thank you, but I like the open air. You think the kid did it?'

'I don't know. His story is believable but he could be lying. He says he got the money together and drove to the motel. He claims a van swung out from the motel just before he arrived. He says the door to unit ten was already open. He pushed in, saw Stokes butchered. He threw up and drove off. The motel people didn't see any van.'

'Doesn't mean he made that up.'

'I know.'

'I've gone back over that night a thousand times in my head. The dance contest, lots of pretty girls. There was one blonde, she was seething.'

'She lost the dance contest.'

'I was drunk. Duck was smoking weed. There was a young girl on a bicycle who had danced.'

Kitty, Doreen's favourite.

Crane reached out and laid his hand on Blake's arm. 'Thanks for believing in me. It was a long time since anybody did. Including myself.'

'I didn't do all that much.'

We need a champion, all of us. Jimmy had been his. And Doreen. He'd promised himself he'd call in on her again, watch television. There were worse things.

The second thing he did when he walked in after she'd opened the door was look around for the TV. The first thing was hand her a bunch of flowers he'd bought at the florist. Jimmy always said that the best gift you can give a woman is flowers.

'They're beautiful, thank you.'

She beamed, began fussing for a vase.

'I wanted to cheer you up. You've looked blue lately.'

'Just tired.' She found a vase under the sink, poured in water.

'Where is it?'

'What?'

'The long-awaited television.'

'I sold it.'

He didn't understand women at all.

'I thought I'd like it but it just wasn't for me. I think I prefer the radio.'

She arranged the flowers. She didn't seem right though.

'Have I been working you too hard?'

'No, not at all.'

But she wasn't looking him in the eye. Maybe it was a personal thing? A boyfriend or some family problem. He'd chosen to know nothing at all about her life outside the Surf Shack.

'Crane's back.' He flexed his toes as he delivered the news.

That made her look at him.

'Sober,' he emphasised.

'I hope he thanked you.'

'He did.'

She placed the flowers on a table near the door. He wanted to spend time with her, couldn't help it. He cleared his throat because if the words caught it would be more awkward.

'We're rehearsing later but I thought … well I *was* thinking TV, but do you want to do something?'

'I'm going to Kitty's school play, *South Pacific*. She's got the lead role. You want to come?'

He wasn't ready to sit on a hard chair listening to a musical, and truth was what he'd really wanted was just some quiet time, him and Doreen, like it had been in the hospital room when they'd been waiting for Andy to get better.

'I'd have to leave halfway. We'll do it another time.'

'Sure.'

'I better let you get ready then. See you tomorrow. Have a good night.'

He let himself out. When he said he couldn't go to the play, in her eyes had been a look he recognised, disappointment. She actually wanted him to go with her. This was confusing, dangerous. He let people down, he was weak. No matter how much he bathed in the river of salt, no matter how much he sought to numb the pain or erase the past, he was the same person who had left Jimmy to have his brains blown out in a cheap room. If you cared about someone, like he did for Doreen, a care that was growing, then you should leave them be, for their own good.

She felt like pinching herself. Everything had worked out since that day at the library when she'd found the code-key to the mysteries of her life. The day, she liked to think of now, as the day she grew up. And here she was tonight, Nellie Forbush for real, sitting in the dressing-room with Mrs Wilson the costume person, fussing over every detail. Vocally she was passable, certainly as good as any of the other girls — and they'd all tried out, even Jenny who couldn't sing the Vegemite jingle, what a joke! It was her dancing, all those hours she'd been spending with Doreen, that had been the clincher. Mr Cobham, who was directing, actually dropped his clipboard. She didn't want to sound big-headed but from day one she knew she was going to get it because it was like following a map, connecting dots. The one thing that was putting a stopper on her excitement was what had been happening lately between her parents. Once she began reading a lot and taking in what she'd learned — listening to the sighs, understanding the import of words not spoken, the *absence* of things — she had come to understand them not as cardboard cut-outs but living, breathing people with their own ambitions and thwarted dreams. Their lives weren't perfect, they lived with disappointment the way some people live with backache. No matter, they had seemed to be able to deal with it. But things had changed recently.

At first, she thought it was simply her new awareness of the intricacies of their hitherto hidden world. But one day sport had been cancelled and she'd come home early and found her mother down the back garden on an old tree stump, dabbing her eyes with tissues. She began to listen out for scraps of telephone conversation between her mum and her friends, noted more frequent times when voices were dropped to exclude prying ears: hers. But it was clear from the lack of maternal harassment of recent times that she wasn't the topic of conversation. Her mum's mind was drifting too. She'd pack no lunch for her, or double. There were more drop-ins from Aunty Muriel, her mum's closest friend, not a real aunty.

More hushed conversations followed. Her first thought, that her mum was sick with some horrible disease, was dismissed when she saw that the same conversations were not repeated with her dad. Oh, there was a hush alright, but the lines on their mouths were drawn tight when she would 'surprise' them. And then they would make up some ridiculous gabble about the car or a neighbour, as if that was what they'd been talking about. One day at the tennis club she had set out to deliberately spy on them and had noted, from the safety of the drinks machine, her mother pull her hand away when her father tried to touch it. But even before then, she had concluded there was only one explanation.

Her father was having or had had an affair.

It was devastating. Her father was her hero. He came to every dance recital, every speech night, every sporting event. They washed the car together, played quoits on the back verandah. Often they shopped while Mum was in the salon having her hair done, selected chocolate to share during the Sunday Theatre on TV. Of course he had flaws. He had sought an alliance with Todd's father because it would have given him a status he wasn't confident of achieving by his own efforts. But if he'd been having an affair, that was just horrible. She was acutely aware of the embarrassment Shelley Unsworth had suffered when it was revealed her father was carrying on with that slut Wendy Avery. Somebody had spied them leaving a motel up near the Heads. Sordid, that was the word that always came to mind. It conjured discarded bras and dark rooms with blinds drawn, stiletto heels and men ripping ties from their work shirts. She shuddered. The Unsworths had divorced. That was even worse. She had speculated without success on who the 'other woman' might be. Her mum might be too stricken to do anything about it but not Kitty. Anyway, tonight her parents had travelled in together and she expected they still had good enough manners not to conduct a skirmish in public. Not on her big night. That would be death.

Kitty looked at herself in the mirror, felt a flush of satisfaction. She was perfect for Nellie Forbush and Nellie was perfect for her. She should have been nervous but she wasn't. She was ready. The boy playing opposite her as Emile was nowhere near as sophisticated as was required by the role but she didn't let that put her off. Nothing, not even her adulterous father, could divert her now.

'Three minutes.'

Henry Weston was the prompt and director's assistant. She took a deep breath, others fretted. Last-minute touches of make-up: boys in sailor suits flicking and punching each other, girls checking the mirror again and again, the babble of the audience rising, Mr Cobham's anxious last cigarette drifting in from the side door, the lights dim, a hush, one loud nervous laugh.

'But what's this one?' Her first lines would be spoken offstage. You nailed the first one, everything else would follow. She knew every line. Not just hers, everybody's. More than once in rehearsal somebody had slipped up and she'd been able to save the day.

Why couldn't husbands and wives love one another forever and ever?

'But what's this one?' She knew how she was going to deliver it with just the right degree of curious inflection. Henry Weston cued her. She got up from her chair and walked to where 'Emile' was jiggling nervously, shaking his fingers out like he was on the diving block for the fifty-five yards. He was the school's best swimmer but she blanked that out. He was Emile. The band finished the overture.

Blackout. She filled her lungs with air.

'But what's this one?'

It's funny how your brain has shadows and something can lurk there, something that should have been flushed out in the open by a patrolman's torch but it never happens, or not until you least expect it. He was out the back of the Surf Shack. He and Panza were already set up but as usual Duck had been late so Blake thought he'd help out by grabbing the kit from the van. Duck carried out the bass drum so Blake just reached in to haul out a floor-tom and a cymbal stand. That's when he smelled the marihuana, still fresh. Duck was late because he had been smoking that weed again. Which Blake'd asked him not to, at least not around the club, and maybe Duck had figured in order to comply he'd smoke his weed before he arrived. It wasn't that though that pricked Blake. It was recalling when he'd asked Duck to stop. That was as a result of the cop, Vernon, who had come to the Surf Shack because a marihuana cigarette had been found in Valerie Stokes' motel room — along with a matchbook from the Surf Shack. Valerie Stokes had never been in the Surf Shack but she could have picked up the matchbook at, say, the Heads. Could have. But she hadn't likely picked it up at Clarke's house. Winston Clarke had never been in to the Surf Shack, nor his son. Not even on that night in question. So, whoever left that matchbook might be her killer. And whoever gave her the dope might be her killer ...

'Sorry I was late, man. Had a blocked drain, last minute.'

He looked at Duck, thinking thoughts he didn't want to think.

They rehearsed one new song he'd written and a bunch of others just to stay across them but his mind was elsewhere the whole time. He told Duck he may as well pack up, he just wanted to run through the new chords again with Panza. Duck didn't need an invitation. Panza and he ran through the chords — a good thing anyway because Panza had one of the changes wrong.

'I was thinking about that night the Stokes girl was killed — in case the police interview me again with the trial and all, or I get called as some sort of witness. When you left, was Crane out the back?'

'Yeah, remember I spoke to the lawyer and he asked me all this stuff. Crane was sitting there when I left.'

'What about Duck? When did he go?'

'He left pretty quickly. There were a few of those contestant girls milling around. I thought Duck must have scored with one of them 'cause he left in a hurry like he was on a promise. He had to jam his brakes on near the exit — nearly hit one of the girls — the sexy blonde. Wasn't his fault actually, she wasn't looking, pulled out in front, she'd just had a barney with the boyfriend.'

Blake remembered the blonde. He searched for a name ... Brenda.

Panza was worried. 'Crane's in the clear, isn't he?'

'I think so, but you know, cops ... I like to get a picture of how it was.'

'The girl that got killed. She was never in here, right?'

'No. Thank God.'

But she had been outside earlier. And so had Duck.

It was almost ten, probably too late to call Nalder, but he called anyway.

'Hello?'

'It's me, Sergeant. Glad you're still up.'

'*Untouchables*, just finished. I told you not to bother me at home.'

'I'm sorry. One thing: what make was the van Thomas Clarke claimed he saw leaving the Ocean View Motel?'

'Why the fuck do you want to know?'

'Please.'

'Bedford. He said it was a Bedford.'

Duck's van was a Bedford.

Even before Doreen took her seat in the school hall, she was feeling the happiest she had in months. Blake had called around with flowers, and though she was sure he didn't mean that in a romantic way, dammit that made it even better, because Blake wasn't trying to woo her, just to do something to make her happy. That was romantic. The school hall doubled as a gymnasium. It was boomy and the rows of school chairs were a bit skew-whiff, having obviously been set up by the junior kids who looked awkward standing around in school uniforms. The parents had dressed up, women in long gloves, men in jackets and ties. She waited till most of them were seated before looking for a single seat. The band consisted of a woman who was likely the music teacher at an upright piano, a boy about fifteen on drums whose hair had been Brylcreemed and parted, and some high-school horn players. She made out two saxophones, a flute and a clarinet. She was guessing they were all music students. It wasn't Duke Ellington but they were in tune and in time enough that you could recognise the songs in the overture. The lights dimmed, the audience hushed and she felt her heart beating fast. She was more nervous for Kitty than she would have been for herself. Lately Kitty had not only got herself back on track but grown stronger. She prayed that it went well, did not want to see Kitty back in that horrible place of a couple of months ago. She was a great kid, funny, talented and she'd worked so hard on her dancing. Kitty spoke offstage.

'But what's this one?'

A moment later Kitty strode on. She was like a fireball sucking oxygen toward her. The other kids weren't in the same league. Even though Kitty didn't have the greatest voice you'd ever heard, she went off here and there, she had so much bounce and confidence and vitality that you didn't care. She made 'A Cockeyed Optimist' her song, and when you knew what had happened to her in the holidays, the triumph was all the sweeter. Kitty had been telling her she wanted to be an actress and now, looking at her on stage you could see it. Doreen wished she'd had that confidence but you have it or you don't. She wasn't a leading lady, she was chorus, good legs, could dance most styles. She remembered all the sensible things your teachers told you: if you're in the chorus you may not get the star on your door but you'll always be in work. The leading ladies were either hot as a bushfire or cold as a Canberra frost. Maybe that was true, she'd not been long enough in stage musicals to know. The money in cabaret and clubs was better. Personally in the play, it wasn't Nellie that she identified with but the Asian girl who fell in love with the American. She felt teary when he was killed but that was quickly smashed away by her applauding palms. Kitty made a point of looking for her. Because she was hidden behind a tall man, she had to move her head so Kitty could see she was there.

Later, everybody milled around in the foyer or spilled out onto the lawn, a few clutching cardboard cups of orange cordial. The vibe was buoyant. Doreen felt like an intruder and would have gone home but she wanted to congratulate Kitty. Kitty emerged, a gaggle of people telling her how wonderful she was but she was only half-listening and when her eyes found Doreen she raced to her.

'What did you think?'

'You were terrific.'

Kitty squeezed the life out of her. 'Thanks to you.'

'No. No thanks to me. That was all you. I showed you a few steps that was all.'

Kitty started dragging her. 'Come and meet my parents. I've told them all about you.'

Doreen allowed herself to be pulled across the lawn to where a couple, their backs to them, were talking.

'Mum, Dad, this is Doreen.'

They turned.

Doreen's heart stopped. Kitty's mum had a little stole around her shoulders and Doreen tried to concentrate on that because Kitty's father was somebody she recognised: Adrian, the man she'd brought back to her place from the golf club.

It was like looking through a haze with everything in slow motion. She saw his recognition, his shock and attempt to kill it but, though her legs were jelly, she fought to smile politely as you would to a stranger, and focused instead on Kitty's mum, a pretty woman who had been to the hairdresser. She extended her hand, they shook. Kitty's mum gushed about how wonderfully she had helped Kitty. The words were a 45 on 33 rpm. Her head was pounding, she wanted to burst into tears. Somewhere in the background some excited members of the cast had broken into 'Some Enchanted Evening'. When she finally risked a glance at Kitty she was met by glacier eyes.

She knew.

Get away, get away, get away. Her heels clipped through the carpark to where she had parked the Beetle. The stars that had seemed to twinkle like sequins were now pennies on a dead man's eyes. She reached the car door, fumbled for a key.

'You bitch.' Kitty ran at her. 'You fucking slut.'

Doreen's cheek reverberated with the power of the slap. Kitty was crying, fists balled, punching her arms now.

'Why my dad? Why? You fucking tramp.'

What could she say? I didn't know, didn't realise? But you had known it was somebody's husband, somebody's father, hadn't you? You'd just used loneliness as a convenient blindfold. She stood there accepting, knowing her pain was nothing to what Kitty was feeling. She wanted the punishment, the more the better. She could not forgive herself, let alone expect forgiveness from others.

15. The First Stone

Blake's knuckles rammed hard on the door of the sleep-out. Duck lived out the back of his grandmother's, what they called here a weatherboard. There was a stumbling, shuffling. He'd no doubt been asleep. It was just after one a.m. Blake had tried to wait for the new day, had driven around the town's near silent grid going out of his head. There was no point heading home trying to catch zeds. He had to know. A bolt scraped on the inside of the door as it was pulled. The old wooden door swung open. Duck was half-asleep, wearing black footy shorts and a fleecy shirt. He rubbed his eyes.

'What's up, mate? What's happened?'

Blake shoved inside. He'd only been here twice before. It reminded him of a teenager's bedroom: comics, an old game of Crow Shoot stacked neatly in a box on top of Scrabble. Duck's parents had moved north years ago but Duck had stayed and learned the plumbing trade. His nanna cooked, did his washing and gave him a rent-free room where he could practise his drums.

'The night Valerie Stokes was killed, where were you?'

Duck blinked. 'What do you mean where was I? We did the gig.'

'After that?'

'I came back here. What is this?'

'You gave that weed to her.'

'No. I told you, maybe somebody else …'

'Don't lie to me, Duck.'

'I'm not. There were kids out the back, I might have given them a joint. For fuck's sake …'

'You screamed out of the carpark, Panza saw you.'

'So?'

'You were meeting Stokes at the motel.'

'You sure you haven't been smoking my joints?'

He grabbed Duck, shoved him against the wall.

'You killed Stokes.'

'What?' Duck couldn't cover the fear in his voice by surprise.

'You lit out after her. You drove up the coast to the motel.'

'I told you, I drove home. You're fucking crazy.'

'Your van was spotted at the motel.'

It was a lie but when you lie to somebody who is lying himself, sometimes the shell hits the magazine. He saw the horror in Duck's face, could almost hear the rush of thoughts through his brain.

'I didn't kill her. Honest, man.'

'Come on, Duck. When the kid turned up, she was already dead. He saw your van leaving.'

Duck was breathing heavily now. Blake realised he should have brought a weapon but he'd been too distracted. He tensed in case Duck made for something.

'I promise you man. I did not see Valerie Stokes. I did not give her dope. I did not kill her.'

'Your van ...'

'Okay. Yes, I was at the motel. But not to see Valerie Stokes. I met with somebody else.'

He was desperate now, throwing out his life jacket to keep the boat afloat.

'You expect me to believe that?'

'It's true. That's why I rushed there.'

'Fine. Who is she? What's her name?'

Duck's eyes bulged, he looked like he was going to throw up.

'Duck, if you're telling the truth, give me her name.'

He went to talk, couldn't. Tried again, weak. 'It's not a she.'

Blake didn't understand. Duck must have read his confusion.

'That's why I couldn't say anything. I was there. With a man.'

Blake stood there, mute, his feet set among two piles of comics on the floor.

'I'm a homo, Blake.'

Blake didn't know any homosexuals. Well, he probably did without knowing it, he figured. In his days hanging around the Mob it wasn't the sort of thing you advertised.'

'You're saying that's why you were at the motel.'

'His name is Michael. He's a family man. Please, the cops have already interviewed him and cleared him. Don't tell them about this, for his sake.'

'This Michael live around here?'

'Toorolong. I can put you in touch if you don't believe me.'

Blake was weighing it slowly. 'Tell me what happened that night from when we finished.'

'I'd met up with Michael earlier that day.'

'Where?'

'Where do you think? The kind of place we have to: dark places that smell or are broken, deserted.'

'So you'd already made a rendezvous?'

'Yes. The motel suited him. I loaded the van and left: nearly hit the blonde from the dance comp. Not my fault, she pulled straight out in front of me. She'd been shouting at her boyfriend, wasn't watching.'

'This was what time?'

'Ten maybe.'

'You went straight to the motel.'

'Yeah. I got there a little before ten-thirty. Michael had been waiting for a couple of hours. Neither of us saw anything down near the far unit where she was. I don't even remember her car.'

'You didn't see or hear any other cars coming or going?'

'I wasn't thinking about other cars. It was quiet though, late Thursday, who's around?'

'You left, when?'

'About half past eleven.'

That jibed with what the Clarke kid said. According to the motel guy, Stokes hadn't checked in till nine forty-five that night. If Clarke was telling the truth and she was dead when he arrived, she was killed between nine forty-five and eleven fifteen. If Duck was telling the truth, she could have been killed while he was doing whatever he was doing.

Duck said, 'This is crazy. I did not kill that girl. I'm not even attracted to women. It's just an act.'

'Why?'

'Why do you think? You were going to have a poofta in your band?'

'If he keeps time.' He told himself that was true but to be honest it was nothing he'd thought about. 'I want to speak to Michael, and I want your fingerprints.'

'You going to tell Panza and Doreen?'

'What you do is your business, Duck. Just don't lie to me.'

'I'm not.' His bottom lip quivered. 'You don't know how hard it is.'

'I get it. But if you're using this as an excuse ...'

'I'm queer, man. That's the simple truth.'

After he left Duck's, he drove to the beach and listened to the waves crashing in the dark. He'd made Duck put his fingers into an inkpad he used for receipts from his plumbing business, made him press them into paper. How else could he eliminate him? If they matched the prints in Stokes' car, he'd know Duck was lying. But he didn't think so. The image of him as some cop, Duck some criminal, poked and prodded him like a school bully. Why couldn't he have let it be? Okay, he'd wanted to clear Crane, there he had justification, but Thomas Clarke wasn't his responsibility. It probably was just the Clarke kid grabbing at straws; he saw Duck's van, he wanted to blow smoke.

Yet something refused to let him leave it like that. He didn't know Val Stokes. She was nothing to him. Sure he'd been to the Cross, he understood her life, sounded like she was on the up and up, had a boyfriend now but she'd lapsed, slid back for the chance of easy money. It was probably a trick gone wrong, a risk of the game. He wasn't judging her, far from it. What he'd done for a living, that was shameful. No, it wasn't because he wanted justice for Val Stokes. It was as if he had to push on, because this was his home now. He'd never felt like he had a home before. Somebody had murdered Val Stokes and in doing so had trashed his turf. That's why it was personal, that's why he had to see this through. Right, Jimmy?

Nalder had been given a copy of the set of prints found in Stokes' car, just in case some local crime generated the same set. Blake had to study these fingerprints closely but he could see pretty clearly that the set of prints the police had found did not match Duck's.

'Whose are they?' Nalder had wanted to know when Blake had laid down the paper with the prints.

'They don't match, so it's not them. That's all that matters.'

'Don't keep me in the dark, son.'

'I find something, you'll get it.'

'I don't want you to find anything,' the cop had said. 'I like everything fine just how it is. The only reason I'm helping you is that if the Clarke kid didn't do it, the murderer is still out there. That's the only reason. No grandstanding.'

Grandstanding was the last thing Blake wanted. He drove up to Toorolong and drove by the house that Duck said was Michael's. Kids' scooters outside an ordinary-looking place. Duck had arranged for Blake to meet Michael at the Toorolong pub and had told him that Michael would wear green. The beer garden was a few pieces of lumpy furniture, a lattice fence. Blake was the only person there. Michael appeared through a little archway that led directly to a rear carpark.

'Don't worry. Duck told me all about you. I knew I'd recognise you. Mind you …'

He gestured at the empty garden. He was younger than Blake would have imagined, thirty-one or two, a cheap suit, jet-black hair. Duck had said he was some kind of salesman. Michael went inside to get himself a beer. It was a little after five, and chilly, but it was private and pleasant under the trees. A labrador wandered past. There was a minigolf course across the way, thinly populated on a weeknight. Michael came back out and sat opposite him on a weathered wooden bench.

'You arrived at the motel at what time?'

'About seven-thirty. I stayed in my room, listened to the radio. I didn't hear anything much — maybe a vehicle coming or going but I wasn't looking. I knew Duck wouldn't be getting there till around ten.'

His story matched Duck's.

'He came straight to your room?'

'Why wouldn't he? You know Duck. You really think he could stab some woman to death?'

Blake didn't answer. He knew lots of people who killed and who looked like a greengrocer or a schoolteacher. There was nothing exclusive about murder. He was living proof.

Crane had his pants rolled to his knees as he waded in the shallows looking for interesting shells or detritus from passing boats.

'You thought it was somebody else?'

'Yeah, but that didn't pan out.'

After Toorolong, Blake had felt in need of companionship. His field of choice had narrowed to Crane or Doreen. Crane was on the way in from Toorolong.

'Why can't you accept it's the kid?' Crane studied a twisting shell, declared it unworthy for collection, tossed it back.

'The blood. The shirt. I saw the photos. She was butchered. I don't buy that an eighteen-year old does that, then showers, puts on a shirt, pukes because now he's thinking about what he's done. If he killed her, then puked, then showered, maybe.'

What he was thinking about was a kid named Maurice Ekerman who had been a year younger than him. Ekerman was weedy, glasses, not super bright. He had a stepfather who treated him like shit. The stepdad used to wash his car on the street every Sunday and he would berate Maurice Ekerman about everything he was doing wrong. Sometimes Ekerman would come down by the railyards where Jimmy and Vin and, if he was lucky enough to get an invite, Blake hung out and drank soda and looked at dog-eared girly magazines. Often Ekerman would have a bruise, on his face, arms. They all knew it was the stepdad but that wasn't unusual. Most of them had bruises from stepdads or real fathers or 'uncles', who were basically men screwing moms. One morning when Blake had been walking down Ekerman's street he saw a whole mob of cops milling around the Ekerman brownstone. There was a squad car too, and a coroner's wagon and, naturally, a crowd. Then the coroner's wagon drove off and he had a real sick feeling in his stomach because he knew it was Maurice Ekerman in there and that they all should have done something long before. *He* should have done something long before. And then there was like a gasp from the crowd and he saw two cops exiting the Ekerman house and between them, hands cuffed behind his back, was Maurice Ekerman. He was covered in blood, even his glasses, his cheeks, chin. Turned out he had taken a kitchen knife and carved up the stepfather. If Tom Clarke had murdered Val Stokes, he was sure that's what he would have looked like.

'If the evidence is that slim, he'll get off.' Crane had finally found a spider shell up to scratch and was wading back to shore.

'Whoever left prints on the ceiling of her car, I think, is our killer. And I would much rather know that than leave it to a jury to acquit the kid because the evidence is weak. You sure you didn't see who it was?'

'Certain. He was just a shape.'

They picked up their sandals and headed towards the beach shack that Crane had mostly rebuilt.

'You're off the booze?'

'For now.'

'How rough is that?'

'A tempest, sir, a veritable tempest.'

'You up to working tomorrow night?'

'I hope you use the term loosely. If so, I'll be there.'

ooo

It was weird doing the gig. Things had changed forever. Neither he nor Duck had addressed their previous meeting before they started. Panza was oblivious. It was probably the best Duck had played and the crowd was the biggest yet. They loved everything they did. Not just 'The Twist' and 'Apache' but even the original songs. When they finally left after two encores, Crane was waiting side of stage.

'Nice set,' he said. 'Now I get to wreck the vibe.'

Crane was received with moderate applause. Those with previous experience of him almost uniformly left for the bar. The ones who stayed were devotees. Crane stood legs apart, took a deep breath, seized the microphone like it was his tango partner.

> Get out of your clothes, get into your scuba
> There's a strange new world, man, happening down in Cuba
> They've got cubists and communists and hotsky-to-Trotskyists
> Staging a revolution that might threaten the constitution
> The peasants are comin' at us with a flower and sickle
> But JF can take 'em down by the thousands for less than a nickel
> He's got missiles pointed in the right direction
> One mighty stratospheric ejection
> JFK's ready to rhumba, all action and A-bomb no time to slumber
> Get out of your clothes and into your scuba
> We'll soon be exploring the lost city of Cuba.

He was side of stage wiping down the guitar when he looked up saw Duck. Crane was still rolling in the background.

'Great gig.'

'That's it, Blake. I'm quitting. I'll see out the weekend.'

Blake stood there with the rag in his hand, not exactly surprised. He said, 'You don't have to do that.'

'Yeah I do. Time I moved on. Sydney or Brisbane. Besides, I'm not good enough for your stuff. I'm a plumber, not a drummer.'

'This is all coming together now. You were great.'

'You don't know how many gigs I wanted to hear you say that.'

Blake felt ashamed in a whole different way.

'Things can't be the same, Blake. You know that. You think about me different now. It's there in your eyes.'

'Hey, what you do ...'

'I don't mean that. I know you're not judging me but you feel I'm different to what I was, but I'm not. We can't put the genie back in the bottle, man. Anyway, like I said, I was just playing at this. You're the real deal.'

'I'm going to miss you.'

Duck nodded. 'Same. I know of a drummer up the Heads who might be right for you. I'll tell him to ring you.'

He hugged Duck, spontaneously, said the words that he'd never had a chance to with Jimmy. 'I'm sorry.'

□□□

Whether that tramp Doreen was the only one her father had been unfaithful with she didn't know but she had seen it in their faces, both of them, the cowardice, the deceit, like a fly frozen in an iceblock. Obviously seeing one another there shocked the hell out of them so until then the tramp clearly didn't know the man she'd fucked was her father. Sordid images grabbed her: faded neon, whisky tumblers, a hump in his car or back at her place. Predatory bitch. No wonder Blake would have nothing to do with her. He probably knew the real Doreen.

Maybe, thought Kitty, I should make a play for Blake? That would really hurt her. But then as quickly as it had leapt, she knocked it down. She learned from the Todd experience that if you go after the best-looking men, you wind up burned. But on the other hand, Blake might not know just how depraved Doreen was. She could send him an anonymous note along the lines of 'your employee fucks married men'. The mere idea gave her a little kick of satisfaction. You couldn't trust anybody, that's what she had learned this year. Not Todd, her father or her so-called best friend. All those hours hanging out together, what a waste of time, what a big fat lie. She'd told that bitch her innermost thoughts and fears. She'd been there after the Todd thing but who was to say that wasn't just prurient interest?

Kitty felt sorry for her mother, tried to pay more attention to her, tell her that her hair looked nice, go shopping with her but her mum was fucking hopeless, just carrying on like nothing had changed. Kitty finally fronted her, told her to her face: I know Dad's been unfaithful. Her mother denied it at first. She was so weak. Told her to go away and stop talking such horrible lies.

This was a dumb place, the stupid 'Heights' bullshit, the one dumb drive-in and the way the hoons revved their engines and stupid girls lay in the back of station wagons and panel vans facing the screen as if they were cool. And everybody collected snow domes. And women wore charm bracelets with stupid little charms from where they had been on holiday, which was mainly nowhere much. She couldn't wait to get out, be an actress. That stupid moll Brenda epitomised — yes, *epitomised*, a word most of these apes wouldn't even know because they read nothing more demanding than *Women's Weekly* or comics — all that was wrong with the place. She'd walk around in her silly white chemist smock as if she was actually a chemist when all she was good for was dispensing jellybeans and Ovaltine. Word was Todd Henley wouldn't have anything to do with her now but she still carried on like he was smitten by her. They deserved each other.

She managed the last few paces to the house, her school bag ridiculously heavy. She took the side path, walked in through the back door, and dropped her bag on her bedroom floor where it made such a thump her little glass and crystal collection vibrated. She headed for the kitchen. Her mum was sitting at the table in a housecoat turning the pages of a magazine. She'd just made herself a Nescafé. How she could drink that muck was unbelievable.

'Hi, love.'

'Hello.'

She opened the fridge, pulled out a large Fanta and poured the fizzy orange liquid into her favourite tumbler, which had pictures of little beach umbrellas and beach balls. She sat at the opposite end of the table to her mother and sipped, watching her mum's eyes following the story of Princess Margaret or Elizabeth Taylor. She suddenly felt a deep warmth towards her. She wondered what Edith Wharton would make of this domestic scene, her sitting there, still child enough to have a favourite glass with transfers on the outside, passing judgement. She faced off with her better self: you have been too embarrassed to tell her about Todd, and yet you expect her to open up about dad's adultery.

What choice did her mum really have? Kick her father out? Demand a divorce? Everybody knew how that ended. The blame wound up as much on the woman: she couldn't satisfy him, she got what she deserved. She'd become an outcast in her own land, be forced to flee to the Gold Coast where all the divorced women seemed to congregate, getting suntans and living in apartment buildings off the proceeds of their house sales until the money was all gone. Eventually they might get a job in a shoe store or a cake shop serving other divorcees. No tennis club, no big Christmas party competing for the honour of best tuna mornay. She got up from her chair, walked to the other end of the table and hugged her mum as tight as she could.

ᗡᗡᗡ

The weekend had been huge. Last night, the Saturday, had turned into a Duck farewell party. Doreen had done up a banner, the band rocked. The replacement drummer had made contact with Blake and driven down to see the show. He liked what he saw. Blake had not risen till nearly nine and by the time he surfed, changed and had finally made it to the Surf Shack it was near eleven. Andy was outside tidying the empties.

'Sorry, haven't had a chance to do the banner yet.'

Blake told him not to worry. He went inside, grabbed a stepladder and set to work. Even with the doors open the smell of booze and smoke never left. Andy came back in to help but Blake told him he was fine. Andy studied the fish.

'The Siamese are behaving themselves.'

'Good to hear.'

'I've been remembering more stuff,' said Andy, still looking into the glowing water of the tank. 'About those guys. Before they beat me up, they smashed the tank with a cricket bat. I tried to stop them, honest.'

'I know you would have.'

Andy was upset, his voice tighter than usual. 'I felt so … weak.'

'You're not weak, Andy.'

He stayed silent for a time. Then he said, 'That's not Audrey, is it?'

'No. It's a new Audrey.'

Andy nodded slowly to himself. 'I'll bag the tablecloths for Doreen.'

Every week Doreen washed the tablecloths in the laundry out back. She'd stripped them the night before and dumped them on the floor, it was the easiest way. Blake thought he might restock the jukebox. People got bored with the same old tracks. He kept a cupboard full of 45s in his office. Whenever somebody was heading to the city or even up to the

Heads he would give them money to buy a couple of new singles. On top of the pile he found a brown paper bag that contained a single he hadn't seen before. He took it out, studied it: The Beatles. Good name. Doreen appeared in the doorway.

'Ah, that, I forgot to tell you, I put it there yesterday.'

She looked a little thin but otherwise great. Doreen kept talking.

'One of the girls I danced with, Joan. She's a stewardess now. She says they're all the rage in London.'

'You okay?'

'Of course.'

'I worry you work too hard. You heard it?'

'Not yet.'

'Let's have a listen.'

They walked to the jukebox.

'I forgot to ask. How was the play the other night?'

'Kitty was fantastic.'

'I hope she appreciated what you did. You've helped her a lot.'

Doreen made a kind of false smile. 'Actually, I didn't help at all.'

Frank Ifield came out and The Beatles went in. The record was called *Please Please Me*. It kicked off with a jangly guitar hook over an R'n'B beat and then the vocals crashed in and grabbed you. Made you want to sing and dance at the same time. He looked at Doreen, she looked at him. This was different. Like Chuck Berry but even more bounce.

When it finished she said, 'It's good.'

'No. It's great.' They spun it again. Blake knew nothing was going to be the same. He knew the music The Twang was playing was already as good as dead.

Doreen said, 'I'm going to do the laundry.'

As she exited, Andy entered, in a pickle. He didn't seem to notice the music at all.

'That washer's gone in the tap. I've looked in the keg-shed but I can't find one.'

Blake said he was pretty sure there were some in the office. Andy followed. Something Andy had said earlier echoed.

'You said you've been remembering stuff?'

'Yeah. Every now and again I remember something.'

'What about the night of the dance competition, that Thursday night. You remember anything more about the guy in the shirt?'

'The police asked me all about that. They said I might be called as a witness.'

'Yeah, but anything new?' They were in the office. He was unstacking wooden soft-drink crates. In the third one down, he had screws and washers. Andy started looking for what he needed.

'I haven't thought. This one.' He held up the washer.

'Did you remember seeing Valerie Stokes arrive?'

'No. But I remember her car because the police showed me photos.'

'You didn't see anybody in it with her?'

He hesitated. 'No.'

'But what?'

'I think … I mean I'm pretty sure …' he shook his head. 'It's hard, I get a bit confused, it's just tiny little pieces of things that I had forgotten.'

Blake was patient. 'I get it. But what?'

'I have one flash. Some bloke walking from the car … or maybe not like out of the seat but from right near there so I think that's where he came from because there weren't any other cars around. Not that I remember. Not there where hers was.'

Blake, keeping his excitement strapped down: 'You recognise this guy?'

'I've seen him once or twice but I don't know him.'

Doreen appeared at the door. 'There's some man here says he wants to speak to the boss.'

She didn't have to spell it out. Doreen's radar was excellent. Whoever it was, she was wary.

Blake pointed at her, an idea had formed. 'You had some photos up from the watusi dance contest, right?'

'Yes. After a week I took them down.'

'You still got them?'

'In a shoebox. In here I think.'

She got down on her knees and started looking in a sliding cupboard.

'Andy, I want you to go through them, see if you can find the man you think you saw near the car.'

'I've got to fix this.' He held up the washer.

'Don't worry about that.'

Blake smelled trouble right away. The man was tall, and the way he leaned against the bar you knew he had a hard body underneath the grey suit. Maybe he was a cop or an ex-cop. Blake looked him in the eye, playing the curious businessman.

'Blake Saunders.'

'How do you do, Mr Saunders.' The man extended his hand for a shake. Blake allowed it.

'How can I help you, Mr …?'

'Smith. It's more how I can help you. I believe some business associates of mine may have spoken to you.'

So Nalder had been right. Here was the back-up plan for the Queensland bookie.

'Yeah. I hope they bought some of the insurance they were selling.'

'Smith' allowed himself a smile.

'Tragic, but it just goes to show, everybody needs insurance, even those selling.'

'You too, Mr Smith?'

'Of course. I come heavily insured.'

And he let his jacket open just enough to show the butt of a revolver. This time they meant business.

'I really don't think I need it.'

'I really think you do, Blake. Imagine if you had a fire here. Imagine if that glorious piece of snatch that showed me in was … scarred for life. You wouldn't live with yourself.'

Easy now. Easy.

'What are you suggesting?'

'Our insurance means you can rest easy. And it's only fifteen pounds a week.'

'Your mates were offering twelve.'

Smith sucked his teeth. 'Sadly they were too nice for their own good. Shall we say a month in advance, cash?'

Blake fought the urge to bite back. 'Seems like a great deal. Nothing bad will ever come my way, right?'

'That's right. You can sleep real easy.'

Doreen was working hard at keeping everything normal. After the blow-up with Kitty, she wanted to crawl into a deep hole, like some reptile. Everything was shit, everything. When she'd walked in the door from the play, the first thing she had seen were the flowers Blake had left. The tears exploded: for all that had been lost, that might have been. She'd stayed in bed all the next day. She'd hoped work might help, told herself be smooth and strong as concrete. And she would be — for an hour or two. After that, she was more a rope whose strands were fraying one by one, feeling the pull and strain with less reserves to resist than a moment before. She retrieved the box of photos and put them on the desk for Andy. She was there but not. Images crashed through her brain like a big dumper: sliding her drink over her coaster at the golf club, listening with amusement to the origin of her name; a doctor's surgery, old thumbed *Pix*; the bare walls of *that* room, the tube light above and the instructions about what to do if bleeding continues while all the time your ears are ringing like a bell at the side of a boxing ring and your face and arms are numb; then Kitty striding across the stage, she's gonna wash that man right out of her hair, the smell of orange cordial and the sting of the slap across her face …

Andy had said something.

'What?'

He was pointing. 'This bloke. I think he was the one.'

16. Match

Blake was looking at the photo, which showed a young guy looking up at the stage where the blonde and Kitty were facing off. He'd sent Andy outside. He and Doreen had the office to themselves.

'Vaguely remember him. Who is he?'

'His name is Todd Henley. Local royalty. Here's the thing, I think it was the next night or maybe the one after he took Kitty to the drive-in, practically raped her. She only escaped because Brenda ...' she tapped the image of Brenda on stage, '... attacked the car with her shoe.'

'Brenda is his girlfriend?'

'Obviously she likes to think so.'

Things were clicking into place like tumblers on a lock. What had Duck said? The blonde, Brenda, had nearly driven into him because she'd been fighting with the boyfriend. Maybe because Todd Henley had been screwing Val Stokes.

Doreen was still talking. 'Todd Henley was the school hot-shot. Kitty and all the girls swooned over him. He was captain of the rugby team, the best swimmer. He goes to university up in Brisbane, I think.'

Blake spoke his thoughts aloud. 'Val Stokes comes here to meet up with Thomas Clarke in the parking lot. While she's waiting, Val and Henley lock eyes. Maybe he's got the readies. They do it right there in the car.'

Doreen joined in. 'Brenda realises he's been having it off with Stokes. They argue. She heads off in a huff.'

'Todd isn't going to take that. He's a sports star. He knows where Stokes is going. She mentioned it, or he follows her. He could be the one who brought the joint. He's a popular guy. Duck gives a joint to one of the girls. They pass it to Todd ...'

Blake was pacing around the room, the picture in his head almost complete. 'He drives to the motel, gets there before Clarke. Stokes lets him in. She demands money or whatever. They argue. He's already furious. He stabs her to death.'

'What about the knife?'

'Maybe he has it in his car anyway. Or, if he's a psycho, he blames Stokes for the problem with Brenda and when he leaves here he goes home to get it, determined to kill her. Which he does. Wipes his prints, showers ...'

An idea crash-tackled him.

'You said he was a sports star.' He opened the drawer, lifted out the melted metal pin he'd found in the incinerator at Clarke's car yard. 'This the kind of the thing they give to school athletes?'

Doreen examined it. 'Sure is. That could easily be the school crest.'

It was charred but faint lines could be discerned.

Doreen said, 'And you know something else? I remember he worked there at the car yard for a while. Washing cars. The girls used to stand by the fence to see him with his shirt off.'

'It's gotta be him.'

Doreen examined the pin. 'You think you can prove it?'

Her blonde hair was pulled back in a ponytail. He'd watched her take her lunch break in the park, home sandwiches, and now her white smock was moving along the footpath back towards the chemist with the unhurried tempo of a sheet of paper caught in the wind.

'Hi, Brenda.'

She swivelled to see who had addressed her, the natural judgement on her pouty mouth, high cheekbones being negative but then the lips curled upwards and a glint appeared in her eye.

'I know you. You're in the band. You own the Surf Shack.'

'That's right. Blake.'

'So what's happening ... Blake.'

She enjoyed rolling the name off her lips. Everything about her was Tuesday Weld sexy.

'I wanted to ask you something ...'

She was anticipating an invitation, a date, he could sense the body language.

'... are you still going out with Todd?'

'Sort of.'

Meaning perhaps she was open to a better offer.

'I don't get it. Pretty girl like you. He screws some babe in the carpark and you haven't dumped him.'

Her chin jutted. 'What are you talking about?'

'You know. That girl. The night of the dance contest.'

Now she was openly suspicious, if not hostile. 'I have to go to work. I don't like people talking trash about Todd.'

'Come on. People heard you arguing. And next thing you know he's taken some other girl to the drive-in?'

'Get lost.'

Blake followed her. 'He's a killer. You need to be careful.'

She swung at him, glared. 'How dare you. He never killed that girl. Tom Clarke did.'

'You don't believe that. Listen, for your own good, go to the police.'

'Why don't you mind your own business?'

'You're playing with fire. He killed Val Stokes, burned his clothes in the incinerator at the car yard.'

'There's no way he killed that slut.'

'And you're sure.'

'I am. He was with me, all night. Now scram like the bug you are.'

Blake watched her stride back to the chemist shop. He didn't believe her for an instant. She'd finished the night of the dance contest on bad terms with Henley, roaring out of the carpark. She didn't seem to care he might have butchered Val Stokes. She was a girl who had planned the engagement and wedding in her head, everything from the bridesmaids' dresses to the waltz. She'd decided where they would own their first home and how many children they would have. She'd probably worked out their names. No stupid Yank was going to upset that dream.

But without Brenda Holsch onside, he did not have enough to take to Nalder. Nalder was swanning around town playing the big man. He was not going to be prepared to alienate town royalty and his new Homicide friends unless he had a lot more than a hunch. Andy's ID was qualified and now Blake had managed to give Henley an alibi. He cursed himself. He'd broken his own rules, jumped in without planning, didn't even have an exit route. He could have played it way smarter, got Doreen to befriend the girl, win her confidence. This was a disaster. First thing Brenda would do would be to tell Henley, prepare him. He had to move fast.

The rat-tat-tat of sprinklers over bowling green lawns, the morning sun glinting off the chrome of new cars: the Heights. Blake cruised past the Henley household, an architect-designed angular house in the most exclusive circle of the suburb. The Heights wasn't the kind of place you could just park your car and wait, somebody would come and investigate. So starting at eleven a.m., he had begun cruising. Mrs Henley drove a Chrysler station wagon. It was still in the garage forty minutes later, but then a little after midday as he was about to turn into the street, he saw a trim woman with dark brown hair emerge from the house and head to the twin garage. He watched her drive off, then he cruised away, parked two streets on by a park where tall gums stood like armed guards. He put on the hat that somebody had left one night at the Shack. It went well with the dark suit he'd bought first thing that morning from Campbell Menswear. The sample briefcase had set him back ten pounds but he figured it was worth it because now he looked like your typical door-to-door salesman.

He walked briskly down the street, worried somebody might actually ask him what he sold. Maybe he could bullshit about insurance. On reflection, he should have grabbed some glasses from the Shack for his sample case, said he sold glassware. Too late now. According to Doreen, Todd had a younger sister. Blake was presuming the girl was at school but when he reached the neat path that led to the Henley front door he realised he couldn't take that for granted. There could also be a cleaning lady, something like that. He rang the bell of the neatly varnished front door and waited, breathed a sigh of relief when there was no response. He retraced his steps and took a path along the side of the house that was conveniently hemmed in by oleander bushes and some other plants he didn't know the names of. A locked, barred gate and fence blocked his way. He threw over the sample bag and scaled the gate easily. He moved quickly, pulling on washing-up gloves he'd kept in his breast pocket, searching the windows, pushing them, got lucky. One wasn't snug. It looked like a simple swing clasp locked the window on the inside. He reached into his pocket, pulled out a strip of thin but strong cardboard and worked it into the gap between the window and fed it up until it reached the bottom of the clasp. Two pushes and the clasp was off, the window open. He scaled quickly, found himself in what must have been the girl's room: dolls on a shelf, snow domes, pink frills. Next door he struck gold, Todd's bedroom, preserved: sporting trophies and medals on a shelf, a rugby ball. He grabbed the ball, and one of the medals and exited the way he came. At the gate he put the ball and the medal in the sample bag and tossed it back over the fence. He followed, grabbed the bag and was at his car in five minutes.

ᴑᴑᴑ

Pretty much as soon as he had dusted the swimming medal Saunders had brought in, he knew the prints were a match to those in Stokes' car. Which was a shit because you didn't take on Richard Henley. He was on the board of the golf club and most other things in Coral Shoals. Henley could destroy a local cop like him.

He asked where Saunders had got the medal and was told it 'fell off the back of a truck'.

He didn't like people's houses being broken into but conceded it was the quickest way to get evidence, so in that sense he didn't bake the Yank like he might have. The pin in the incinerator had cleaned up well and almost certainly showed the high-school crest. It added weight to Saunders' theory but would be hard to prove beyond doubt it was Henley's. Approaching the girl had been reckless. She'd probably already warned Todd Henley. And all the prints proved was that Henley had been in Stokes' car, especially now Brenda Holsch had given Saunders an alibi.

'She's lying,' Saunders had protested, and likely she was but it was still an alibi so before he contacted Vernon or did anything else, he'd paid Brenda Holsch a visit himself, playing the dumb local cop who had been forced to ask these unpleasant things.

'I'm sure you understand?'

The girl had told him what she'd told Saunders. Like Saunders he didn't believe her.

With a lot of embarrassment she had told him how she and Todd had been 'together' till the early hours.

'At your place?'

'No, I live with my parents.'

'At his parents' place?'

'No, down at the lagoon in his car.'

'This was from …'

'About eleven at night till two the next morning.'

Covering the important hours like that. It might have ended there, except that when he got back to the station he was able to check the log of the diligent Constable Denham, part of whose duties included patrolling lover's lane down by the lagoon and recording the numberplates of the vehicles. This was only partly police work. In fact it was Nalder's own insurance scheme should any people of importance ever attempt to move against him. 'Tell me, Bob, what you were doing down at the lagoon at three a.m.?' Coral Shoals was a small place. There weren't many places people could slip away for a liaison. Constable Denham's log showed no number plate of either the girl's car or Todd Henley's. They weren't there. Now he was on firmer ground. He could destroy the kid's alibi. There was still the matter of how he approached Homicide though. It couldn't look like he was a smart-arse. In the end he had decided to go with the tried and true. He'd called Vernon, said he'd had an anonymous call claiming a young local man, Todd Henley, had been in the car with Stokes just hours before she was murdered. He mentioned that Henley's girlfriend had likely seen them together but when questioned had denied it and instead provided an alibi which he had since discredited.

'Just two nights later this same kid was involved in what might have amounted to a sexual assault had the girlfriend not turned up.'

Vernon was as annoyed as he was grateful. 'Where is this Henley now?'

'Brisbane. University. I'm thinking the Brisbane cops could likely find something with his prints on and you could check to see if they match those in the car.'

He was told that was exactly what Vernon was thinking, and thanked for his time.

Vernon had called back twenty-four hours later, confirming the match.

That's when Nalder expanded his theory to the incineration of the murder clothes at the car yard where Henley had worked over summer washing cars.

'I found a pin that could be an athletics pin. Won't stand up as clear evidence probably but it might help.'

'We've made some inquiries. The kid is coming back home for the weekend.'

Vernon and Apollonia arrived on the Friday night. He'd made reservations for them at Mrs Lawson's guest house. She cooked them steak and vegetables and they ate in the parlour on a fine rosewood table polished with the dedication of a widow.

'The kid is at the parents' house, now. We'll go in first thing tomorrow.'

'What's for dessert?' asked Apollonia.

'Stewed apples and ice cream, I believe.'

ᗧᗧᗧ

Blake arrived to find Nalder sitting at a picnic table with a large bottle of beer opened. It was close to six p.m. and the place was deserted except for litter left by earlier picnickers who were now home running hot baths for tired kids. He had a gig to play with the new drummer but there was plenty of time.

'Help yourself.' Nalder offered the beer bottle.

Word had already spread around town that Todd Henley had been arrested but details were sketchy. It was the first time they'd shared a drink. Blake took a slug.

'How did it go?'

'We turned up at six in the morning. They were prepared. Obviously Brenda Holsch had tipped them off. They had a lawyer waiting on the phone instructing them to say nothing. Todd did what he was told, said nothing except he was with Brenda Holsch at the lagoon. Vernon and Apollonia have driven him to Sydney for questioning.'

'Has he been charged?'

'Not yet. But if the kid isn't going to crack, there's no point holding off.'

'What about Thomas Clarke?'

'He's still sitting in remand. Vernon has no doubt it is Henley. Maybe Clarke or somebody else will remember seeing Henley's car near the motel. That's all they really need. When the girl realises she could go to jail if she keeps lying, she'll change her tune. You did alright, Saunders.'

They each swigged again. Blake thought he would feel something, a sense of triumph, satisfaction, but he was a void. He had murdered people in cold blood, which maybe was worse than what Henley had done. Henley was just a fucked-up psycho. What was he — a hired killer, a fucking amoeba. A few weeks ago he'd been prepared to kill again, silence an innocent woman to keep his secret. He craved absolution but knew he did not deserve it.

He said, 'You were right. The bookie sent somebody else.'

Nalder moaned. 'I'm sorry. I'd like to help you but …'

He could fill in the missing words. If Nalder helped him where did it stop? Like the first time you pick up a gun with darkness in your heart.

If only he could go back, hand the gun back to Jimmy, say, 'No, let's find another way.' He could have got a job, loading trucks or hanging curtains. Something that had not let the darkness in. He put the bottle down.

'I've gotta go play some music.'

17. I Wanna Hold Your Hand

It was a Sunday, that hour when the sun has been rolled flat and televisions like glow-worms start to appear as families settle in for *The Flintstones* with a dinner of rissoles or fish and chips. She felt a pang just thinking about it, family, blocked it out, tried to concentrate on Blake across the way. No TV for him. He was in his lounge room sitting on a kitchen chair, hunched over playing guitar. Last night with the new drummer, he'd been sensational. She wondered what was on his mind right now. Probably music, or perhaps the end of the Stokes case. Todd Henley was going to get his just deserts. It made her angry just thinking about him and what he had done, or tried to do, to Kitty. Thank God the jealous Barbie doll had got involved. Imagine if Kitty had wound up like Val Stokes. She shuddered involuntarily.

Thinking about Kitty made her feel empty, guilty. She'd imagined herself as a big sister, was able to convince herself for a while there that all the mistakes she'd made in her past weren't wasted because she could impart wisdom to her. What a fucking disaster in the end.

Something pricked her brain, something about Kitty that made her suddenly … uneasy. But then, what didn't? You find out you've screwed the father of somebody you are trying to mentor, that's a first-class *Titanic* disaster right there. Of course Kitty was going to resent her. However, she wasn't sure that was the buried insight her detector had just buzzed deep in her brain. It wasn't something personal, or at least she didn't feel that it was, but it did involve Kitty. It was a bit like when you drop a shilling, you hear it bounce but you're not sure exactly where to look: Kitty and Todd … Brenda. Oh well, it was no use, it wouldn't come and it wasn't important.

Now she was shivering for real. It was cool with that sea breeze, no cardigan, no sun. Earlier today she had tried to finish the month's bookkeeping but given up, deciding to take a break. She'd go back to the Surf Shack now, knock it on the head, give herself two full days off. Blake was still practising something over and over.

Blake's fingers strolled through The Shadows and The Ventures. He imagined Jimmy sitting opposite him sipping a beer while he brought Jimmy up to speed.

'We were really good last night. The new guy is actually better than Duck but you know the ironical thing? It doesn't matter now, we're stuck out in the backwater and all the action is ahead of us. There's a new sound and it's not my sound. No tremolo guitars, tom-toms, none of that, more R'n'B. And vocals. The surf sound is dead, Jimmy. Like you.'

Jimmy laughed at that, raised the beer bottle in a salute. Life was a wild bull you could never corral. It just kicked in the walls like they were matchsticks. Blake had explained to himself his determination to find Stokes' killer as a desire to protect his patch, but maybe it was even simpler.

If the killer was still out there, they might harm Doreen. Last night they'd been together like they always were after the last person left the Surf Shack, like they were the only two people in the world. He'd snatched glimpses of her crinkles around her eyes when she laughed, imagined they were on a desert island, just the two of them under a big white moon with waves crashing on the sand where they slept. He imagined pressing his body next to hers as they lay on the beach, their hearts pumping so he could hear the beat from hers travel back up through the sand. The two of them, one pulse. Because it was just the two of them, no bad things could ever happen. Nobody could turn up demanding you pay them. Nobody could step out of the shadows to harm you, and there would be no choice but to be together because there would be nowhere else to go, no guitar to play, no record to listen to, no excuse. There would be nothing except her heartbeat, the stars above their heads and the hush of waves.

It was while looking for the ledgers that she came across the solicitor Harvey's file about the Stokes case again. She flicked through it, her mind brushing against the fragility of life, the horror of murder, the loneliness of death. With a false step here or there, she could have been Val Stokes. She looked at the typed list of personal belongings, feeling compassionate ... pulled herself up. No, that didn't make sense. There were two pairs of shoes listed, both high heels. Come on, she'd been away nearly a week. Were there tights? Yes. Then she had to have slip-ons of some sort. Or sandshoes. But they weren't mentioned. Maybe the cops made a mistake? She checked up the rest of the clothes. Two evening dresses, one pair of tights, one blouse but no casual top. No woman packed like that. An idea roared out of the mist like a train.

What if somebody had taken them?

And now her head was spinning, she couldn't believe what she was thinking but it all fitted. The notion she'd sensed before with Kitty, about there being something hidden, now revealed itself. She rummaged through Blake's desk looking for the pin he'd found in the incinerator but it wasn't there. Must have given it to Nalder. She went to the next drawer down, pulled out the photos of the dance competition Blake had made her find for Andy, skimmed fast, the prints spilling on the floor till she found one she wanted. She grabbed the phone, dialled a number she hadn't forgotten yet. A woman's voice answered.

'Ferguson residence.'

'May I speak to Kitty, please.'

'Just one moment. Kitty!'

The phone was placed on a cradle that played a mechanical tune: 'Fascination'. The music gave way to Kitty's voice.

'Hello.'

'Kitty it's me.'

The receiver slammed in her ear.

Blake put the guitar down. He wasn't that hungry but he figured he could scramble some eggs. He was toying with the idea that he should go visit Doreen anyway. That's who he really wanted to hang out with. He reached into the tray under the stove for the heavy frypan. It would be nice, just the two of them. He was taking out two eggs and some butter from the fridge when his doorbell rang. It was funny but he immediately thought maybe it's Doreen thinking the same thing? He was only wearing shorts and a striped shirt but she wouldn't expect much different. He opened the door and was surprised.

'I hope you don't mind me calling on you.' Brenda Holsch stood there in black tights, short dress and a sweater, her hair in a ponytail.

He wasn't too sure how to respond, only managed to come out with, 'No.'

She took that as an invitation and stepped into the room.

He said, 'Can I get you anything?'

'A Coke?'

He had a small one in the fridge, popped the top, found a clean glass in the overhead cupboard.

'Please have a seat. Sorry about the mess.'

Of course he wasn't sorry, this was his place but he guessed that's what you were supposed to say.

'You need a woman here.'

She said it brightly, sat neatly on one of the kitchen chairs, her hands folded across her lap. She was a good-looking young woman. He handed her the glass, leaned back against the kitchen bench.

She said, 'I owe you an apology. I was being stupid. I just couldn't believe that Todd ...' She shook her head and sipped her Coke.

Blake said, 'It's hard to believe. Have you got people around you?'

'My mum is an alcoholic. My father left years ago. All the girls have it in for me because, well, I don't want to seem ... they'd kill for my figure, put it that way.'

'You've got the chemist job.'

'Mmm. That's what I wanted to talk to you about. If I could get some night work I might be able to get my own place.'

'My manager, Doreen, does all the hiring.'

'Yeah, see that's the problem.'

'Doreen is fair ...'

'But she's thick with Kitty Ferguson. I've seen them together, and me and Kitty have a bit of history. So ...' she put the glass down on the table, leaned back to emphasise her bust. '... I thought I should come straight to the boss. I'd be really, really grateful.'

There was no mistaking the emphasis. Her tongue rolled around her bottom lip, her foot swayed back and forth.

Blake said, 'Doreen will be fair. I promise you that. Now, I was just about to make myself some eggs.'

As if she didn't hear him, Brenda got to her feet and moved to where the Fender leaned against the wall.

'Is this your guitar? I would love to play the guitar.'

Blake didn't want this to drag on. He wanted her out. He stepped towards her.

'Brenda, I think ...'

He didn't get out another word. All he saw was a blur and then he felt a mighty crack in the head.

She'd driven to the Heights, determined to try something, anything, maybe knock on Kitty's bedroom window. She'd been to Kitty's twice, knew her room was closest to the back. One street away from the house, though, she got lucky, recognised the familiar small stature of Kitty walking the family dog. She pulled into the kerb on the wrong side of the road, jumped out.

Kitty snarled, 'Stay away from me.'

Kitty tried to pull the dog but it had locked onto an interesting scent.

'Please, Kitty. This is important.'

'I'm not listening.'

'That essay you wrote for school ...'

'Are you mental?'

She was literally dragging the dog. Doreen grabbed hold of her.

'Let me go or I'll scream.'

'I'm sorry. If I could change anything, I would.'

Kitty yanked herself away.

Doreen called after her, 'You talked about Brenda as a witch, stabbing you with some pin. Was that Todd's?'

Only then did Kitty swivel back. 'That creep has been arrested. I don't want to think about him, or you, ever again.'

'Did Todd give Brenda his badge?'

There must have been something in the urgency that got through to Kitty.

'Yes. One of his rugby badges. She wore it everywhere.'

Doreen pulled the eight-by-ten black and white from her pocket, unfolded it. It showed Duck before the competition began surrounded by the girls. Beneath the lamppost there was just enough light to make out something on Brenda's blouse above her right breast.

'This thing?'

'Yes. I'm glad you're obsessed with her now. Don't bother me again.'

She started to jog away, the dog having to canter to keep up. Doreen wanted to call after her, tell her it was all a terrible mistake and she loved her, but what would have been the point?

Blake's world was fuzzy, inverted, a demon's face staring down, yelling words he couldn't hear because of the sound in his head, high and dull bells all at the same time. His field of vision grew wider, the triple images became one: the ceiling of his lounge room, the demon revealed — Brenda clothed only in her underwear, blood smeared on her cheeks, his large kitchen knife in her hands. He was on the floor, his head throbbed. He sensed the blood was his. No strength yet, he tried to haul himself up, realised his hands were tied back and anchored to something, maybe the table. When he tried to raise his head, a bare heel slammed down onto his forehead like it was squashing a bug. Grey filter, almost black, the image in negative ... his ears working again, 'Apache' playing on the turntable, words raining down on him now.

'... was everything to me and you took him from me, you fucking bastard. You told the cops, didn't you? You were the one trying to split me and Todd. Like that fucking slut, bitch, whore, and you're going to die the same way as she did, like a fucking dog. Everything was working out. That dickhead Tom Clarke was going to get blamed. Todd was mine. As if *he* killed that ugly bitch.' She straddled him, then suddenly dropped, all her weight on him. Her crotch ground into his.

'Like that, do you?'

Doreen recognised the car at the end of the cul-de-sac, and just knew. She went through the garage and began up the back stairs, wary. Music was playing. She reached the back landing, heard a woman's voice screaming above guitars. She opened the door and walked in, took it in: Brenda straddling Blake, a knife raised, held double-handed, ready to plunge.

'You. Wrecked. Everything.'

Brenda's back muscles tensed to drive the knife down. Doreen threw herself at her. Her hands gripped Brenda's, keeping the blade pointed upwards. Brenda screamed and tried to get free but Doreen held on with everything she had. They rolled off Blake. She was bigger than Brenda but Brenda was wiry strong. Both slipped on the polished boards. Doreen flashed images: Val Stokes at the mercy of this banshee. Brenda got to one knee, gained leverage, Doreen was still only on her hip, pushing up with a longer reach but Brenda was gradually turning the knife towards her, extending her back leg. Doreen couldn't hold. She let go, rolled fast, the knife drove down, glanced her somewhere on the side, she tried to crawl, get to her feet, turned to see Brenda standing, grinning ... until Blake's left leg swept wide, taking her foot. Brenda went down. Doreen stood, swung the hardest punch she could into Brenda's face, heard the knife clatter. Brenda, a mad cat, hissed, pushed off like a sprinter, hurling herself towards the open door and balcony. Doreen watched her jump, cycling in midair. Then she dropped out of sight. Even with the needle bumping the record label you could hear the smack of a body hitting concrete.

Doreen turned, saw Blake had hoisted himself to sitting position, his head seeping blood. She crawled to him, pressed her chest to his as she reached around and began untying the knotted stocking that bound his hands.

'Are you okay?' She felt her lips moving, couldn't recall forming words. His mouth drew close to her ear. She got the knot undone. He pulled her to him.

'I'm sorry. I'm sorry,' he whispered.

And then she kissed him.

ㅁㅁㅁ

That Blake's neighbours were so engrossed in their Sunday night television movie that they didn't hear anything of the ruckus did not surprise Doreen. Given the option, she would have chosen Ray Milland playing the devil over wrestling a knife-wielding psycho. Doreen was the first to reach Brenda while Blake dialled for an ambulance. She was lying like a broken doll on the concrete driveway, blood pooling around her head in something that looked like a map of Queensland. Remarkably, she had a pulse. When the ambulance came, she was still alive but whatever Brenda Holsch had been was history. Nalder told them later that the doctors said she would likely be brain dead from here on, and maybe never walk again. Doreen had totally forgotten that she had been grazed by the knife. The hospital put a dressing on it and she was fine within a few days. Blake's skull had a minor crack from being hit by his guitar, but the lacerations were fairly superficial. They ran through the basics while Nalder drove them to hospital. Doreen told how she figured some of Val Stokes' clothes were missing, along with a pair of slip-on shoes.

'First I was thinking it was something weird, you know, Henley taking her clothes with him because he was a psycho, and then, I thought: what if it was a woman? And it all made sense. If a woman killed Stokes, she would be covered in blood. She could shower and just dress in Stokes' clothes and burn her own.'

She told them about how she'd read a story by Kitty where Brenda, 'the witch in the story', was stabbing at the heroine with the 'prince's' pin.

Nalder said, 'She was smart. By giving Henley an alibi, she gave herself one.'

Later Henley admitted he'd had sex with Stokes in her car, paid her with a joint one of the girls had slipped him and given her the matchbook.

But after the fight with Brenda he'd gone straight home. His parents and sister had been away that weekend and he was worried that he would be a sitting duck, so when Brenda offered an alibi, he grabbed it.

Personally Doreen was disappointed that Henley would get away with no punishment but she realised that wasn't so true. He wasn't the golden boy any more, never would be. That other creep Winston Clarke couldn't be charged over his blue movie seeing as he had never distributed it but she'd heard his ex had made sure their son would never visit him again. In truth, none of that mattered all that much since — in the heat of that awful moment — she had kissed Blake.

And he had kissed her back.

18. The Nineteenth Hole

Winter had passed the way a headcold does. The winters here were really nothing. Not like back in Philly, stomping your feet to keep warm. That local band The Atlantics had released a hit record, a surf track, 'Bombora', good as anything he had heard from the States. Maybe he was wrong, maybe the guitar sound wasn't dead yet, although The Beatles were getting bigger by the minute. It was November now and he couldn't believe it but he was lying on the beach beside Doreen, his right arm around her body listening to her heart, just like he'd imagined. The days were warm again and the nights scented, the moon a big pearl on black velvet. Nobody else was around. It could have been a desert island.

'I used to sit on the sandhill opposite your house and watch you,' she confessed, her thumb moving across his palm.

'I know.' He had seen movement one time, pretended to move off, found some binoculars, crouched down behind the sofa and checked out who was watching him, his heart in his mouth because he'd half-expected it could be Peste or somebody like him, somebody sent from home.

'No! You knew all that time? Why didn't you say something?'

'I didn't want to break the spell. I liked knowing you were there.'

'This is better.'

'Yes.'

'I had an abortion,' she said. 'Earlier this year.'

He remembered when she'd seemed wan, not herself.

'I don't want to keep secrets from you.'

It was the perfect time to tell her about Jimmy. He started. 'I ...' It was too hard.

'Don't feel you have to tell me stuff.'

He let go. 'I killed my brother, Jimmy.'

He felt her stiffen, even though she tried not to.

'I mean, I didn't actually pull the trigger but I ratted him out.'

He held his breath. This was where he always imagined she left him with nothing but the smell of her perfume on his skin. She turned around, stroked his face. He wanted to spell it out. 'I understand if you want nothing to do with me. I do. I was a miserable coward.'

'I love you,' she said, and kissed him again. 'And you're not a coward. There's nothing cowardly about the truth.'

ロロロ

'An Englishman, an Irishman and a Jew walk into a bar ...'

They all leaned in, even though they could hear perfectly well, because when George Gardiner told a joke you didn't want to miss anything. Nalder allowed himself to drift temporarily, to view the tableau as if he was an angel on the wall looking down at this fraternity. Sunday morning, the sun heating the greens, producing the most wonderful smell, exceeded only by that from the skin of a newborn baby. He saw Gardiner, his knees in their check pants pointing forward, whisky tumbler at the ready as his animated hands enlivened the joke. Parker, who had taken to wearing all black like his hero Gary Player, a smile of anticipation already in his dimples, Johnson with his straight back, just out of the circle because he was smoking Kool and was polite enough not to want to puff directly into somebody's face, and himself, more a Kel Nagle type with his rotund torso and set off to the side the jaunty hat with the little feather. It was a wonderful thing indeed to be part of all this, better than he had imagined. When Edith and the boys wanted to give him a Father's Day or birthday gift, they didn't just have to go to socks, no, they could give him a set of golf balls or gloves. Marvellous. It was not lost on him that the sublime had come from horror and blood. Wasn't that the way it always had been, whether it was the British in India or the Incas? The two are the flip sides of the same coin, the trick in life was to make the right call.

□□□

Kitty had been surprised at how quickly Brenda's notoriety had faded. She had finally died two weeks ago, never having regained consciousness. The local paper had run a big story and a reporter had tried to interview Todd's mum but had got nowhere. Her own parents never openly reflected on their eagerness to match her up with Todd. That episode had been forgotten or swept under the carpet — apart from her mum making some comment about Kitty having 'good instincts'. Yeah right. She was less certain now about being an actress, didn't think she was pretty enough and, sure, you could play those support roles like Ethel in *I Love Lucy* but that wasn't where the fun was. She was going to leave town though, as soon as she could. Maybe there would be something else she could do, like television. At university she could at least join a drama society. Her mum and dad seemed to get on better now, or maybe they were just more careful around her. She had glimpsed Doreen a few times in town. At first she had made sure she crossed the road or went into an arcade, anything to get away from her, but those hours they had trained in the Surf Shack, the afternoons they'd had tea at the Victoria Tearooms and laughed and talked, they were still with her like germs from a flu you couldn't shake. Somewhere while listening to *Please Please Me*, out from the vinyl grooves crawled the embarrassing memory of the aftermath of the Todd fiasco when it had been Doreen who had driven her home. She hadn't wanted to admit it but she missed her.

The other day she had seen Doreen near Gannons and for the first time she hadn't walked away. She'd stood there and looked at Doreen who, emerging with her shopping, had looked up and seen her, and you could tell it surprised her, and she just stopped stone dead and their eyes had met. Then Doreen had waved at her, just a small little wave with four fingers while her thumb held the shopping bag, like she was cleaning a tiny window. Kitty hadn't waved back, but she hadn't left either. She watched Doreen walk away and was still watching when Doreen turned back, and she was pretty sure she smiled, and to be honest, inside, she was smiling too.

It was a funny thing but each day now seemed further and further away from the day before. All that mattered was ahead of her. She rolled over on her bed and put down her book. Lately she'd really started pushing herself: French authors, Steinbeck. She looked up and saw the transistor radio she had won in the dance contest and she was filled with joy. Wow, she had actually won. It was funny how you could forget triumphs. She'd been darn good as Nellie Forbush too. She was ready to finish school, to get out, but she knew she was going to miss it, was going to one day long for these hours of utter boredom — spinning the wheel of your bicycle while mothers played slowed rallies on the warm grass tennis courts, dreaming of a future that you'd be lucky if it turned out half as good as your past, of gossip on school playgrounds and decorating your schoolbag with woven plastic strips and badges of Mousketeers, of the joy of opening a new bottle of Fanta, and the scratch of chalk on a blackboard while you wrote the names of the Beatles in your exercise book using three different coloured pens at once.

She turned on the radio. 'Ask Me Why' was playing. The Beatles made you feel great, no matter what. The past was like the poor old fido you had to bury in the backyard. You'd never love another dog as much as the one you had from when you were ten years old but you had to embrace your future: the possibilities were infinite.

19. The Other Side Of Dallas

They ate breakfast together, ham and eggs. He cooked, though she'd offered like she always did. The breeze came in through the back door, a westerly today, and leaves gathered at the bottom step. He liked watching her eat whatever he cooked, wondered how she could have such a large appetite but stay so slim.

'When will you be back do you think?' she asked.

'Tomorrow night, probably. I reckon before you close up.'

'Shame you can't play this weekend.'

'It's no big deal. It's good to take a break.'

Last month he'd missed a weekend and that hadn't done the band's popularity any harm. He began to clear up.

He said, 'Panza's coming down to keep an eye on you.'

'Don't trust me?'

'Don't trust a bunch of thieving knuckleheads out there who decide to rip off somebody else's hard-earned.'

His concern for her prompted reciprocation. 'I don't want you speeding. That highway is a death trap. And watch out in Sydney too, the traffic is crazy.'

He promised he would be fine. He kissed her on the forehead and the lips.

She looked up into his eyes. 'You really thinking of buying this club?'

He'd told her that's why he needed to go to Sydney, check on the business firsthand.

'I want to keep my options open.'

She kissed him again. He broke away and walked down to the car, carrying his overnight bag. He drove out slowly with a toot and a wave. She stood on the balcony and blew him a kiss. He headed south out of town but then turned right up to Belvedere, where he laid another right heading north. She wouldn't check the odometer.

He'd already made sure he had a full tank, didn't want to be stopping. It took him five hours give or take to make Brisbane, getting in before the Friday five o'clock traffic. Last month he'd arrived on the Thursday and camped outside the mark's house, following him all through Thursday, Friday and Saturday. Reason and logic told him that the mark was going to be most predictable on a Saturday. But you never took anything for granted. He parked outside of the main city area and walked six blocks. The pubs were rollicking, the smell of hops and the sound of Friday laughter coming out in a whoosh every time a door opened onto the street. He kept his eyes on the opposite side of the street, an office one floor up. The mark should be in there till late, doing his numbers, getting everything down for the next day.

A little after nine p.m., the streets now quieter, the light in the office finally went out. Four minutes later an old-fashioned, broad-shouldered, pinhead goon appeared and checked the street. He wore a heavy, dark suit, had a nose that had been busted more than once, likely an ex-pug. He hardly paid any attention to the young guy across the road with the flowers, vainly waiting for a date who must have stiffed him. The goon opened the door to the building and the mark stepped out. A short man with a gut, broad shoulders. His suit and hat were expensive and he was carrying a Gladstone bag that Blake guessed was full of cash. The goon waited while his boss opened the door of a Mercedes parked directly in front of the building. The mark climbed in and drove off. Last time Blake had been forced to follow. This time he was pretty sure the mark was heading home.

Blake retrieved his car and drove. Fifteen minutes later he cruised past the iron fence that protected the big gabled house in the green suburb. The Mercedes was visible, parked nose first in a garage, its rear to the street.

He'd seen enough. He drove to the YMCA, parking his car two streets away, and took a bed at the Y, giving the name John Paterson. The advantage of the Y was there were another five guys who could have passed for him and vice versa. He didn't like the shared bathroom, the cold tile floor, the scummy shower stall but then he didn't need to use anything but the urinal. He closed his eyes, slept lightly, alert to the sound of doors opening and closing and footsteps down the hallway. He was out of there by five. To kill time he drove to the river and watched fishermen. There was something timeless and relaxing about watching a man fish.

Even though it was only nine thirty in the morning, the first race still hours off, the carpark was not unpopulated. He sat in his car and waited until he saw the Mercedes enter and peel off to the area reserved for bookmakers. Then he climbed out, put on a pair of cheap sunglasses and the long white cotton coat. The beauty of the coat was it made him invisible, just another parking attendant. He walked straight into the bookies' carpark past the old boy with the bifocals and the hearing aid.

'Morning, Roy,' he called as he went through. Last time he'd made a point of catching the man's name. Roy grinned and waved, pretending he knew him. Twenty yards on, the brakelights of the Mercedes went out: freshly parked. A dozen other cars waited in a line, at a glance empty, but he couldn't be certain. He strode quickly now, arriving perfectly on time as the driver door of the Mercedes opened on the man whose office he had been watching last night.

'Mr Hennessy?'

'Yes?'

The faintest trace of suspicion, a cunning man whose bookie's brain was used to calculating odds in a split second, realising too late that the odds were all wrong.

Blake had decided on the Beretta. 'Say hi to Jimmy for me.'

He fired close up into the forehead, knew it was a kill shot but fired another to the chest just in case of a miracle. Another car was arriving as he closed the driver door and strode off. In the distance he noticed a man in a suit swivelling. He knew he had heard something, just not exactly what. He waved goodbye to Roy, who had not heard a thing. At his car he removed the white jacket and tossed it on the ground. Then he climbed in and drove away.

Near Southport he parked. Watched by a lone circling gull, he got out and hurled the Beretta into the river of salt. He hoped he would never have need of it, but if he did, there was still the Browning. He drove back, respectful of the thirty-five mile per hour speed limit, enjoying the shadows of gums on the tar. He looked over and saw Jimmy sitting beside him.

'So what do you think?'

'You done pretty good.'

'We done pretty good.'

Then the seat was vacant again and he was imagining other souls from his journey. Jim the pilot who had flown him to Australia, Carol a hot body making milkshakes, Edward with his swag and Duck thumping his toms always just a little out of time. Once he was south of the Heads, he stopped at the first service station he found, a little store with one pump and ice-cream signage out the front. He might treat himself to an ice cream, he thought. When no one came to fill up the car, he decided to do it himself. He finished and was almost at the office when a sandy-haired man about fifty, wearing a stained grey uniform shirt emerged, flustered.

'I'm sorry, I just … I couldn't believe it. I was listening to the radio.'

'What's happened?'

'Somebody shot JFK. They're saying he's dead.'

Yeah, life was a big mean wave. Just when you think you have it licked, it kicks you in the teeth. That could have been you pulling that trigger, he thought to himself. You never asked how or why, you just did what you were told for a steak dinner. You don't deserve any goodness in your life. You have brought misery and death and despair. And sure, they might bring it on themselves with greed or malice, and if you didn't do it, somebody else surely would. But that didn't make it right. How can you live like that?

The answer, he knew, was waiting around three hours away. He leaned back into his seat and kept his foot even on the accelerator, cocooned in the smell of leather and a lingering odour of leaking oil. The crazy thing about the crazy world we live in, is that anything is possible. One day we might even put a man on the moon. He'd volunteer for that. Just so long as he could take Doreen with him.

Acknowledgements

On p.75, Crane quotes from Percy Bysshe Shelley's poem 'Adonais'. Lines from 'A Cockeyed Optimist', p. 86, © Rodgers and Hammerstein, 1958.

I am very fortunate to work with Georgia Richter of Fremantle Press as my editor. Everything is better for having her eye across the manuscript and I thank her for her input. Thanks also in advance to Jane Fraser, Claire Miller and everybody else at Fremantle Press who I know will be working very hard on my behalf to bring *River of Salt* to the widest readership possible. The idea of this book came when I went to an Atlantics' gig where my friend and colleague Martin Cilia, Australia's premier surf-guitarist, was playing with the original members of that amazing band. This is a good chance to thank Martin for all the times we've sat around working out chords, bars and other licks. Finally my greatest appreciation to my wife and most ardent supporter Nicole, who gives everything of herself to her family and friends. Hopefully we'll record her album next and she can thank Martin and me before heading to Philly and meeting Vin, Marcello and the gang in the flesh — if they haven't been rubbed out.

WA PREMIER'S AWARD WINNER

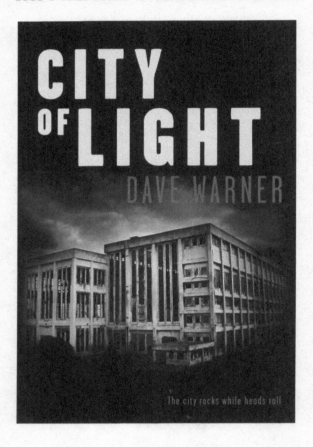

'Jesus Christ. I found one.' These words are blurted over the phone to Constable Snowy Lane, who is preoccupied with no more than a ham sandwich and getting a game with the East Fremantle league side on Saturday. They signal the beginning of a series of events that are to shake Perth to its foundations. It is 1979, and Perth is jumping with pub bands and overnight millionaires. 'Mr Gruesome' has just taken another victim. Snowy's life and career are to be forever changed by the grim deeds of a serial killer, and the dark bloom spreading across the City of Light.

'Lively, funny, with enough plot for three novels.' *Sun-Herald.*

FROM FREMANTLEPRESS.COM.AU

NED KELLY AWARD WINNER

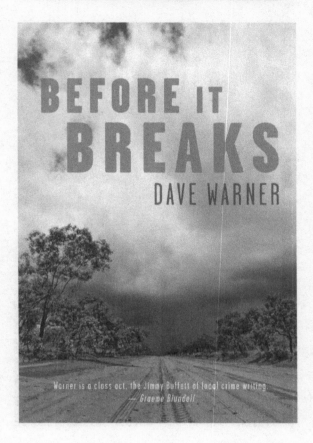

Detective Daniel Clement is back in Broome, licking his wounds from a busted marriage and struggling to be impressed by his new team of small-town cops. Here, in the oasis on the edge of the desert, life is as stagnant as Clement's latest career move. But when a body is discovered at a local fishing spot, it is clearly not the result of a crocodile attack. Somewhere in Broome is a hunter of a different kind. As more bodies are found, Clement races to solve a decades-old mystery before a monster cyclone hits.

'Laid-back and laconic, with sentences as snappy as a nutcracker.' *Books+Publishing*

AND ALL GOOD BOOKSTORES

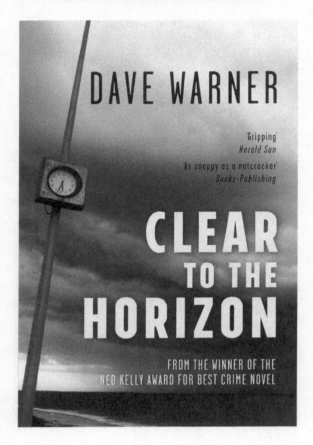
In 1999 and 2000, three women disappear from outside a nightclub in Perth. Snowy Lane is hired as a private investigator but neither he nor the cops can find the abductor. Seventeen years on, the daughter of a wealthy mining magnate goes missing, and Snowy is hired to find her. In the tropical town of Broome, a spate of local thefts puts Snowy and DI Daniel Clement back on the trail of the cold-case killer. Snowy is determined that this time he will get his man, even if it costs him his life.

'A fast-paced plot and writing that is dense with colourful vernacular and Aussie humour.' *Sun-Herald*.

FROM FREMANTLEPRESS.COM.AU

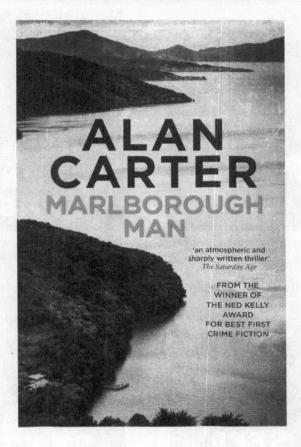

THE CATO KWONG CRIME SERIES

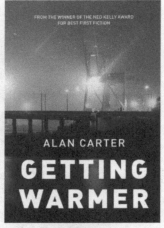

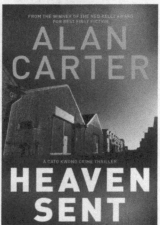

From the winner of the Ned Kelly Award for best first fiction, and winner of the Ngaio Marsh Award.

'*Bad Seed* is hard to beat.' *Weekend Australian*

'Accomplished and entertaining.' *Sydney Morning Herald*

'*Getting Warmer* is a winner.' *The Saturday Age*

'Compelling crime drama.' *OUTinPerth*

FROM FREMANTLEPRESS.COM.AU